THE LITERARY WEREWOLF

Information Hertfordshire

# Reference Only

# Not For Loan

# THE LITERARY WEREWOLF

*An Anthology*

Edited by CHARLOTTE F. OTTEN

Syracuse University Press

Copyright © 2002 by Syracuse University Press
Syracuse, New York 13244-5160

*All Rights Reserved*

First Edition 2002

07          6  5  4  3  2

The paper used in this publication meets the minimum requirements
of American National Standard for Information Sciences—Permanence
of Paper for Printed Library Materials, ANSI Z39.48–1984.∞™

**Library of Congress Cataloging-in-Publication Data**

The literary werewolf : an anthology / [compiled by] Charlotte F. Otten.—1st ed.
p. cm.
ISBN 0–8156–2965–6 (cloth : alk. paper)—ISBN 0–8156–0753–9 (pbk. : alk. paper)
1. Werewolves—Fiction. I. Otten, Charlotte F.
PN6120.95.W47 L58 2002
808.83'9375—dc21
2002009335

*Manufactured in the United States of America*

In those that are possessed with 't there o'erflows
Such melancholy humor they imagine
Themselves to be transformed into wolves;
Steal forth to church-yards in the dead of night
And dig dead bodies up: as two nights since
One met the Duke 'bout midnight in a land
Behind Saint Mark's church, with the leg of a man
Upon his shoulder; and he howled fearfully;
Said he was a wolf, only the difference
Was, a wolf's skin was hairy on the outside,
His on the inside; bade them take their swords,
Rip up his flesh, and try . . .

—JOHN WEBSTER

(1623), *The Duchess of Malfi* (v.ii)

**Charlotte F. Otten** is professor of English (emerita), Calvin College, and the author of *A Lycanthropy Reader: Werewolves in Western Culture* (Syracuse University Press), *English Women's Voices, 1540–1700,* and *Environ'd with Eternity: God, Poems, and Plants in Sixteenth and Seventeenth Century England.* Professor Otten has published widely in journals such as the *Huntington Library Quarterly, English Literary Renaissance,* and *Shakespeare Quarterly.*

# Contents

# Preface

*A LYCANTHROPY READER: Werewolves in Western Culture*, which appeared in 1986, paved the way for this anthology of werewolf fiction, *The Literary Werewolf: An Anthology*. Readers of the medical cases, trial records, historical accounts, philosophical and theological approaches to metamorphosis, critical studies of lycanthropy, a few myths and legends, and an allegory in *A Lycanthropy Reader* wondered aloud about fictive accounts of werewolves. I wondered with them and decided to check it out.

After beginning a search for werewolf fiction, I discovered that there were more werewolf stories than I had ever dreamed of finding, that writers throughout the centuries, including some of the greatest, had written fiction about werewolves, and that in selecting the stories to include in the anthology I would have to grapple with difficult choices. In going over the stories, however, I found individual characteristics and identities of werewolves that challenged the assumption that all werewolves are the same and that they can be safely packed away in the genre called *horror*.

A pattern of selection emerged. There are, I discovered, erotic, rapacious, diabolical, supernatural, victimized, avenging, guilty, unabsolved, and voluntary werewolves, all of whom deserved to be included in this anthology and to be rescued from stereotyping. Representative figures of each kind are included in the sections that follow. If in some cases there is an overlap of characteristics, the defining feature of the werewolf determined the placement.

Werewolf fiction is not a breeding ground for trivial or sensational or blood-curdling stories but is a deep pool that mirrors aspects of human life that can only be faced by looking into that pool. Whether the story is by the ancient Ovid or by the contemporary Brian Stableford, each is arresting as it reveals aspects of human nature hidden in the psyche. The tradition of werewolf fiction is a long-lived, compelling one, worthy of survival and continuing attention.

A book that has been long in the making accumulates debts. I wish to thank Beverley Kemp, a member of the Humanities Reference Service of the British Library, and David Smith, librarian in the General Research Division of the New York Public Library, for tracing a biographical entry; Kathleen Struck of the Hekman Library at Calvin College for obtaining interlibrary loans; and my children and my husband for supporting me in this long quest.

# Acknowledgments

EVERY EFFORT has been made to trace copyright holders in all copyright material in this book. We gratefully acknowledge the following permissions:

"Wolves Don't Cry," by Bruce Elliott. Copyright © 1954, by Mercury Press, Inc. Copyright renewed 1982. Originally appeared in *The Magazine of Fantasy & Science Fiction*, April 1954. Reprinted by permission of Scott Meredith Literary Agency, LP.

"The Kill," by Peter Fleming. Copyright © 1931 by Peter Fleming. First published in *A Story to Tell and Other Tales*, published by Jonathan Cape, Ltd. Reprinted by permission of Kate Grimond, executor of the Estate of Peter Fleming.

"February, Cycle of the Werewolf," by Stephen King. First published by New American Library in *Cycle of the Werewolf*, 1983. "Reprinted With Permission. © Stephen King. All rights reserved."

"The Bitang," by Mihai I. Spariosu and Dezsö Benedek. Copyright © 1994 by Mihai I. Spariosu and Dezsö Benedek. First published in *Ghosts, Vampires, and Werewolves: Eerie Tales from Transylvania*, published by Orchard Books. Reprinted by permission of Mihai I. Spariosu.

*The Werewolves of London*, by Brian Stableford. Copyright © 1992 by Brian Stableford, published by Carroll & Graf Publishers, Inc. Reprinted by permission of Carroll & Graf Publishers, Inc.

"Green Messiah," by Jane Yolen. Copyright © 1988, by Jane Yolen and Martin H. Greenberg. First published in *Werewolves*, published by HarperCollins. Reprinted by permission of Curtis Brown, Ltd.

# Contributors

**Manly Banister** (1914– ), a fireman, an oiler on ships, a continuity writer for radio, has spent his life exploring many areas. He is an expert on bookbinding and etching. Two of his books on these subjects have been kept in print for many years: *The Craft of Bookbinding* and *Practical Guide to Etching and Other Intaglio Printmaking Techniques*. For a time Banister also wrote stories for *Weird Tales*.

**Dezsö Benedek** was born in Romania. Since emigrating to the United States, he has been affiliated with the University of Georgia and is currently director of the university's program in Tokyo. His academic work in cultural anthropology and comparative literature has taken him all over the world since he left Romania. His most extensive project involved several years studying the Yami, who preserve a Stone Age lifestyle on a small island off Taiwan.

**Gerald Biss** (1876–1922) is the author of *The White Rose Mystery* (1907), *The Dupe* (1909), *The Fated, Five* (1910), and *The Door of the Unreal* (1919, 1920). His werewolf novel (excerpted in section 3) was praised by H. P. Lovecraft in *Supernatural Horror in Literature* (1945) as being the "first such work to incorporate the folkloristic elements of lycanthropy into a modern mystery plot successfully."

**Algernon Blackwood** (1869–1951) was born in England, spent time in Canada as a writer for a Canadian magazine, moved to New York and became a reporter first for the *Evening Sun* and later for the *New York Times*, and returned to England in 1899 to become a writer of stories of ghosts, horror, and the supernatural. He wrote more than 150 stories, many of which are still being reprinted.

Although Blackwood spent most of his life in big cities, he felt the mystic power of nature on his frequent visits to remote islands, deep woods and forests, lakes and streams. He describes his love of nature as a passion: "I had one yearning only, intense and passionate: to get away into the woods and forests by myself. Nature, apparently, gave me something that human nature could not give." Many of his stories are based on his own experiences.

In later life, Blackwood enjoyed appearances as reader of stories on radio and television. At age seventy-nine he received an award from the Television Society for his distinguished contribution to television.

**August W. Derleth** (1909–1971), an editor, publisher, and prolific writer of fantasy fiction, collaborated with Mark Schorer on twenty "supernatural" stories that appeared in *Weird Tales*, a magazine that began in 1923 and ceased publication in 1954. *Weird Tales* was host to many of the great writers of fantasy of the twentieth century, including Ray Bradbury and H. P. Lovecraft.

Early in his life, Derleth showed an interest in stories of the supernatural. When he was seventeen years old, his first story, "Bat's Belfry," was published in *Weird Tales*. In 1930 he wrote his thesis for the B.A. degree at the University of Wisconsin on "The Weird Tale in English Since 1890." His discovery of the stories of H. P. Lovecraft led him in 1939 to found Arkham House, a small press specializing in the publication of supernatural fiction. Arkham House has outlived Derleth and is still publishing today.

**Bruce Elliott** (1915–1973) spent his short life as a novelist, short story writer, editor and publisher of *The Phoenix* (a trade journal for magicians), author of several standard texts on magic that have been translated into many languages, editor of a variety of magazines, editor of *The Best* (an anthology that included John Steinbeck, Oscar Wilde, Benjamin Franklin, and Elliott himself), and writer of detective and science fiction novels (under several pseudonyms). His most famous novel is *The Rivet in Grandfather's Neck*.

"Wolves Don't Cry" (see section 9), which appeared in 1954 in *The Magazine of Fantasy and Science Fiction*, has frequently been anthologized. The editor of the magazine described Elliott's story as "at once moving, plausible . . . and completely unlike any other you have ever read."

**Eugene Field** (1850–1895) held many journalism positions during his short lifetime. As a reporter, editor, and columnist, he worked for the *St. Louis Evening Journal*, the *St. Joseph Gazette*, the *Kansas City Times*, and the *Denver Tribune*. In his final job as a columnist for the *Chicago Morning News,* he wrote "Sharps and Flats," producing more than 7 million words in the column that he wrote six days a week. This column became famous throughout the United States and earned him a reputation as a satirist, humorist, and realist. Also an antiquarian and bibliophile who reveled in dialects, Old English ballads, and the myths of long-gone cultures, he wrote fiction set in the past.

This is the same Eugene Field who wrote poetry for children. Today, more than a hundred years after his poems were written, children still read and recite "Little Boy Blue," "Over the Hills and Far Away," and "Wynken, Blynken, and Nod." His memorials, often visited by children, can be found in Lincoln Park, Chicago; Washington Park, Denver; and the Eugene Field House in St. Louis.

**Peter Fleming** (1907–1971) had a life that was marked by adventure. An author and an explorer, even his approach to writing was an adventure. In response to an ad in the *Times* of London, he joined a search party to hunt for three men who had disappeared in the jungles of Brazil. While in Brazil he discovered that he had no aptitude for penetrating the jungle. Returning to London, he wrote *Brazilian Adventure,* a parody of travel adventure stories. In the 1930s he traveled extensively in Asia and the Soviet Union and wrote books about his experiences there.

With the coming of World War II, Fleming joined the Grenadier Guards and made his major contribution in the Asian theater where he devised a complex series of phony battle plans that deceived the Japanese in the Indian and Burmese theaters of engagement. He wrote several books about the war, including a study of Hitler's plans for the invasion of England and *The Siege at Peking.*

In his introduction to a collection of his short stories, *A Story to Tell,* Fleming stresses the importance of plot: "The art of story-telling is based on invention; and the first thing you have to invent is the plot, the skeleton of the story as I think Maugham calls it somewhere." His short stories reveal his preoccupation with what he described as "the dramatic or the would-be dramatic twist."

**Marie de France** (*fl.* 1160–1215) tells her readers that she was born in France and that she doesn't want any clerics to claim her writings as their own. Like most medieval writers, she left no biographical information and no dates of birth or death. Considered the greatest woman writer of the Middle Ages, she wrote short stories—"lays"—before Chaucer and Boccaccio made short fiction famous. While male writers of her time were writing long "romances" about the adventures and the loves of people like King Arthur, and Lancelot and Guinevere, Marie de France was writing psychologically complex short tales seen through the eyes of a woman.

Her stories reveal that she was probably a noblewoman, since her writing focuses on the complicated lives of the nobility. Since she spent time in the court of Henry II and Eleanor of Aquitaine, there is speculation that she may have been the sister of Henry II.

**Clemence Housman** (1861–1955) was known not so much as a writer and artist but as the sister of two famous brothers: A. E. Housman (classics scholar and poet) and Laurence Housman (artist and writer of poetry, plays, and art criticism). Coming to London in 1883 to study art with her brother Laurence, she focused on the fine art of wood engraving, with her engravings appearing in many books, including her own, *The Were-Wolf* (after a drawing by Laurence Housman). Many of her wood engravings are now in the Victoria and Albert Museum in London.

An elusive figure all her life (even jailed as a suffragette protestor of taxes in 1911), at the time of her death at age ninety-four, Clemence Housman had retired from wood engraving and spent her time gardening and being the companion of her brother Laurence, who died four years later, also at the age of ninety-four. In 1975 there was an exhibition at the National Book League (London) of the works of A. E. Housman, Laurence Housman, and Clemence Housman.

**Joseph Jacobs** (1854–1916) was born in Australia, emigrated to England in 1872, and to the United States in 1900. His interests in literature, anthropology, history, and ethnology led him to collecting, adapting, and retelling folklore. Before moving to the United States, Jacobs spent much of his time either listening to and recording oral versions of the tales (along with their many variants), or reading numerous written versions of the tales. His daughter said that every morning he would "take his bowler hat from the hall-stand, place the crook of his umbrella over his left arm, and start out for the British Museum to find more stories to put in his fairy books."

Well-known and respected among folklorists, he was president of the Folk-Lore Society and editor of *Folk-Lore* from 1890 to 1893.

**Stephen King** (1947– ) had his first story ("I Was a Teenage Graverobber") published in 1965 when he was eighteen years old. Since then, Stephen King's name is recognized everywhere, not only by readers of his books but also by filmgoers. With more than 70 million copies of his books in print and a wide distribution of films based on his books, he is considered the world master of the horror genre.

King's early fame came in 1974 with the publication of his first book, *Carrie,* which sold more than 3.5 million copies; his reputation was enhanced by Brian De Palma's film adaptation, *Carrie,* in 1976. Since then new titles appear frequently, among them *The Shining* (1977), *The Dead Zone* (1979), *Pet Sematary* (1983), *Misery* (1987), and most recently *The Girl Who Loved Tom Gordon* (1999).

King's books cut across cultural boundaries. Articles about his work appear in journals as diverse as *Journal of American Culture, Esquire, English Journal, Artes Liberales,* and *Connecticut Onomastic Review.* Books that attempt to guide his readers (and viewers) into the densely populated fantasy world of King are readily available: *The Reader's Guide to Stephen King, The Complete Stephen King Encyclopedia, The Stephen King Concordance, The Stephen King Phenomenon.*

**Rudyard Kipling** (1865–1936) was born in Bombay, lived in England from age six to seventeen, and returned after an eleven-year absence to India to work as a journalist. On assignment for the Allahabad *Pioneer,* he traveled widely through India, meeting civil and military leaders and observing all aspects of Indian life. When the newspaper had room for fillers, Kipling wrote poems and stories to fill the empty spots. After accumulating a number of stories, he collected them for publication. They were published in paperback in India and sold at railway bookstalls there.

With the success of his stories and poems, Kipling decided to become a full-time writer and to leave journalism and India. Although he stayed in India as a journalist for only seven years, those years provided him with such a storehouse of material that India became the source and substance of most of his writing for the rest of his life.

A prolific and popular writer of fiction and poetry, at the time of his death his reputation rested mainly on his books for children: *The Jungle Book* (1894), *Kim* (1901), and the *Just So Stories* (1902). His poems, especially those in *Barrack-Room Ballads* (1892), enjoyed wide popularity throughout the British empire. Poems like "Recessional," "Mandalay," "Danny Deever," and "If—" were recited and sung by people of all ranks and classes. Kipling was the first English writer to be awarded the Nobel Prize for literature (1907).

**Fritz Leiber** (1910–1992), born in Chicago early in the twentieth century, was to become one of the century's great names in fantasy literature. The list of awards he received is long: the Hugo Award five times, the Nebula Award three times, the World Fantasy Award, the GrandMaster Award of the Science Fiction Writers of America, the GrandMaster Award of the Horror Writers of America, and the World Fantasy Award for Life Achievement.

Before beginning his writing career, Leiber was an actor for a brief time. He joined his actor-father's road company for two years (1934–1936), appearing on stage and in film. In 1936 he began writing fantasy; throughout his life he wrote "sword and sorcery" fiction, science fiction, and horror fiction, which appeared in magazines and as hardcover and paperback books. The readership of his more than forty books (including collections of short stories) numbers in the millions.

Long before Richard Matheson and Stephen King were writing about horror in modern cities, Leiber focused on urban terror. As early as 1940 he wrote about a gun in an urban setting that did its own automated killing ("The Automatic Pistol"), and in 1941 he wrote about a disturbing urban phantom ("Smoke Ghost"). His 1943 novel about witchcraft at a modern university (*Conjure Wife*) was filmed in 1962 as *Night of the Eagle*.

**Guy de Maupassant** (1850–1893) was plagued by ill health most of his life. Suffering from delusions, hallucinations, seizures, convulsions, and delirium in the third stage of syphilis, he slit his throat in January 1892 and said to his valet, "See what I have done. I have cut my throat, it is an absolute case of madness." He spent the last eighteen months of his life in a mental hospital in

Passy. It is not surprising, then, to discover that a number of his stories focus on madness.

Fearless in his exploration of the human psyche (although he tried, not always successfully, to hide autobiographical elements in the stories), Maupassant wrote about ghosts, monsters, mutilation, masochism, alienation, diabolic possession, suicide, insanity, the pathology of death, the struggle between Saint Michael and Satan, and eternal damnation.

In spite of being plagued by ill health, Maupassant was a prolific writer. His works include poetry, plays, six novels, three travel journals, and, as he himself observed, "It was I who brought back the short story and the novelette into great vogue in France. My volumes have been translated all over the world and sell in large quantities; for newspaper publication I am paid the highest rates ever known, receiving a franc a line for my novels and five hundred francs for a single tale. . . . More editions of my works have been sold than of anyone else's except Zola's."

His short stories, most of which were written in the ten years between 1880 and 1890, have been ranked with those of Turgenev, Chekhov, Poe, and Henry James. His influence can be traced beyond France to the short stories of Kipling, Conrad, Maugham, Saroyan, and D'Annunzio. His mentor was Flaubert.

**Ovid** (43 B.C.–A.D. 18) is the Roman poet of love and myth. His poems about love, *Amores*, and his poetic manual of instructions on the art of love, *Ars amatoria*, have for centuries been the rich source of material for writers of various cultures and backgrounds. Even more famous, and more heavily borrowed from, is Ovid's *Metamorphoses*. Published about the time of the birth of Christ, it is a collection of 250 transformation myths. Fourteen centuries after Ovid, Chaucer gave the *Metamorphoses* the ultimate praise by using it in *The Canterbury Tales*. By the Renaissance, the *Metamorphoses* had been appropriated by artists, poets, and dramatists, who adapted it, translated it, and used it as the subject of their own original creations. Shakespeare's borrowings from the *Metamorphoses* in *A Midsummer Night's Dream* is only one of his appropriations; in his long poem, *Venus and Adonis*, two of Ovid's transformation myths appear, almost unaltered from their originals.

The popularity of the *Metamorphoses* seems never to have waned. The most recent translation of twenty-four of the most disturbing of Ovid's tales is by the former poet laureate of England, Ted Hughes. In the introduction to his translation, Hughes captures the continuing cultural appeal of Ovid's transformation myths: "The act of metamorphosis, which at some point touches each of the tales, operates as the symbolic guarantee that the passion has become mythic, has achieved the unendurable intensity that lifts the whole episode onto the supernatural or divine plane."

**Seabury Quinn** (1889–1969), both a practicing lawyer and a writer, was also a medical doctor (though he seems not to have practiced medicine). With this expertise in at least three fields, he took on still another field—the editorship of an undertakers' trade journal, *Casket and Sunnyside*. He quickly became known as a specialist in mortuary jurisprudence and was asked to lecture on that subject at New York's Renard School. Recognized as an acute observer of human life and death, Quinn was invited in 1950 to serve as an intelligence specialist for the US Air Force; in 1964 he was awarded a medal for meritorious civilian service.

Quinn's writing reflects his lifelong interest in psychology, in death and burial practices, and in the role of the supernatural in human life. He became the most prolific contributor of short stories and essays to *Weird Tales*: 182 items in all, beginning in its first year of publication (1923) and extending over its thirty-year life. In 1933 one appreciative reader of *Weird Tales* described Quinn as "the best writer since Poe."

**Saki** (H. H. Munro) (1870–1916), who adopted the pseudonym Saki for his writing, was born in Akyab, Burma, but from the age of two lived in England with his two aunts. At the age of twenty-three, Munro joined the military police in Burma. Seven illnesses in thirteen months forced him to return to England. He recovered quickly, moved to London, took rooms in Mortimer Street, and set out "to earn his living by writing." His stories and articles began to appear in a number of publications, including the *Westminster Gazette*, the *Morning Post*, and the *Bystander*. His work for the *Morning Post* brought him as a foreign correspondent to the Balkans to the cover the outbreak of war there. He was later sent to Macedonia, Warsaw, and St. Petersburg. While in St. Petersburg, he completed a "Saki" book that was published in London as *Reginald*.

By 1908 he was back in London in Mortimer Street as a writer and journalist. He published *The Chronicles of Clovis* in 1911 and *Beasts and Super-Beasts* in 1914.

At the beginning of World War I, Munro (at age forty-four) enlisted in the army, convinced that he should serve his country as a soldier. Refusing to accept a commission or to qualify as a German speaker, which would have gotten him an easier assignment, he was sent to France in 1914, where he saw much fighting. In November 1916, although having been down with malaria, he insisted on returning to the battlefield. After a rendezvous in no-man's-land, he returned to the trenches. Seeing a soldier light up a cigarette, he shouted, "Put that bloody cigarette out." Immediately after shouting, Munro (not the other soldier) was shot through the head by a sniper's bullet.

**Mark Schorer** (1908–1977), biographer, renowned literary scholar, and novelist, collaborated with August W. Derleth on twenty "supernatural" stories that appeared in *Weird Tales*, a magazine that was published from 1923 to 1954. *Weird Tales* was host to many of the great writers of fantasy of the twentieth century, including Ray Bradbury and H. P. Lovecraft.

Schorer is known for his definitive biography of Sinclair Lewis—a biography that is also social history—and for his long critical study titled *William Blake: The Politics of Vision.* He was the author of three novels, *A House Too Old* (1935), *The Hermit Place* (1941), and *The Wars of Love* (1954). As a writer of more than fifty short stories, thirty-two of which were collected under the title *The State of Mind* (1947), Schorer was quick to defend fantasy's postmodern appeal to a nonelitist audience; he did not hesitate to write in a genre for which traditional academic critics had a deep-rooted antipathy.

**Mihai I. Spariosu** was born in Romania. Since emigrating to the United States, he has taught at several universities. Currently a professor of comparative literature at the University of Georgia, he has written or edited several collections of stories which were published in Romania. He is also the author of studies in comparative literature, *The Wreath of Wild Olive* and *God of Many Names.*

**Brian Stableford** (1948– ) is a sociologist, a writer of science fiction novels, and a literary critic on science fiction. He has received a number of awards: the

Distinguished Scholarship Award by the International Association for the Fantastic in the Arts (1987); the J. Lloyd Easton Award for Scientific Romance in Britain, 1890–1950 (1987); the Pioneer Award by the Science Fiction Research Association for "How Should a Science Fiction Story End?" (1996).

A contributing editor to *The Encyclopedia of Science Fiction* (1979), Stableford has also contributed to numerous reference books on science fiction and fantasy literature. His *The Dictionary of Science Fiction Places* (1999) identifies and describes more than 1500 places in the intricate but vast world of science fiction. His many novels include the six-volume *Halcyon Drift* series and *The Hunger and Ecstasy of Vampires* (1996). *The Werewolves of London* (excerpted here) is followed by *The Angel of Pain* (1995) and *The Carnival of Destruction* (1996).

**Jane Yolen** (1939– ) comes from a family of writers. Her father's grandfather was a storyteller in his Finno-Russian village, her father was a journalist, and her mother wrote short stories. Yolen's own extensive writing includes children's books (*Owl Moon* won the Caldecott Award in 1988), nonfiction, screenplays, poetry, and science fiction. Among the many awards she has received are the World Fantasy Award (1988), the Mythopoeic Society Award (1986), and the Daedalus Award for the body of short fantasy fiction (1987). Her original fairy tales have earned her the title "America's Hans Christian Andersen." She is a past president of the Science Fiction Writers of America.

Yolen's writing career began early. When she was in first grade she wrote the class musical, and on her twenty-second birthday she sold her first book. Wide-ranging in her choice of subjects, Yolen writes about the Holocaust, the millennium, religious cults, dragons, ghosts, unicorns, vampires, witches, space travel, marine animals, birds, and werewolves.

# Introduction

WEREWOLVES ARE ALIVE. They live in the twentieth century. Cases of lycanthropy—of human beings who believe themselves transformed into a wolf and who exhibit wolf characteristics and behavior—have been reported in recent psychiatric literature.

When medical researchers at McLean Hospital in Belmont, Massachusetts, came across four reports of lycanthropy in the psychiatric literature, they decided to review the number of cases that they had seen in their hospital in the twelve years from 1974 to 1986. They discovered, to their surprise, that they had treated twelve cases of animal transformation. Several cases were of metamorphosis into a wolf, but there were also cases where the patient had adopted the characteristics and behavior of a cat, rabbit, bird, gerbil, dog, or tiger.

Medical cases of lycanthropic behavior, however, are nothing new, and the diagnoses of lycanthropy over the centuries have remained relatively constant. Today's psychiatrists link lycanthropy to a number of psychoses: paranoid schizophrenia, chronic brain syndrome, pseudoneurotic schizophrenia, schizoid personality traits, delusional depression, bipolar disorder, obsessive-compulsive disorder, borderline personality disorder, hysterical neurosis of the dissociative type, psychomotor epilepsy, drug abuse (hallucinogen), alcohol abuse, autism connected with feral manifestations in children.

Yesterday's psychiatrists gave similar diagnoses. Paulos Aigina, for example, a physician who lived in seventh-century Alexandria, attributed the causes of lycanthropy to brain malfunction, to humoral pathology, and to the use of hallucinogenic drugs. Ten centuries later in seventeenth-century England, Robert Burton, an avid student of psychology and abnormal mental behavior, analyzed and diagnosed all the mental illnesses that he could locate through extensive research in the vast literature of abnormal psychology. In his book *Anatomy of Melancholy*, he classified lycanthropy as a form of insanity (melancholia).

Theories about the origin and nature of lycanthropy have also abounded over the centuries. Ongoing debates continue about whether a human being can actually, metaphysically, be metamorphosed into an animal form. As early as the fifth century, St. Augustine denied the possibility of the actual physical metamorphosis of a human being into a wolf:

> It is very generally believed that by certain witches' spells and the power of the Devil men may be changed into wolves . . . but they do not lose their human reason and understanding, nor are their minds made the intelligence of a mere beast. Now this must be understood in this way: namely, that the Devil creates no new nature, but that he is able to make something appear to be which in reality is not. For by no spell nor evil power can the mind, nay, not even the body corporeally, be changed into the material limbs and features of any animal . . . but a man is fantastically and by illusion metamorphosed into an animal, albeit he to himself seems to be a quadruped.

The debate about the role of the devil in metamorphosis was continued by such luminaries as St. Boniface, Thomas Aquinas, and King James I of England, among many other prominent thinkers throughout the ages.

In the environment in which these debates were carried on in sixteenth-century Europe, many werewolves were brought to trial and condemned to death. In France, Henri Boguet, Supreme Judge of the St. Claude district in Burgundy, wrote a book, *Discours des Sorciers* (1608), that recounts in vivid detail the werewolf trials of the sixteenth century, many of which he had presided over. Those werewolves who were pronounced guilty of monstrous crimes, including cannibalism, were condemned to death by burning at the stake; their ashes were ordered to be scattered. All traces of them were to be obliterated so that no one in the community could be contaminated by the presence of their bones.

In nineteenth-century post-Civil War Pennsylvania, werewolves were also seen. According to Henry W. Shoemaker, the wolfish creatures which infested Elk Creek Gap in Centre County between Throne's Farm in Brush Valley and Millheim were probably werewolves. There was twenty-four-hour hauling of lumber through the gap and at night what seemed to be gigantic dogs or wolves came off Hundsrick Mountain and got on the loaded sledges;

they were of such weight that they bogged down the horses, making hauling an almost impossible task. Others put their front paws on the back of the sleds, holding them down as if they were iron, and making the horses balk after their frantic efforts under the driver's cruel *sjamboks* or blacksnake whips. . . .

> In Lingle Valley, between Centre and Mifflin counties, in the log cabin where Edgar Allan Poe is said to have spent a night on his hunt for a legacy in Poe Valley, 1838, a boy child was born who developed long hairs between his fingers and on the sides of his feet. "He will do no good; he will become a garol," said his great-grandmother. When he was eight years old, he began running away, becoming restless on nights when the wolves were out. He was usually found near the wolves' hairy beds. (*New York Folklore Quarterly* 1952)

In our contemporary world, the psychologist C. G. Jung approached the phenomenon of metamorphosis not from the standpoint of demonic influence but from the standpoint of the role of the personality in dissociation. Uncovering autonomous psychic factors in the human personality, Jung identified an autonomous factor that he labeled "the beast within us all." His official designation of this archetype was the "shadow." Under this rubric Jung placed lycanthropy, recognizing that werewolfism is a phenomenon which has been occurring for millennia.

Anne Rice, our contemporary world's leading writer of vampire fiction, proposes still another theory for the metamorphosis of a human being into a wolf:

> I would like to suggest that the werewolf in many instances embodies a potent blending of masochistic and sadistic elements. On the one hand, man is degraded as he is forced to submit to the bestial metamorphosis; on the other hand, he emerges as a powerful sadistic predator who can, without regret, destroy other men. The werewolf as both victim and victimizer, wrapped in magic, may arouse emotions in us that are hard to define.

In today's popular psychology, we frequently hear references to the

"Other," to the "Outsider," not only as a psychological reality but especially in connection with criminal behavior, where attempts to explain horrific acts reach out for the concept of an Other. The Other is identified as the kind of person who has never been socially assimilated, who feels rejected by the community and even by the family, and, hence, is one who reverts to the violent behavior commonly associated with animals, not with civilized human beings.

In addition to theories of lycanthropy—its causes, nature, and cures—journalistic reports regularly appear of so-called werewolf crimes. On 17 December 1976, for example, the *London Daily Mail* carried the headline "We Have Werewolf Killer, Say Police," reporting on the capture of the multiple murderer known as "The Werewolf of Paris." The first paragraph of the article reads: "A man was charged last night with the 'werewolf' murders of seven women in seven years."

Where it is applied in criminal instances, the word *werewolf* functions as a powerful moral metaphor. The designation *werewolf* seems to be a linguistic attempt to face the unfathomable: it projects into the word *werewolf* what is submoral, subrational, subhuman, that is, multiple murders, sexual attacks, cannibalism, torture, sadomasochism, satanism. The irony is that wolves (except in cases of injury or hunger) do not kill, attack, mutilate, or in any way harm other wolves. According to recent research, wolves live in packs and establish congenial, bonding relationships and a society founded on trust. If one of their number develops killer instincts, that criminal wolf is destroyed for the good of the community.

ALONGSIDE the medical, theological, psychological, and popular notions of lycanthropy, a body of stories grew up. One of the earliest stories of a human being turned into a werewolf appeared in ancient Greece. In a fourth-century dialog, the philosopher Plato makes a reference to a werewolf. It is the story of the metamorphosis of Lycaon, retold here by the Roman poet Ovid (see section 7) four centuries after Plato. Among the Greek and Roman mythologists, historians, narrators, and poets who told their own versions of the myths of metamorphosis are Homer, Pausanias, Herodotus, Pliny, Marcellus Sidetes, and Petronius.

The Hebrew Old Testament also gives an early account of metamorphosis. Because of his offensive *hubris*, the Babylonian king Nebuchadnezzar (d.

562 BC) was transformed by God into a man-beast. For a year he lived with the beasts of the field, eating grass like an ox, growing hair like eagles' feathers, sprouting nails like birds' claws (Daniel 4:33).

In the medieval period, stories of werewolves were not uncommon. Giraldus Cambrensis, an ecclesiastic who was elected to be bishop of St. David's in 1198, tells a compassionate story of a werewolf pair who requested last rites for the dying female werewolf. Marie De France's "Lai de Bisclavret" is a twelfth-century story of a nobleman condemned to a life as a werewolf by his wife (see section 6). Another twelfth-century narrative is the story of "Guillaume de Palerne," a boy whose stepmother rubbed him with a magic ointment and turned him into a werewolf. And the Arthurian legends include a story (though an unfamiliar tale not included in standard editions) told to King Arthur by King Gorlagon of his transformation into a werewolf by his adulterous wife.

In Shakespeare's day, stories of metamorphosis found their way into drama. Who can forget the delightfully humorous transformation of Bottom, a "hempen homespun" who talks like a human being but has the head of an ass, in *A Midsummer Night's Dream*? Or the erotomanic Duke Ferdinand, transformed into a werewolf in John Webster's *The Duchess of Malfi*, where "lycanthropia" is described by Duke Ferdinand's doctor:

> In those that are possessed with 't there o'erflows
> Such melancholy humor they imagine
> Themselves to be transformed into wolves;
> Steal forth to church-yards in the dead of night
> And dig dead bodies up: as two nights since
> One met the Duke 'bout midnight in a land
> Behind Saint Mark's church, with the leg of a man
> Upon his shoulder; and he howled fearfully;
> Said he was a wolf, only the difference
> Was, a wolf's skin was hairy on the outside,
> His on the inside; bade them take their swords,
> Rip up his flesh, and try.
>
> V.ii

In the nineteenth century, werewolf novels had to compete with Mary

Shelley's *Frankenstein*, a "supernatural" story of a human being created from charnel-house bones by the Genevan student Frankenstein. (Its popularity continues today as a novel, but especially in its many film versions.) Serialization, a common form of narrative writing in the nineteenth century, contributed to the popularity of a werewolf novel titled *Wagner: The Wehr-Wolf*, by George W. M. Reynolds; it appeared in seventy-seven chapters in *Reynold's Miscellany*. While a number of writers joined the "werewolf novelists"— Clemence Housman (see section 1), Charles Maturin, and Samuel Rutherford Crockett among them—many more joined the ranks of the short story writers: Catharine Crowe, Sutherland Menzies, Guy de Maupassant (see section 2); Sir Gilbert Campbell, Count Eric Stenbok, Rudyard Kipling (see section 4); Robert Louis Stevenson.

In the early twentieth century, a few werewolf novels were published. One of the most enduring of those novels is Guy Endore's *The Werewolf of Paris*, which was published in 1933, was made into a Hollywood film in 1935 with the same title, and into a British-made film in 1961 titled *Curse of the Werewolf*. Other novels include Gerald Biss's *The Door of the Unreal* (see section 3), Charles Swem's *Were Wolf*, Frederick Marryat's *The White Wolf of the Harz Mountains*, and *The Wolf Demon* by a person described as "the Author of *Buffalo Bill*."

SHORT STORY WRITERS of the early twentieth-century werewolves include Eugene Field (see section 5), Saki (see sections 2 and 9), Algernon Blackwood (see section 8), and Peter Fleming (see section 6). Many werewolf stories appeared in *Weird Tales*, a fantasy magazine that was published from 1923 to 1954. Among the writers who appeared in it were Seabury Quinn (see sections 3 and 8), August Derleth and Mark Schorer (see section 5), Manly Banister (see section 1), and Fritz Leiber (see section 4).

A renewed interest in the werewolf novel in the latter part of the twentieth century has seen writers like Stephen King (see section 1), Brian Stableford (see section 3), Alice Borchardt (Anne Rice's sister), Bruce Lowery, Pat Murphy, and Henry Garfield adding novels to the age-old collections of werewolf fiction. (There is also a rash of werewolf novels for young adult readers appearing in the "horror" genre, either as individual titles or in series.)

Short story writers have been returning to the werewolf theme. The international scene includes the young Russian writer Victor Pelevin's "A Werewolf Problem in Central Russia," the South African writer J. A. Rio-Neuhof's "Die

Weerwolf," the Romanian writers Mihai I. Spariosu and Dezsö Benedek's "The Bitang" (see section 7), and the American writers Bruce Elliott's "Wolves Don't Cry" and Jane Yolen's "Green Messiah" (see section 9).

ALTHOUGH THIS ANTHOLOGY is not about actual medical cases of were-wolfism, the etiology of lycanthropy, the theological analyses of metamorphosis, or psychological theories of mental and social aberration, it does contain stories that venture into this territory. There is no doubt that the writers of these stories touched the many possible causes of lycanthropy. And whether or not the writers believed that a human being can actually metamorphose into a wolf, they have created stories that make the reader suspend disbelief: inside the stories werewolves are alive.

It is dizzying, however, to enter the world of the fictive werewolf. It is not an isolated, artificially constructed world. Outside the fictive world of werewolves there exists a world in which the actuality of werewolves has been validated: the medical profession has observed and treated them, the legal profession has in the past brought them to trial, released them, or sentenced them to death. Although many characters in the horror genre are constructs that have no counterparts in the actual world, the world of werewolf fiction is so unsettling because lurking in the culture are documented instances of lycanthropy. The distinction between fiction and actual life blurs. The horror intensifies.

Fictive werewolves can be upsetting, both morally and psychologically. Contrary to popular opinion (often based on preconceived notions of the evil nature of the werewolf, or on the stereotypical, cosmetically altered murdering werewolf of the movies), not all werewolves are alike, either in fiction or in actuality. Werewolves shift, change, deviate from the expected. The werewolves in this anthology may destabilize readers, forcing them to perceive werewolves in a new, perhaps uncomfortable, way.

Another unforeseen eventuality is that the readers of these stories may find themselves identifying with the werewolf. Something in human beings longs for transformation—whether to a higher or to a lower form. One of the most ecstatic writings by St. Paul in the New Testament is his contemplation of, and desire to participate in, the mystery of transformation: "We shall all be changed, in a moment, in the twinkling of an eye, at the last trump: for the trumpet shall sound, and the dead shall be raised incorruptible, and we shall be changed (I Corinthians 15:51–52). The poet J. D. McClatchy echoes this innate desire: "Still, doesn't everyone long to be changed, / Transformed to, no matter, a higher or lower state" ("My Mammogram," *Ten Commandments*).

In Jungian psychology, life's *shadows* are the darker impulses that all human beings experience—the direct opposites of love, joy, peace, patience, gentleness, goodness, faith, meekness, temperance. Autonomous darker impulses are vividly displayed in Shakespeare's dramatic image of the abhorrent man-beast Caliban in *The Tempest,* who harbors unrestrained desires to rape Miranda and to murder her father, Prospero. At the end of the play, however, there is a startling revelation: Prospero acknowledges that Caliban, this "shadow," is his own darker self: "This thing of darkness I / acknowledge mine" (V.i 275–76), an acknowledgment that strikes a resonating chord within the audience.

Another aspect of being transformed into a lower state—into a were-wolf—may not call for ecstatic utterances but may give moral relief to the metamorphosed. Legitimate moral doubts arise. How responsible is a human being for horrible acts done as a werewolf? Should involuntary werewolves, those who have become werewolves through no fault of their own, be punished for crimes committed as subhumans? Is a genetic inheritance unalterable? Is there no moral or metaphysical antibiotic for an infectious werewolf bite?

Writers express these concerns and entertain these doubts in the nine sections of the anthology: "The Erotic Werewolf," "The Rapacious Werewolf," "The Diabolical Werewolf," "The Supernatural Werewolf," "The Victimized Werewolf," "The Avenging Werewolf," "The Guilty Werewolf," "The Unabsolved Werewolf," "The Voluntary Werewolf." The stories transcend the merely sensational, titillating shape-shifting of throwaway horror fiction that exists in its own pathless desert. But they do capture the eeriness, the terror, the exhilaration, and the dread of metamorphosis. The nine categories are meant to enhance the reader's pleasure, not to mar that pleasure by dissection.

Here are stories told by master storytellers whose range of narrative technique is apparent in the subtlety, variety, depth, and range of their stories. They give insight into the human condition, probing the psychological, physical, moral, spiritual, medical, and philosophical aspects of transformation into a werewolf. Their stories defy simplistic analysis and challenge the reader to complex emotions—even empathy—while they awaken horror, distaste, fear, anxiety, and love.

# PART ONE

# The Erotic Werewolf

The word erotic has an aura—the atmosphere around it is sexual and associated with the female seductress, with the male predator, and with menacing images of violence. In this section, one erotic werewolf is a male predator and two are female, one a seductress, the other an innocent lover who hunts down the erotic memory of human love with a tenderness not usually associated with werewolves.

Stephen King's male werewolf is a part of the horror genre that King is famous for. "When you read horror," King writes in his introduction to Night Shift (1993), "you don't really believe what you read. You don't believe in vampires, werewolves, trucks that suddenly start up and drive themselves. The horrors that we all do believe in are . . . hate, alienation, growing lovelessly old, tottering out into a hostile world on the unsteady legs of adolescence."

King's Cycle of the Werewolf (1983) of which this excerpt is a part, takes place in the small town of Tarker's Mills, Maine. It begins in January in a blizzard that has trapped Arnie Westrum, flagman on the railroad, in a small shack nine miles out of town. The murderous attack of a wolf on Arnie Westrum signals the beginning of the werewolf cycle that will end in December. King's emphasis on the ordinariness of the town invaded by a werewolf intensifies the horror. This is a town where "baked beans church suppers are a weekly event . . . where the Nature Outings of the Senior Citizens' Club are religiously reported in the weekly paper."

At full moon each month there is a fresh victim of an attack by a wolflike beast. Baffled by the murders, the small town cannot admit that the murderer is one of them, that perhaps even the murderer does not know who he is. The horror springs from the internal mystery and the painful depths of probing necessary to solve it.

In February Stella Randolph, an aging virgin, celebrates her longing for sexual fulfillment by sending herself valentines from Paul Newman, Robert Redford, John Travolta, and Ace Frehley, and by fantasizing about a lover who will ravish her in a night of love. One night in bed she hears a scratching at the window—not a fantasy scratching but a real scratching. Jumping to her feet, she lets in the cold wind and snow and, to her surprise but not dismay, she sees a wolf ready to leap in. Memories of the January murder are forgotten and dim shadowings of a werewolf in the community do not surface: Stella finds this beast irresistibly erotic. His overwhelming lust does not repel her but draws a warm response from her. His eroticism is the eroticism of a wolf who smells a receptive female in heat. Her response to the erotic werewolf may mean death, but death drips with love. Dying, she believes she has found love at last.

Manly Banister's female werewolf story (1947) was one of two werewolf stories that he wrote for the magazine Weird Tales. His is the story of a tender love between an albino she-werewolf named Eena and a man of extraordinary sensibility. Living in a region of the country where there is a bounty on wolves, Joel Cameron kills a large she-wolf, not realizing that she has a whelp beside her. When he sees the young wolfling trying to escape and hears her whim-pering, Cameron scoops her up in his arms and takes her home to his cabin. He confines her to a pen, feeds her, talks to her, and loves her. When she is six months old, he agrees to sell her to a friend who plans to breed her with his best dogs. Before Eena can be sold, however, she burrows under the chicken wire fence of her pen and escapes.

After her escape, Banister shifts the viewpoint of the story from Carpenter to Eena. Banis-ter enters into Eena's consciousness and captures the ambiguous erotic feelings that hover be-tween animal and human in the breast of a female werewolf. Although Eena becomes the leader of a wolf pack, she is subject to restless moments when her memory moves hazily back to a cross-species life. She dimly remembers "kindness and something that amounted to a friendship with a creature who was called man."

Banister explores the wonder of Eena's metamorphosis into a human being. Unlike many stories of werewolf transformation when a human being is changed into a wolf at full moon, Eena experiences a reverse transformation: she changes from a wolf into a human being at full moon. The change fills her with ecstasy. Like Eve in Paradise Lost, she catches sight of her own reflection in the dark surface of the lake, and, like Eve, delights in her puzzlingly exquisite image:

> As I bent down to look, just opposite,
> A Shape within the wat'ry gleam appear'd
> Bending to look on me, I started back,
> It started back, but pleas'd I soon return'd,
> Pleas'd it return'd as soon with answering looks
> Of sympathy and love
>
> IV.460–65

And, like Eve, she falls in love with her male human counterpart.

Near the end of the story, Banister's viewpoint shifts back to Joel Cameron and the trau-matic impact that loving a werewolf has on him. The most beautiful woman he has ever seen and ever loved is also the wolf who kills cattle and humans. Her necessary death breaks his heart.

The other female werewolf, White Fell, was created by Clemence Housman to amuse her fellow students at an art school in London (first published in Atalanta magazine in 1890 and as a book in 1896). White Fell is an exquisite femme fatale cast as a beautiful woman who awakens erotic desire in a vulnerable young man. Succumbing to the magnetic power of White Fell's erotic love, Sweyn, her prey, is unable to recognize her true identity. His brother, Christian, senses immediately that White Fell is attracting his brother so that she may eventually devour him.

Housman's story, rooted in Norse mythology, channels the reader's imagination into the realm of the numinous. Set in the northern lands of ice and snow, the farmhouse and its inhabitants create a warm environment. The shadow of something sinister, however, gives a chill to the air inside the farmhouse and creates the feeling that horror lurks in corners of the room and just outside the door.

The conflict between Christian and White Fell takes place under the dark sky of a northern winter. Pursuing her beyond human endurance, Christian clings to White Fell, after miles and hours of running; and, though maimed and suffering great pain, triumphs over her in death—his a sacrificial one, hers the death of a large female white wolf at midnight.

Christian allegory frames the story. There are two opposing forces: the Good represented by the hero, Christian, and the Evil represented by the white female werewolf. The beautiful young woman dressed in white furs is the temptress-werewolf who has supernatural strength to destroy those she can get in her clutches, including a child, an old woman, and the young man who loves her. Christian's quiet heroism springs from a humility that forces him to challenge the decision of his brother to love the erotic White Fell. Christian draws his strength to destroy Evil in life and his comfort in death from the source of Love, Agape, not Eros.

Housman's story of an erotic female werewolf is often referred to as "the greatest story of lycanthropy ever written."

# February, Cycle of the Werewolf

STEPHEN KING (1947– )

*LOVE,* STELLA RANDOLPH THINKS, lying in her narrow virgin's bed, and through her window streams the cold blue light of a St. Valentine's Day full moon.

*Oh love love love, love would be like—*

This year Stella Randolph, who runs the Tarker's Mills Set 'n Sew, has received twenty Valentines—one from Paul Newman, one from Robert Redford, one from John Travolta . . . even one from Ace Frehley of the rock group Kiss. They stand open on the bureau across the room from her, illuminated in the moon's cold blue light. She sent them all to herself, this year as every year.

*Love would be like a kiss at dawn . . . or the last kiss, the real one, at the end of the Harlequin romance stories . . . love would be like roses in twilight . . .*

They laugh at her in Tarker's Mills, yes, you bet. Small boys joke and snigger at her from behind their hands (and sometimes, if they are safe across the street and Constable Neary isn't around, they will chant Fatty-Fatty-Two-by-Four in their sweet, high mocking sopranos), but she knows about love, and about the moon. Her store is failing by inches, and she weighs too much, but now, on this night of dreams with the moon a bitter blue flood through frost-traced windows, it seems to her that love is still a possibility, love and the scent of summer as he comes . . .

*Love would be like the rough feel of a man's cheek, that rub and scratch—*

And suddenly there is a scratching at the window.

She starts up on her elbows, the coverlet falling away from her ample bosom. The moonlight has been blocked out by a dark shape—amorphous

Steven King, *Cycle of the Werewolf* (New York: New American Library, 1985; copyright hardcover edition, 1983), 21–24.

5

but clearly masculine, and she thinks: *I am dreaming . . . and in my dreams, I will let him come . . . in my dreams I will let myself come. They use the word dirty, but the word is clean, the word is right; love would be like coming.*

She rises, convinced that this is a dream, because there *is* a man crouched out there, a man she *knows*, a man she passes on the street nearly every day. It is—

*(love love is coming, love has come)*

But as her pudgy fingers fall on the cold sash of the window, she sees it is not a man at all; it is an animal out there, a huge, shaggy wolf, his forepaws on the outer sill, his rear legs buried up to the haunches in the snowdrift which crouches against the west side of her house, here on the outskirts of town.

*But it's Valentine's day and there will be love,* she thinks; her eyes have deceived her even in her dream. It is a man, *that* man, and he is so wickedly handsome.

*(wickedness yes love would be like wickedness)*

and he has come this moon-decked night and he will take her. He will—

She throws the window up, and it is the blast of cold air billowing her filmy blue nightgown out behind that tells her that *this is no dream.* The man is gone and with a sensation like swooning she realizes he was never there. She takes a shuddering, groping step backward and the wolf leaps smoothly into her room and shakes itself, spraying a dreamy sugarpuff of snow in the darkness.

*But love! Love is like . . . is like . . . like a scream—*

Too late she remembers Arnie Westrum, torn apart in the railroad shack to the west of town only a month before. Too late . . .

The wolf pads toward her, yellow eyes gleaming with cool lust. Stella Randolph backs slowly toward her narrow virgin's bed until the backs of her pudgy knees strike the frame and she collapses upon it.

Moonlight parts the beast's shaggy fur in a silvery streak.

On the bureau the Valentine cards shiver minutely in the breeze from the open window; one of them falls and seesaws lazily to the floor, cutting the air in big silent arcs.

The wolf puts its paws up on the bed, one on either side of her, and she can smell its breath . . . hot, but somehow not unpleasant. Its yellow eyes stare into her.

"Lover," she whispers, and closes her eyes.

It falls upon her.

Love is like dying.

# Eena

MANLY BANISTER (1914– )

THE SHE-WOLF was silhouetted sharply against the moon-gilded waters of Wolf Lake. Silent as Death in the cover of a rotting log, Joel Cameron sighted along a dully gleaming rifle barrel. He squeezed the trigger.

The gray-tipped wolf leaped high, cavorted grotesquely in midair. The beast threshed in short-lived agony upon the ground and lay still. Joel ejected the cartridge from the smoking chamber.

"Five bucks, and all profit!" he grunted, anticipating the state bounty.

In the act of legging over the log, he stopped and swiftly raised his weapon. His attention had been so intent upon the she-wolf as she slunk from the forest edge, he had not noticed the whelp that followed her. Terrified, the whimpering wolf cub galloped toward the safety of the woods. Joel dropped his rifle and sprinted.

"I'll be darned!" he panted, scooping the wolfling up into his arms. "An albino whelp!"

In this manner, Eena the she-wolfling was introduced to the world and the ways of men.

JOEL'S CABIN was a mile down the lakeshore, hidden in a wooded draw that protected it from wind and weather, and separated from the edge of the lake by a thin screen of timber.

Joel Cameron had been born and raised in the high pine woods. Later fortune, through the medium of a battered typewriter and a skillful ability to weave a fanciful yarn, had led him to life in the city. But every Spring he re-

In *Weird Tales* (September, 1947).

turned to the cabin he had built in the hills and stayed there until the crispness of early Autumn presaged the coming of snow.

It was an ideal life, one to which Joel's temperament was ideally suited. When editorial favor inclined to the lean side, which it often did, he could depend upon the cabin in the mountains for refuge from the palsied palms of greedy landlords. The state wolf bounty kept the figurative wolf from his door by inviting the literal one within.

Eena proved to be different from the usual wolfkind. Joel recognized this from the first. Even her albinism was different. She lacked the red eyes usually associated with the lack of pigmentation. They were gray-hazel, and they gave Joel a weird sense being somehow human. They were distinctly out of place in the snow-white lupine visage of the wolflet.

She grew rapidly and prodigiously. At one time or another, every homesteader in the valley below passed by to see the albino. Some admired her look of intelligence, the growing strength of her. Some deplored the thought that a wolf so handy for killing should be allowed to live.

Pierre Lebrut, a trapper who had a tumbledown cabin a mile away, rubbed his palms on his greasy overalls and spat toward the caged wolf.

"Cameroon," said he, "I catch her, I keel you bat!" He scowled at the white wolf, Eena's hackles raised in response. "She bad one all right," Pierre growled. "She bring bad luck. You see!"

The man went away, and Joel crouched by the chicken-wire fence of Eena's pen. He had got into the practice of talking softly to the animal.

"Kill you? Not you, my beauty!" He chuckled fondly. The half-grown wolf cocked her head at him and stared with unblinking, gray-hazel eyes.

"Sometimes I wonder if you'd let me scratch your ears?" He smiled through the fence. Eena lolled her tongue with a friendly grin. "On the other hand," Joel told her, "I need both my hands to type with! You're an independent she-cuss. Maybe that's why I like you!"

Eena furnished Joel with material for several stories that went over well. As the Summer drifted somnolently past, he regarded her with increasing fondness. By the time Fall came around, Joel considered himself on friendly terms with the wolf, though he never dared venture close enough to touch her.

By this time, too, the curiosity of the countryside was more or less satiated in regard to the albino wolf, and the traffic of visitors had long since returned to normal . . . one every two weeks.

Pete Martin worked the first homestead on the country road that led to Valley Junction. Pete Martin was the valley's pride as a wolf hunter.

"Sent three sons an' a daughter through college on wolf hides!" he often asserted, referring to the monthly bounty checks from the state.

"I'll give you fifty bucks fer that wolf-bitch," Pete told Joel. "You'll be winterin' in the city pretty soon, an' you can't take the hellion with you. I want to cross her with some o' my best dogs, an' raise me a breed o' good wolf hunters."

Eena, six months old now and as big as a grown wolf, snoozed in the shade of the kennel Joel had built for her. Joel frowned.

"If I could think of some way to keep her," he told the homesteader, "I'd never part with her. Under the circumstances, I'll take your offer. I'll be driving to the city within three days. I'll bring her by then."

The two men shook hands solemnly on the agreement.

That night, Eena burrowed under the chicken wire fence of her enclosure. Like a silent wraith, she disappeared into the trackless wilds of the pine forest.

Joel drove his battered coupe back to the city, fifty dollars poorer than he might have been.

October winds rustled the waters of Wolf Lake. Deciduous trees turned red and gold and brown. The foothills blazed with Nature's paint pot.

November skies were leaden. The frost giants awakened in the earth. Snow smothered the valley and the hills. Existence in the wild turned bleak and harrowing. On silent pads the wolf pack stole into the haunts of men. They followed the lead of a great, white she-wolf, the largest and most cunning wolf ever seen.

The wolves swept down from the hills and lurked in the swirling skirts of the blizzard to strike and kill. They took a costly toll from the livestock that pastured in the valley. The homesteaders cursed the white she-leader of the pack. Joel Cameron's name was anathema on every tongue.

Eena was a year old the following spring. The handful of wolfling Joel Cameron had carried to his cabin a year before was now twice the size of the largest, sturdiest male in her pack. It was to this, and to her wise cunning, that she owed her leadership.

Eena regarded the black wolves lolling around her in the warm sun. These were her kind, yet not her kind. She knew she was different in more ways than size and the color of her pelt. For weeks she had felt a restlessness stirring inside her, an inexplicable thrilling of unknown significance.

Across the lake, which glittered like a turquoise jewel in its setting of forest emerald, the sun sparkled upon the snowy mantilla of the mountain that thrust bare, stone shoulders up from a clinging bodice of pine woods.

Memory stirred the mind of the white she-wolf. She was thinking of a cabin hidden in a woodsy draw, hard by the waters of the lake. She remembered a clean-lined young face, a soothing voice that had spoken to her in pleasing, unintelligible syllables. She remembered kindness and something that amounted to friendship with a creature who was called man. Eena whimpered and got up.

The wolves rose with her and ringed around expectantly. A long moment Eena stood poised and silent, dwarfing the members of her pack. A thought, feeling . . . a command . . . went from her to them. The wolves sank back upon their haunches, tongues lolling. Eena turned and trotted alone into the forest.

The white wolf padded silently along sun-barred aisles of the forest. Her path led in an easy circle around the lake. Near sunset, she came unerringly upon the clearing occupied by Joel Cameron's cabin.

She crept into a thicket of elderberry trees and peered expectantly forth. Not toward the cabin, for that with the setting sun was at her back. Her questing glance winged across the darkening blue waters of the lake and fixed upon the glowing summit of the mountain.

Fascinated, Eena watched the fading beauty of it. The sky turned smoky-hued, a star or two glittered diamond-hard. A golden glow paled the sable sky beyond the shoulder of the mountain.

Crouched in the voiceless shadows, Eena held her breath and tingled with suspense. Instinct gave her thrilling warning. She was about to witness the essence of her difference from the wolfkind.

The moon came up full, a pumpkin-yellow disk, and rested its chin upon the mountain to ponder the scene thoughtfully before commencing its climb into the sky . . . and Eena *changed*.

The change shook her with ecstasy. Bubbling rapture accompanied the smooth flowing of supple muscles, the adjusting of bones in their sockets. An excitement of sensual pleasure engulfed every nerve and sinew. Afterward, she lay for long supine, one arm flung across her eyes to bar the eldritch glare of the moon, panting, trembling with remembered delight.

She sat up at last and thrilled to the shapely beauty of her form. Eena knew she was a woman, and she was content. She did not question how this had come about.

Eena crept down to the water's edge and surveyed her reflection in the dark surface of the lake. A faint breeze stirred the platinum tresses against round, golden shoulders. Her face was eager, full-lipped with flaring brows accenting her gray-hazel eyes. Her body was high of breast and long of leg, and the moonlight caressed her with a touch of mystery and magic.

The cabin was still, highlighted and shadowed in the moon-brimming canyon. Eena padded around it in a cautious circle. The air was dead, without scent. The man with the kind face and soothing voice was not here.

Puzzled and hurt, Eena turned away. She swam a while in the icy waters of the lake, reveling in the tonic effect of the chill.

Later, she roamed aimlessly, enjoying the easy response of her nerves and muscles. Once, her keen wolf sense detected a rabbit quaking in a patch of brush. She started it up. As the frightened animal ran out, she sprinted swiftly and seized it in her hands. The rabbit uttered a thin, terrorized shriek, and died.

Eena sank her teeth in the rabbit's throat and exulted to the gushing warmth of blood. She sat down upon the needled turf, methodically tore the animal to pieces, and ate it.

From time to time in her wandering, Eena responded to her woman's nature and crept down to the lake to admire her reflection.

The night was short . . . too short. Eena's aimless peregrination brought her just before dawn to another cabin. Pierre Lebrut lived here. Eena's sensitive nose caught the trapper's reek strong upon the air. A sluggish memory stirred in her brain. Eena snarled without sound and retreated with the prickling of invisible hackles stirring the length of her spine.

A twig snapped under Eena's foot. Steel piano wire sang, and a bent sapling straightened with a rush. Eena was flung to earth, one foot jerked high in the wire noose of a snare. She threshed in wild panic, clawing and snapping wolf-fashion at the searing pain in her ankle.

Within the musty cabin, Lebrut sat up in his tumbled bunk.

"By gar, she sound like bear in dat trap!" He slipped into heavy boots—he slept in his pants and undershirt—seized his rifle and hurried outside.

Gray dawn lighted the east, reflected palely into the forest. Lebrut saw the woman caught in his snare, laid down his rifle, and hurried to release her.

"Sacre nom d'un loup!" he muttered, slackening the wire to remove the noose from Eena's threshing ankle. "Lady, you pick fine time an' place for peec-neec—an' w'at you do wit' no clo'es on?"

Pierre was excited and his voice shrill. The scent of him was overpowering in Eena's nostrils. She bit him savagely on the calf.

Pierre yelled in sudden fright. He fell heavily on the wolf-girl, and she snapped and clawed in renewed terror. The man grunted with anger and fought her, pinioned her arms.

"You wild one, *hein?*" Eena's body was closed, arched and quivering. Pierre grinned. "Maybe Pierre tame you wit' a kees, *hein?*"

The sun came up over the shoulder of the mountain and tinged the lake with blood. . . . And Eena *changed.*

It was no sensation of pleasure to return to the wolf. Eena felt the agony of the change in every muscle and nerve. She screamed with the horrid crunching and grinding of bones in her head, lengthening into the lupine muzzle. Albino fur sprouted like a million thorny barbs from her tender skin.

Pierre was still wide-eyed and frozen with horror when the fangs of the agonized wolf ripped the life from his terror-stricken body.

PETE MARTIN LOOKED GRIM as he pried open the stiffened fingers of the dead trapper. The wind stirred a tuft of albino fur on the dead man's palm.

"Your albino bitch, Joel," the homesteader said.

Joel bit his lip.

"It's a devil of a thing for a man to come back to, Pete." He looked stolidly down at the dead man. "Poor Pierre! He died hard." Joel brought his glance up to meet the kindly stare of the homesteader. "I know the valley blames me for not killing Eena when she was a pup."

Martin shrugged. "It's too late now for blame, Joel. Maybe I'm to blame for not takin' her with me the day I offered to buy her. I dunno." He scratched his long jaw. "Well, we better see about gettin' Pierre properly planted, I guess."

Joel's expression was darkly stormy. "I feel responsible for the cattle . . . for Pierre." He wondered silently when and where the white wolf would kill again. He tongued dry lips. "I'll track her down and destroy her."

"There's a thousand dollars on her hide, Joel. Every homesteader in the valley chipped in."

"If I bring in her hide," Joel clipped, "it won't cost the homesteaders a cent!"

The homesteader's gray eyes lighted with a friendly gleam.

"Figured you'd look at it like that, Joel. I'll give you what help I can. . ."

Joel spent the following month in the hinterland, returning to his cabin at intervals only to replenish supplies. The wolves were wary. He seldom came upon wolf sign, and saw no wolves at all. But he heard them. By night their lonesome song rang eerily through the forest and echoed from the mountains.

Joel made a final return to his cabin, and that night drove his coupe down a moonlit road to the Martin homestead.

"Reckoned you wouldn't find her," the homesteader acknowledged Joel's acquiescence to defeat. "She knows she's hunted an' will always manage to be someplace else. She was here night before last with her pack an' got my prize heifer."

Joel made a gesture of despair. "You see what I'm up against? Besides, I'm behind in my work. I came up here to finish a book. The publisher is yelling his head off for it. How can I write a book and hunt wolves, too?"

The homesteader spat a fine stream of tobacco juice. "You go ahead an' write your book, son. You've made your try, an' 'twarn't your fault you failed. Some of us are gittin' together in the mornin'. We'll take to the wolf trail an' stick it out till we git her!"

Joel's heart felt heavy. He still had a fond memory of the white she-wolf he had nursed from babyhood. He remembered her attitude of sage intelligence, her qualities that had made her seem almost human. Then he remembered she had turned killer, and he peered into the moon shadows as he drove along the county road, half afraid he might spy her lurking there.

He turned down the indistinct ruts that led to his lakeside cabin, and another mile of bumpy going brought him home. The wobbling headlights swept across the cabin front, revealed an open door.

Joel suffered mild panic. Had a bear forced entry? He could imagine the shambles the animal had made of the interior. He sprang out and approached the house cautiously, rifle ready. Everything inside was in order. He lit the mantle of the kerosene lamp, went out and shut off the car lights, and reentered the cabin.

Eena lay curled on a bearskin rug in front of the stone fireplace. Her platinum curls glistened silver contrast against the dusky gold of her naked skin. She supported her chin with her hands and watched him with wide, wary eyes. A patch of full-moon brilliance, brighter than the lamplight, puddled the floor at her feet.

Joel stared. She was a dream come to life. The shock of seeing her there dismayed him.

"Who are you?" he essayed at last.

Eena stirred languidly. Her expression mimicked a wolfish grin. Hot blood surged into Joel's cheeks. He caught up a dressing gown and flung it to her.

"Put it on," he ordered.

Eena sobered, regarded the garment, and swung her level glance back to the man.

"Haven't you ever seen clothes before?" he asked sarcastically. He crossed over and adjusted the robe hastily about her shoulders. "Suppose one of the neighbors came by?"

The possibility was not likely, he knew. He said things simply to cover up his own shock and embarrassment. He sat down heavily in a leather club chair and stared at her. Eena stared back with friendly indifference.

Joel's mind boiled with fantastic questions. The girl remained silent. Only her eyes spoke, and their meaning was not clear to the beleaguered man.

He gave up trying to draw a word from her. Was she a deaf-mute? Who was she? Why was she here? He recalled stories he had heard of white savages; but those were found only in the wilds of the South American jungle, or in some hidden Shangri-la of Tibet. He tried to place her racial type and was unsuccessful. There was something familiar about the shape and look of her eyes, but what it was eluded him.

He knew only that she was very beautiful, and that he wanted her as he had never wanted another human being before. He could not know that Eena was not quite . . . human.

"I can't sit here all night, just looking at you," he said at last. He grinned with wry humor. "It's an idea, though, at that!" He stood up. "Lady, if you will consent to occupy the guest room tonight, the hotel can accommodate you."

Joel held out his hand to help her rise. Eena moved like a flash, shaking off the encumbering dressing gown. She paused at the door and smiled at him. The lamplight made molten gold of her body, a tawny silhouette against the moon-silvered outdoors.

Then she was gone, like a wolf goes, on swift, silent pads.

And with her, the warmth went from the cabin. Joel felt a chill, followed by a helpless feeling of immeasurable loss.

In the cold, gray light of dawn, the cabin shivered to a thunderous knocking. Joel tumbled from bed, threw on a dressing gown, and greeted Pete Martin at the door. Martin was backed by half a dozen husky homesteaders.

"Thought I'd let you know we're headin' along the wolf trail."

Joel grumpily asserted the idea was a fine one, he was glad to know it, and now would they go away and let him sleep?

"We wouldn't have stopped," Martin apologized, "except we wondered about your visitor last night."

Joel's jaw cracked in the middle of a yawn. He swallowed hard and flushed blackly.

"Visitor? What visitor?" he hedged.

The homesteader crooked a finger, and Joel followed out upon the porch. Martin pointed out the wolf tracks that crossed and crossed the yard.

"Those are the tracks of your white bitch, Joel. She came home last night. Didn't see her, did you?"

Joel closed his eyes. He felt a swimming sensation in his head.

"No. No, I didn't see her." Fantastically, he thought of the visitor he had seen, and thought of her body mutilated and torn by sharp wolf fangs. He shuddered.

The homesteader shrugged. "Keep a lookout for her, Joel. She'll be back again . . . if we don't git her first!"

He gestured to his companions, and they filed off into the forest. Joel stood alone, looking down at the tracks . . . at one track that had gone unnoticed by the others—the single print of a woman's shapely foot.

JOEL CAMERON WAS PLEASED with his own industry. He finished proof-reading the final chapter of his book, gathered the manuscript together, and wrapped it for shipment. There, it was off his mind.

He took the manuscript down to the village post office, collected a few necessary supplies. Toward sunset, he legged into his car and chugged away up the county road toward home.

Night shadows fell swiftly. The sky turned smoky, then sequinned. The moon came up full over the roof of the forest.

Joel turned into the ruts that meandered through the woods to his cabin. Wobbling headlamps bored a tunnel through the gloom. The night was eerily still throughout the pine woods. Joel slewed the machine around a bumpy turn. The wolf-woman stood starkly illumined in the glare of the headlights.

Joel jammed a foot on the brakes. He scrambled from his seat, calling. Eena flashed into the shadows. After two minutes struggle with the whipping underbrush, Joel gave up and went back to his car.

He was suddenly lonesome and despondent. He ground the coupe through the final furlong and killed the motor in front of the cabin.

Eena sat quietly upon the porch.

Even with the lights off, Joel could see her there. Her form was tawny gold in the moonlight. Her hair was a flashing silver aura enhaloing her laughing face.

Joel started toward her, thought better of it, and sat on the running board. Eena was less than ten feet away. Joel said nothing. Eena answered in kind.

After a while, Joel began to talk to her, softly. He mused and wondered aloud, letting his thoughts drift with the association of his words. Eena cocked her head attentively. She appeared to be listening, but he knew that his words held no meaning for her.

What language would serve him? What syllables would convey to her knowledge of the tumultuous beating in his breast her simple presence evoked?

He moved toward her, murmuring softly. He took the firm, golden flesh of her arm in his grasp. Eena looked up into Joel's strong kindly face. Her eyes spoke the thought her tongue could not.

Joel drew her gently to her feet. She swayed, and he caught her to him. Her lips were as tender and responsive as he had dreamed they would be. He took them, hungrily. . . .

EENA PROWLED the forest resentfully. She hated to be hunted. Twice, now, the coming of the full moon had brought her only pangs of frustration. The hunters who swarmed in the woods prevented her going to the man she loved.

The pine woods shimmered in the heat of midsummer. Hunters from all over the state, attracted by the enormous price on Eena's hide, came to blunder among the hills. When they went away, defeated, others came instead of them.

Eena had no rest. She was hounded and harried. By night, the forest twin-
kled with campfires.

Once, a hunter reckless enough to hunt alone had cornered the she-wolf.
Braving the fire of his weapon, Eena attacked and ripped the man to shreds of
bloody ruin. The price on Eena's life doubled overnight.

Once, too, she had been trapped by a horde of hunters and their dogs at
the lip of a precipice, overlooking Wolf Lake. The she-wolf leaped, and swam
to safety through a hail of lead. The rock thereafter was called Wolf Leap, and
Eena's character became legendary.

The swelling moon nightly presaged the approach of the change. Eena
longed for it, longed for the pleasure of her human form, and gladly paid with
the pangs of her return to the wolf. All the savage ferocity of her wolf nature
rebelled at the restriction the presence of hunters imposed. Then cunning asserted itself.

Joel's cabin lay westward. Eena turned her pointed muzzle into the east.
On silent pads she fled through the silver and dross of the moonlit forest. At
dawn, she rested.

Facing northward, she took up her way for a number of hours; then she
turned into the west.

It was not easy running. The way led up steep mountainsides, down precipitous proclivities. She swam mountain torrents, crossed ravines on fallen pines.
When she hungered, she pulled down a white-tail deer and gorged on the kill.

In midafternoon, Eena made her way southward. She had completely en-
circled the hunters that swarmed in the forest.

The white wolf came at last into familiar territory at the west end of the
lake. She slackened her pace, although a frantic urge to hurry assailed her. She
knew the limitations of her human form, and with moonrise tonight the
Change would be visited upon her. She wanted to be close by the cabin when
that came to pass.

She had slightly more than an hour to span the miles that yet lay between.

Eena skulked along in the shadowy underbrush, pausing at intervals to
scent danger. She soon paralleled the lakeshore, a hurrying white wraith in the
green-gray shadows of the forest. The wind brought a smell of dampness off
the lake, a formless breath of stale fishiness. The pines cast long shadows upon
the water. The sky darkened in the east.

A rifle cracked. The whistling missile spent itself far out over the lake, and Eena gathered her muscles, with the instant response of spring steel, and lunged ahead. A man yelled, and dogs began to bark frantically. Eena doubled away from the lake, putting on a fresh burst of speed.

The wind had betrayed her. It had come to her nostrils from the sterile face of the water, while her danger lay on the other hand.

A rifle spat livid flame in the green glare ahead. Eena leaped, snarling and snapping at the trenchant pain in her shoulder. Spurting blood reddened her muzzle, staining the snowy pelt of her side.

Other rifles cracked all around her. Rifle balls whined nastily through the woods. The yelping of dogs was bedlam.

The white wolf recovered her stride, in spite of her searing wound. She ran with desperation and terror hounding her; her goal an idea interlocked with the memory of a kindly face and a soothing voice.

Eena fled for the protection of the only being in all the forest whom she loved, the one man among men who loved her.

Joel Cameron heard the flat racketing of gunfire, the distant shouting and yelping. A strange uneasiness held him motionless, listening. He caught up his rifle and hurried to the door.

The noise swelled louder by the moment. Twilight pressed down upon the forest, swirled into the clearing about the cabin. Joel saw the men, then, flitting silhouettes between the pines, limned against the tarnished silver of the lake. The forest trembled with the belling of the dog pack.

His ears caught another sound, nearer . . . more terrifying. He heard the swift whisper of racing pads, the sound of a heavy body hurtling through the undergrowth.

The enormous, pale form of the wolf leaped from the forest edge, charged relentlessly toward him. A mental gong sounded in the man's clamoring brain. Joel's rifle snapped automatically into the hollow of his shoulder. The report ripped echoes from the hills.

The murderous shock of the ball lifted the white wolf, flung her with bleeding breast back upon her haunches. Gathering the last atom of her strength, Eena lunged and fell kicking at Joel Cameron's feet.

The man sighted carefully for the mercy shot that would send a bullet crashing into Eena's brain. The moon came up full over the shoulder of the mountain, bridged the lake with its golden track, thrust a questing beam though a gap in the pines.

The effulgent glow caressed Eena's wolf form. Eena died with the ecstasy of the Change soothing the agony of her hurts.

Joel stared, uncomprehending. The rifle fell from his nerveless grasp. Slowly, his knees buckled. He dropped beside the huddled girl-shape, gathered limp, tawny shoulders against his chest, and buried his face in the silver cloud of her hair.

He was holding her like that when the hunters burst into the moonlit clearing. He did not look up, even when they went silently away.

# The Were-Wolf

CLEMENCE HOUSMAN (1861–1955)

THE GREAT FARM HALL was ablaze with firelight, and noisy with laughter and talk. None could be idle but the very young and the very old: little Rol, who was hugging a puppy, and old Trella, whose palsied hand fumbled over her knitting. The early evening had closed in, and the farm servants, come from their outdoor work, had assembled in the ample hall, which gave space for a score or more of workers. Several of the men were engaged in carving, and to these were yielded the best place and light; others made or repaired fishing tackle, and a great seine net occupied three pairs of hands. Of the women most were sorting and mixing eider feathers and chopping straw to add to it. Looms were there, though not in present use, but three wheels whirred, and the finest and swiftest thread of the three ran between the fingers of the house mistress. Near her were some children, busy too, plaiting wicks for candles and lamps. Each group of workers had a lamp in its center, and those farthest from the fire had live heat from two braziers filled with glowing wood embers, replenished now and again from the generous hearth. But the flicker of the great fire was manifest to remotest corners, and prevailed beyond the limits of the weaker lights.

Little Rol grew tired of his puppy, dropped it, and made an onslaught on Tyr, the old wolfhound, who basked dozing, whimpering and twitching in his hunting dreams. Prone went Rol beside Tyr, his young arms round the shaggy neck, his curls against the black jowl. Tyr gave a perfunctory lick, and stretched with a sleepy sigh. Rol growled and rolled and shoved invitingly, but could only gain from the old dog placid toleration and a half-observant blink.

*The Were-Wolf* (London: John Lane at the Bodley Head, Chicago: Way and Williams, 1896).

"Take that then!" said Rol, indignant at this ignoring of his advances, and sent the puppy sprawling against the dignity that disdained him as a playmate. The dog took no notice, and the child wandered off to find amusement elsewhere. . . .

Rol sprawled forward to survey the room. . . . As he slipped in among the men, they looked up to see that their tools might be, as far as possible, out of reach of Rol's hands, and close to their own. Nevertheless, before long he managed to secure a fine chisel and take off its point on the leg of the table. The carver's strong objections to this disconcerted Rol, who for five minutes thereafter effaced himself under the table.

During this seclusion he contemplated the many pairs of legs that surrounded him, and almost shut out the light of the fire. . . . A few moments later Sweyn of the long legs felt a small hand caressing his foot, and looking down, met the upturned eyes of his little cousin Rol. Lying on his back, still softly patting and stroking the young man's foot, the child was quiet and happy for a good while. He watched the movement of the strong deft hands, and the shifting of the bright tools. Now and then, minute chips of wood, puffed off by Sweyn, fell down upon his face. At last he raised himself, very gently, lest a jog should wake impatience in the carver, and crossing his own legs round Sweyn's ankle, clasping with his arms too, laid his head against the knee. . . . Sweyn forgot he was near, hardly noticed when his leg was gently released, and never saw the stealthy abstraction of one of his tools.

Ten minutes thereafter was a lamentable wail from low on the floor, rising to the full pitch of Rol's healthy lungs; for his hand was gashed across, and the copious bleeding terrified him. Then was there soothing and comforting, washing and tending, and a modicum of scolding, till the loud outcry sank into occasional sobs, and the child, tear-stained and subdued, was returned to the chimney-corner settle, where Trella nodded.

In the reaction after pain and fright, Rol found that the quiet of that firelit corner was to his mind. Tyr, too, disdained him no longer, but, roused by his sobs, showed all the concern and sympathy that a dog can by licking and wistful watching. A little shame weighed also upon his spirits. He wished he had not cried quite so much. He remembered how once Sweyn had come home with his arm torn down from the shoulder, and a dead bear, and how he had never winced nor said a word, though his lips turned white with pain. Poor little Rol gave another sighing sob over his own fainthearted shortcomings.

The light and motion of the great fire began to tell strange stories to the child, and the wind in the chimney roared a corroborative note now and then. The great black mouth of the chimney, impending high over the hearth, received as into a mysterious gulf murky coils of smoke and aspiring sparks, and beyond, in the high darkness, were muttering and wailing and strange doings, so that sometimes the smoke rushed back in panic, and curled out and up to the roof, and condensed itself to invisibility among the rafters. And then the wind would rage after its lost prey, and rush round the house, rattling and shrieking at window and door.

In a lull, after one such loud gust, Rol lifted his head in surprise and listened. A lull had also come on the babel of talk, and thus could be heard with strange distinctness a sound outside the door—the sound of a child's voice, a child's hands. "Open, open, let me in!" piped the little voice from low down, lower than the handle, and the latch rattled as though a tiptoe child reached up to it, and soft small knocks were struck. One near the door sprang up and opened it. "No one is here," he said. Tyr lifted his head and gave utterance to a howl, loud, prolonged, most dismal.

Sweyn, not able to believe that his ears had deceived him, got up and went to the door. It was a dark night, the clouds were heavy with snow that had fallen fitfully when the wind lulled. Untrodden snow lay up on the porch, there was no sight nor sound of any human being. Sweyn strained his eyes far and near, only to see dark sky, pure snow, and a line of black fir trees on a hill brow, bowing down before the wind. "It must have been the wind," he said, and closed the door.

Many faces looked scared. The sound of a child's voice had been so distinct—and the words "Open, open, let me in!" The wind might creak the wood, or rattle the latch, but could not speak with a child's voice, nor knock with the soft plain blows that a plump fist gives. And the strange unusual howl of the wolfhound was an omen to be feared. Strange things were said by one and another, till the rebuke of the house-mistress quelled them into far-off whispers. For a time after there was uneasiness, constraint, and silence; then the chill fear thawed by degrees, and the babble of talk flowed on again.

Yet half an hour later a very slight noise outside the door sufficed to arrest every hand, every tongue. Every head was raised, every eye fixed in one direction. "It is Christian; he is late," said Sweyn.

No, no; this is a feeble shuffle, not a young man's tread. With the sound of uncertain feet came the hard tap-tap of a stick against the door, and the high-pitched voice of eld, "Open, open, let me in!" Again Tyr flung up his head in a long doleful howl.

Before the echo of the tapping stick and the high voice had fairly died away, Sweyn had sprung across to the door and flung it wide. "No one again," he said in a steady voice, though his eyes looked startled as he stared out. He saw the lonely expanse of snow, the clouds swagging low, and between the two the line of dark fir trees bowing in the wind. He closed the door without a word of comment, and recrossed the room.

A score of blanched faces were turned to him as though he must be solver of the enigma. He could not be unconscious of this mute eye-questioning, and it disturbed his resolute air of composure. He hesitated, glanced towards his mother, the house-mistress, then back at the frightened folk, and gravely, before them all, made the sign of the cross. There was a flutter of hands as the sign was repeated by all, and the dead silence was stirred as by a huge sigh, for the held breath of many was freed as though the sign gave magic relief.

Even the house-mistress was perturbed. She left the wheel and crossed the room to her son, and spoke with him for a moment in a low tone that none could overhear. But a moment later her voice was high-pitched and loud, so that all might benefit by her rebuke of the "heathen chatter" of one of the girls. Perhaps she essayed to silence thus her own misgivings and forebodings.

No other voice dared speak now with its natural fulness. Low tones made intermittent murmurs, and now and then silence drifted over the whole room. The handling of tools was as noiseless as might be, and suspended on the instant if the door rattled in a gust of wind. After a time Sweyn left his work, joined the group nearest the door, and loitered there on the pretense of giving advice and help to the unskillful.

A man's tread was heard outside in the porch. "Christian!" said Sweyn and his mother simultaneously, he confidently, she authoritatively, to set the checked wheels going again. But Tyr flung up his head with an appalling howl.

"Open, open, let me in!"

It was a man's voice, and the door shook and rattled as a man's strength beat against it. Sweyn could feel the planks quivering, as on the instant his hand was upon the door, flinging it open, to face the blank porch, and beyond only snow and sky, and firs aslant in the wind.

He stood for a long minute with the open door in his hand. The bitter wind swept in with its icy chill, but a deadlier chill of fear came swifter, and seemed to freeze the beating of hearts. Sweyn stepped back to snatch up a great bearskin cloak.

"Sweyn, where are you going?"

"No farther than the porch, Mother," and he stepped out and closed the door.

He wrapped himself in the heavy fur, and leaning against the most sheltered wall of the porch, steeled his nerves to face the devil and all his works. No sound of voices came from within, the most distinct sound was the crackle and roar of the fire.

IT WAS BITTERLY COLD. His feet grew numb, but he forbore stamping them into warmth lest the sound should strike panic within, nor would he leave the porch, nor print a footmark on the untrodden white that declared so absolutely how no human voices and hands could have approached the door since snow fell two hours or more ago. "When the wind drops there will be more snow," thought Sweyn.

For the best part of an hour he kept his watch, and saw no living thing— heard no unwonted sound. "I will freeze here no longer," he muttered, and reentered.

One woman gave a half-suppressed scream as his hand was laid on the latch, and then a gasp of relief as he came in. No one questioned him, only his mother said, in a tone of forced unconcern, "Could you not see Christian coming?" as though she were made anxious only by the absence of her younger son. Hardly had Sweyn stamped near to the fire than clear knocking was heard at the door. Tyr leapt from the hearth, his eyes red as the fire, his fangs showing white in the black jowl, his neck ridged and bristling, and, overleaping Rol, ramped at the door, barking furiously.

Outside the door a clear mellow voice was calling. Tyr's bark made the words undistinguishable.

No one offered to stir towards the door before Sweyn.

He stalked down the room, resolutely lifted the latch, and swung back the door.

A white-robed woman glided in.

No wraith! Living—beautiful—young.

Tyr leapt upon her.

Lithely she baulked the sharp fangs with folds of her long fur robe, and snatching from her girdle a small two-edged axe, whirled it up for a blow of defense.

Sweyn caught the dog by the collar, and dragged him off yelping and struggling.

The stranger stood in the doorway motionless, one foot set forward, one arm flung up, till the house-mistress hurried down the room, and Sweyn, relinquishing to others the furious Tyr, turned again to close the door, and offer excuse for so fierce a greeting. Then she lowered her arm, slung the axe in its place at her waist, loosened the furs about her face, and shook over her shoulders the long white robe—all as it were with the sway of one movement.

She was a maiden, tall and fair. The fashion of her dress was strange, half masculine, yet not unwomanly. A fine fur tunic, reaching but little below the knee, was all the skirt she wore; below were the cross-bound shoes and leggings that a hunter wears. A white fur cap was set low upon the brows, and from its edge strips of fur fell lappet-wise about her shoulders, two of these at her entrance had been drawn forward and crossed about her throat, but now, loosened and thrust back, left unhidden long plaits of fair hair that lay forward on shoulder and breast, down to the ivory-studded girdle where the axe gleamed.

Sweyn and his mother led the stranger to the hearth without a question or a sign of curiosity, till she voluntarily told her tale of a long journey to distant kindred, a promised guide unmet, and signals and landmarks mistaken.

"Alone!" exclaimed Sweyn in astonishment. "Have you journeyed thus far, a hundred leagues, alone?"

She answered "Yes" with a little smile.

"Over the hills and the wastes! Why, the folk there are savage and wild as beasts."

She dropped her hand upon her axe with a laugh of some scorn.

"I fear neither man nor beast; some few fear me." And then she told strange tales of fierce attacks and defense, and of the bold free huntress life she had led.

Her words came a little slowly and deliberately, as though she spoke in a scarce familiar tongue, now and then she hesitated, and stopped in a phrase, as though for lack of some word.

She became the center of a group of listeners. The interest she excited dissipated, in some degree, the dread inspired by the mysterious voices. There was nothing ominous about this young, bright, fair reality, though her aspect was strange.

Little Rol crept near, staring at the stranger with all his might. Unnoticed, he softly stroked and patted a corner of her soft white robe that reached to the floor in ample folds. He laid his cheek against it caressingly, and then edged up close to her knees.

"What is your name?" he asked.

The stranger's smile and ready answer, as she looked down, saved Rol from the rebuke merited by his unmannerly question.

"My real name," she said, "would be uncouth to your ears and tongue. The folk of this country have given me another name, and from this" (she laid her hand on the fur robe) "they call me 'White Fell.' "

Little Rol repeated it to himself, stroking and patting as before. "White Fell, White Fell."

The fair face, and soft, beautiful dress pleased Rol. He knelt up, with his eyes on her face and an air of uncertain determination, like a robin's on a doorstep, and plumped his elbows into her lap with a little gasp at his own audacity.

Rol!" exclaimed his aunt, but "Oh, let him!" said White Fell, smiling and stroking his head; and Rol stayed.

He advanced farther, and panting at his own adventurousness in the face of his aunt's authority, climbed up on her knees. Her welcoming arms hindered any protest. He nestled happily, fingering the head, the ivory studs in her girdle, the ivory clasp at her throat, the plaits of fair hair, rubbing his head against the softness of her fur-clad shoulder, with a child's full confidence in the kindness of beauty.

White Fell had not uncovered her head, only knotted the pendant fur loosely behind her neck. Rol reached up his hand toward it, whispering her name to himself, "White Fell, White Fell," then slid his arms round her neck, and kissed her—once—twice. She laughed delightedly, and kissed him again.

"The child plagues you?" said Sweyn.

"No, indeed," she answered with an earnestness so intense as to seem disproportionate to the occasion.

Rol settled himself again on her lap, and began to unwind the bandage bound round his hand. He paused a little when he saw where the blood had soaked through, then went on till his hand was bare and the cut displayed, gaping and long, though only skin deep. He held it up towards White Fell, desirous of her pity and sympathy.

At sight of it, and the blood-stained linen, she drew in her breath suddenly, clasped Rol to her—hard, hard—till be began to struggle. Her face was hidden behind the boy, so that none could see its expression. It had lighted up with a most awful glee.

Afar, beyond the fir grove, beyond the low hill behind, the absent Christian was hastening his return. From daybreak he had been afoot, carrying notice of a bear hunt to all the best hunters of the farms and hamlets that lay within a radius of twelve miles. Nevertheless, having been detained till a late hour, he now broke into a run, going with a long smooth stride of apparent ease that fast made the miles diminish.

He entered the midnight blackness of the fir grove with scarcely slackened pace, though the path was invisible, and passing through into the open again, sighted the farm lying a furlong off down the slope. Then he sprang out freely, and almost on the instant gave one great sideways leap, and stood still. There in the snow was the track of a great wolf.

His hand went to his knife, his only weapon. He stopped, knelt down, to bring his eyes to the level of the beast, and peered about, his teeth set, his heart beat a little harder than the pace of his running insisted on. A solitary wolf, nearly always savage and of large size, is a formidable beast that will not hesitate to attack a single man. This wolf track was the largest Christian had ever seen, and, so far as he could judge, recently made. It led from under the fir trees down the slope. Well for him, he thought, was the delay that had so vexed him before: well for him that he had not passed through the dark fir grove when that danger of jaws lurked there. Going warily, he followed the track.

It led down the slope, across a broad ice-bound stream, along the level beyond, making towards the farm. A less precise knowledge had doubted, and guessed that here might have come straying big Tyr or his like, but Christian was sure, knowing better than to mistake between footmark of dog and wolf.

Straight on—straight on towards the farm.

Surprised and anxious grew Christian, that a prowling wolf should dare so near. He drew his knife and pressed on, more hastily, more keen-eyed. Oh, that Tyr were with him!

Straight on, straight on, even to the very door, where the snow failed. His heart seemed to give a great leap and then stop. There the track ended.

Nothing lurked in the porch, and there was no sign of return. The firs stood straight against the sky, the clouds lay low, for the wind had fallen and a few snowflakes came drifting down. In a horror of surprise, Christian stood dazed a moment: then he lifted the latch and went in. His glance took in all the old familiar forms and faces, and with them that of the stranger, fur-clad and beautiful. The awful truth flashed upon him: he knew what she was.

Only a few were startled by the rattle of the latch as he entered. The room was filled with bustle and movement, for it was the supper hour, when all tools were laid aside, and trestles and tables shifted. Christian had no knowledge of what he said and did; he moved and spoke mechanically, half thinking that soon he must wake from this horrible dream. Sweyn and his mother supposed him to be cold and dead tired, and spared all unnecessary questions. And he found himself seated beside the hearth, opposite that dreadful Thing that looked like a beautiful girl, watching her every movement, curdling with horror to see her fondle the child Rol.

Sweyn stood near them both, intent upon White Fell also, but how differently! She seemed unconscious of the gaze of both—neither aware of the chill dread in the eyes of Christian, nor of Sweyn's warm admiration.

These two brothers, who were twins, contrasted greatly, despite their striking likeness. They were alike in regular profile, fair brown hair, and deep blue eyes, but Sweyn's features were perfect as a young god's, while Christian's showed faulty details. Thus, the line of his mouth was set too straight, the eyes shelved too deeply back, and the contour of the face flowed in less generous curves than Sweyn's. Their height was the same, but Christian was too slender for perfect proportion while Sweyn's well-knit frame, broad shoulders, and muscular arms, made him preeminent for manly beauty as well as for strength. As a hunter Sweyn was without rival; as a fisher without rival. All the country-side acknowledged him to be the best wrestler, rider, dancer, singer. Only in speed could he be surpassed, and in that only by his younger brother. All others Sweyn could distance fairly, but Christian could outrun him easily. Ay, he could keep pace with Sweyn's most breathless burst, and laugh and talk the while. Christian took little pride in his fleetness of foot, counting a man's legs to be the least worthy of his members. He had no envy of his brother's athletic superiority, though to several feats he had made a moderate second. He loved as only a twin can love— proud of all that Sweyn did, content with all that Sweyn was; humbly content also that his own great love should not be so exceedingly returned, since he knew himself to be so far less love-worthy.

Christian dared not, in the midst of women and children, launch the horror that he knew into words, tell anyone what he knew about the girl in white fur. He waited to consult his brother, but Sweyn did not, or would not, notice the signal he made, and kept his face always turned towards White Fell. Christian drew away from the hearth, unable to remain passive with that dread upon him.

"Where is Tyr?" he said suddenly. Then, catching sight of the dog in a distant corner, "Why is he chained there?"

"He flew at the stranger," one answered.

Christian's eyes glowed. "Yes?" he said, interrogatively.

"He was within an ace of having his brain knocked out."

"Tyr?"

"Yes; she was nimbly up with that little axe she has at her waist. It was well for old Tyr that his master throttled him off."

Christian went without a word to the corner where Tyr was chained. The dog rose up to meet him, as piteous and indignant as a dumb beast can be. He stroked the black head. "Good Tyr! brave dog!"

They knew, they only; and the man and the dumb dog had comfort of each other.

Christian's eyes turned again towards White Fell. Tyr's also, and he strained against the length of the chain. Christian's hand lay on the dog's neck, and he felt it ridge and bristle with the quivering of impotent fury. Then he began to quiver in like manner, with a fury born of reason, not instinct, as impotent morally as was Tyr physically. Oh! the woman's form that he dare not touch! Anything but that, and he with Tyr would be free to kill or be killed.

Then he returned to ask fresh questions.

"How long has the stranger been here?"

"She came about half an hour before you."

"Who opened the door to her?"

"Sweyn. No one else dared."

The tone of the answer was mysterious.

"Why?" queried Christian. "Has anything strange happened? Tell me."

For answer he was told in a low undertone of the summons at the door, of Tyr's howls, and of Sweyn's fruitless watch outside.

Christian turned towards his brother in a torment of impatience for a word apart. The board was spread, and Sweyn was leading White Fell to the guest's place. This was more awful: she would break bread with them under the roof-tree!

He started forward and touching Sweyn's arm, whispered an urgent entreaty. Sweyn stared, and shook his head in angry impatience.

Thereupon Christian would take no morsel of food.

His opportunity came at last. White Fell questioned of the landmarks of the country, and of one Cairn Hill, which was an appointed meeting place at which she was due that night. The house-mistress and Sweyn both exclaimed.

"It is three long miles away," said Sweyn, "with no place for shelter but a wretched hut. Stay with us this night, and I will show you the way tomorrow."

White Fell seemed to hesitate. "Three miles," she said, "then I should be able to see or hear a signal."

"I will look out," said Sweyn, "then if there be no signal, you must not leave us."

He went to the door. Christian rose silently, and followed him out.

"Sweyn, do you know what she is?"

Sweyn, surprised at the vehement grasp, and low, hoarse voice, made answer:

"She? Who? White Fell?"

"Yes."

"She is the most beautiful girl I have ever seen."

"She is a Were-Wolf."

Sweyn burst out laughing. "Are you mad?" he asked.

"No, here, see for yourself."

Christian drew him out of the porch, pointing to the snow where the footmarks had been. Had been, for now they were not. Snow was falling fast, and every dint was blotted out.

"Well?" asked Sweyn.

"Had you come when I signed to you, you would have seen for yourself."

"Seen what?"

"The footprints of a wolf leading up to the door; none leading away."

It was impossible not to be startled by the tone alone, though it was hardly above a whisper. Sweyn eyed his brother anxiously, but in the darkness could make nothing of his face. Then he laid his hands kindly and reassuringly on Christian's shoulders and felt how he was quivering with excitement and horror.

"One sees strange things," he said, "when the cold has got into the brain behind the eyes; you came in cold and worn out."

"No," interrupted Christian. "I saw the track first on the brow of the slope, and followed it down right here to the door. This is no delusion."

Sweyn in his heart felt positive that it was. Christian was given to day-dreams and strange fancies, though never had he been possessed with so mad a notion before.

"Don't you believe me?" said Christian desperately. "You must. I swear it is sane truth. Are you blind? Why, even Tyr knows."

"You will be clearer headed tomorrow after a night's rest. Then come too, if you will, with White Fell, to the Hill Cairn, and if you have doubts still, watch and follow, and see what footprints she leaves."

Galled by Sweyn's evident contempt, Christian turned abruptly to the door. Sweyn caught him back.

"What now, Christian? What are you going to do?"

"You do not believe me; my mother shall."

Sweyn's grasp tightened. "You shall not tell her," he said authoritatively.

Customarily Christian was so docile to his brother's mastery that it was now a surprising thing when he wrenched himself free, vigorously, and said as determinedly as Sweyn, "She shall know!" but Sweyn was nearer the door and would not let him pass.

"There has been scare enough for one night already. If this notion of yours will keep, broach it tomorrow." Christian would not yield.

"Women are so easily scared," pursued Sweyn, "and are ready to believe any folly without shadow of proof. Be a man, Christian, and fight this notion of a Were-Wolf by yourself."

"If you would believe me," began Christian.

"I believe you to be a fool," said Sweyn, losing patience. "Another, who was not your brother, might believe you to be a knave, and guess that you had transformed White Fell into a Were-Wolf because she smiled more readily on me than on you."

The jest was not without foundation, for the grace of White Fell's bright looks had been bestowed on him, on Christian never a whit. Sweyn's cox-combery was always frank, and most forgivable, and not without fair color.

"If you want an ally," continued Sweyn, "confide in old Trella. Out of her stores of wisdom, if her memory holds good, she can instruct you in the orthodox manner of tackling a Were-Wolf. If I remember aright, you should watch the suspected person till midnight, when the beast's form must be resumed, and retained ever after if a human eye sees the change; or, better still, sprinkle hands and feet with holy water, which is certain death. Oh! never fear, but old Trella will be equal to the occasion."

"You speak of them as old wives' tales, but if you had seen the proof I have seen, you would be ready at least to wish them true, if not also to put them to the test."

"Well," said Sweyn with a laugh that had a little sneer in it, "put them to the test! I will not object to that, if you will only keep your notions to yourself. Now, Christian, give me your word for silence, and we will freeze here no longer."

Christian remained silent.

Sweyn put his hands on his shoulders again and vainly tried to see his face in the darkness.

"We have never quarreled yet, Christian?"

"I have never quarreled," returned the other, aware for the first time that his dictatorial brother had sometimes offered occasion for quarrel, had he been ready to take it.

"Well," said Sweyn emphatically, "if you speak against White Fell to any other, as tonight you have spoken to me—we shall."

He delivered the words like an ultimatum, turned sharp round, and reentered the house. Christian, more fearful and wretched than before, followed.

"Snow is falling fast; not a single light is to be seen."

White Fell's eyes passed over Christian without apparent notice, and turned bright and shining upon Sweyn.

"Nor any signal to be heard?" she queried. "Did you not hear the sound of a sea-horn?"

"I saw nothing, and heard nothing, and signal or no signal, the heavy snow would keep you here perforce."

She smiled her thanks beautifully. And Christian's heart sank like lead with a deadly foreboding, as he noted what a light was kindled in Sweyn's eyes by her smile. That night, when all others slept, Christian, the weariest of all, watched outside the guest chamber till midnight was past. No sound, not the faintest, could be heard. Could the old tale be true of the midnight change? What was on the other side of the door, a woman or a beast? He would have given his right hand to know. Instinctively he laid his hand on the latch, and drew it softly, though believing that bolts fastened the inner side. The door yielded to his hand; he stood on the threshold, a keen gust of air cut at him; the window stood open, the room was empty.

So Christian could sleep with a somewhat lightened heart.

In the morning there was surprise and conjecture when White Fell's absence was discovered. Christian held his peace. Not even to his brother did he say how he knew that she had fled before midnight, and Sweyn, though evidently greatly chagrined, seemed to disdain reference to the subject of Christian's fears.

All that day, and for many a day after, Christian would never go out of sight of his home. Sweyn alone noticed how he maneuvered for this, and was clearly annoyed by it. White Fell's name was never mentioned between them, though not seldom was it heard in general talk. Hardly a day passed but little Rol asked when White Fell would come again: pretty White Fell, who kissed like a snowflake. And if Sweyn answered, Christian would be quite sure that the light in his eyes, kindled by White Fell's smile, had not yet died out.

Little Rol! Naughty, merry, fair-haired little Rol. A day came when his feet raced over the threshold never to return, when his chatter and laugh were heard no more; when tears of anguish were wept by eyes that never would see his bright head again: never again, living or dead.

He was seen at dusk for the last time, escaping from the house with his puppy, in freakish rebellion against old Trella. Later, when his absence had begun to cause anxiety, his puppy crept back to the farm, cowed, whimpering and yelping, a pitiful, dumb lump of terror, without intelligence or courage to guide the frightened search.

Rol was never found, nor any trace of him. Where he had perished was never known; how he had perished was known only by an awful guess—a wild beast had devoured him.

Christian heard the conjecture "a wolf"; and a horrible certainty flashed upon him that he knew what wolf it was. He tried to declare what he knew, but Sweyn saw him start at the words with white face and struggling lips, and guessing his purpose, pulled him back, and kept him silent, hardly, by his imperious grip and wrathful eyes, and one low whisper.

That Christian should retain his most irrational suspicion against beautiful White Fell was, to Sweyn, evidence of a weak obstinacy of mind that would but thrive upon expostulation and argument. But this evident intention to direct the passions of grief and anguish to a hatred and fear of the fair stranger, such as his own, was intolerable, and Sweyn set his will against it. Again Christian yielded to his brother's stronger words and will, and against his own judgment consented to silence.

Repentance came before the new moon, the first of the year, was old. White Fell came again, smiling as she entered, as though assured of a glad and kindly welcome, and, in truth, there was only one who saw again her fair face and strange white garb without pleasure. Sweyn's face glowed with delight, while Christian's grew pale and rigid as death. He had given his word to keep silence, but he had not thought that she would dare to come again. Silence was impossible, face to face with that Thing, impossible. Irrepressibly he cried out:

"Where is Rol?"

Not a quiver disturbed White Fell's face. She heard, yet remained bright and tranquil. Sweyn's eyes flashed round at his brother dangerously. Among the women some tears fell at the poor child's name, but none caught alarm from its sudden utterance, for the thought of Rol rose naturally. Where was little Rol, who had nestled in the stranger's arms, kissing her, and watched for her since, and prattled of her daily?

Christian went out silently. . . . The swiftest runner of the countryside had started on his hardest race: little less than three leagues and back, which he reckoned to accomplish in two hours, though the night was moonless and the way rugged. He rushed against the still cold air till it felt like a wind upon his face. . . . He took no conscious heed of landmarks, not even when all sign of a path was gone under depths of snow. His will was set to reach his goal with unexampled speed, and thither by instinct his physical forces bore him, without one definite thought to guide.

And the idle brain lay passive, inert, receiving into its vacancy restless siftings of past sights of that dreadful Thing. Tyr—O Tyr!—white fangs in the black jowl: the women who wept on the foolish puppy, precious for the child's last touch: footprints from pine wood to door: the smiling face among furs, of such womanly beauty—smiling—smiling: and Sweyn's face.

"Sweyn, Sweyn, O Sweyn, my brother!"

Sweyn's angry laugh possessed his ear within the sound of the wind of his speed; Sweyn's scorn assailed more quick and keen than the biting cold at his throat. And yet he was unimpressed by any thought of how Sweyn's anger and scorn would rise, if this errand were known.

Sweyn was a skeptic. His utter disbelief in Christian's testimony regarding the footprints was based upon positive skepticism. His reason refused to bend in accepting the possibility of the supernatural materialized. That a living beast could ever be other than palpably bestial—pawed, toothed, shagged, and eared as such, was to him incredible; far more than a human presence could be transformed from its godlike aspect, upright, freehanded, with brows, and speech, and laughter. The wild and fearful legends that he had known from childhood and then believed he regarded now as built upon facts distorted, overlaid by imagination, and quickened by superstition. Even the strange summons at the threshold, that he himself had vainly answered, was, after the first shock of surprise, rationally explained by him as malicious foolery on the part of some clever trickster, who withheld the key to the enigma.

To the younger brother, all life was a spiritual mystery, veiled from his clear knowledge by the density of flesh. Since he knew his own body to be linked to the complex and antagonistic forces that constitute one soul, it seemed to him not impossibly strange that one spiritual force could possess diverse forms for widely various manifestation. Nor, to him, was it great effort to believe that as pure water washes away all natural foulness, so water, holy by consecration, must needs cleanse God's world from that supernatural evil Thing. Therefore, faster than ever man's foot had covered those leagues, he sped under the dark, still night, over the waste, trackless snow ridges to the faraway church, where salvation lay in the holy-water stoup at the door. His faith was as firm as any that wrought miracles in days past, simple as a child's wish, strong as a man's will.

He was hardly missed during these hours, every second of which was by him fulfilled to its utmost extent by extremist effort that sinews and nerves could attain. Within the homestead the while, the easy moments were bright with words and looks of unwonted animation, for the kindly, hospitable instincts of the inmates were roused into cordial expression of welcome and interest by the grace and beauty of the returned stranger.

But Sweyn was eager and earnest, with more than a host's courteous warmth. The impression that at her first coming had charmed him, that had lived since through memory, deepened now in her actual presence. Sweyn, the matchless among men, acknowledged in this fair White Fell a spirit high and bold as his own, and a frame so firm and capable that only bulk was lacking for equal strength. Yet the white skin was molded most smoothly, without such muscular swelling as made his might evident. Such love as his frank self-love could concede was called forth by an ardent admiration for this supreme stranger. More admiration than love was in his passion, and therefore he was free from a lover's hesitancy and delicate reserve and doubts. Frankly and boldly he courted her favor by looks and tones, and an address that came of natural ease, needless of skill by practice.

Nor was she a woman to be wooed otherwise. Tender whispers and sighs would never gain her ear; but her eyes would brighten and shine if she heard of a brave feat, and her prompt hand in sympathy fall swiftly on the axe-haft and clasp it hard. That movement ever fired Sweyn's admiration anew; he watched for it, strove to elicit it, and glowed when it came. Wonderful and beautiful was that wrist, slender and steel-strong; also the smooth shapely hand, that curved so fast and firm, ready to deal instant death.

Desiring to feel the pressure of these hands, this bold lover schemed with palpable directness, proposing that she should hear how their hunting songs were sung, with a chorus that signaled hands to be clasped. So his splendid voice gave the verses, and as the chorus was taken up, he claimed her hands, and even through the easy grip, felt, as he desired, the strength that was latent, and the vigor that quickened the very fingertips, as the song fired her, and her voice was caught out of her by the rhythmic swell, and rang clear on the top of the closing surge.

Afterwards she sang alone. For contrast, or in the pride of swaying moods by her voice, she chose a mournful song that drifted along in a minor chant, sad as a wind that dirges.

Old Trella came tottering from her corner, shaken to additional palsy by an aroused memory. She strained her dim eyes towards the singer, and then bent her head, that the one ear yet sensible to sound might avail of every note. At the close, groping forward, she murmured with the high-pitched quaver of old age:

"So she sang, my Thora, my last and brightest. What is she like, she whose voice is like my dead Thora's? Are her eyes blue?"

"Blue as the sky."

"So were my Thora's! Is her hair fair, and in plaits to the waist?"

"Even so," answered White Fell herself, and met the advancing hands with her own, and guided them to corroborate her words by touch.

"Like my dead Thora's," repeated the old woman, and then her trembling hands rested on the fur-clad shoulders, and she bent forward and kissed the smooth fair face that White Fell upturned, nothing loath, to receive and return the caress.

So Christian saw them as he entered.

He stood a moment. After the starless darkness and the icy night air, and the fierce silent two hours' race, his senses reeled on sudden entrance into warmth, and light, and the cheery hum of voices. A sudden unforeseen anguish assailed him, as now first he entertained the possibility of being overmatched by her wiles and her daring, if at the approach of pure death she should start up at bay transformed to a terrible beast, and achieve a savage glut at the last. He looked with horror and pity on the harmless, helpless folk, so unwitting of outrage to their comfort and security. The dreadful Thing in their midst, that was veiled from their knowledge by womanly beauty, was a center of pleasant interest. There, before him, signally impressive, was poor old Trella, weakest and feeblest of all, in fond nearness. And a moment might bring about the revelation of a monstrous horror—a ghastly, deadly danger, set loose and at bay, in a circle of girls and women and careless defenseless men so hideous and terrible a thing as might crack the brain, or curdle the heart stone dead.

And he alone of the throng prepared.

For one breathing space he faltered, no longer than that, while over him swept the agony of compunction that yet could not make him surrender his purpose.

He alone? Nay, but Tyr also, and he crossed to the dumb sole sharer of his knowledge.

So timeless is thought that a few seconds only lay between his lifting of the latch and his loosening of Tyr's collar, but in those few seconds succeeding his first glance, as lightning-swift had been the impulses of others, their motion as quick and sure. Sweyn's vigilant eye had darted upon him, and instantly his every fiber was alert with hostile instinct, and, half divining, half incredulous, of Christian's object in stooping to Tyr, he came hastily, wary, wrathful, resolute to oppose the malice of his wild-eyed brother.

But beyond Sweyn rose White Fell, blanching white as her furs, and with eyes grown fierce and wild. She leapt down the room to the door, whirling her long robe closely to her. "Hark!" she panted. "The signal horn! Hark, I must go!" as she snatched at the latch to be out and away.

For one precious moment Christian had hesitated on the half-loosened collar, for, except the womanly form were exchanged for the bestial, Tyr's jaws would gnash to rags his honor of manhood. Then he heard her voice, and turned—too late.

As she tugged at the door, he sprang across grasping his flask, but Sweyn dashed between, and caught him back irresistibly so that a most frantic effort only availed to wrench one arm free. With that, on the impulse of sheer despair, he cast at her with all his force. The door swung behind her, and the flask flew into fragments against it. Then, as Sweyn's grasp slackened, and he met the questioning astonishment of surrounding faces, with a hoarse inarticulate cry: "God help us all!" he said: "She is a Were-Wolf."

Sweyn turned upon him. "Liar, coward!" he shouted, and his hands gripped his brother's throat with deadly force, as though the spoken word could be killed so; and as Christian struggled, lifted him clear off his feet and flung him crashing backward. So furious was he, that, as his brother lay motionless, he stirred him roughly with his foot, till their mother came between, crying shame; and yet then he stood by, his teeth set, his brows knit, his hands clenched, ready to enforce silence again violently, as Christian rose staggering and bewildered.

But utter silence and submission were more than he expected, and turned his anger into contempt for one so easily cowed and held in subjection by mere force. "He is mad!" he said, turning on his heel as he spoke, so that he lost his mother's look of pained reproach at this sudden free utterance of what was a lurking dread within her.

Christian was too spent for the effort of speech. His hard-drawn breath labored in great sobs, his limbs were powerless and unstrung in utter relax and after hard service. Failure in his endeavor induced a stupor of misery and despair. In addition was the wretched humiliation of open violence and strife with his brother, and the distress of hearing misjudging contempt expressed without reserve; for he was aware that Sweyn had turned to allay the scared excitement half by imperious mastery, half by explanation and argument, that showed painful disregard of brotherly consideration. All this unkindness of his twin he charged upon the fell Thing who had wrought this their first dissension, and, ah! most terrible thought, interposed between them so effectually, that Sweyn was wilfully blind and deaf on her account, resentful of interference, arbitrary beyond reason.

Dread and perplexity unfathomable darkened upon him; unshared the burden was overwhelming: a foreboding of unspeakable calamity, based upon his ghastly discovery, bore down with him, crushing out hope of power to withstand impending fate.

Sweyn the while was observant of his brother. . . . Observation set him wondering on Christian's exhausted condition. The heavy laboring breath and the slack inert fall of the limbs told surely of unusual and prolonged exertion. And then why had close upon two hours' absence been followed by open hostility against White Fell?

Suddenly, the fragments of the flask giving a clue, he guessed all, and faced about to stare at his brother in amaze. He forgot that the motive scheme was against White Fell, demanding derision and resentment from him, that was swept out of remembrance by astonishment and admiration for the feat of speed and endurance. In eagerness to question he inclined to attempt a generous part and frankly offer to heal the breach; but Christian's depression and sad following gaze provoked him to self-justification by recalling the offense of that outrageous utterance against White Fell, and the impulse passed.

That night Sweyn and his mother talked long and late together, shaping into certainty the suspicion that Christian's mind had lost its balance, and discussing the evident cause. For Sweyn, declaring his own love for White Fell, suggested that his unfortunate brother, with a like passion, they being twins in loves as in birth, had through jealousy and despair turned from love to hate, until reason failed at the strain, and a craze developed, which the malice and treachery of madness made a serious and dangerous force.

So Sweyn theorized, convincing himself as he spoke, convincing afterwards others who advanced doubts against White Fell, fettering his judgment by his advocacy, and by his staunch defense of her hurried flight silencing his own inner consciousness of the unaccountability of her action.

But a little time and Sweyn lost his vantage in the shock of a fresh horror at the homestead. Trella was no more, and her end a mystery. The poor old woman crawled out in a bright gleam to visit a bedridden gossip living beyond the fir grove. Under the trees she was last seen, halting for her companion, sent back for a forgotten present. Quick alarm sprang, calling every man to the search. Her stick was found among the brushwood only a few paces from the path, but no track or stain, for a gusty wind was sifting the snow from the branches, and hid all sign of how she came by her death.

So panic-stricken were the farm folk that none dared go singly on the search. Known danger could be braced, but not this stealthy Death that walked by day invisible, that cut off alike the child in his play and the aged woman so near to her quiet grave.

"Rol she kissed, Trella she kissed!" So rang Christian's frantic cry again and again, till Sweyn dragged him away and strove to keep him apart, albeit in his agony of grief and remorse he accused himself wildly, as answerable for the tragedy, and gave clear proof that the charge of madness was well founded, if strange looks and desperate, incoherent words were evidence enough.

But thenceforward all Sweyn's reasoning and mastery could not uphold White Fell above suspicion. He was not called upon to defend her from accusation when Christian had been brought to silence again, but he well knew the significance of the fact, that her name, formerly uttered freely and often, he never heard now: it was huddled away into whispers that he could not catch.

The passing of time did not sweep away the superstitious fears that Sweyn despised. He was angry and anxious, eager that White Fell should return, and, merely by her bright gracious presence, reinstate herself in favor, but doubtful if all his authority and example could keep from her notice an altered aspect of welcome, and he foresaw clearly that Christian would prove unmanageable, and might be capable of some dangerous outbreak.

Christian's surveillance galled him incessantly, and embarrassment and danger he foresaw as the outcome. Therefore, that suspicion might be lulled, he judged it wise to make overtures for peace. Most easily done. A little kindliness, a few evidences of consideration, a slight return of the old brotherly imperiousness, and Christian replied by a gratefulness and relief that might have touched him had he understood all, but instead, increased his secret contempt.

So successful was this finesse, that when, late on a day, a message summoning Christian to a distance was transmitted by Sweyn, no doubt of its genuineness occurred. When his errand proved useless, he set out to return, mistake or misapprehension was all that he surmised. Not till he sighted the homestead, lying low between the night-grey snow ridges, did vivid recollection of the time when he had tracked that horror to the door rouse an intense dread, and with it a hardly defined suspicion.

His grasp tightened on the bear spear that he carried as a staff; every sense was alert, every muscle strung; excitement urged him on, caution checked him, and the two governed his long stride, swiftly, noiselessly, to the climax he felt was at hand. As he drew near to the outer gates, a light shadow stirred and went, as though the grey of the snow had taken detached motion. A darker shadow stayed and faced Christian, striking his lifeblood chill with utmost despair.

Sweyn stood before him, and surely, the shadow that went was White Fell. They had been together—close. Had she not been in his arms, near enough for lips to meet?

There was no moon, but the stars gave light enough to show that Sweyn's face was flushed and elated. The flush remained, though the expression changed quickly at sight of his brother. How, if Christian had seen all, should one of his frenzied outbursts be met and managed: by resolution? by indifference? He halted between the two, and as a result, he swaggered.

"White Fell?" questioned Christian, hoarse and breathless.

"Yes?"

Sweyn's answer was a query, with an intonation that implied he was clearing the ground for action.

From Christian came: "Have you kissed her?" like a bolt direct, staggering Sweyn by its sheer prompt temerity.

He flushed yet darker, and yet half smiled over this earnest of success he had won. Had there been really between himself and Christian the rivalry that he imagined, his face had enough of the insolence of triumph to exasperate jealous rage.

"You dare ask this?"

"Sweyn, O Sweyn, I must know! You have!"

The ring of despair and anguish in his tone angered Sweyn, misconstruing it as jealousy. Jealousy urging to such presumption was intolerable.

"Mad fool," he said, constraining himself no longer. "Win for yourself a woman to kiss. Leave mine without question. Such an one as I should desire to kiss is such an one as shall never allow a kiss to you."

Then Christian fully understood his supposition.

"I—I!" he cried. "White Fell—that deadly Thing! Sweyn, are you blind, mad? I would save you from her: a Were-Wolf!"

Sweyn maddened again at the accusation—a dastardly way of revenge, as he conceived, and instantly, for the second time, the brothers were at strife violently. But Christian was now too desperate to be scrupulous, for a dim glimpse had shot a possibility into his mind, and to be free to follow it the striking of his brother was a necessity. Thank God! he was armed, and so Sweyn's equal.

Facing his assailant with the bear spear, he struck up his arms, and with the butt end hit hard so that he fell. The matchless runner leapt away on the instant, to follow a forlorn hope.

Sweyn, on regaining his feet, was as amazed as angry at this unaccountable flight. He knew in his heart that his brother was no coward, and that it was unlike him to shrink from an encounter because defeat was certain, and cruel humiliation from a vindictive victor probable. Of the uselessness of pursuit he was well aware: he must abide his chagrin, content to know that his time for advantage would come. Since White Fell had parted to the right, Christian to the left, the event of a sequent encounter did not occur to him.

And now Christian, acting on the dim glimpse he had had, just as Sweyn turned upon him, of something that moved against the sky along the ridge behind the homestead, was staking his only hope on a chance, and his own superlative speed. If what he saw was really White Fell, he guessed she was bending her steps toward the open wastes; and there was just a possibility that, by a straight dash, and a desperate perilous leap over a sheer bluff, he might yet meet her or head her. And then he had no further thought.

It was past, the quick, fierce race, and the chance of death at the leap; and he halted in a hollow to fetch his breath and to look: did she come? had she gone?

She came.

She came with a smooth, gliding, noiseless speed, that was neither walking nor running; her arms were folded in her furs that were drawn tight about her body; the white lappets from her head were wrapped and knotted closely beneath her face; her eyes were set on a far distance. So she went till the even sway of her going was startled to a pause by Christian.

"Fell."

She drew a quick, sharp breath at the sound of her name thus mutilated, and faced Sweyn's brother. Her eyes glittered, her upper lip was lifted, and she showed the teeth. The half of her name, impressed with an ominous sense as uttered by him, warned her of the aspect of a deadly foe. Yet she cast loose her robes till they trailed ample, and spoke as a mild woman.

"What would you?"

Then Christian answered with his solemn dreadful accusation. "You kissed Rol—and Rol is dead! You kissed Trella: she is dead! You have kissed Sweyn, my brother, but he shall not die!"

He added, "You may live till midnight."

The edge of the teeth and the glitter of the eyes stayed a moment, and her right hand also slid down to the axe haft. Then, without a word, she swerved from him, and sprang out and away swiftly over the snow.

And Christian sprang out and away, and followed her swiftly over the snow, keeping behind, but half-a-stride's length from her side.

So they went running together, silent, towards the vast wastes of snow, where no living thing but they two moved under the stars of night.

Never before had Christian so rejoiced in his powers. The gift of speed, and the training of use and endurance were priceless to him now. Though midnight was hours away, he was confident that, to where that Fell Thing would, hasten as she would, she could not escape from him. Then, when came the time for transformation, when the woman's form was no longer a shield against a man's hand, he would slay or be slain to save Sweyn. He had struck his dear brother in dire extremity, but he could not, though reason urged, strike a woman.

For one mile, for two miles they ran: White Fell ever foremost, Christian ever at equal distance from her side, so near that, now and again, her outflying furs touched him. She spoke no word, nor he. She never turned her head to look at him, nor swerved to evade him; but with face looking forward, sped straight on, over rough, over smooth, aware of his nearness by the regular beat of his feet, and the sound of his breath behind.

In a while she quickened her pace. From the first, Christian had judged of her speed as admirable, yet with exulting security in his own excelling and enduring whatever her efforts. But, when the pace increased, he found himself put to the test as never had he been before in any race. Her feet, indeed, flew faster than his; it was only by the length of stride that he kept his place as her side. But his heart was high and resolute, and he did not fear failure yet.

So the desperate race flew on. . . . White Fell held on without slack. She, it was evident, with confidence in her speed proving matchless, was as resolute to outrun her pursuer as he to endure till midnight and fulfil his purpose. And Christian held on, still self-assured. He could not fail; he would not fail. To avenge Rol and Trella was motive enough for him to do what man could do; but for Sweyn more. She had kissed Sweyn, but he should not die too: with Sweyn to save he could not fail. Never before was such a race as this; no, not when in old Greece man and maid raced together with two fates at stake, for the hard running was sustained unabated, while star after star rose and went wheeling up towards midnight, for one hour, for two hours.

Then Christian saw and heard what shot him through with fear. Where a fringe of trees hung round a slope he saw something dark moving, and heard a yelp, followed by a full horrid cry, and the dark spread out upon the snow, a pack of wolves in pursuit.

Of the beasts alone he had little cause for fear; at the pace he held he could distance them, four-footed though they were. But of White Fell's wiles he had infinite apprehension, for how might she not avail herself of the savage jaws of these wolves, akin as they were to half her nature. She vouchsafed to them nor look nor sign; but Christian, on an impulse to assure himself that she should not escape him, caught and held the back-flung edge of her furs, running still.

She turned like a flash with a beastly snarl, teeth and eyes gleaming again. Her axe shone, on the upstroke, on the downstroke, as she hacked at his hand. She had lopped it off at the wrist, but that he parried with the bear spear. Even then, she shore through the shaft and shattered the bones of the hand at the same blow, so that he loosed perforce.

Then again they raced on as before, Christian not losing a pace, though his left hand swung useless, bleeding and broken.

The snarl, indubitable, though modified from a woman's organs, the vicious fury revealed in teeth and eyes, the sharp arrogant pain of her maiming blow, caught away Christian's heed of the beasts behind, by striking into him close vivid realization of the infinitely greater danger than ran before him in that deadly Thing.

When he bethought him to look behind, lo! the pack had but reached their tracks, and instantly slunk aside, cowed, the yell of pursuit changing to yelps and whines. So abhorrent was that fell creature to beast as to man.

She had drawn her furs more closely to her, disposing them so that, instead of flying loose to her heels, no drapery hung lower than her knees, and this without a check to her wonderful speed, nor embarrassment by the cumbering of the folds. She held head as before; her lips were firmly set, only the tense nostrils gave her breath, not a sign of distress witnessed to the long sustaining of that terrible speed.

But on Christian by now the strain was telling palpably. His head weighed heavy, and his breath came in great sobs; but such a dullness oppressed his brain, that it was only by degrees he could realize his helpless state; wounded and weaponless, chasing that terrible Thing, that was a fierce, desperate, axe-armed woman, except she should assume the beast with fangs yet more formidable.

And still the far slow stars went lingering nearly an hour from midnight.

So far was his brain astray that an impression took him that she was fleeing from the midnight stars, whose gain was by such slow degrees that a time equaling days and days had gone in the race round the northern circle of the world, and days and days as long might last before the end—except she slackened, or except he failed.

But he would not fail yet.

How long had he been praying so? He had started with a self-confidence and reliance that had felt no need for that aid, and now it seemed the only means by which to restrain his heart from swelling beyond the compass of his body, by which to cherish his brain from dwindling and shriveling quite away. Some sharp-toothed creature kept tearing and dragging on his maimed left hand; he never could see it, he could not shake if off, but he prayed it off at times.

The clear stars before him took to shuddering, and he knew why they shuddered at sight of what was behind him. He had never divined before that strange things hid themselves from men under pretense of being snow-clad mounds or swaying trees; but now they came slipping out from their harmless covers to follow him, and mock at his impotence to make a kindred Thing resolve to truer form. He knew the air behind him was thronged; he heard the hum of innumerable murmurings together, but his eyes could never catch them, they were too swift and nimble. Yet he knew they were there, because, on a backward glance, he saw the snow mounds surge as they groveled flatlings out of sight; he saw trees reel as they screwed themselves rigid past recognition among the boughs.

And after such glance the stars for awhile returned to steadfastness, and an infinite stretch of silence froze upon the chill grey world, only deranged by the swift even beat of the flying feet, and his own—slower from the longer stride, and the sound of his breath. And for some clear moments he knew that his only concern was to sustain his speed regardless of pain and distress, to deny with every nerve he had her power to outstrip him or to widen the space between them, till the stars crept up to midnight. Then out again would come that crowd invisible, humming and hustling behind, dense and dark enough, he knew, to blot out the stars at his back, yet ever skipping and jerking from his sight.

A hideous check came to the race. White Fell swirled about and leapt to the right, and Christian, unprepared for so prompt a lurch, found close at his feet a deep pit yawning, and his own impetus past control. But he snatched at her as he bore past, clasping her right arm with his one whole hand, and the two swung together upon the brink.

And her straining away in self-preservation was vigorous enough to counterbalance his headlong impulse, and brought them reeling together to safety.

Then, before he was verily sure that they were not to perish so, crashing down, he saw her gnashing in wild pale fury as she wrenched to be free; and since her right hand was in his grasp, used her axe left-handed, striking back at him.

The blow was effectual enough even so; his right arm dropped powerless, gashed, and with the lesser bone broken, that jarred with horrid pain when he let it swing as he leaped out again, and ran to recover the few feet she had gained from his pause at the shock.

The near escape and this new quick pain made again every faculty alive and intense. He knew that what he followed was most surely Death animate: wounded and helpless, he was utterly at her mercy if so she should realize and take action. Hopeless to avenge, hopeless to save, his very despair for Sweyn swept him on to follow, and follow, and precede the kiss-doomed to death. Could he yet fail to hunt that Thing past midnight, out of the womanly form alluring and treacherous, into lasting restraint of the bestial, which was the last shred of hope left from the confident purpose of the outset?

"Sweyn, Sweyn, O Sweyn!" He thought he was praying, though his heart wrung out nothing but this: "Sweyn, Sweyn, O Sweyn!"

The last hour from midnight had lost half its quarters, and the stars went

lifting up to the great minutes, and again his greatening heart, and his shrinking brain, and the sickening agony that swung at either side, conspired to ap-
pall the will that had only seeming empire over his feet.

Now White Fell's body was so closely enveloped that not a lap nor an
edge flew free. She stretched forward strangely aslant, leaning from the upright poise of a runner. She cleared the ground at times by long bounds, gaining an increase of speed that Christian agonized to equal.

Because the stars pointed that the end was nearing, the black brood came
behind again, and followed, noising. . . . What shape had they? Should he
ever know? If it were not that he was bound to compel the fell Thing that ran
before him into her truer form, he might face about and follow them. No—
no—not so, if he might do anything but what he did—race, race, and racing
bear this agony, he would just stand still and die, to be quit of the pain of
breathing. . . .

Why did the stars stop to shudder? Midnight else had surely come!

THE LEANING, LEAPING THING looked back at him with a wild, fierce
look, and laughed in savage scorn and triumph. He saw in a flash why, for
within a time measurable by seconds she would have escaped him utterly. As
the land lay, a slope of ice sunk on the one hand; on the other hand a steep
rose, shouldering forwards; between the two was space for a foot to be
planted, but none for a body to stand; yet a juniper bough, thrusting out, gave
a handhold secure enough for one with a resolute grasp to swing past the perilous place, and pass on safe.

Though the first seconds of the last moment were going, she dared to flash
back a wicked look, and laugh at the pursuer who was impotent to grasp.

The crisis struck convulsive life into his last supreme effort; his will surged
up indomitable, his speed proved matchless yet. He leapt with a rush, passed
her before her laugh had time to go out, and turned short, barring the way, and
braced to withstand her.

SHE CAME hurling desperate, with a feint to the right hand, and then
launched herself upon him with a spring like a wild beast when it leaps to kill.
And he, with one strong arm and a hand that could not hold, with one strong
hand and an arm that could not guide and sustain, he caught and held her even
so. And they fell together. And because he felt his whole arm slipping, and his

whole hand loosing, to slack the dreadful agony of the wrenched bone above, he caught and held with his teeth the tunic at her knee, as she struggled up and wrung off his hands to overleap him victorious.

Like lightning she snatched her axe, and struck him on the neck, deep— once, twice—his lifeblood gushed out, staining her feet.

The stars touched midnight.

The death scream was not his, for his set teeth had hardly yet relaxed when it rang out; and the dreadful cry began with a woman's shriek, and changed and ended as the yell of a beast. And before the final blank overtook his dying eyes, he saw She gave place to It; he saw more, that Life gave place to Death—causelessly, incomprehensibly.

For he did not presume that no holy water could be more holy, more po- tent to destroy an evil thing than the lifeblood of a pure heart poured out for another in free willing devotion.

His own true hidden reality that he had desired to know grew palpable, recognizable. It seemed to him just this: a great glad abounding hope that he had saved his brother; too expansive to be contained by the limited form of a sole man, it yearned for a new embodiment infinite as the stars.

What did it matter to that true reality that the man's brain shrank, shrank, till it was nothing; that the man's body could not retain the huge pain of his heart, and heaved it out through the red exit riven at the neck, that the black noise came again hurtling from behind, reinforced by that dissolved shape, and blotted out forever the man's sight, hearing, sense.

IN THE EARLY GRAY OF DAY Sweyn chanced upon the footprints of a man—a runner, as he saw by the shifted snow; and the direction they had taken aroused curiosity, since a little farther their line must be crossed by the edge of a sheer height. He turned to trace them. And so doing, the length of the stride struck his attention—a stride long as his own if he ran. He knew he was following Christian.

In his anger he had hardened himself to be indifferent to the nightlong ab- sence of his brother, but now, seeing where the footsteps went, he was seized with compunction and dread. He had failed to give thought and care to his poor frantic twin, who might—was it possible?—have rushed to a frantic death.

His heart stood still when he came to the place where the leap had been taken. A piled edge of snow had fallen too, and nothing but snow lay below when he peered. Along the upper edge he ran for a furlong, till he came to a dip where he could slip and climb down, and then back again on the lower level to the pile of fallen snow. There he saw that the vigorous running had started afresh.

He stood pondering, vexed that any man should have taken that leap where he had not ventured to follow, vexed that he had been beguiled to such painful emotions, guessing vainly at Christian's object in this mad freak. He began sauntering along, half unconsciously following his brother's track; and so in a while he came to the place where the footprints were doubled.

Small prints were these others, small as a woman's, though the pace from one to another was longer than that which the skirts of women allow.

Did not White Fell tread so?

A dreadful guess appalled him, so dreadful that he recoiled from belief. Yet his face grew ashy white, and he gasped to fetch back motion to his checked heart. Unbelievable? Closer attention showed how the smaller foot-fall had altered for greater speed, striking into the snow with a deeper onset and a lighter pressure on the heels. Unbelievable? Could any woman but White Fell run so? Could any man but Christian run so? The guess became a certainty. He was following where alone in the dark night White Fell had fled from Christian pursuing.

Such villainy set heart and brain on fire with rage and indignation: such villainy in his own brother, till lately love-worthy, praiseworthy, though a fool for meekness. He would kill Christian; had he lives many as the footprints he had trodden, vengeance should demand them all. In a tempest of murderous hate he followed on in haste, for the track was plain enough, starting with such a burst of speed as could not be maintained, but brought him back soon to a plod for the spent, sobbing breath to be regulated. He cursed Christian aloud and called White Fell's name on high in a frenzied expense of passion. His grief itself was a rage, being such an intolerable anguish of pity and shame at the thought of his love, White Fell, who had parted from his kiss free and radiant, to be hounded straightway by his brother mad with jealousy, fleeing for more than life while her lover was housed at his ease. If he had but known, he raved, in impotent rebellion at the cruelty of events, if he had but known that his strength and love might have availed in her defense; now the only service to her that he could render was to kill Christian.

As a woman he knew she was matchless in speed, matchless in strength, but Christian was matchless in speed among men, nor easily to be matched in strength. Brave and swift and strong though she were, what chance had she against a man of his strength and inches, frantic, too, and intent on horrid revenge against his brother, his successful rival?

Mile after mile he followed with a bursting heart; more piteous, more tragic, seemed the case at this evidence of White Fell's splendid supremacy, holding her own so long against Christian's famous speed. So long, so long that his love and admiration grew more and more boundless, and his grief and indignation therewith also. Whenever the track lay clear he ran, with such reckless prodigality of strength, that it soon was spent, and he dragged on heavily, till, sometimes on the ice of a mere, sometimes on a windswept place, all signs were lost, but, so undeviating had been their line that a course straight on, and then short questing to either hand, recovered them again.

Hour after hour had gone by through more than half that winter day, before ever he came to the place where the trampled snow showed that a scurry of feet had come—and gone! Wolves' feet—and gone most amazingly! Only a little beyond he came to the lopped point of Christian's bear spear; farther on he would see where the remnant of the useless shaft had been dropped. The snow here was dashed with blood, and the footsteps of the two had fallen closer together. Some hoarse sound of exultation came from him that might have been a laugh had breath sufficed. "O White Fell, my poor, brave love! Well struck!" he groaned, torn by his pity and great admiration, as he guessed surely how she had turned and dealt a blow.

On—on—on—through the aching time, toiling and straining in the track of those two superb runners, aware of the marvel of their endurance, but unaware of the marvel of their speed, that, in the three hours before midnight had overpassed all that vast distance that he could only traverse from twilight to twilight. For clear daylight was passing when he came to the edge of an old marl-pit, and saw how the two who had gone before had stamped and trampled together in desperate peril on the verge. And here fresh blood stains spoke to him of a valiant defense against his infamous brother, and he followed where the blood had dripped till the cold had staunched its flow, taking a savage gratification from this evidence that Christian had been gashed deeply, maddening afresh with desire to do likewise more excellently, and so slake his murderous hate. And he began to know that through all his despair he had entertained a germ of hope, that grew apace, rained upon by his brother's blood.

He strove on as best he might, wrung now by an access of hope, now of despair, in agony to reach the end, however terrible, sick with the aching of the toiled miles that deferred it.

And light went lingering out of the sky, giving place to uncertain stars.

He came to the finish.

Two bodies lay in a narrow place. Christian's was one, but the other beyond not White Fell's. There, where the footsteps ended, lay a great white wolf.

At the sight Sweyn's strength was blasted; body and soul he was struck down groveling.

The stars had grown sure and intense before he stirred from where he had dropped prone. Very feebly he crawled to his dead brother, and laid his hands upon him, and crouched so, afraid to look or stir farther.

Cold, stiff, hours dead. Yet the dead body was his only shelter and stay in that most dreadful hour. His soul, stripped bare of all skeptic comfort, cowered, shivering, naked, abject; and the living clung to the dead out of piteous need for grace from the soul that had passed away.

He rose to his knees, lifting the body. Christian had fallen face forward in the snow, with his arms flung up and wide, and so had the frost made him rigid: strange, ghastly, unyielding to Sweyn's lifting, so that he laid him down again and crouched above, with his arms fast round him, and a low heart-wrung groan.

When at last he found force to raise his brother's body and gather it in his arms, tight clasped to his breast, he tried to face the Thing that lay beyond. The sight set his limbs in a palsy with horror and dread. His senses had failed and fainted in utter cowardice, but for the strength that came from holding dead Christian in his arms, enabling him to compel his eyes to endure the sight, and take into the brain the complete aspect of the Thing. No wound, only blood stains on the feet. The great grim jaws had a savage grin, though dead-stiff. And his kiss: he could bear it no longer, and turned away, nor ever looked again.

And the dead man in his arms, knowing the full horror, had followed and faced it for his sake; had suffered agony and death for his sake; in the neck was the deep death gash, one arm and both hands were dark with frozen blood, for his sake! Dead he knew him, as in life he had not known him, to give the right meed of love and worship. Because the outward man lacked perfection and strength equal to his, he had taken the love and worship of that great pure heart as his due, he, so unworthy in the inner reality, so mean, so despicable, callous, and contemptuous towards the brother who had laid down his life to save him. He longed for utter annihilation, that so he might lose the agony of knowing himself so unworthy such perfect love. The frozen calm of death on the face appalled him. He dared not touch it with lips that had cursed so lately, with lips fouled by kiss of the horror that had been death.

He struggled to his feet, still clasping Christian. The dead man stood upright within his arm, frozen rigid. The eyes were not quite closed; the head had stiffened, bowed slightly to one side; the arms stayed straight and wide. It was the figure of one crucified, the blood-stained hands also conforming.

So living and dead went back along the track that one had passed in the deepest passion of love, and one in the deepest passion of hate. All that night Sweyn toiled through the snow, bearing the weight of dead Christian treading back along the steps he before had trodden, when he was wronging with vilest thoughts, and cursing with murderous hatred, the brother who all the while lay dead for his sake.

Cold, silence, darkness encompassed the strong man bowed with the dolorous burden, and yet he knew surely that that night he entered hell, and trod hellfire along the homeward road, and endured through it only because Christian was with him. And he knew surely that to him Christian had been as Christ, and had suffered and died to save him from his sins.

# PART TWO

# The Rapacious Werewolf

*The rapacious werewolves in this section live to kill. Both are males. De Maupassant's werewolf is an old male who has eluded capture for many years; Saki's werewolf is a young male who seems relatively new to killing. Both werewolves, driven by voracious appetites for flesh, are as apt to devour humans as animals; they may, in fact, prefer human flesh to animal flesh. Serial killers, they attack easy prey, destroying all evidence, except a skull or bones or clothes left after a killing.*

*Guy de Maupassant's story is set against the backdrop of sixteenth- and seventeenth-century France. Werewolves were prosecuted in those centuries. Court records give detailed (sometimes lurid) accounts of individuals accused of lycanthropic acts of cannibalism and rapacious crimes that took place in the jurisdictions of judges Henri Boguet, Jean Bodin, and Nicolas Remy. In the eighteenth century, half of France was terrorized by a werewolf who attacked (and in most instances consumed) more than a hundred people. This werewolf was finally shot and killed.*

*De Maupassant chose an appropriate time and place—eighteenth-century France—for his story. Lurking in the dense forests surrounding a comfortable chateau is a "colossal wolf, with gray fur, almost white, who had eaten two children, gnawed off a woman's arms, strangled all the dogs of garde du pays, and penetrated without fear into the farmyards to come snuffling under the doors." The wolf, who slips away from the most experienced hunters and bloodhounds, is described as "thinking like a human being." The two brothers who live in the chateau vow to kill this werewolf. The story is the tale of their pursuit of the werewolf, of their relentless hunting of a prey that is powerfully and horrifyingly attractive, and of a disturbing passion that overcomes both brothers.*

*The gothic ending, a triumph marred with blood, has cinematic touches: the reader sees the surviving brother propping up the bleeding head and body of the dead brother against a tree; sees the surviving brother luring the werewolf into a fight and strangling the werewolf with his bare hands; and sees the horse carrying the two dead bodies, human and werewolf, back to the chateau, touching each other in death. The reader is left with the distinct impression that rapacity is as present in the hearts of the human beings in the story as it is in the heart of the werewolf.*

*Saki is a writer whose distinctive, sophisticated narrator's voice leads the reader into an en-*

ticing, slightly repulsive world where the macabre is juxtaposed with gentility, where the lurid smolders under civility, where the ghastly is covered over with good breeding. His story about an apparently guileless young boy who lives, uninvited, in the woods on Van Cheele's estate has a disquietingly sinister quality that is buried under a deliberate flippancy of tone. Discovering the boy basking in the sun after a swim in the pool, Van Cheele is startled to hear the boy admit to eating "flesh," adding ingenuously that he prefers the taste of "child-flesh" to animal flesh. Baffled by the boy's chatter, doubting his credibility, and yet wary of its moral implications, Van Cheele remembers that lambs and poultry have been disappearing in the neighborhood. Suddenly he also recalls that a local, rather disposable, child has been missing for two months. The boy's shameless bragging about his cannibalistic conquests, however, makes Van Cheele wonder whether the boy is fantasizing and deters Van Cheele from giving the matter serious thought. Even to contemplate action against a boy-werewolf would, like any psychological intruder, disturb Van Cheele's tranquil but frivolous life.

When Van Cheele's aunt discovers the boy, she clothes him, feeds him, and christens him "Gabriel-Ernest," a name weighty with innocence. Van Cheele begins to realize the danger neighboring children are in, especially since his aunt has placed the "homeless child," whom she does not recognize as a werewolf, in charge of the young children in her Sunday-school class.

The ironic closing shows Saki's brilliant awareness of the subtext of his story. It is society's preoccupation with surface reality and its inability to recognize the dark, rapacious forces lurking under the smooth surface of conventional goodness that are just as alarming as the actions of a boy-werewolf.

# The Wolf

GUY DE MAUPASSANT (1850–1893)

HERE IS WHAT the old Marquis d'Arville told us towards the end of St. Hubert's dinner at the house of the Baron des Ravels.

We had killed a stag that day. The marquis was the only one of the guests who had not taken any part in this chase, for he never hunted.

All through that long repast we had talked about hardly anything but the slaughter of animals. The ladies themselves were interested in tales sanguinary and often unlikely, and the orators imitated the attacks and the combats of men against beasts, raised their arms, romanced in a thundering voice.

M. d'Arville talked well, with a certain poetry of style somewhat high-sounding, but full of effect. He must have repeated this story often, for he told it fluently, not hesitating on words, choosing them with skill to produce a picture—

Gentlemen, I have never hunted; neither did my father, nor my grandfather, nor my great-grandfather. This last was the son of a man who hunted more than all of you put together. He died in 1764. I will tell you how.

His name was Jean. He was married, father of that child who became my ancestor, and he lived with his younger brother, Francois d'Arville, in our castle in Lorraine, in the middle of the forest.

Francois d'Arville had remained a bachelor for love of the chase.

They both hunted from one end of the year to the other, without repose, without stopping, without fatigue. They loved only that, understood nothing else, talked only of that, lived only that.

They had at heart that one passion, which was terrible and inexorable. It consumed them, having entirely invaded them, leaving place for no other.

They had given orders that they should not be interrupted in the chase, for any reason whatever. My great-grandfather was born while his father was following a fox, and Jean d'Arville did not stop his pursuit, but he swore: "Name of a name, that rascal there might have waited till after the view-halloo!"

His brother Francois showed himself still more infatuated. On rising he went to see the dogs, then the horses; then he shot little birds about the castle until the moment for departing to hunt down some great beast.

In the countryside they were called M. le Marquis and M. le Cadet, the nobles then not doing at all like the chance nobility of our time, which wishes to establish an hereditary hierarchy in titles; for the son of a marquis is no more a count, nor the son of a viscount a baron, than the son of a general is a colonel by birth. But the mean of vanity of today finds profit in that arrangement.

I return to my ancestors.

They were, it seems, immeasurably tall, bony, hairy, violent, and vigorous. The younger, still taller than the older, had a voice so strong that, according to a legend of which he was proud, all the leaves of the forests shook when he shouted.

And when they both mounted to go off to the hunt, that must have been a superb spectacle to see those two giants straddling their huge horses.

Now towards the midwinter of the year, 1764, the frosts were excessive, and the wolves became ferocious.

They even attacked belated peasants, roamed at night about the houses, howled from sunset to sunrise, and depopulated the stables.

And soon a rumor began to circulate. People talked of a colossal wolf, with gray fur, almost white, who had eaten two children, gnawed off a woman's arm, strangled all the dogs of the *garde du pays,* and penetrated without fear into the farmyards to come snuffling under the doors. The people in the houses affirmed that they had felt his breath, and that it made the flame of the lights flicker. And soon a panic ran through all the province. No one dared go out anymore after nightfall. The shades seemed haunted by the image of the beast.

The brothers d'Arville resolved to find and kill him, and several times they assembled all the gentlemen of the country to a great hunting.

In vain. They might beat the forest and search the coverts; they never met him. They killed wolves, but not that one. And every night after a *battue,* the beast, as if to avenge himself, attacked some traveler or devoured someone's cattle, always far from the place where they had looked for him.

Finally one night he penetrated into the pigpen of the Chateau d'Arville and ate the two finest pigs.

The brothers were inflamed with anger, considering this attack as a bravado of the monster, an insult direct, a defiance. They took their strong bloodhounds used to pursue formidable beasts, and they set off to hunt, their hearts swollen with fury.

From dawn until the hour when the empurpled sun descended behind the great naked trees, they beat the thickets without finding anything.

At last, furious and disconsolate, both were returning, walking their horses along an *allee* bordered with brambles, and they marveled that their woodcraft should be crossed so by this wolf, and they were seized suddenly with a sort of mysterious fear.

The elder said: "That beast there is not an ordinary one. You would say it thought like a man."

The younger answered: "Perhaps we should have a bullet blessed by our cousin, the bishop, or pray some priest to pronounce the words which are needed."

Then they were silent.

Jean continued: "Look how red the sun is. The great wolf will do some harm tonight."

He had hardly finished speaking when his horse reared; that of Francois began to kick. A large thicket covered with dead leaves opened before them, and a colossal beast, quite gray, sprang up and ran off across the wood.

Both uttered a kind of groan of joy, and, bending over the necks of their heavy horses, they threw them forward with an impulse from their whole bodies, hurling them on at such a pace, exciting them, hurrying them away, maddening them so with the voice, with gesture, and with spur that the strong riders seemed rather to be carrying the heavy beasts between their thighs and to bear them off as if they were flying.

Thus they went, *ventre a terre*, bursting the thickets, cleaving the beds of streams, climbing the hillsides, descending the gorges, and blowing on the horn with full lungs to attract their people and their dogs.

And now, suddenly, in that mad race, my ancestor struck his forehead against an enormous branch which split his skull; and he fell stark dead on the ground, while his frightened horse took himself off, disappearing in the shade which enveloped the woods.

The cadet of Arville stopped short, leaped to the earth, and seized his brother in his arms. He saw that the brains ran from the wound with the blood.

Then he sat down beside the body, rested the head, disfigured and red, on his knees, and waited, contemplating that immobile face of the elder brother. Little by little a fear invaded him, a strange fear which he had never felt before, the fear of the dark, the fear of solitude, the fear of the deserted wood, and the fear also of the fantastic wolf who had just killed his brother to avenge himself upon them both.

The shadows thickened; the acute cold made the trees crack. Francois got up, shivering, unable to remain there longer, feeling himself almost growing faint. Nothing was to be heard, neither the voice of the dogs nor the sound of the horns—all was silent along the invisible horizon; and this mournful silence of the frozen night had something about it frightening and strange.

He seized in his colossal hands the great body of Jean, straightened it and laid it across the saddle to carry it back to the chateau; then he went on his way softly, his mind troubled as if he were drunken, pursued by horrible and surprising images.

And abruptly, in the path which the night was invading, a great shape passed. It was the beast. A shock of terror shook the hunter; something cold, like a drop of water, glided along his veins, and like a monk haunted of the devil, he made a great sign of the cross, dismayed at this abrupt return of the frightful prowler. But his eyes fell back upon the inert body laid before him, and suddenly, passing abruptly from fear to anger, he shook with an inordinate rage.

Then he spurred his horse and rushed after the wolf.

He followed it by the copses, the ravines, and the tall trees, traversing woods which he no longer knew, his eyes fixed on the white speck which fled before him through the night now fallen upon the earth.

His horse also seemed animated by a force and an ardor hitherto unknown. It galloped, with outstretched neck, straight on, hurling against the trees, against the rocks, the head and the feet of the dead man thrown across the saddle. The briers tore out the hair; the brow, beating the huge trunks, spattered them with blood; the spurs tore their ragged coats of bark. And suddenly the beast and the horseman issued from the forest and rushed into a valley, just as the moon appeared above the mountains. This valley was stony, closed by enormous rocks, without possible issue; and the wolf was cornered and turned round.

Francois then uttered a yell of joy which the echoes repeated like a rolling of thunder, and he leaped from his horse, his cutlass in his hand.

The beast, with bristling hair, the back arched, awaited him; its eyes glistened like two stars. But, before offering battle, the strong hunter, seizing his brother, seated him on a rock, and, supporting with stones his head, which was no more than a blot of blood, he shouted in the ears as if he was talking to a dead man, "Look, Jean; look at this!"

Then he threw himself upon the monster. He felt himself strong enough to overturn a mountain, to bruise stones in his hands. The beast tried to bite him, seeking to strike in at his stomach; but he had seized it by the neck, without even using his weapon, and he strangled it gently, listening to the stoppage of the breathings in its throat and the beatings of its heart. And he laughed, rejoicing madly, pressing closer and closer his formidable embrace, crying in a delirium of joy, "Look, Jean, look!" All resistance ceased; the body of the wolf became lax. He was dead.

Then Francois, taking him up in his arms, carried him off and went and threw him at the feet of the elder brother, repeating, in a tender voice, "There, there, there, my little Jean, see him!"

Then he replaced on the saddle the two bodies, one upon the other; and he went his way.

He returned to the chateau, laughing and crying, like Gargantua at the birth of Pantagruel, uttering shouts of triumph and stamping with joy in relating the death of the beast, and moaning and tearing his beard in telling that of his brother.

And often, later, when he talked again of that day, he said, with tears in his eyes, "If only that poor Jean could have seen me strangle the other, he would have died content. I am sure of it!"

The Marquis d'Arville was silent. Someone asked: "That story is a legend, isn't it?

And the storyteller answered: "I swear to you that it is true from one end to the other."

Then a lady declared, in a little soft voice: "All the same, it is fine to have passions like that."

# Gabriel-Ernest

SAKI (H. H. MUNRO, 1870–1916)

"THERE IS A WILD BEAST in your woods," said the artist Cunningham, as he was being driven to the station. It was the only remark he had made during the drive, but as Van Cheele had talked incessantly his companion's silence had not been noticeable.

"A stray fox or two and some resident weasels. Nothing more formidable," said Van Cheele. The artist said nothing.

"What did you mean about a wild beast?" said Van Cheele later, when they were on the platform.

"Nothing. My imagination. Here is the train," said Cunningham.

That afternoon Van Cheele went for one of his frequent rambles through his woodland property. He had a stuffed bittern in his study, and knew the names of quite a number of wild flowers, so his aunt had possibly some justification in describing him as a great naturalist. At any rate, he was a great walker. It was his custom to take mental notes of everything he saw during his walks, not so much for the purpose of assisting contemporary science as to provide topics for conversation afterwards. When the bluebells began to show themselves in flower, he made a point of informing everyone of the fact; the season of the year might have warned his hearers of the likelihood of such an occurrence, but at least they felt that he was being absolutely frank with them.

What Van Cheele saw on this particular afternoon was, however, something far removed from his ordinary range of experience. On a shelf of smooth stone overhanging a deep pool in the hollow of an oak coppice, a boy of about sixteen lay asprawl, drying his wet brown limbs luxuriously in the sun. His wet

From *The Complete Short Stories of Saki (H. H. Munro)* (New York: Viking 1930, 1958).

hair, parted by a recent dive, lay close to his head, and his light-brown eyes, so light that there was an almost tigerish gleam in them, were turned towards Van Cheele with a certain lazy watchfulness. It was an unexpected apparition, and Van Cheele found himself engaged in the novel process of thinking before he spoke. Where on earth could this wild-looking boy hail from? The miller's wife had lost a child some two months ago, supposed to have been swept away by the millrace, but that had been a mere baby, not a half-grown lad.

"What are you doing there?" he demanded.

"Obviously, sunning myself," replied the boy.

"Where do you live?"

"Here, in these woods."

"You can't live in the woods," said Van Cheele.

"They are very nice woods," said the boy, with a touch of patronage in his voice.

"But where do you sleep at night?"

"I don't sleep at night; that's my busiest time."

Van Cheele began to have an irritated feeling that he was grappling with a problem that was eluding him.

"What do you feed on?" he asked.

"Flesh," said the boy, and he pronounced the word with slow relish, as though he were tasting it.

"Flesh! What flesh?"

"Since it interests you, rabbits, wildfowl, hares, poultry, lambs in their season, children when I can get any; they're usually too well locked in at night, when I do most of my hunting. It's quite two months since I tasted child-flesh."

Ignoring the chaffing nature of the last remark, Van Cheele tried to draw the boy on the subject of possible poaching operations.

"You're talking rather through your hat when you speak of feeding on hares." (Considering the nature of the boy's toilet, the simile was hardly an apt one.) "Our hillside hares aren't easily caught."

"At night I hunt on four feet," was the somewhat cryptic response.

"I suppose you mean that you hunt with a dog?" hazarded Van Cheele.

The boy rolled over on his back, and laughed a weird low laugh, that was pleasantly like a chuckle and disagreeably like a snarl. "I don't fancy any dog would be very anxious for my company, especially at night."

Van Cheele began to feel that there was something positively uncanny

about the strange-eyed, strange-tongued youngster. "I can't have you staying in these woods," he declared authoritatively.

"I fancy you'd rather have me here than in your house," said the boy.

The prospect of the wild, nude animal in Van Cheele's primly ordered house was certainly an alarming one. "If you don't go, I shall have to make you," said Van Cheele.

The boy turned like a flash, plunged into the pool, and in a moment had flung his wet and glistening body halfway up the bank where Van Cheele was standing. In an otter the movement would not have been remarkable; in a boy Van Cheele found it sufficiently startling. His foot slipped as he made an involuntary backward movement, and he found himself almost prostrate on the slippery weed-grown bank, with those tigerish yellow eyes not very far from his own. Almost instinctively he half raised his hand to his throat. The boy laughed again, a laugh in which the snarl had nearly driven out the chuckle, and then, with another of his astonishing lightning movements, plunged out of view into a yielding tangle of weed and fern.

"What an extraordinary wild animal!" said Van Cheele as he picked himself up. And then he recalled Cunningham's remark, "There is a wild beast in your woods."

Walking slowly homeward, Van Cheele began to turn over in his mind various local occurrences which might be traceable to the existence of this astonishing young savage.

Something had been thinning the game in the woods lately, poultry had been missing from the farms, hares were growing unaccountably scarcer, and complaints had reached him of lambs being carried off bodily from the hills. Was it possible that this wild boy was really hunting the countryside in company with some clever poacher dog? He had spoken of hunting "four-footed" by night, but then, again, he had hinted strangely at no dog caring to come near him, "especially at night." It was certainly puzzling. And then, as Van Cheele ran his mind over the various depredations that had been committed during the last month or two, he came suddenly to a dead stop, alike in his walk and his speculations. The child missing from the mill two months ago— the accepted theory was that it had tumbled into the millrace and been swept away; but the mother had always declared she had heard a shriek on the hill side of the house, in the opposite direction from the water. It was unthinkable, of course, but he wished that the boy had not made that uncanny remark about this child-flesh eaten two months ago. Such dreadful things should not be said even in fun.

Van Cheele, contrary to his usual wont, did not feel disposed to be communicative about his discovery in the wood. His position as a parish councillor and justice of the peace seemed somehow compromised by the fact that he was harboring a personality of such doubtful repute on his property; there was even a possibility that a heavy bill of damages for raided lambs and poultry might be laid at his door. At dinner that night he was quite unusually silent.

"Where's your voice gone to?" said his aunt. "One would think you had seen a wolf."

Van Cheele, who was not familiar with the old saying, thought the remark rather foolish; if he *had* seen a wolf on his property his tongue would have been extraordinarily busy with the subject.

At breakfast next morning Van Cheele was conscious that his feeling of uneasiness regarding yesterday's episode had not wholly disappeared, and he resolved to go by train to the neighboring cathedral town, hunt up Cunningham, and learn from him what he had really seen that had prompted the remark about a wild beast in the woods. With this resolution taken, his usual cheerfulness partially returned, and he hummed a bright little melody as he sauntered to the morning room for his customary cigarette. As he entered the room the melody made way abruptly for a pious invocation. Gracefully asprawl on the ottoman, in an attitude of almost exaggerated repose, was the boy of the woods. He was drier than when Van Cheele had last seen him, but no other alteration was noticeable in his toilet.

"How dare you come here?" asked Van Cheele furiously.

"You told me I was not to stay in the woods," said the boy calmly.

"But not to come here. Supposing my aunt should see you!"

And with a view to minimizing that catastrophe, Van Cheele hastily obscured as much of his unwelcome guest as possible under the folds of a *Morning Post*. At that moment his aunt entered the room.

"This is a poor boy who has lost his way—and lost his memory. He doesn't know who he is or where he comes from," explained Van Cheele desperately, glancing apprehensively at the waif's face to see whether he was going to add inconvenient candor to his other savage propensities.

Miss Van Cheele was enormously interested.

"Perhaps his underlinen is marked," she suggested.

"He seems to have lost most of that, too," said Van Cheele, making frantic little grabs at the *Morning Post* to keep it in its place.

A naked, homeless child appealed to Miss Van Cheele as warmly as a stray kitten or derelict puppy would have done.

"We must do all we can for him," she decided, and in a very short time a messenger, dispatched to the rectory, where a page boy was kept, had returned with a suit of pantry clothes, and the necessary accessories of shirt, shoes, collar, etc. Clothed, clean and groomed, the boy lost none of his uncanniness in Van Cheele's eyes, but his aunt found him sweet.

"We must call him something till we know who he really is," she said. "Gabriel-Ernest, I think; those are nice suitable names."

Van Cheele agreed, but he privately doubted whether they were being grafted on to a nice suitable child. His misgivings were not diminished by the fact that his staid and elderly spaniel had bolted out of the house at the first incoming of the boy, and now obstinately remained shivering and yapping at the farther end of the orchard, while the canary, usually as vocally industrious as Van Cheele himself, had put itself on an allowance of frightened cheeps. More than ever he was resolved to consult Cunningham without loss of time.

As he drove off to the station, his aunt was arranging that Gabriel-Ernest should help her to entertain the infant members of her Sunday-school class at tea that afternoon.

Cunningham was not at first disposed to be communicative.

"My mother died of some brain trouble," he explained, "so you will understand why I am averse to dwelling on anything of an impossibly fantastic nature that I may see or think that I have seen."

"But what *did* you see?" persisted Van Cheele.

"What I thought I saw was something so extraordinary that no really sane man could dignify it with the credit of having actually happened. I was standing, the last evening I was with you, half hidden in the hedgegrowth by the orchard gate, watching the dying glow of the sunset. Suddenly I became aware of a naked boy, a bather from some neighboring pool, I took him to be, who was standing out on the bare hillside also watching the sunset. His pose was so suggestive of some wild faun of Pagan myth I instantly wanted to engage him as a model, and in another moment I think I should have hailed him. But just then the sun dipped out of view, and all the orange and pink slid out of the landscape, leaving it cold and gray. And at the same moment an astounding thing happened—the boy vanished too!"

"What! Vanished away into nothing?" asked Van Cheele excitedly.

"No; that is the dreadful part of it," answered the artist; "on the open hill-side where the boy had been standing a second ago, stood a large wolf, black-ish in color, with gleaming fangs and cruel, yellow eyes. You may think—"

But Van Cheele did not stop for anything as futile as thought. Already he was tearing at top speed towards the station. He dismissed the idea of a telegram. "Gabriel-Ernst is a werewolf" was a hopelessly inadequate effort at conveying the situation, and his aunt would think it was a code message to which he had omitted to give her the key. His one hope was that he might reach home before sundown. The cab which he chartered at the other end of the railway journey bore him with what seemed exasperating slowness along the country roads, which were pink and mauve with the flush of the sinking sun. His aunt was putting away some unfinished jams and cake when he arrived.

"Where is Gabriel-Ernest?" he almost screamed.

"He is taking the little Toop child home," said his aunt. "It was getting so late, I thought it wasn't safe to let it go back alone. What a lovely sunset isn't it?"

But Van Cheele, although not oblivious of the glow in the western sky, did not stay to discuss its beauties. At a speed for which he was scarcely geared he raced along the narrow lane that led to the home of the Toops. On one side ran the swift current of the millstream, on the other rose the stretch of bare hillside. A dwindling rim of red sun showed still on the skyline, and the next turning must bring him in view of the ill-assorted couple he was pursuing. Then the color went suddenly out of things, and a gray light settled itself with a quick shiver over the landscape. Van Cheele heard a shrill wail of fear, and stopped running.

Nothing was ever seen of the Toops' child or Gabriel-Ernest, but the latter's discarded garments were found lying in the road, so it was assumed that the child had fallen into the water, and that the boy had stripped and jumped in, in a vain endeavor to save it. Van Cheele and some workmen who were nearby at the time testified to having heard a child scream loudly just near the spot where the clothes were found. Mrs. Toop, who had eleven other chil-dren, was decently resigned to her bereavement, but Miss Van Cheele sincerely mourned her lost foundling. It was on her initiative that a memorial brass was put up in the parish church to "Gabriel-Ernest, an unknown boy, who bravely sacrificed his life for another."

Van Cheele gave way to his aunt in most things, but he flatly refused to subscribe to the Gabriel-Ernest memorial.

# PART THREE

# The Diabolical Werewolf

The stories in this section reach back into lycanthropic history and myth to show the werewolf's diabolic origins and the malignity of their originator. These werewolves owe their metamorphosis to the Devil, who is able, and more than willing, to transform human flesh into animal flesh in order to create moral chaos in the world. Dedicated to transforming the world into a place where evil conquers good, the Devil creates the werewolf—a ferocious human-wolf (either male or female) whose depraved activities display the master's power.

Seabury Quinn's interest in law, medicine, and death and burial practices led him into writing stories about the supernatural. Creating the French detective Jules de Grandin and his physician friend, Dr. Trowbridge, Quinn launched de Grandin and Trowbridge in 1925 in a story, "The Horror on the Links," which appeared in Weird Tales. Its immense popularity encouraged him to write ninety-three de Grandin stories in all.

"The Thing in the Fog" shows de Grandin as an unusually erudite detective who, at crucial moments, parcels out his knowledge of the history of lycanthropy to Trowbridge, always insisting that lycanthropy is rooted in diabolism. At one point de Grandin observes, "Werewolves sometimes become werewolves by the aid of Satan, that they may kill their enemies while in lupine form, or satisfy their natural lust for blood and cruelty while disguised as beasts. Some are transformed as the result of a curse upon themselves or their families, a few are metamorphosed by accident. These are the most unfortunate of all. In certain parts of Europe, notably in Greece, Russia and the Balkan states, the very soil seems cursed with lycanthropic power. . . . Certain streams and springs there are which, if drunk from, will render the drinker liable to transformation at the next full moon, and regularly thereafter."

The male werewolf in this story is a mature Greek who charms a beautiful young Englishwoman, then living in Smyrna, into drinking from an enchanted pool at midnight. Instantly transformed into a young she-werewolf, she accompanies this powerful male werewolf on his deadly hunts. After she leaves Smyrna, he pursues her to England, where, as a werewolf, he kills several Englishmen in his attempt to reclaim her and to prevent her imminent marriage.

Unable to gain access to her, the werewolf attempts to gain power over her by transforming her again into a she-wolf. He accomplishes this by sending her, anonymously, the gift of a lycanthropy-inducing perfume made from "wolf flowers." As de Grandin observes, "It is a *highly concentrated venom of their devilishness. One applying it to her person, anointing lips, ears, hair, and hands with it, as women wont, would as surely be translated into wolfish form as though she wore the cursed flower whence the perfume comes."*

*It is de Grandin's vast knowledge of the poisons and diabolic magic of lycanthropy that rescues the innocent young woman (though not before she is metamorphosed into a sleek young werewolf) from both the pursuing werewolf and from the horrors of periodic metamorphosis. Her savior shares with the reader some of the ancient techniques of inducing and conquering diabolic lycanthropy.*

*Brian Stableford's story, "The Werewolves of London," is an excerpt from the first novel of his eschatological trilogy. The story opens in Victorian England in 1872 at the height of the Industrial Revolution. Fallen angels of Biblical narrative roam the streets of London as werewolves. Having been asleep for a long time, the werewolves must acclimate themselves to this strange new world. Although they scheme and war among themselves, they do agree on their quest: to bring their own Hell into the human world.*

*Stableford draws from the story of the fallen angel of Genesis who transformed himself into a serpent and brought strife and death into the world of Adam and Eve in Paradise—and to the human race yet unborn. Stableford shows that the power of the demonic is constantly reborn. No human being can escape from this diabolic power, even though centuries have elapsed and the world has progressed technologically far beyond the simple garden of Eden.*

*In this excerpt, David Lydyard awakens in an unfamiliar, squalid place. The setting is surreal: an "awesomely beautiful woman," whose glamour attracts him, has made him her prisoner. At first she flatters him and lies to him in an effort to seduce him into confessing what he knows about the secrets of the universe. The female werewolf declares, "Poor man-child, you think that you have only dreamed of being in Hell, but you do not know how real your dreams now are. You are hostage to the powers of Creation and Destruction, whose reality is unimagined in your knowledge and your language."*

*Torture is her weapon. She scratches deep into his cuts, reopening them and making them bleed; she burns a candle on the sole of his foot; she taunts him with the promise of more intense pain and with the question of how long it takes to die by burning his flesh inch by inch with a candle. These are the diabolical weapons (Stableford knows that the reader will recognize these as familiar human weapons) she uses while verbally trying to convince David that giving up his secret will guarantee him a painless imprisonment.*

*Although the story is futuristic science fiction, Stableford's werewolves are not far from the werewolves of earlier centuries. During the time when werewolves were regularly brought to trial, some theoreticians were sure that werewolves were actually fallen angels in disguise. Others thought that fallen angels entered the consciousness of a human being, creating in the psyche* the illusion of being a werewolf, and thus forcing a human being into diabolical acts of destruction. In Stableford's story, werewolves have demonic origins and their only aim is to obliterate human society—in as painful a way as possible.

The two old werewolves in Gerald Biss's story are a male professor, Lycurgus Wolff, who is a specialist in lycanthropy, and his female servant, Anna Brunnolf. He regularly transforms himself and Anna into werewolves and murders travelers who accidentally enter into his territory. The two of them have taken the professor's young stepdaughter, Dorothy, captive, forcing her to engage in ancient lycanthropic rites and turning her into a werewolf on the night of a full moon. She explains the ritual of metamorphosis to her friends: "He made me dip my hands and face in special water that he brought with his own hands. . . . Then he placed round my waist a girdle of dark plaited hair with a queer old gold buckle, and put flowers—these horrible yellow ones with the black pustules . . . and red and white ones as well: and then in the old oak hall, empty and lit only by the light of the moon through the mullioned windows, with white chalk he drew a circle some six or seven feet in diameter, and placed me in the center, sprinkling my forehead, my hands, and my breast with some of the same water. . . . [H]e began in his rough guttural voice to chant a weird incantation, moving slowly round and round me all the while. . . . And then it seemed that out of the half darkness there rose a tall, pillar-like phantom. . ."

The professor is admittedly in league with the Devil; the evil in his house is as serpentine as the evil in the Garden of Eden. Only a person who is equally familiar with the diabolism of lycanthropy can thwart the professor and free the young woman from the bondage of werewolfism. This savior is Lincoln Osgood, an American whose knowledge of lycanthropy rivals that of Dr. Lycurgus Wolff.

Saving Dorothy means that the professor and his servant must die and that his house, barn, the lycanthropic plants growing in the garden, and the noxious pools must be burned down in a ritual conflagration. After eliminating all traces of the professor and his servant, Osgood arranges an exorcism for Dorothy in order to remove all traces of the evil spirits that have been introduced into her soul by the demonic werewolves. In an elaborate ceremony (reminiscent of earlier ceremonies to exorcise werewolf-demonic possession), Osgood calls on "God's grace to be able to exorcise this impregnated evil," and the "unspeakable elemental who had defiled the temple of her body by taking up its dwelling therein" exits Dorothy's body in a "pyramid of foul smoke, disappearing and disintegrating into the air."

# The Thing in the Fog

SEABURY QUINN (1889–1969)

"*TIENS, ON SUCH A NIGHT AS THIS* the Devil must congratulate himself!" Jules de Grandin forced his chin still deeper in the upturned collar of his trench coat, and bent his head against the whorls of chilling mist which eddied upward from the bay in token that autumn was dead and winter come at last.

"Congratulate himself?" I asked in amusement as I felt before me for the curbstone with the ferrule of my stick. "Why?"

"Why? *Pardieu,* because he sits at ease beside the cozy fires of hell, and does not have to feel his way through this eternally-to-be-execrated fog! If we had but the sense—

"*Pardon, Monsieur,* one of us is very clumsy, and I do not think that it is I!" he broke off sharply as a big young man, evidently carrying a heavier cargo of ardent spirits than he could safely manage, lurched against him in the smothering mist, then caromed off at an unsteady angle to lose himself once more in the enshrouding fog.

"Dolt!" the little Frenchman muttered peevishly. "If he can not carry liquor he should abstain from it. Me, I have no patience with these—*grand Dieu,* what is that?"

Somewhere behind us, hidden in the curtains of the thick, gray vapor, there came a muffled exclamation, half of fright, half of anger, the sound of something fighting threshingly with something else, and a growling, snarling noise, as though a savage dog had leapt upon its prey, and, having fleshed its teeth, was worrying it; then: "Help!" The cry was muffled, strangled, but laden with a weight of helpless terror.

In *Weird Tales* (March 1933).

71

"Hold fast, my friend, we come!" de Grandin cried, and, guided by the sounds of struggle, breasted through the fog as if it had been water, brandishing his silver-headed sword-stick before him as a guide and a defense.

A score of quick steps brought us to the conflict. Dim and indistinct as shadows on a moonless night, two forms were struggling on the sidewalk, a large one lying underneath, while over it, snarling savagely, was a thing I took for a police dog which snapped and champed and worried at the other's throat.

"Help!" called the man again, straining futilely to hold the snarling beast away and turning on his side the better to protect his menaced face and neck.

"*Cordieu*, a war-dog!" exclaimed the Frenchman. "Stand aside, Friend Trowbridge, he is savage, this one; mad, perhaps, as well." With a quick, whipping motion he ripped the chilled-steel blade from the barrel of his stick and, point advanced, circled round the struggling man and beast, approaching with a cautious, catlike step as he sought an opportunity to drive home the sword.

By some uncanny sense the snarling brute divined his purpose, raised its muzzle from its victim's throat and backed away a step or two, regarding de Grandin with a stare of utter hatred. For a moment I caught the smoldering glare of a pair of fire-red eyes, burning through the fog folds as incandescent charcoal might burn through a cloth, and: "A dog? *Non, pardieu*, it is—" began the little Frenchman, then checked himself abruptly as he lunged out swiftly with his blade, straight for the glaring, fiery eyes which glowered at him through the mist.

The great beast backed away with no apparent haste, yet quickly enough to avoid the needle point of Jules de Grandin's blade, and for an instant I beheld a row of gleaming teeth bared savagely beneath the red eyes' glare; then, with a snarling growl which held more defiance than surrender in its throaty rumble, the brute turned lithely, dodged and made off through the fog, disappearing from sight before the clicking of its nails against the pavement had been lost to hearing.

"Look to him, Friend Trowbridge," de Grandin ordered, casting a final glance about us in the mist before he put his sword back in its sheath. "Does he survive, or is he killed to death?"

"He's alive, all right," I answered as I sank to my knees beside the supine man, "but he's been considerably chewed up. Bleeding badly. We'd best get him to the office and patch him up before—"

"Wha— what was it?" our mangled patient asked abruptly, rising on his elbow and staring wildly round him. "Did you kill it—did it get away? D'ye think it had hydrophobia?"

"Easy on, son," I soothed, locking my hands beneath his arms and helping him to rise. "It bit you several times, but you'll be all right as soon as we can stop the bleeding. Here"—I snatched a handkerchief from the breast pocket of my dinner coat and pressed it into his hand—" hold this against the wound while we're walking. No use trying to get a taxi tonight, the driver'd never find his way about. I live only a little way from here and we'll make it nicely if you'll lean on me. So! That's it!"

The young man leant heavily upon my shoulder and almost bore me down, for he weighed a good fourteen stone, as we made our way along the vapor-shrouded street.

"I say, I'm sorry I bumped into you, sir," the youngster apologized as de Grandin took his other arm and eased me somewhat of my burden. "Fact is, I'd taken a trifle too much and was walkin' on a side hill when I passed you." He pressed the already-reddened handkerchief closer to his lacerated neck as he continued with a chuckle: "Maybe it's a good thing I did, at that, for you were within hearing when I called because you'd stopped to cuss me out."

"You may have right, my friend," de Grandin answered with a laugh. "A little drunkenness is not to be deplored, and I doubt not you had reason for your drinking—not that one needs a reason, but—"

A sudden shrill, sharp cry for help cut through his words, followed by another call which stopped half uttered on a strangled, agonizing note; then, in a moment, the muffled echo of a shot, another, and immediately afterward, the shrilling signal of a police whistle.

"*Tete bleu*, this night is full of action as a pepper pot is full of spice!" exclaimed de Grandin, turning toward the summons of the whistle. "Can you manage him, Friend Trowbridge? If so I—"

Pounding of heavy boots on the sidewalk straight ahead told us that the officer approached, and a moment later his form, bulking gigantically in the fog, hove into view. "Did any o' yez see—" he started, then raised his hand in half-formal salute to the visor of his cap as he recognized de Grandin.

"I don't suppose ye saw a dar-rg come runnin' by this way, sor?" he asked. "I wuz walkin' up th' street a moment since, gettin' ready to report at th' box, when I heard a felly callin' for help, an' what should I see next but th' biggest,

ugliest baste of a dar-rg ye iver clapped yer eyes upon, a'worryin' at th' pore
lad's throat. I wuz close to it as I'm standing to you, sor, pretty near, an' I shot
at it twict, but I'm damned if I didn't miss both times, slick as a whistle—an' me
holdin' a pistol expert's medal from th' department, too!"

"U'm?" de Grandin murmured. "And the unfortunate man beset by this
great beast your bullets failed to hit, what of him?"

"Glory be to God; I plumb forgot 'im!" the policeman confessed. "Ye see,
sor, I wuz that overcome wid shame, as th' felly says, whin I realized I'd missed
th' baste that I run afther it, hopin' I'd find it agin an' maybe put a slug into it
this time, so—"

"Quite so, one understands," de Grandin interrupted, "but let us give attention to the man; the beast can wait until we find him, and—*mon Dieu!* It is as
well you did not stay to give him the first aid, my friend, your efforts would
have been without avail. His case demands the coroner's attention."

He did not understate the facts. Stretched on his back, hands clenched to
fists, legs slightly spread, one doubled partly under him, a man lay on the sidewalk; across the white expanse of evening shirt his opened coat displayed
there spread a ruddy stickiness, while his starched white-linen collar was already sopping with the blood which oozed from his torn and mangled throat.
Both external and anterior jugulars had been ripped away by the savagery
which had torn the integument of the neck to shreds, and so deeply had the
ragged wound gone that a portion of the hyoid bone had been exposed. A
spate of blood had driveled from the mouth, staining lips and chin, and the
eyes, forced out between the lids, were globular and fixed and staring, though
the film of death had hardly yet had time to set upon them.

"Howly Mither!" cried the officer in horror as he looked upon the body.
"Sure, it were a hound from th' Divil's own kennels done this, sor!"

"I think that you have right," de Grandin nodded grimly. "Call the department, if you will be so good. I will stand by the body." He took a kerchief from
his pocket and opened it, preparatory to veiling the poor, mangled face which
stared appealingly up at fog-bound night, but:

"My God, it's Suffrige!" the young man at my side exclaimed. "I left him
just before I blundered into you, and—oh, what could have done it?"

"The same thing which almost did as much for you, *Monsieur,*" the Frenchman answered in a level, toneless voice. "You had a very narrow escape from
being even as your friend, I do assure you."

"You mean that dog—" he stopped, incredulous, eyes fairly starting from his face as he stared in fascination at his friend's remains.

"The dog, yes, let us call it that," de Grandin answered.

"But—but—" the other stammered, then, with an incoherent exclamation which was half sigh, half groaning hiccup, slumped heavily against my shoulder and slid unconscious to the ground.

De Grandin shrugged in irritation. "Now we have two of them to watch," he complained. "Do you recover him as quickly as you can, my friend, while I—" he turned his back to me, dropped his handkerchief upon the dead man's face and bent to make a closer examination of the wounds in the throat.

I took the handkerchief from my overcoat pocket, ran it lightly over the trunk of a leafless tree which stood beside the curb and wrung the moisture from it on the unconscious man's face and forehead. Slowly he recovered, gasped feebly, then, with my assistance, got upon his feet, keeping his back resolutely turned to the grisly thing upon the sidewalk. "Can—you—help—me—to—your—office? he asked slowly, breathing heavily between the words.

I nodded, and we started toward my house, but twice we had to stop; for once he became sick, and I had to hold him while he retched with nausea, and once he nearly fainted again, leaning heavily against the iron balustrade before a house while he drew great gulps of chilly, fog-soaked air into his lungs.

At last we reached my office, and helping him up to the examination table I set to work. His wounds were more extensive than I had at first supposed. A deep cut, more like the raking of some heavy, blunt-pointed claw than a bite, ran down his face from the right temple almost to the angle of the jaw, and two deep parallel scores showed on his throat above the collar. A little deeper, a little more to one side, and they would have nicked the anterior jugular. About his hands were several tears, as though they had suffered more from the beast's teeth than had his face and throat, and as I helped him with his jacket I saw his shirtfront had been slit and a long, raking cut scored down his chest, the animal's claws having ripped through the stiff, starched linen as easily as though it had been muslin.

The problem of treatment puzzled me. I could not cauterize the wounds with silver nitrate, and iodine would be without efficiency if the dog were rabid. Finally I compromised by dressing the chest and facial wounds with potassium permanganate solution and using an electric hot-point on the hands, applying laudanum immediately as an anodyne.

"And now, young fellow," I announced as I completed my work, "I think you could do nicely with a tot of brandy. You were drunk enough when you ran into us, heaven knows, but you're cold sober now, and your nerves have been badly jangled, so—"

"So you would be advised to bring another glass," de Grandin's hail sounded from the surgery door. "My nerves have been on edge these many minutes, and in addition I am suffering from an all-consuming thirst, my friend."

The young man gulped the liquor down in one tremendous swallow, seeing which de Grandin gave a shudder of disgust. Drinking fifty-year-old brandy was a rite with him, and to bolt it as if it had been common bootlegged stuff was grave impropriety, almost sacrilege.

"Doctor, do you think that dog had hydrophobia?" our patient asked half diffidently. "He seemed so savage—"

"Hydrophobia is the illness human beings have when bitten by a rabid dog or other animal, *Monsieur*," de Grandin broke in with a smile. "The beast has rabies, the human victim develops hydrophobia. However, if you wish, we can arrange for you to go to Mercy Hospital early in the morning to take the Pasteur treatment; it is effective and protective if you are infected, quite harmless if you are not."

"Thanks," replied the youth. "I think we'd better, for—"

"*Monsieur*," the Frenchman cut him short again, "is your name Maxwell, by any chance? Since I first saw you I have been puzzled by your face; now I remember, I saw your picture in *le journal* this morning."

"Yes," said our visitor, "I'm John Maxwell, and, since you saw my picture in the paper, you know that I'm to marry Sarah Leigh on Saturday; so you realize why I'm so anxious to make sure the dog didn't have hydro—rabies, I mean. I don't think Sallie'd want a husband she had to muzzle for fear he'd bite her on the ankle when she came to feed him."

The little Frenchman smiled acknowledgment of the other's pleasantry, but through his lips drew back in the mechanics of a smile, his little, round, blue eyes were fixed and studious.

"Tell me, *Monsieur*," he asked abruptly, "how came this dog to set upon you in the fog tonight?"

Young Maxwell shivered at the recollection. "Hanged if I know," he answered. "Y'see, the boys gave me a farewell bachelor dinner at the Carteret this evening, and there was the usual amount of speech making and toast drinking, and by the time we broke up I was pretty well paralyzed—able to find my way about, but not very steadily, as you know. I said good-night to the bunch at the hotel and started out alone, for I wanted to walk the liquor off. You see"—a flush suffused his blond, good-looking face—"Sallie said she'd wait up for me to telephone her—just like old married folks!—and I didn't want to talk to her while I was still thick-tongued. Ray Suffrige, the chap who—the one you saw later, sir—decided he'd walk home, too, and started off in the other direction, and the rest of 'em left in taxis.

"I'd walked about four blocks, and was getting so I could navigate pretty well, when I bumped into you, then brought up against the railing of a house. While I was hanging onto it, trying to get steady on my legs again, all of a sudden, out of nowhere, came that big police dog and jumped on me. It didn't bark or give any warning till it leaped at me; then it began growling. I flung my hands up, and it fastened on my sleeve, but luckily the cloth was thick enough to keep its teeth from tearing my arm.

"I never saw such a beast. I've had a tussle or two with savage dogs before, and they always jumped away and rushed in again each time I beat 'em off, but this thing stood on its hind legs and fought me *like a man*. When it shook its teeth loose from my coat sleeve it clawed at my face and throat with its forepaws—that's where I got most of my mauling—and kept snapping at me all the time; never backed away or even sank to all fours once, sir.

"I was still unsteady on my legs, and the brute was heavy as a man; so it wasn't long before it had me down. Every time it bit at me I managed to get my arms in its way; so it did more damage to my clothes than it did to me with its teeth, but it surely clawed me up to the Queen's taste, and I was beginning to tire when you came running up. It would have done me as it did poor Suffrige in a little while, I'm sure."

He paused a moment, then, with a shaking hand, poured out another drink of brandy and tossed it off at a gulp. "I guess I *must* have been drunk," he admitted with a shamefaced grin, "for I could have sworn the thing *talked* to me as it growled."

"Eh? The Devil!" Jules de Grandin sat forward suddenly, eyes wider and rounder than before, if possible, the needle points of his tightly waxed wheat-blond mustache twitching like the whiskers of an irritated tomcat. "What is it that you say?"

"Hold on," the other countered, quick blood mounting to his cheeks. "I didn't say it; I said it *seemed* as if its snarls were words."

"*Precisement, exactement,* quite so," returned the Frenchman sharply. "And what was it that he *seemed* to snarl at you, *Monsieur?* Quickly, if you please."

"Well, I was drunk, I admit, but—"

"Ten thousand small blue devils! We bandy words. I have asked you a question; have the courtesy to reply, *Monsieur.*"

"Well, it sounded—sort of—as if it kept repeating Sallie's name, like this—" he gave an imitation of a throaty, growling voice: " 'Sarah Leigh, Sarah Leigh—you'll never marry Sarah Leigh!'

"Ever hear anything so nutty? I reckon I must have had Sallie in my mind, subconsciously, while I was having what I thought was my death struggle."

It was very quiet for a moment. John Maxwell looked half sullenly, half defiantly from de Grandin to me. De Grandin sat as though lost in contemplation, his small eyes wide and thoughtful, his hands twisting savagely at the waxed ends of his mustache, the tip of his patent-leather evening shoe beating a devil's tattoo on the white-tiled floor. At length, abruptly: "Did you notice any smell, any peculiar odor, when we went to Monsieur Maxwell's rescue this evening, Friend Trowbridge?" he demanded.

"Why—" I bent my brows and wagged my head in an effort at remembrance. "Why, no, I didn't—" I stopped, while somewhere from the file cases of my subconscious memory came a hint of recollection: Soldiers' Park—a damp and drizzling day—the open-air dens of the menagerie. "Wait," I ordered, closing both eyes tightly while I bade my memory catalogue the vague, elusive scent; then: "Yes, there was an odor I've noticed at the zoo in Soldiers' Park; it was the smell of the damp fur of a fox, or wolf!"

De Grandin beat his small, white hands together softly, as though applauding at a play. "Capital, perfect!" he announced. "I smelled it too, when first we did approach, but our senses play strange tricks on us at times, and I needed the corroboration of your nose's testimony, if it could be had. Now—" he turned his fixed, unwinking stare upon me as he asked: "Have you ever seen a wolf's eyes—or a dog's—at night?"

"Yes, of course," I answered wonderingly.

"*Tres bien.* And they gleamed with a reflected greenness, something like Madame Pussy's, only not so bright, *n'est-ce pas?*"

"Yes."

"*Tres bon.* Did you see the eyes of what attacked Monsieur Maxwell this evening? Did you observe them?"

"I should say I did," I answered, for never would I forget those fiery, glaring orbs. "They were red, red as fire!"

"Oh, excellent Friend Trowbridge; oh, prince of all the recollectors of the world!" de Grandin cried delightedly. "Your memory serves you perfectly, and upholds my observations to the full. Before, I guessed; I said to me, 'Jules de Grandin, you are generally right, but once in many times you may be wrong. See what Friend Trowbridge has to say.' And you, *parbleu,* you said the very thing I needed to confirm me in my diagnosis.

"*Monsieur,*" he turned to Maxwell with a smile, "you need not fear that you have hydrophobia. No. You were very near to death, a most unpleasant sort of death, but not to death by hydrophobia. *Morbleu,* that would be an added refinement which we need not take into consideration."

"Whatever are you talking about?" I asked in sheer amazement. "You ask me if I noticed the smell that beast gave off, and if I saw its eyes, then tell Mr. Maxwell he needn't fear he's been inoculated. Of all the hare-brained—"

He turned his shoulder squarely on me and smiled assuringly at Maxwell. "You said that you would call your *amoureuse* tonight, *Monsieur;* have you forgotten?" he reminded, then nodded toward the 'phone.

The young man picked the instrument up, called a number and waited for a moment; then: "John speaking, honey," he announced as we heard a subdued *click* sound from the monophone. Another pause, in which the buzzing of indistinguishable words came faintly to us through the quiet room; then Maxwell turned and motioned me to take up the extension 'phone.

"—and please come right away, dear," I heard a woman's voice plead as I clapped the instrument against my ear. "No, I can't tell you over the 'phone, but I must see you right away, Johnny—I must! You're sure you're all right? Nothing happened to you?"

"Well," Maxwell temporized, "I'm in pretty good shape, everything considered. I had a little tussle with a dog, but—"

"A—*dog?*" Stark, incredulous horror sounded in the woman's fluttering voice. "What sort of dog?"

"Oh, just a dog, you know; not very big and not very little, sort o' betwixt and between, and—"

"You're sure it was a *dog?* Did it look like a—a police dog, for instance?"

"Well, now you mention it, it *did* look something like a police dog, or collie, or airedale, or something, but—"

"John, dear, don't try to put me off that way. This is terribly, dreadfully important. Please hurry over—no, don't come out at night—yes, come at once, but be sure not to come alone. Have you a sword, or some sort of steel or iron weapon you can carry for defense when you come?"

Young Maxwell's face betrayed bewilderment. "A sword?" he echoed. "What d'ye think I am, dear, a knight of old? No, I haven't a sword to my name, not even a jackknife, but—I say, there's a gentleman I met tonight who has a bully little sword; may I bring him along?"

"Oh, yes, please do, dear; and if you can get someone else, bring him, too. I'm terribly afraid to have you venture out tonight, dearest, but I have to see you right away!"

"All right," the young man answered. "I'll pop right over, honey."

As he replaced the instrument, he turned bewilderedly to me. "Wonder what the deuce got into Sally?" he asked. "She seemed all broken up about something, and I thought she'd faint when I mentioned my set-to with that dog. What's it mean?"

Jules de Grandin stepped through the doorway connecting surgery with consulting room, where he had gone to listen to the conversation from the desk extension. His little eyes were serious, his small mouth grimly set. "*Monsieur*," he announced gravely, "it means that Mademoiselle Sarah knows more than any of us what this business of the Devil is about. Come, let us go to her without delay."

As we prepared to leave the house he paused and rummaged in the hall coat closet, emerging in a moment, balancing a pair of blackthorn walking sticks in his hands.

"What—" I began, but he cut me short.

"These may prove useful," he announced, handing one to me, the other to John Maxwell. "If what I damn suspect is so, he will not greatly relish a thwack from one of these upon the head. No, the thornbush is especially repugnant to him."

"Humph, I should think it would particularly repugnant to anyone," I answered, weighing the knotty bludgeon in my hand. "By the way, who is 'he'?"

"Mademoiselle Sarah will tell us that," he answered enigmatically. "Are we ready? *Bon*, let us be upon our way."

The mist which had obscured the night an hour or so before had thinned to a light haze, and a drizzle of rain was commencing as we set out. The Leigh house was less than half a mile from my place, and we made good time as we marched through the damp, cold darkness.

I had known Joel Leigh only through having shared committee appointments with him in the local Republican organization and at the archdeaconry. He had entered the consular service after being retired from active duty with the Marine Corps following a surgeon's certificate of disability, and at the time of his death two years before had been rated as one of the foremost authorities on Near East commercial conditions. Sarah, his daughter, whom I had never met, was by all accounts a charming young woman, equally endowed with brains, beauty, and money, and keeping up the family tradition in the big house in Tuscarora Avenue, where she lived with an elderly maiden aunt as duenna.

Leigh's long residence in the East was evidenced in the furnishings of the long, old-fashioned hall, which was like a royal antechamber in miniature. In the softly diffused light from a brass-shaded Turkish lamp, we caught gleaming reflections from heavily carved blackwood furniture and the highlights of a marvelously inlaid Indian screen. A carved table flanked by dragon chairs stood against the wall; the floor was soft as new-mown turf with rugs from China, Turkey and Kurdistan.

"Mis' Sarah's in the library," announced the Negro butler who answered our summons at the door, and led us through the hall to the big, high-ceilinged room where Sarah Leigh was waiting. Books lined the chamber's walls from floor to ceiling on three sides; the fourth wall was devoted to a bulging bay window which overlooked the garden. Before the fire of cedar logs was drawn a deeply padded divan, while flanking it were great armchairs upholstered in red leather. The light which sifted through the meshes of a brazen lamp shade disclosed a tabouret of Indian mahogany on which a coffee service stood. Before the fire the mistress of the house stood waiting for us. She was rather less than average height, but appeared taller because of her fine carriage. Her mannishly close-cropped hair was dark and inclined toward curliness, but as she moved toward us I saw it showed bronze glints in the lamplight. Her eyes were large, expressive, deep hazel, almost brown. But for the look of cynicism, almost hardness, around her mouth, she would have been something more than merely pretty.

Introductions over, Miss Leigh looked from one of us to the other with something like embarrassment in her eyes. "If—" she began, but de Grandin divined her purpose, and broke in:

"*Mademoiselle*, a short time since, we had the good fortune to rescue *Monsieur* your fiancé from a dog which I do not think was any dog at all. That same creature, I might add, destroyed a gentleman who had attended Monsieur Maxwell's dinner within ten minutes of the time we drove it off. Furthermore, Monsieur Maxwell is under the impression that this dog-thing talked to him while it sought to slay him. From what we overheard of your message on the telephone, we think you hold the key to this mystery. You may speak freely in our presence, for I am Jules de Grandin, physician and occultist, and my friend, Doctor Trowbridge, has most commendable discretion."

The young woman smiled, and the transformation in her taut, strained face was startling. "Thank you," she replied; "if you're an occultist you will understand, and neither doubt me nor demand explanations of things I can't explain."

She dropped cross-legged to the hearth rug, as naturally as though she were more used to sitting that way than reclining in a chair, and we caught the gleam of a great square garnet on her forefinger as she extended her hand to Maxwell.

"Hold my hand while I'm talking, John," she bade. "It may be for the last time." Then, as he made a gesture of dissent, abruptly: "I cannot marry you— or anyone," she announced. Maxwell opened his lips to protest, but no sound came. I stared at her in wonder, trying futilely to reconcile the agitation she had shown when telephoning with her present deadly, apathetic calm.

Jules de Grandin yielded to his curiosity. "Why not, *Mademoiselle?*" he asked. "Who has forbid the banns?"

She shook her head dejectedly and turned a sad-eyed look upon him as she answered: "It's just the continuation of a story which I thought was a closed chapter in my life." For a moment she bent forward, nestling her cheek against young Maxwell's hand; then: "It began when Father was attached to the consulate in Smyrna," she continued. "France and Turkey were both playing for advantage, and Father had to find out what they planned, so he had to hire secret agents. The most successful of them was a young Greek named George Athanasakos, who came from Crete. Why he should have taken such employment was more than we could understand; for he was well educated, apparently a gentleman, and always well supplied with money. He told us he took the work because of his hatred of the Turks, and as he was always successful in getting information, Father didn't ask questions.

"When his work was finished he continued to call at our house as a guest, and I—I really didn't love him, I *couldn't* have, it was just infatuation, meeting him so far from home, and the water and that wonderful Smyrna moonlight, and—"

"Perfectly, *Mademoiselle*, one fully understands," de Grandin supplied softly as she paused, breathless; "and then—"

"Maybe you never succumbed to moonlight and water and strange, romantic poetry and music," she half whispered, her eyes grown wider at the recollection, "but I was only seventeen, and he was very handsome, and—and he swept me off my feet. He had the softest, most musical voice I've ever heard, and the things he said sounded like something written by Byron at his best. One moonlit night when we'd been rowing, he begged me to say I loved him, and—and I did. He held me in his arms and kissed my eyes and lips and throat. It was like being hypnotized and conscious at the same time. Then, just before we said good-night he told me to meet him in an old garden on the outskirts of the city where we sometimes rested when we'd been out riding. The rendezvous was made for midnight, and though I thought it queer that he should want to meet me at that time in such a place—well, girls in love don't ask questions, you know. At least, I didn't.

"There was a full moon the next night, and I was fairly breathless with the beauty of it all when I kept the tryst. I thought I'd come too early, for George was nowhere to be seen when I rode up, but as I jumped down from my horse and looked around I saw something moving in the laurels. It was George, and he'd thrown a cape or cloak of some sort of fur across his shoulders. He startled me dreadfully at first; for he looked like some sort of prowling beast with the animal's head hanging half down across his face, like the beaver of an ancient helmet. It seemed to me, too, that his eyes had taken on a sort of sinister greenish tinge, but when he took me in his arms and kissed me I was reassured.

"Then he told me he was the last of a very ancient clan which had been wiped out warring with the Turks, and that it was a tradition of their blood that the woman they married take a solemn oath before the nuptials could be celebrated. Again I didn't ask questions. It all seemed so wonderfully romantic," she added with a pathetic little smile.

"He had another skin cloak in readiness and dropped it over my shoulders, pulling the head well forward above my face, like a hood. Then he built a little fire of dry twigs and threw some incense on it. I knelt above the fire and inhaled the aromatic smoke while he chanted some sort of invocation in a tongue I didn't recognize, but which sounded harsh and terrible—like the snarling of a savage dog.

"What happened next I don't remember clearly, for that incense did things to me. The old garden where I knelt seemed to fade away, and in its place appeared a wild and rocky mountain scene where I seemed walking down a winding road. Other people were walking with me, and all were clothed in cloaks of hairy skin like mine. Suddenly, as we went down the mountainside, I began to notice that my companions were dropping to all fours, like beasts. But somehow it didn't seem strange to me; for, without realizing it, I was running on my hands and feet, too, Not crawling, you know, but actually running—like a dog. As we neared the mountain's foot we ran faster and faster; by the time we reached a little clearing in the heavy woods which fringed the rocky hill we were going like the wind, and I felt myself panting, my tongue hanging from my mouth.

"In the clearing other beasts were waiting for us. One great, hairy creature came trotting up to me, and I was terribly frightened at first, for I recognized it as a mountain wolf, but it nuzzled me with its black snout and licked me, and somehow it seemed like a caress—I liked it. Then it started off across the unplowed field, and I ran after it, caught up with it, and ran alongside. We came to a pool and the beast stopped to drink, and I bent over the water too, lapping it up with my tongue. Then I saw our images in the still pond, and almost died of fright, for the thing beside me was a mountain wolf, and I was a she-wolf!

"My astonishment quickly passed, however, and somehow I didn't seem to mind having been transformed into a beast; for something deep inside me kept urging me on, on to something—I didn't quite know what.

"When we'd drunk we trotted through a little patch of woodland and suddenly my companion sank to the ground in the underbrush and lay there, red tongue lolling from its mouth, green eyes fixed intently on the narrow, winding path beside which we were resting. I wondered what we waited for, and half rose on my haunches to look, but a low, warning growl from the thing beside me warned that something was approaching. It was a pair of farm laborers, Greek peasants I knew them to be by their dress, and they were talking in low tones and looking fearfully about, as though they feared an ambush. When they came abreast of us the beast beside me sprang—so did I.

"I'll never forget the squeaking scream the nearer man gave as I leaped upon him, or the hopeless, terrified expression in his eyes as he tried to fight me off. But I bore him down, sank my teeth into his throat and began slowly tearing at his flesh. I could feel the blood from his torn throat welling up in my mouth, and its hot saltiness was sweeter than the most delicious wine. The poor wretch's struggles became weaker and weaker, and I felt a sort of fierce elation. Then he ceased to fight, and I shook him several times, as a terrier shakes a rat, and when he didn't move or struggle, I tore at his face and throat and chest till my hairy muzzle was one great smear of blood.

"Then, all at once, it seemed as though a sort of thick, white fog were spreading through the forest, blinding me and shutting out the trees and undergrowth and my companion beasts, even the poor boy whom I had killed, and—there I was, kneeling over the embers of the dying fire in the old Smyrna garden, with the clouds of incense dying down to little curly spirals.

"George was standing across the fire from me, laughing, and the first thing I noticed was that *his lips were smeared with blood.*

"Something hot and salty stung my mouth, and I put my hand up to it. When I brought it down the fingers were red with a thick, sticky liquid.

"I think I must have started to scream; for George jumped over the fire and clapped his hand upon my mouth—*ugh*, I could taste the blood more than ever, then!—and whispered, 'Now you are truly mine, Star of the Morning. Together we have ranged the woods in spirit as we shall one day in body, O true mate of a true *vrykolakas!*'

"*Vrykolakas* is a Greek word hard to translate into English. Literally it means 'the restless dead,' but it also means a vampire or a werewolf, and the *vrykolakes* are the most dreaded of all the host of demons with which Greek peasant legends swarm.

"I shook myself free from him. 'Let me go; don't touch me; I never want to see you again!' I cried.

" 'Nevertheless, you shall see me again—and again and again—Star of the Sea!' he answered with a mocking laugh. 'You belong to me, now, and no one shall take you from me. When I want you I will call, and you will come to me, for'—he looked directly into my eyes, and his own seemed to merge and run together, like two pools of liquid, till they were one great disk of green fire— 'thou shalt have no other mate than me, and he who tries to come between us dies. See, I put my mark upon you!'

"He tore my riding shirt open and pressed his lips against my side, and next instant I felt a biting sting as his teeth met in my flesh. See—"

With a frantic, wrenching gesture she snatched at the low collar of her red silk lounging pajamas, tore the fabric asunder and exposed her ivory flesh. Three inches or so below her left axilla, in direct line with the gently swelling bulge of her firm, high breast, was a small whitened cicatrix, and from it grew a little tuft of long, grayish-brown hair, like hairs protruding from a mole, but unlike any body hairs which I had ever seen upon a human being.

"*Grand Dieu,*" exclaimed de Grandin softly. "*Poil de loup!*"

"Yes," she agreed in a thin, hysterical whisper, "it's wolf's hair! I know. I cut it off and took it to a biochemist in London, and he assured me it was unquestionably the hair of a wolf. I've tried and tried to have the scar removed, but it's useless. I've tried cautery, electrolysis, even surgery, but it disappears for only a little while, then comes again."

For a moment it was still as death in the big dim-lighted room. The little French-gilt clock upon the mantelpiece ticked softly, quickly, like a heart that palpitates with terror, and the hissing of a burning resined log seemed loud and eerie as night wind whistling round a haunted tower. The girl folded the torn silk of her pajama jacket across her breast and pinned it into place; then, simply, desolately, as one who breaks the news of a dear friend's death: "So I can not marry you, you see, John, dear," she said.

"Why?" asked the young man in a low, fierce voice. "Because that scoundrel drugged you with his devilish incense and made you think you'd turned into a wolf? Because—"

"Because I'd be your murderess if I did so," she responded quaveringly.

"Don't you remember? He said he'd call me when he wanted me, and anyone who came between him and me would die. He's come for me, he's called me, John; it was he who attacked you in the fog tonight. Oh, my dear, my dear, I love you so; but I must give you up. It would be murder if I were to marry you!"

"Nonsense!" began John Maxwell brusquely. "If you think that man can—"

Outside the house, seemingly from underneath the library's bow window, there sounded in the rain-drenched night a wail, long-drawn, pulsating, doleful as the cry of an abandoned soul: "O-u-o—o-u-oo—o-u-o—o-u-oo!" It rose and fell, quavered and almost died away, then resurged with increased force. "O-u-o—o-u-oo—o-u-o—o-u-oo!"

The woman on the hearth rug cowered like a beaten beast, clutching frantically with fear-numbed fingers at the drugget's pile, half crawling, half writhing toward the brass bars where the cheerful fire burned brightly. "Oh," she whimpered as the mournful ululation died away, "that's he; he called me once before today; now he's come again, and—"

"*Mademoiselle*, restrain yourself," de Grandin's sharp, whiplike order cut through her mounting terror and brought her back to something like normality. "You are with friends," he added in a softer tone; "three of us are here, and we are a match for any *sacre loup-garou* that ever killed a sheep or made night hideous with his howling. *Parbleu*, but I shall say damn yes. Did I not, all single-handed, already put him to flight once tonight? But certainly. Very well, then, let us talk this matter over calmly, for—"

With the suddenness of a discharged pistol a wild, vibrating howl came through the window once again. "O-u-o—o-u-oo—o-u-o!" It rose against the stillness of the night, diminished to a moan, then suddenly crescendoed upward, from a moan to a wail, from a wail to a howl, despairing, pleading, longing as the cry of a damned spirit, fierce and wild as the rally call of the fiends of hell.

"*Sang du diable*, must I suffer interruption when I wish to talk? *Sang des tous les saints*—it is not to be borne!" de Grandin cried furiously, and cleared the distance to the great bay window in two agile, catlike leaps.

"*Allez!*" he ordered sharply, as he flung the casement back and leaned far out into the rainy night. "Be off, before I come down to you. You know me, *hein?* A little while ago you dodged my steel, but—"

A snarling growl replied, and in the clump of rhododendron plants which fringed the garden we saw the baleful glimmer of a pair of fiery eyes.

"*Parbleu*, you dare defy me—*me?*" the little Frenchman cried, and vaulted nimbly from the window, landing surefooted as a panther on the rain-soaked garden mold, then charging at the lurking horror as though it had been harmless as a kitten.

"Oh, he'll be killed; no mortal man can stand against a *vrykolakas!*" cried Sarah Leigh, wringing her slim hands together in an agony of terror. "Oh, God in heaven, spare—"

A fusillade of crackling shots cut through her prayer, and we heard a short, sharp yelp of pain, then the voice of Jules de Grandin hurling imprecations in mingled French and English. A moment later: "Give me a hand, Friend Trowbridge," he called from underneath the window. "It was a simple matter to come down, but climbing back is something else again.

"*Merci*," he acknowledged as he regained the library and turned his quick, elfin grin on each of us in turn. Dusting his hands against each other, to clear them of the dampness from the windowsill, he felt for his cigarette case, chose a "Maryland" and tapped it lightly on his fingernail.

"*Tiens*, I damn think he will know his master's voice in future, that one," he informed us. "I did not quite succeed in killing him to death, unfortunately, but I think that it will be some time before he comes and cries beneath this lady's window again. Yes. Had the *sale poltron* but had the courage to stand against me, I should certainly have killed him; but as it was"—he spread his hands and raised his shoulders eloquently—"it is difficult to hit a running shadow, and he offered little better mark in the darkness. I think I wounded him in the left hand, but I can not surely say."

He paused a moment, then, seeming to remember, turned again to Sarah Leigh with a ceremonious bow. "*Pardon, Mademoiselle*," he apologized, "you were saying, when we were so discourteously interrupted—" he smiled at her expectantly.

"Doctor de Grandin," wondering incredulity was in the girl's eyes and voice as she looked at him, "you shot him—wounded him?"

"Perfectly, *Mademoiselle*," he patted the waxed ends of his mustache with affectionate concern, "my marksmanship was execrable, but at least I hit him. That was something."

"But in Greece they used to say—I've always heard that only silver bullets were effective against a *vrykolakas*; either silver bullets or a sword of finely tempered steel, so—"

"*Ah bah!*" he interrupted with a laugh. "What did they know of modern ordnance, those old-time ritualists? Silver bullets were decreed because silver is a harder metal than lead, and the olden guns they used in ancient days were not adapted to shoot balls of iron. The pistols of today shoot slugs encased in cupro-nickel, far harder than the best of iron, and with a striking force undreamed of in the days when firearms were a new invention. *Tiens*, had the good Saint George possessed a modern military rifle he could have slain the dragon at his leisure while he stood a mile away. Had Saint Michel had a machine gun, his victory over Lucifer could have been accomplished in thirty seconds by the watch."

Having delivered himself of this scandalous opinion, he reseated himself on the divan and smiled at her, for all the world like the family cat which has just breakfasted on the household canary. "And how was it that this so valiant runner-away-from-Jules-de-Grandin announced himself to you, *Mademoiselle?*" he asked.

"I was dressing to go out this morning," she replied, "when the 'phone rang, and when I answered it no one replied to my 'hello.' Then, just as I began to think they'd given someone a wrong number, and was about to put the instrument down, there came one of those awful, wailing howls across the wire. No word at all, sir, just that long-drawn, quavering howl, like what you heard a little while ago.

"You can imagine how it frightened me. I'd almost managed to put George from my mind, telling myself that the vision of lycanthropy which I had in Smyrna was some sort of hypnotism, and that there really weren't such things as werewolves, and even if there were, this was practical America, where I needn't fear them—then came that dreadful howl, the sort of howl I'd heard— and given!—in my vision in the Smyrna garden, and I knew there *are* such things as werewolves, and that one of them possessed me, soul and body, and that I'd have to go to him if he demanded it.

"Most of all, though, I thought of John, for if the werewolf were in America he'd surely read the notice of our coming marriage, and the first thing I remembered was his threat to kill anyone who tried to come between us."

She turned to Maxwell with a pensive smile. "You know how I've been worrying you all day, dear," she asked, "how I begged you not to go out to that dinner tonight, and when you said you must, how I made you promise that you'd call me as soon as you got home, but on no account to call me before you were safely back in your apartment?

"I've been in a perfect agony of apprehension all evening," she told us, "and when John called from Doctor Trowbridge's office I felt as though a great weight had been lifted from my heart."

"And did you try to trace the call?" the little Frenchman asked.

"Yes, but it had been dialed from a downtown pay station, so it was impossible to find it."

De Grandin took his chin between his thumb and forefinger and gazed thoughtfully at the tips of his patent-leather evening shoes. "U'm?" he murmured; then: "What does he look like, this so gallant persecutor of women,

*Mademoiselle?* 'He is handsome,' you have said, which is of interest, certainly, but not especially instructive. Can you be more specific? Since he is a Greek, one assumes that he is dark, but—"

"No, he's not," she interrupted. "His eyes are blue and his hair is rather light, though his beard—he used to wear one, though he may be smooth-shaven now—is quite dark, almost black. Indeed, in certain lights it seems to have an almost bluish tinge."

"Ah, so? *Une barbe bleu?*" de Grandin answered sharply. "One might have thought as much. Such beards, *ma chere*, are the sign manual of those who traffic with the Devil. Gilles de Retz, the vilest monster who ever cast insult on the human race by wearing human form, was light of hair and blue-black as to beard. It is from him we get the most unpleasant fairy tale of Bluebeard, though the gentleman who dispatched his wives for showing too much curiosity was a lamb and sucking dove beside the one whose name he bears.

"Very well. Have you a photograph of him, by any happy chance?"

"No; I did have one, but I burned it years ago."

"A pity, *Mademoiselle;* our task would be made easier if we had his likeness as a guide. But we shall find him otherwise."

"How?" asked Maxwell and I in chorus.

"There was a time," he answered, "when the revelations of a patient to his doctor were considered privileged communications. Since prohibition came to blight your land, however, and the gangster's gun has written history in blood, the physicians are required to note the names and addresses of those who come to them with gunshot wounds, and this information is collected by the police each day. Now, we know that I have wounded this one. He will un-doubtlessly seek medical assistance for his hurt. *Voila,* I shall go down to the police headquarters, look upon the records of those treated for injuries from bullets, and by a process of elimination we shall find him. You apprehend?"

"But suppose he doesn't go to a physician?" young Maxwell interposed.

"In that event we have to find some other way to find him," de Grandin an-swered with a smile, "but that is a stream which we shall cross when we have arrived upon its shore. Meantime"—he rose and bowed politely to our host-ess—"it is getting late, *Mademoiselle,* and we have trespassed on your time too long already. We shall convoy Monsieur Maxwell safely home, and see him lock his door, and if you will keep your doors and windows barred, I do not think that you have anything to fear. The gentleman who seems also to be a wolf has his wounded paw to nurse, and that will keep him busy the remainder of the night."

With a movement of his eyes he bade me leave the room, following closely on my heels and closing the door behind him. "If we must separate them the least which we can do is give them twenty little minutes for good-night," he murmured as we donned our mackintoshes.

"Twenty minutes?" I expostulated. "Why, he could say good-night to twenty girls in twenty minutes!"

"Oui-da, certainement; or a hundred," he agreed, "but not to the one girl, my good friend. Ah bah, Friend Trowbridge, did you never love; did you never worship at the small, white feet of some beloved woman? Did you never feel your breath come faster and your blood pound wildly at your temples as you took her in your arms and put your lips against her mouth? If not—grand Dieu des porcs—then you have never lived at all, though you be older than Methuselah!"

Running our quarry to earth proved a harder task than we had anticipated. Daylight had scarcely come when de Grandin visited the police, but for all he discovered he might have stayed at home. Only four cases of gunshot wounds had been reported during the preceding night, and two of the injured men were Negroes, a third a voluble but undoubtedly Italian laborer who had quarreled with some fellow countrymen over a card game, while the fourth was a thin-faced, tight-lipped gangster who eyed us saturninely and murmured, "Never mind who done it; I'll be seein' im," evidently under the misapprehension that we were emissaries of the police.

The next day and the next produced no more results. Gunshot wounds there were, but none in the hand, where de Grandin declared he had wounded the nocturnal visitant, and though he followed every lead assiduously, in every case he drew a blank.

He was almost beside himself on the fourth day of fruitless search; by evening I was on the point of prescribing triple bromides, for he paced the study restlessly, snapping his fingers, tweaking the waxed ends of his mustache till I made sure he would pull the hairs loose from his lip, and murmuring appalling blasphemies in mingled French and English.

At length, when I thought that I could stand his restless striding no longer, diversion came in the form of a telephone call. He seized the instrument peevishly, but no sooner had he barked a sharp *"Allo?"* then his whole expression changed and a quick smile ran across his face, like sunshine breaking through a cloud.

"But certainly; of course, assuredly!" he cried delightedly. Then, to me:

"Your hat and coat, Friend Trowbridge, and hurry, *pour l'amour d'un tetard—* they are marrying!"

"Marrying?" I echoed wonderingly. "Who—"

"Who but Mademoiselle Sarah and Monsieur Jean, *parbleu?"* he answered with a grin. *"Oh, la, la,* at last they show some sense, those ones. He has broken her resistance down, and she consents, werewolf or no werewolf. Now we shall surely make the long nose at that *sacre singe* who howled beneath her window when we called upon her!"

The ceremony was to be performed in the sacristy of St. Barnabas Church, for John and Sarah, shocked and saddened by the death of young Fred Suffrige, who was to have been their best man, had recalled the invitations and decided on a private wedding with only her aunt and his mother present in addition to de Grandin and me.

"Dearly beloved, we are gathered together here in the sight of God and in the face of this company to join together this man and this woman in holy matrimony," began the rector, Doctor Higginbotham, who, despite the informality of the occasion, was attired in all the panoply of a high church priest and accompanied by two gorgeously accoutered and greatly interested choirboys who served as acolytes. "In this holy estate these two persons come now to be joined. If any man can show just cause why they should not lawfully be joined together, let him now speak, or else hereafter forever hold his peace—"

"Jeez!" exclaimed the choir youth who stood upon the rector's left, letting fall the censer from his hands and dodging nimbly back, as from a threatened blow.

The interruption fell upon the solemn scene like a bombshell at a funeral, and one and all of us looked at the cowering youngster, whose eyes were fairly bulging from his face and whose ruddy countenance had gone a sickly, pasty gray, so that the thick-strewn freckles started out in contrast, like spots of rouge upon a corpse's pallid cheeks.

"Why, William—" Doctor Higginbotham began in a shocked voice; but:

*Rat, tat-tat!* sounded the sudden sharp clatter of knuckles against the windowpane, and for the first time we realized it had been toward this window the boy had looked when his sacrilegious exclamation broke in on the service.

Staring at us through the glass we saw a great, gray wolf! Yet it was not a wolf, for about the lupine jaws and jowls was something hideously reminiscent of a human face, and the greenish, phosphorescent glow of those great, glaring eyes had surely never shone in any face, animal or human. As I looked, breathless, the monster raised its head, and strangling horror gripped my throat with fiery fingers as I saw a human-seeming neck beneath it. Long and grisly thin it was, corded and sinewed like the desiccated gula of a lich, and, like the face, covered with a coat of gray-brown fur. Then a hand, hair-covered like the throat and face, slim as a woman's—or a mummy's!—but terribly misshapen, fingers tipped with blood-red talon-nails, rose up and struck the glass again. My scalp was fairly crawling with sheer terror, and my breath came hot and sulfurous in my throat as I wondered how much longer the frail glass could stand against the impact of those bony, hair-gloved hands.

A strangled scream behind me sounded from Sarah's aunt, Miss Leigh, and I heard the muffled thud as she toppled to the floor in a dead faint, but I could no more turn my gaze from the horror at the window than the fascinated bird can tear its eyes from the serpent's numbing stare.

Another sighing exclamation and another thudding impact. John Maxwell's mother was unconscious on the floor beside Miss Leigh, but still I stood and stared in frozen terror at the thing beyond the window.

Doctor Higginbotham's teeth were chattering, and his ruddy, plethoric countenance was death-gray as he faced the staring horror, but he held fast to his faith.

"*Conjuro te, sceleratissime, abire ad tuum locum*"—he began the sonorous Latin exorcism, signing himself with his right hand and advancing his pectoral cross toward the thing at the window with his left—"I exorcise thee, most foul spirit, creature of darkness—"

The corners of the wolf-thing's devilish eyes contracted in a smile of malevolent amusement, and a rim of scarlet tongue flicked its black muzzle. Doctor Higginbotham's exorcism, bravely begun, ended on a wheezing, stifled syllable, and he stared in round-eyed fascination, his thick lips, blue with terror, opening and closing, but emitting no sound.

"*Sang d'un cochon*, not that way, *Monsieur*—this!" cried Jules de Grandin, and the roar of his revolver split the paralysis of quiet which had gripped the little chapel. A thin, silvery tinkle of glass sounded as the bullet tore through the window, and the grisly face abruptly disappeared, but from somewhere in the outside dark there echoed back a braying howl which seemed to hold a sort of obscene laughter in its quavering notes.

"*Sapristi!* Have I missed him?" de Grandin asked incredulously. "No matter; he is gone. On with the service, *Monsieur le Cure.* I do not think we shall be interrupted further."

"No!" Doctor Higginbotham backed away from Sarah Leigh as though her breath polluted him. "I can perform no marriage until that thing has been explained. Someone here is haunted by a devil—a malign entity from hell which will not heed the exorcism of the Church—and until I'm satisfied concerning it, and that you're all good Christians, there'll be no ceremony in this church!

"*Eh bien, Monsieur,* who can say what constitutes a good Christian?" de Grandin smiled unpleasantly at Doctor Higginbotham. "Certainly one who lacks in charity as you do can not be competent to judge. Have it as you wish. As soon as we have recovered these fainting ladies, we shall leave, and may the Devil grill me on the grates of hell if ever we come back until you have apologized."

Two hours later, as we sat in the Leigh library, Sarah dried her eyes and faced her lover with an air of final resolution: "You see, my dear, it's utterly impossible for me to marry you, or anyone," she said. "That awful thing will dog my steps, and—"

"My poor, sweet girl, I'm more determined than ever to marry you!" John broke in. "If you're to be haunted by a thing like that, you need me every minute, and—"

"*Bravo!*" applauded Jules de Grandin. "Well said, *mon vieux,* but we waste precious time. Come, let us go."

"Where?" asked John Maxwell, but the little Frenchman only smiled and shrugged his shoulders.

"To Maidstone Crossing, quickly, if you please, my friend," he whispered when he had led the lovers to my car and seen solicitously to their comfortable seating in the tonneau. "I know a certain justice of the peace there who would marry the Witch of Endor to the Emperor Nero though all the wolves which ever plagued Red Riding Hood forbade the banns, provided only we supply him with sufficient fee."

Two hours' drive brought us to the little hamlet of Maidstone Crossing,. and de Grandin's furious knocking on the door of a small cottage evoked the presence of a lank, lean man attired in a pair of corduroy trousers drawn hastily above the folds of a canton-flannel nightshirt.

A whispered colloquy between the rustic and the slim, elegant little Parisian; then: "O. K., Doc," the justice of the peace conceded. "Bring 'em in; I'll marry 'em an'—hey, Sam'l!" he called up the stairs. "C'mon down, an' bring yer shotgun. There's a weddin' goin' to be pulled off, an' they tell me some fresh guys may try to interfere!"

"Sam'l," a lank, lean youth whose costume duplicated that of his father, descended the stairway grinning, an automatic shotgun cradled in the hollow of his arm. "D'ye expect any real rough stuff?" he asked.

"Seems like they're apt to try an' set a dawg on 'em," his father answered, and the younger man grinned cheerfully.

"Dawgs, is it?" he replied, "Dawgs is my dish. Go on, Pap, do yer stuff. Good luck, folks," he winked encouragingly at John and Sarah and stepped out on the porch, his gun in readiness.

"Do you take this here woman fer yer lawful, wedded wife?" the justice inquired of John Maxwell, and when the latter answered that he did:

"An' do you take this here now man to be yer wedded husband?" he asked Sarah.

"I do," the girl responded in a trembling whisper, and the roaring bellow of a shotgun punctuated the brief pause before the squire concluded:

"Then by virtue of th' authority vested in me by th' law an' constitootion of this state, I do declare ye man an' wife—an' whoever says that ye ain't married lawfully 's a danged liar," he added as a sort of afterthought.

"What wuz it that ye shot at, Sam'l?" asked the justice as, enriched by fifty dollars, and grinning appreciatively at the evening's profitable business, he ushered us from the house.

"Durned if I know, Pap," the other answered. "Looked kind o' funny to me. He wuz about a head taller'n me—an' I'm six foot two—an' thin as Job's turkey-hen, to boot. His clothes looked skintight on 'im, an' he had on a cap, or sumpin with a peak that stuck out over his face. I first seen 'im comin' up th' road, kind o' lookin' this way an' that, like as if he warn't quite certain o' his way. Then, all of a suddent, he kind o' stopped an' threw his head back, like a dawg sniffin' th' air, an' started to go down on his all-fours, like he wuz goin' to sneak up on th' house. So I hauls off an' lets 'im have a tickle o' buckshot. Don't know whether I hit 'im or not, an' I'll bet he don't, neether; he sure didn't waste no time stoppin' to find out. Could he run! I'm tellin' ye, that feller must be in Harrisonville by now, if he kep' on goin' like he started!"

Two days of feverish activity ensued. Last-minute traveling arrangements had to be made, and passports for "John Maxwell and wife, Harrisonville, New Jersey, USA," obtained. De Grandin spent every waking hour with the newly married couple and even insisted on occupying a room in the Leigh house at night; but his precautions seemed unnecessary, for not so much as a whimper sounded under Sarah's window, and though the little Frenchman searched the garden every morning, there was no trace of unfamiliar footprints, either brute or human, to be found.

"Looks as if Sallie's Greek boyfriend knows when he's licked and has decided to quit following her about," John Maxwell grinned as he and Sarah, radiant with happiness, stood upon the deck of the *Ile de France.*

"One hopes so," de Grandin answered with a smile. "Good luck, *mes amis,* and may your *lune de miel* shine as brightly throughout all your lives as it does this night.

"*La lune*—ha?" he repeated half musingly, half with surprise, as though he just remembered some important thing which had inadvertently slipped his memory. "May I speak a private warning in your ear, Friend Jean?" He drew the bridegroom aside and whispered earnestly a moment.

"Oh, bosh!" the other laughed as they rejoined us. "That's all behind us, Doctor; you'll see; we'll never hear a sound from him. He's got *me* to deal with now, not just poor Sarah."

"Bravely spoken, little cabbage!" the Frenchman applauded. "*Bon voyage.*" But there was a serious expression on his face as we went down the gangway.

"What was the private warning you gave John?" I asked as we left the French Line piers. "He didn't seem to take it very seriously."

"No," he conceded. "I wish he had. But youth is always brave and reckless in its own conceit. It was about the moon. She has a strange influence on lycanthropy. The werewolf metamorphoses more easily in the full of the moon than at any other time, and those who may have been affected with his virus, though even faintly, are most apt to feel its spell when the moon is at the full. I warned him to be particularly careful of his lady on moonlit nights, and on no account to go anywhere after dark unless he were armed.

"The werewolf is really an inferior demon," he continued as we boarded the Hoboken ferry. "Just what he is we do not know with certainty, though we know he has existed from the earliest times; for many writers of antiquity mention him. Sometimes he is said to be a magical wolf who has the power to become a man. More often he is said to be a man who can become a wolf at times, sometimes of his own volition, sometimes at stated seasons, even against his will. He has dreadful powers of destructiveness; for the man who is also a wolf is ten times more deadly than the wolf who is only a wolf. He has the wolf's great strength and savagery, but human cunning with it. At night he quests and kills his prey, which is most often his fellow man, but sometimes sheep or hares, or his ancient enemy, the dog. By day he hides his villainy—and the location of his lair—under human guise.

"However, he has this weakness: strong and ferocious, cunning and malicious as he is, he can be killed as easily as any natural wolf. A sharp sword will slay him, a well-aimed bullet puts an end to his career; the wood of the thornbush and the mountain ash are so repugnant to him that he will slink away if beaten or merely threatened with a switch of either. Weapons efficacious against an ordinary physical foe are potent against him, while charms and exorcisms which would put a true demon to flight are powerless.

"You saw how he mocked at *Monsieur* Higginbotham in the sacristy the other night, by example. But he did not stop to bandy words with me. Oh, no. He knows that I shoot straight and quick, and he had already felt my lead on one occasion. If young Friend Jean will always go well-armed, he has no need to fear; but if he be taken off his guard—*eh bien*, we can not always be on hand to rescue him as we did the night when we first met him. No, certainly."

"But why do you fear for Sarah?" I persisted.

"I hardly know," he answered. "Perhaps it is that I have what you Americans so drolly call the hunch. Werewolves sometimes become werewolves by the aid of Satan, that they may kill their enemies while in lupine form, or satisfy their natural lust for blood and cruelty while disguised as beasts. Some are transformed as the result of a curse upon themselves or their families, a few are metamorphosed by accident. These are the most unfortunate of all. In certain parts of Europe, notably in Greece, Russia, and the Balkan states, the very soil seems cursed with lycanthropic power. There are certain places where, if the unwary traveler lies down to sleep, he is apt to wake up with the curse of werewolfism on him. Certain streams and springs there are which, if drunk from, will render the drinker liable to transformation at the next full moon, and regularly thereafter. You will recall that in the dream, or vision, which *Madame* Sarah had while in the Smyrna garden so long ago, she beheld herself drinking from a woodland pool? I do not surely know, my friend, I have not even good grounds for suspicion, but something—something which I can not name—tells me that in some way this poor one, who is so wholly innocent, has been branded with the taint of lycanthropy. How it came about I can not say, but—"

My mind had been busily engaged with other problems, and I had listened to his disquisition on lycanthropy with something less than full attention. Now, suddenly aware of the thing which puzzled me, I interrupted:

"Can you explain the form that werewolf—if that's what it was—took on different occasions? The night we met John Maxwell he was fighting for his life with as true a wolf as any there are in the zoological gardens. O'Brien, the policeman, saw it, too, and shot at it, after it had killed Fred Suffrige. It was a sure-enough wolf when it howled under Sarah's window and you wounded it; yet when it interrupted the wedding it was an awful combination of wolf and man, or man and wolf, and the thing the justice's son drove off with his shotgun was the same, according to his description."

Surprisingly, he did not take offense at my interruption. Instead, he frowned in thoughtful silence at the dashboard lights a moment; then; "Sometimes the werewolf is completely transformed from man to beast," he answered; "sometimes he is a hideous combination of the two, but always he is a fiend incarnate. My own belief is that this one was only partly transformed when we last saw him because he had not time to wait complete metamorphosis. It is possible he could not change completely, too, because—" he broke off and pointed at the sky significantly.

"Well?" I demanded as he made no further effort to proceed.

"*Non*, it is not well," he denied, "but it may be important. Do you observe the moon tonight?"

"Why, yes."

"What quarter is it in?"

"*Precisement.* As I was saying, it may be that his powers to metamorphose himself were weakened because of the waning of the moon. Remember, if you please, his power for evil is at its height when the moon is at the full, and as it wanes, his powers become less and less. At the darkening of the moon, he is at his weakest, and then is the time for us to strike—if only we could find him. But he will lie well hidden at such times, never fear. He is clever with a devilish cunningness, that one."

"Oh, you're fantastic!" I burst out.

"You say so, having seen what you have seen?"

"Well, I'll admit we've seen some things which are mighty hard to explain," I conceded, "but—"

"But we are arrived at home; Monsieur and Madame Maxwell are safe upon the ocean, and I am vilely thirsty," he broke in. "Come, let us take a drink and go to bed, my friend."

With midwinter came John and Sarah Maxwell, back from their honeymoon in Paris and on the Riviera. A week before their advent, notices in the society columns told of their homecoming, and a week after their return an engraved invitation apprised de Grandin and me that the honor of our presence was requested at a reception in the Leigh mansion, where they had taken residence. ". . . and please come early and stay late; there are a million things I want to talk about," Sarah pencilled at the bottom of our card.

Jules de Grandin was more than usually ornate on the night of the reception. His London-tailored evening clothes were knife-sharp in their creases; about his neck hung the insignia of the *Legion d'Honneur*; a row of miniature medals, including the French and Belgian war crosses, the *Medaille Militaire* and the Italian Medal of Valor, decorated the left breast of his faultless evening coat; his little, wheat-blond mustache was waxed to needle sharpness and his sleek blond hair was brilliantined and brushed till it fitted flat upon his shapely little head as a skullcap of beige satin.

Lights blazed from every window of the house as we drew up beneath the porte-cochere. Inside all was laughter, staccato conversation and the odd, not unpleasant odor rising from the mingling of the hundred or more individual scents affected by the women guests. Summer was still near enough for the men to retain the tan of mountain and seashore on their faces and for a velvet vestige of veneer of painfully acquired suntan to show upon the women's arms and shoulders.

We tendered our congratulations to the homing newlyweds; then de

Grandin plucked me by the sleeve. "Come away, my friend," he whispered in an almost tragic voice. "Come quickly or these thirsty ones will have drunk up all the punch containing rum and champagne and left us only lemonade!"

The evening passed with pleasant swiftness, and guests began to leave. "Where's Sallie—seen her?" asked John Maxwell, interrupting a rather Rabelaisian story which de Grandin was retailing with gusto to several appreciative young men in the conservatory. "The Carter-Brooks are leaving, and—"

De Grandin brought his story to a close with the suddenness of a descending theater curtain, and a look of something like consternation shone in his small, round eyes. "She is not here?" he asked sharply. "When did you last see her?"

"Oh," John answered vaguely, "just a little while ago; we danced the 'Blue Danube' together, then she went upstairs for something, and—"

"Quick, swiftly!' de Grandin interrupted. *"Pardon, messieurs,"* he bowed to his late audience and, beckoning me, strode toward the stairs.

"I say, what's the rush—" began John Maxwell, but:

"Every reason under heaven," the Frenchman broke in shortly. To me: "Did you observe the night outside, Friend Trowbridge?"

"Why, yes," I answered. "It's a beautiful moonlit night, almost bright as day, and—"

"And there you are, for the love of ten thousand pigs!" he cut in. "Oh, I am the stupid-headed fool, me! Why did I let her from my sight?"

We followed in wondering silence as he climbed the stairs, hurried down the hall toward Sarah's room and paused before her door. He raised his hand to rap, but the portal swung away, and a girl stood staring at us from the threshold.

"Did it pass you?" she asked, regarding us in wide-eyed wonder.

*"Pardon, Mademoiselle?"* de Grandin countered. "What is it that you ask?"

"Why, did you see that lovely collie, it—"

*"Cher Dieu,"* the words were like a groan upon the little Frenchman's lips as he looked at her in horror. Then, recovering himself: "Proceed, *Mademoiselle,* it was of a dog you spoke?"

"Yes," she returned. "I came upstairs to freshen up, and found I'd lost my compact somewhere, so I came to Sallie's room to get some powder. She'd come up a few moments before, and I was positive I'd find her here, but—" she paused in puzzlement a moment; then: "But when I came in there was no one here. Her dress was lying on the chaise longue there, as though she'd slipped it off, and by the window, looking out with its paws up on the sill, was the loveliest silver collie.

"I didn't know you had a dog, John," she turned to Maxwell. "When did you get it? It's the loveliest creature, but it seemed to be afraid of me; for when I went to pat it, it slunk away, and before I realized it had bolted through the door, which I'd left open. It ran down the hall."

"A dog?" John Maxwell answered bewilderedly. "We haven't any dog, Nell; it must have been—"

"Never mind what it was," de Grandin interrupted as the girl went down the hall, and as she passed out of hearing he seized us by the elbows and fairly thrust us into Sarah's room, closing the door quickly behind us.

"What—" began John Maxwell, but the Frenchman motioned him to silence.

"Behold, regard each item carefully; stamp them upon your memories," he ordered, sweeping the charming chamber with his sharp, stocktaking glance.

A fire burned brightly in the open grate, parchment-shaded lamps diffused soft light. Upon the bed there lay a pair of rose silk pajamas, with a sheer crepe negligee beside them. A pair of satin mules were placed toes in upon the bedside rug. Across the chaise longue was draped, as though discarded in the utmost haste, the white satin evening gown that Sarah had worn. Upon the floor beside the lounge were crumpled wisps of ivory crepe de chine, her bandeau and trunks. Sarah, being wholly modern, had worn no stockings, but her white-and-silver evening sandals lay beside the lingerie, one on its sole, as though she had stepped out of it, the other on its side, gaping emptily, as though kicked from her little pink-and-white foot in panic haste. There was something ominous about that silent room; it was like a body from which the spirit had departed, still beautiful and warm, but lifeless.

"Humph," Maxwell muttered, "the Devil knows where she's gone—"

"He knows very, exceedingly well, I have no doubt," de Grandin interrupted. "But we do not. Now—ah? Ah-ah-ah?" his exclamation rose steadily, thinning to a sharpness like a razor's cutting edge. "What have we here?"

Like a hound upon the trail, guided by scent alone, he crossed the room and halted by the dressing table. Before the mirror stood an uncorked flask of perfume, a lovely thing of polished crystal decorated with silver basketwork. From its open neck there rose a thin but penetrating scent, not wholly sweet nor wholly acrid, but a not unpleasant combination of the two, as though musk and flower scent had each lent it something of their savors.

The little Frenchman put it to his nose, then set it down with a grimace. "Name of an Indian pig, how comes this devil's brew here?" he asked.

"Oh, that?" Maxwell answered. "Hanged if I know. Some unknown admirer of Sallie's sent it to her. It came today, all wrapped up like something from a jeweler's. Rather pleasant smelling, isn't it?"

De Grandin looked at him as Torquemada might have looked at one accusing him of loving Martin Luther. "Did you by any chance make use of it, *Monsieur?*" he asked in an almost soundless whisper.

"I? Good Lord, do I look like the sort of he-thing who'd use perfume?" the other asked.

*"Bien,* I did but ask to know," de Grandin answered as he jammed the silver-mounted stopper in the bottle and thrust the flask into his trousers pocket.

"But where the deuce *is* Sallie?" the young husband persisted. "She's changed her clothes, that's certain; but what did she go out for, and if she didn't go out, where is she?"

"Ah, it may be that she had a sudden feeling of faintness, and decided to go out into the air," the Frenchman temporized. "Come, *Monsieur,* the guests are waiting to depart, and you must say *adieu.* Tell them that your lady is indisposed, make excuses, tell them anything, but get them out all quickly; we have work to do."

John Maxwell lied gallantly, de Grandin and I standing at his side to prevent any officious dowager from mounting the stairs and administering homemade medical assistance. At last, when all were gone, the young man turned to Jules de Grandin, and: "Now, out with it," he ordered gruffly. "I can tell by your manner something serious has happened. What is it, man; what is it?"

De Grandin patted him upon the shoulder with a mixture of affection and commiseration in the gesture. "Be brave, *mon vieux,*" he ordered softly. "It is the worst. He has her in his power; she has gone to join him, for—*pitie de Dieu!*—she has become like him."

"Wha—what?" the husband quavered. "You mean she—that Sallie, my Sallie, has become a were—" his voice balked at the final syllable, but de Grandin's nod confirmed his guess.

*"Helas,* you have said it, my poor friend," he murmured pitifully.

"But how?—when?—I thought surely we'd driven him off—" the young man faltered, then stopped, horror choking the words back in his throat.

"Unfortunately, no," de Grandin told him. "He was driven off, certainly, but not diverted from his purpose. Attend me."

From his trousers pocket he produced the vial of perfume, uncorked it and let its scent escape into the room. "You recognize it, *hein?*" he asked.

"No, I can't say I do," Maxwell answered.

"Do you, Friend Trowbridge?"

I shook my head.

"Very well. I do, to my sorrow."

He turned once more to me. "The night Monsieur and Madame Maxwell sailed upon the *Ile de France,* you may recall I was explaining how the innocent became werewolves at times?" he reminded.

"Yes, and I interrupted to ask about the different shapes that thing assumed," I nodded.

"You interrupted then," he agreed soberly, "but you will not interrupt now. Oh, no. You will listen while I talk. I had told you of the haunted dells where travelers may unknowingly become werewolves, of the streams from which the drinker may receive contagion, but you did not wait to hear of *les fleurs des loups,* did you?"

"*Fleurs les loups*—wolf flowers?" I asked.

"*Precisement,* wolf flowers. Upon those cursed mountains grows a kind of flower which, plucked and worn at the full of the moon, transforms the wearer into a *loup-garou.* Yes. One of these flowers, known popularly as the *fleur de sang,* or blood-flower, because of its red petals, resembles the marguerite, or daisy, in form; the other is a golden yellow, and is much like the snapdragon. But both have the same fell property, both have the same strong, sweet, fascinating scent.

"This, my friends," he passed the opened flagon underneath our noses, "is a perfume made from the sap of those accursed flowers. It is the highly concentrated venom of their devilishness. One applying it to her person, anointing lips, ears, hair, and hands with it, as women wont, would as surely be translated into wolfish form as though she wore the cursed flower whence the perfume comes. Yes.

"That silver collie of which the young girl spoke, *Monsieur*"—he turned a fixed, but pitying look upon John Maxwell—"she was your wife, transformed into a wolf-thing by the power of this perfume.

"Consider: Can you not see it all? Balked, but not defeated, the vile *vryko-lakas* is left to perfect his revenge while you are on your honeymoon. He knows that you will come again to Harrisonville; he need not follow you. Accordingly, he sends to Europe for the essence of these flowers, prepares a philter from it, and sends it to Madame Sarah today. Its scent is novel, rather pleasing; women like strange, exotic scents. She uses it. Anon, she feels a queerness. She does not realize that it is the metamorphosis which comes upon her, she only knows that she feels vaguely strange. She goes to her room. Perhaps she puts the perfume on her brow again, as women do when they feel faint; then, *pardieu*, then there comes the change all quickly, for the moon is full tonight, and the essence of the flowers very potent.

"She doffed her clothes, you think? *Mais non*, they fell from her! A woman's raiment does not fit a wolf; it falls off from her altered form, and we find it on the couch and on the floor.

"That other girl comes to the room, and finds poor Madame Sarah, transformed to a wolf, gazing sadly from the window—*la pauvre*, she knew too well who waited outside in the moonlight for her, and she must go to him! Her friend puts out a hand to pet her, but she shrinks away. She feels she is 'unclean,' a thing apart, one of 'that multitudinous herd not yet made fast in hell'—*les loups-garous!* And so she flies through the open door of her room, flies where? Only *le bon Dieu*—and the Devil, who is master of all werewolves—know!"

"But we must find her!" Maxwell wailed. "We've *got* to find her!"

"Where are we to look?" de Grandin spread his hands and raised his shoulders. "The city is wide, and we have no idea where this wolf-man makes his lair. The werewolf travels fast, my friend; they may be miles away by now."

"I don't care a damn what you say, I'm going out to look for her!" Maxwell declared as he rose from his seat and strode to the library table, from the drawer of which he took a heavy pistol. "You shot him once and wounded him, so I know he's vulnerable to bullets, and when I find him—"

"But certainly," the Frenchman interrupted. "We heartily agree with you, my friend. But let us first go to Doctor Trowbridge's house where we, too, may secure weapons. Then we shall be delighted to accompany you upon your hunt."

As we started for my place he whispered in my ear: "Prepare the knockout drops as soon as we are there, Friend Trowbridge. It would be suicide for him to seek that monster now. He cannot hit a barn-side with a pistol, cannot even draw it quickly from his pocket. His chances are not one in a million if he meets the wolf, and if we let him go we shall be playing right into the adversary's hands."

I nodded agreement as we drove along, and when I'd parked the car, I turned to Maxwell. "Better come in and have a drink before we start," I invited. "It's cold tonight, and we may not get back soon."

"All right," agreed the unsuspecting youth. "But make it quick, I'm itching to catch sight of that damned fiend. When I meet him he won't get off as easily as he did in his brush with Doctor de Grandin."

Hastily I concocted a punch of Jamaica rum, hot water, lemon juice and sugar, adding fifteen grains of chloral hydrate to John Maxwell's and hoping the sugar and lemon would disguise its taste while the pungent rum would hide its odor. "To our successful quest," de Grandin proposed, raising his steaming glass and looking questioningly at me for assurance that the young man's drink was drugged.

Maxwell raised his goblet, but ere he set it to his lips there came a sudden interruption. An oddly whining, whimpering noise it was, accompanied by a scratching at the door, as though a dog were outside in the night and importuning for admission.

"Ah?" de Grandin put his glass down on the hall table and reached beneath his left armpit where the small but deadly Belgian automatic pistol nestled in its shoulder holster. "Ah-ha? We have a visitor, it seems." To me he bade: "Open the door, wide and quickly, Friend Trowbridge; then stand away, for I shall likely shoot with haste, and it is not your estimable self that I desire to kill."

I followed his instructions, but instead of the gray horror I had expected at the door, I saw a slender canine form with hair so silver-gray that it was almost white, which bent its head and wagged its tail, and fairly fawned upon us as it slipped quickly through the opening, then looked at each of us in turn with great, expressive topaz eyes.

"Ah, mon Dieu," exclaimed the Frenchman, sheathing his weapon and starting forward, "it is Madame Sarah!"

"Sallie?" cried John Maxwell incredulously, and at his voice the beast leaped toward him, rubbed against his knees, then rose upon his hind feet and strove to lick his face.

"*Oh, quel dommage!*" de Grandin looked at them with tear-filled eyes; then: "Your pardon, Madame Sarah, but I do not think you came to us without a reason. Can you lead us to the place where he abides? If so we promise you shall be avenged within the hour."

The silver wolf dropped to all fours again, and nodded its sleek head in answer to his question; then, as he hesitated, came slowly up to him, took the cuff of his evening coat gently in its teeth and drew him toward the door.

"*Bravo, ma chere,* lead on, we follow!" he exclaimed; then, as we donned our coats, he thrust a pistol in my hand and cautioned: "Watch well, my friend, she seems all amiable, but wolves are treacherous, man-wolves a thousand times more so; it may be he has sent her to lead us to a trap. Should anything untoward transpire, shoot first and ask your foolish questions afterward. That way you shall increase your chances of dying peacefully in bed."

The white beast trotting before us, we hastened down the quiet, moonlit street. After forty minutes' rapid walk, we stopped before a small apartment house. As we paused to gaze, the little wolf once more seized Jules de Grandin's sleeve between her teeth and drew him forward.

It was a little house, only three floors high, and its front was zigzagged with iron fire escapes. No lights burned in any of the flats, and the whole place had an air of vacancy, but our lupine guide led us through the entranceway and down the ground floor hall until we paused before the door of a rear apartment.

De Grandin tried the knob cautiously, found the lock made fast, and after a moment dropped to his knees, drew out a ringful of fine steel instruments and began picking the fastening as methodically as though he were a professional burglar. The lock was "burglar-proof," but its makers had not reckoned with the skill of Jules de Grandin. Before five minutes had elapsed he rose with a pleased exclamation, turned the knob, and thrust the door back.

"Hold her, Friend Jean," he bade John Maxwell, for the wolf was trembling with a nervous quiver, and straining to rush into the apartment. To me he added: "Have your gun ready, good Friend Trowbridge, and keep by me. He shall not take us unawares."

Shoulder to shoulder we entered the dark doorway of the flat, John Maxwell and the wolf behind us. For a moment we paused while de Grandin felt along the wall, then *click;* the snapping of a wall switch sounded, and the dark room blazed with sudden light.

The wolf-man's human hours were passed in pleasant circumstances. Every item of the room proclaimed it the abode of one whose wealth and tastes were well matched. The walls were hung with light gray paper, the floor was covered with a Persian rug, and wide, low chairs upholstered in long-napped mohair invited the visitor to rest. Beneath the arch of a marble mantelpiece a wood fire had been laid, ready for the match, while upon the shelf a tiny French-gilt clock beat off the minutes with sharp, musical clicks. Pictures in profusion lined the walls, a landscape by an apt pupil of Corot, an excellent imitation of Botticelli, and, above the mantel, a single life-sized portrait done in oils.

Every item of the portrait was portrayed with photographic fidelity, and we looked with interest at the subject, a man in early middle life, or late youth, dressed in the uniform of a captain of Greek cavalry. His cloak was thrown back from his braided shoulders, displaying several military decorations, but it was the face which captured the attention instantly, making all the added detail of no consequence. The hair was light, worn rather long, and brushed straight back from a high, wide forehead. The eyes were blue, and touched with an expression of gentle melancholy. The features were markedly Oriental in cast, but neither coarse nor sensual. In vivid contrast to the hair and eyes was the pointed beard upon the chin; for it was black as coal, yet by some quaint combination of the artist's pigments it seemed to hide blue lights within its sable depths. Looking from the blue-black beard to the sad blue eyes it seemed to me I saw a hint, the merest faint suggestion, of wolfish cruelty in the face.

"It is undoubtlessly he," de Grandin murmured as he gazed upon the portrait. "He fits poor Madam Sarah's description to a nicety. But where is he in person? We can not fight his picture; no, of course not."

Motioning us to wait, he snapped the light off and drew a pocket flashlight from his waistcoat. He tiptoed through the door, exploring the farther room by the beam of his searchlight, then rejoined us with a gesture of negation.

"He is not here," he announced softly; "but come with me, my friends, I would show you something."

He led the way to the adjoining chamber, which, in any other dwelling, would have been the bedroom. It was bare, utterly unfurnished, and as he flashed his light around the walls we saw, some three or four feet from the floor, a row of paw prints, as though a beast had stood upon its hind legs and pressed its forefeet to the walls. And the prints were marked in reddish smears—blood.

"You see?" he asked, as though the answer to his question were apparent. "He has no bed; he needs none, for at night he is a wolf, and sleeps denned down upon the floor. Also, you observe, he has not lacked for provender—*le bon Dieu* grant it was the blood of animals that stained his claws!"

"But where is he? asked Maxwell, fingering his pistol.

"S-S-sh!" warned the Frenchman. "I do not think that he is far way. The window, you observe her?"

"Well?"

"*Precisement*. She is scant four feet from the ground, and overlooks the alley. Also, though she was once fitted with bars, they have been removed. Also, again, the sash is ready-raised. Is it not all perfect?"

"Perfect? For what?"

"For him, *parbleu!* For the werewolf's entrances and exits. He comes running down the alley, leaps agilely through the open window, and *voila*, he is here. Or leaps out into the alleyway with a single bound, and goes upon his nightly hunts. He may return at any moment; it is well that we await him here."

The waiting minutes stretched interminably. The dark room where we crouched was lighted from time to time, then cast again into shadow, as the racing clouds obscured or unveiled the full moon's visage. At length, when I felt I could no longer stand the strain, a low, harsh growl from our four-footed companion brought us sharply to attention. In another moment we heard the soft patter-patter, scratch-scratch of a long-clawed beast running lightly on the pavement of the alleyway outside, and in a second more a dark form bulked against the window's opening and something landed upon the floor.

For a moment there was breathless silence; then: "*Bonsoir, Monsieur Loup-garou,*" de Grandin greeted in a pleasant voice. "You have unexpected visitors.

"Do not move," he added threateningly as a hardly audible growl sounded from the farther corner of the room, and we heard the scraping of long nails upon the floor as the wolf-thing gathered for a spring; "there are three of us, and each one is armed. Your reign of terror draws to a close, *Monsieur.*"

A narrow, dazzling shaft of light shot from his pocket torch, clove through the gloom and picked the crouching wolf-thing's form out of the darkness. Fangs bared, black lips drawn back in bestial fury, the gaunt gray thing was backed into the corner, and from its open jaws we saw a thin trickle of slabber mixed with blood. It had been feeding, so much was obvious. "But what had been its food?" I wondered with a shudder.

"It is your shot, Friend Jean," the little Frenchman spoke. "Take careful aim, and do not jerk the pistol when you fire." He held his flashlight steadily upon the beast, and a second later came the roar of Maxwell's pistol.

The acrid smoke stung in our nostrils, the reverberation of the detonation almost deafened us, and—a little fleck of plaster fell down from the wall where Maxwell's bullet was harmlessly embedded.

"Ten thousand stinking camels!" Jules de Grandin cried, but got no further, for with a maddened, murderous growl the wolf-man sprang, his lithe body describing a graceful arc as it hurtled through the air, his cruel, white fangs flashing terribly as he leaped upon John Maxwell and bore him to the floor before he could fire a second shot.

"*Nom de Dieu de nom de Dieu de mon de Dieu!*" de Grandin swore, playing his flashlight upon the struggling man and brute and leaping forward, seeking for a chance to use his pistol.

But to shoot the wolf would have meant that he must shoot the man, as well; for the furry body lay upon the struggling Maxwell, and as they thrashed and wrestled on the floor it was impossible to tell, at times, in the uncertain light, which one was man and which was beast.

Then came a deep, low growl of pent-up, savage fury, almost an articulate curse, it seemed to me, and like a streak of silver-plated vengeance the little she-wolf leaped upon the gray-born brute which growled and worried at the young man's throat.

We saw the white teeth bared, we saw them flesh themselves in the wolf-thing's shoulder, we saw her loose her hold, and leap back, avoiding the great wolf's counterstroke, then close with it again, sinking needle-fangs in the furry ruff about its throat.

The great wolf shook her to and fro, battered her against the walls and floor as a vicious terrier mistreats a luckless rat, but she held on savagely, though we saw her left forepaw go limp and knew the bone was broken.

De Grandin watched his chance, crept closer, closer, till he almost straddled the contending beasts; then, darting forth his hand he put his pistol to the tawny-gray wolf's ear, squeezed the trigger and leaped back.

A wild, despairing wail went up, the great, gray form seemed suddenly to stiffen, to grow longer, heavier, to shed its fur and thicken in limbs and body structure. In a moment, as we watched the horrid transformation, we beheld a human form stretched out upon the floor; the body of a handsome man with fair hair and black beard, at the throat of which a slender silver-gray she-wolf was worrying.

"It is over, finished, little brave one," de Grandin announced, reaching out a hand to stroke the little wolf's pale fur. "Right nobly have you borne yourself this night; but we have much to do before our work is finished."

The she-wolf backed away, but the hair upon her shoulders was still bristling, and her topaz eyes were jewel-bright with the light of combat. Once or twice, despite de Grandin's hand upon her neck, she gave vent to throaty growls and started toward the still form which lay upon the floor in a pool of moonlight, another pool fast gathering beneath its head where de Grandin's bullet had crashed through its skull and brain.

John Maxwell moved and moaned a tortured moan, and instantly the little wolf was by his side, licking his cheeks with her pink tongue, emitting little pleading whines, almost like the whimpers of a child in pain.

When Maxwell regained consciousness it was pathetic to see the joy the wolf showed as he sat up and feebly put a groping hand against his throat.

"Not dead, my friend, you are not nearly dead, thanks to the bravery of your noble lady," de Grandin told him with a laugh. Then, to me:

"Do you go home with them, Friend Trowbridge. I must remain to dispose of this"—he prodded the inert form with his foot—"and will be with you shortly.

"Be of good cheer, *ma pauvre*," he told the she-wolf, "you shall be soon released from the spell which binds you; I swear it; though never need you be ashamed of what you did this night, whatever form you might have had while doing it."

John Maxwell sat upon the divan, head in hands, the wolf crouched at his feet, her broken paw dangling pitifully, her topaz eyes intent upon his face. I paced restlessly before the fire. De Grandin had declared he knew how to release her from the spell—but what if he should fail? I shuddered at the thought. What booted it that we had killed the man-wolf if Sarah must be bound in wolfish form henceforth?

"*Tiens*, my friends," de Grandin announced himself at the library door, "he took a lot of disposing of, that one. First I had to clean the blood from off his bedroom floor, then I must lug his filthy carcass out into the alley and dispose of it as though it had been flung there from a racing motor. Tomorrow I doubt not the papers will make much of the mysterious murder. 'A gangster put upon the spot by other gangsters,' they will say. And shall we point out their mistake? I damn think no."

He paused with a self-satisfied chuckle; then: "Friend Jean, will you be good enough to go and fetch a negligee for Madame Sarah?" he asked. "Hurry, *mon vieux*, she will have need of it anon."

As the young man left us: "Quick, my friends," he ordered. "You, Madame Sarah, lie upon the floor before the fire, thus. *Bien*.

"Friend Trowbridge, prepare bandages and splints for her poor arm. We can not set it now, but later we must do so. Certainly.

"Now, my little brave one," he addressed the wolf again, "this will hurt you sorely, but only for a moment."

Drawing a small flask from his pocket he pulled the cork and poured its contents over her.

"It's holy water," he explained as she whined and shivered as the liquid soaked into her fur. "I had to stop to steal it from a church."

A knife gleamed in the firelight, and he drove the gleaming blade into her head, drew it forth and shook it toward the fire, so that a drop of blood fell hissing in the leaping flames. Twice more he cut her with the knife, and twice more dropped her blood into the fire; then, holding the knife lightly by the handle, he struck her with the flat of the blade between the ears three times in quick succession, crying as he did so: "Sarah Maxwell, I command that you once more assume your native form in the name of the Most Holy Trinity!"

A shudder passed through the wolf's frame. From nose to tail-tip she trembled, as though she lay in her death agony; then suddenly her outlines seemed to blur. Pale fur gave way to paler flesh, her dainty lupine paws became dainty human hands and feet, her body was no more that of a wolf, but of a soft, sweet woman.

But life seemed to have gone from her. She lay flaccid on the hearth rug, her mouth a little open, eyes closed, no movement of her breast perceptible. I looked at her with growing consternation, but:

"Quickly, my friends, the splints, the bandages!" de Grandin ordered.

I set the broken arm as quickly as I could, and as I finished young John Maxwell rushed into the room.

"Sallie, beloved!" he fell beside his wife's unconscious form, tears stream-ing down his face.

"Is she—is she—" he began, but could not force himself to finish, as he looked imploringly at Jules de Grandin.

"Dead?" the little man supplied. "By no means; not at all, my friend. She is alive and healthy. A broken arm mends quickly, and she has youth and stam-ina. Put on her robe and bear her up to bed. She will do excellently when she has had some sleep.

"But first observe this, if you please," he added, pointing to her side. Where the cicatrix with its tuft of wolf-hair had marred her skin, there was now only smooth, unspotted flesh. "The curse is wholly lifted," he declared delightedly. "You need no more regard it, except as an unpleasant memory."

"John, dear," we heard the young wife murmur as her husband bore her from the room, "I've had such a terrible dream. I dreamed that I'd been turned into a wolf, and—"

"Come, quickly, good Friend Trowbridge," de Grandin plucked me by the arm. "I, too, would dream."

"Dream? Of what?" I asked him.

"Perchance of youth and love and springtime, and the joys that might have been," he answered, something like a tremble in his voice. "And then, again, perchance of snakes and toads and elephants, all of most unauthentic color—such things as one may see when he has drunk himself into the blissful state of delirium tremens. I do not surely know that I can drink that much, but may the Devil bake me if I do not try!"

# The Werewolves of London

## BRIAN STABLEFORD (1948– )

LONDON IS AFIRE *with uncanny light, its buildings dissolving into colored smoke as the stars tumble from the sky like bright rain. The people are frozen where they stand, and as the transforming light dances about them it smooths away their features; they are melted into awkward lumpish shapes, in one and twos and whole crowds, mothers and babies melting together, lovers becoming one at last.*

*Through the changing streets the wolves are running. They are white and silver-grey and black, fleet of foot and light of heart. And the fallen angels which hate mankind parade across the sky like wheels of fire, exulting in their freedom from the darkest prisons of matter, space, and time.*

*In Hell, Satan weeps, watching helplessly as the world above him is lit from within like a crystal ball, all flame and flux and fury. He would reach out and touch it, if he only could.*

*Outside Creation, God's image shifts; helpless in his omnipotence, he is remade, and cannot call to judgement those whose very souls are consumed in the cauldron of potentiality.*

THE MAN IN THE CAVE *confronts the smiling cat, whose jaws gape wide and whose eyes are ablaze with dreadful wrath, and who speaks to say:* What you have stolen from my soul I will take back, else I will poison all the world and wreck Creation itself.

*And the man cries:* Sed libera nos a malo, sed libera nos a malo, sed libera . . .

*Unheard.*

LYDYARD OPENED HIS EYES, which were awash with tears of pain, and said: "Cordelia?"

There was no answer.

Excerpt from Brian Stableford, *The Werewolves of London* (New York: Carrol and Graf, 1992, with arrangement with Simon and Schuster, London, 1990), 315–25.

His head was pounding and he felt sick to his stomach, but the inner sight had let go of him, and left him to the unalloyed misery of his discomforts. The bright imaginary light which had been dazzling him faded into mere yellow lamplight, and he saw the walls which confined him, and the bed on which he lay.

His wrists were closely bound together by thin cord, whose coils were also knotted about one of the iron bars which supported the bedhead. His ankles were bound in similar fashion and tightly tied to a bar beneath the lower rail which was at the foot of the bed, so that his bare feet projected beyond the rail. He was held in such a way that he could not make himself comfortable no matter how he squirmed or tried to change his position. The mattress upon which he lay was very uneven.

He was not alone; beside him, sitting on the bed and looking down at him, was the awesomely beautiful woman he had seen once before. Her neatly formed teeth were just visible between her gently smiling lips; her eyes, which had violet irises, were fixed upon him. Her expression was mockingly affectionate. In the lamplight her silken, glimmering hair seemed more honey-colored than when illuminated by pale sunlight.

He could not take his eyes from her face.

"You would not come with me when I asked," she said, in a teasingly reproachful fashion. "You let my jealous lover take you away. Poor Pelorus has lately become quite mad, as you must have guessed—his will is not his own. My will is entirely my own, and cannot be denied by mere mortals, as you see."

"You are the queen of the werewolves, I presume," he said, gritting his teeth to sustain the angry irony, "and I dare say that you have learned much by the example of our own dear queen."

She laughed, in a curiously mock-polite fashion. "Have you a queen of your own? It is so difficult to keep count of your ephemeral monarchs that I no longer try. I have not been entertained at court for . . . some time."

Lydyard looked about him, at the walls darkened by soot and fungus, which nevertheless contrived to gleam in the lamplight because they were so enslimed. The mortar between the bricks was crumbling, and the brick itself gave the appearance of being rotten to the core. The floor was as brightly lit as the walls, because an oil lamp stood upon it; it was dirt, not even flagstoned, and it stank of excrement. The chair upon which Mandorla Soulier sat was sturdy and plain. Apart from the bed on which he lay, the only other piece of furniture in the room was a low table by the bedhead, on which stood a candle tray; its candle was lit but had already burned low, and its coarse wax had melted into a bizarrely misshapen lump.

In the midst of all this squalor, Mandorla Soulier was ostentatiously costumed in colored silks, like some Drury Lane actress dressed to play Cleopatra—or Salome.

"If this is how you entertain at your own court," he said, "I hope that as many years might pass before I am invited again."

This time, her smile seemed more genuinely amused. "There have been times, Mr. Lydyard, when I could have welcomed you to a finer place by far. But a beautiful woman who does not age is too often flattered by accusations of witchcraft. You do not know what it is like to burn, my darling David, and if you were ever to find out, you could not wake again to cherish the memory. I know, and I sometimes wish that I did not. It is an experience which might teach Pelorus a salutary lesson about those who he holds in such foolishly high regard."

"We never burned witches in England," said Lydyard, fighting against the many pains in his cut and aching head, and also against an insistent nausea in his belly, "and we have not hanged one for a century and more. Had you kept in better touch with our affairs, you might know that."

"I had slept for a while," Mandorla said, regretfully, "and those who guarded me were obliged to be careful. The world had changed when I returned, more than I had thought possible. It had become black and ugly, choked with smoke, flatulent with steam, and drenched with cheap gin, with manners and morals to match. And yet, it has greater potential for its own destruction than I have ever seen before. In these crowded streets, famine and disease are ever close at hand . . . and there is cause for hope that a glorious transformation of the business of war might increase the toll of its slaughter in a most pleasing manner. There is such a wonderful profusion of new engines of destruction!"

"How is Calan?" he asked, bluntly.

"Asleep," she replied, easily enough. "Asleep, and dreaming. Do not think that your leaden bullets can poison or corrupt him, even though your vile liquor has begun to make him stupid. He will wake again, refreshed and renewed, and if I can, I will refresh and renew the world for him, so that he may have a more joyous awakening than he has ever had before. It is the way of the wolf pack, you see, that I am mother and protector to my siblings and my cousins as well as my whelps. We are more faithful and loving than your own kind."

Lydyard yanked at the cords which secured him, squinting against the shock of pain, and said, "I cannot believe it."

She smiled yet again, more coldly than before, and said: "But this is just appearance, my darling David. I am not really human at all—I am a wolf, and humans are my prey, as little to me as rats and frogs. I am loving with my own kind, as you are with yours, but you are as little to me as the beasts which you send to your own slaughterhouses. I might make a pet of you, if the whim took me, and favor you with the kind of affection which you might give to a sleek and pretty cat, but I could not offer you that purer love which a she-wolf feels for her kin.

"I ask you to understand this, David, for I know that you are clever by the standards of your kind, and capable of philosophical detachment. I would not have you think me cruel, when I am a reasoning creature like yourself. You do understand me, David, do you not? Unless you do, you will not understand your own situation, and I want you to see that however I may use you, I do no wrong. I owe you no mercy, no pity, no charity, for I am a wolf, David, no matter what I seem to be in the sight of your poor deluded eyes."

The earnestness of it had the power of speech and thought; would human beings approach them in like fashion? Would the predator expect his prey to understand the logic of the abattoir? Would he have the right to demand that his explanation be accepted—that the justice of murder be admitted, that the rectitude of the slaughterer be recognized?

"Whatever you want from me," he whispered, "I will deny you. By torture you might make me see, and you might also make me speak, but if you hope to separate truth from delusion, reality from dream, you will surely be disappointed. It has ever been the way with oracles, has it not?"

"I know far more of oracles than you do," she told him. "Has Pelorus told you about the way of pain? Even if he did, I doubt that he told you enough. With me to guide you, you will learn to dream the truest dreams of all, and in the end, you will be grateful for the chance to serve my ends. I know the way of pain, you see, far better than any of your kind ever could. I know its persuasiveness as well as its rewards."

He could not doubt that she did, and was forced to swallow a lump in his throat.

Mandorla was still smiling. "Do not be afraid," she said. "You are a little more than human now, and you must not think as a cold-souled coward. I ask for your understanding, and that is not something which I have asked of many men. Different we are, but still we might be allied. I am honest with you because I hope that you might be honest with me. I do not seek to use my disguise in deception or seduction, not because you know what I really am—the power of your eyes to see falsely is so great that I could deceive and seduce you in spite of what you know—but because I see in you authentic intelligence and genuine curiosity."

He knew that it was lie. He knew, beyond the shadow of a doubt, that it was a mere stratagem, a seduction which sought to succeed by disowning the intention to seduce.

He knew, too, that it was a kind of play. She did not speak to him thus because she truly thought it to be the best way of attaining her end, but rather because she rejoiced in her own deceptiveness. Behind her flattery there was a special contempt.

"Do not lose yourself in delight," he told her, with sufficient asperity to take her by surprise, "for something is coming after me, and there is none who can bar its way or force its hand. Neither you nor Harkender can keep Gabriel from the one to whom his soul truly belongs—and it is not for you to command the conflicts of the gods."

She was taken aback, but only for a moment. "Poor oracle," she said. "The poison in your soul will hurt you, if you cannot contain it better than that."

He shook his aching head, as though he might clear it by throwing off his confusion. Unsurprisingly, the shaking worsened his distress. The world seemed to fade and blur. Even through his clothing he could feel the coarseness of the blanket on which he lay, and the chafing of the cords about his bleeding wrists, and these sensations were very sharp indeed—but the face of Mandorla Soulier had lost some fraction of its glamour, and the dismal walls of his prison seemed to have retreated into a distant haze.

"Was any other hurt?" he asked, more harshly than he had intended.

"No," she replied. "Amalax panicked, but his foolishness was contained by his determination to escape. Sir Edward and his daughter are safe and well— for the time being."

Lydyard heard and understood the implied threat, but did not react.

"It may not be as easy as you think to keep me here," he said. "Sir Edward is an influential man, and kidnapping is a serious crime. There is also Pelorus to be reckoned with."

"The police cannot find us here," she assured him, so casually that he believed it, "and if Pelorus cares to come to your aid, he may indeed meet with a reckoning of sorts. I would not hurt him for the world—he is one of us, by nature and by true inclination, and I love him as dearly and inescapably as he loves me—but he must be protected from the alien will which works its evil way within him. He regrets as bitterly as any that his will is not his own. He cannot surrender to me, no matter that he longs to do it, and so I must capture him, as any who loved him half as much would be bound to do. If he comes to save you, his dearest and most secret wish will be to fail, and to be allowed to fall into the sleep of centuries. I would be a poor she-wolf if I did not seek to grant that wish."

Lydyard breathed carefully and deeply, trying to prevent his hand from trembling and his teeth from chattering. The pain in his head was dull but all-consuming. Everything which Mandorla said seemed to reek of mockery and deceit.

"Pelorus may not come alone," he said. "He might make common cause with Sir Edward. And you must not forget the other who might come to help me—that Sphinx whose toy I am. It reduced Pelorus to helplessness in Egypt, and it will do the same to you, if the whim takes it. I will do all I can to bring it here—that I promise you—but I will not bring it to be seduced or teased, I will bring it to exercise its wrath!"

He was glad to see that Mandorla's eyes narrowed then, and knew that he had frightened her, a little. She could not know what measure of mastery he had over his power, or how intimate his connection was with the Sphinx.

"Do not overreach yourself," she murmured. "You might fall into the trap which has claimed poor Harkender. He thinks himself a stealer of souls, but his own soul is imprisoned in a web which he cannot begin to comprehend. Do not think yourself the master, or even the favored slave, of that thing whose eyes you are. I have tried to show you what you are to me, but you are less than that by far to the being which has warmed your soul. You cannot command it, or even dare to hope that it will listen to your prayers.

"Poor man-child, you think that you have only dreamed of being in Hell, but you do not know how real your dreams now are. You are hostage to the powers of Creation and Destruction, whose reality is unimagined in your knowledge and your language. What owns you now had vanished from the reach of outer sight when the world was very young, perhaps before the race of men had been created. Reincarnate, it is free to make what it can of this dreadful, cold and desolate world, and my hope and expectation is that it needs only to see what men are, and what they have made, to be persuaded to turn its power to the breaking and the withering of everything which exists."

He knew that she dared not really believe it. Hope was speaking, not conviction—and even the hope was reaching far beyond her expectations, no matter what she said. In her own way, she was afraid—not of death, but of her own helplessness. She had stolen Gabriel Gill to give her the illusion of power, the illusion of control, but in her heart of hearts she knew that she was no commander of Creation, but only a wolf denied the joy and comfort of her own true being.

She had asked him to understand her, but he suspected that he understood far better than she had intended him to. He had the power of sight, still growing within him. He was a magician, however reluctant, and his power to dream the truth—and know the truth when he dreamed it—was greater than she knew. But his wrists were tightly bound and his body was racked with miseries, and whatever powers she claimed without having, she certainly had the power to deliver him into the untender arms of the dark angel of pain.

She reached out her hand, and put it to his forehead. The ache in his head flared up again, as though the contact had sent a shock through his brain, which seemed unjust, for he believed that she had genuinely sought to soothe and not to inflame. Wolf though she was, there was sufficient humanity in her to corrupt the wholeheartedness of her desire to hurt him. But then she ran her fingertips along the line of the cut which Amalax's knife had made, and there was no doubt that she meant to hurt; her sharpened nails opened the cut again, and he felt blood trickling into his ears.

He tried to move away, but found that he could not. He was too well secured; she and not he had control of his movements.

For the first time, he felt the extreme of fear: all loneliness and pain were in it, all misery and desperation, though first and foremost it was helplessness. That ultimate fear froze him, made him a mere toy of external force, forbade him to act, or even to exert his will against inaction.

"It is not for my own pleasure that I do this," she said to him, "but for your own education. You must learn the way of pain, and I know that you have not the courage to tread that path alone, as Jacob Harkender has."

She took up the grotesquely molten candle from the table, and stood up. She moved unhurriedly to the foot of the bed, so that he would see and understand what she intended.

"It is only a candle," she said to him. "A very tiny flame, which cannot really hurt you. Do you know how long it would take to burn a man to death, if one had only a candle to accomplish the task? It would be a long time, David, whether measured in hours or by the intensity of pain. That pain is best which can be most cleverly prolonged, which hurts without destroying, so that it may be constantly renewed."

She set the flame to the naked soles of Lydyard's feet. She moved it up and down, teasingly, so that the pain would grow slowly.

For a few seconds, the sensation was so dull and distant that he was more inclined to laugh than to scream—but then it began to build, and its sharpness grew in a gradual crescendo. The calluses on his feet were singeing, the dead skin shriveling away to expose the living flesh beneath.

He could not tell how long he fought before he finally screamed. As soon as he cried out, though, she took the flame away. The pain did not stop, but the crescendo began to wind down again.

She came back to the bedhead, and put the candle close to his face so that he could look into the heart of its tiny malevolent flame. She let him look at it for a minute or more, while he hoped fervently that her intention was to set it down and let him rest. But the hope, too, was part of her scheme, encouraged in order that it might be dashed, and when she was ready she moved again to the foot of the bed.

"Dream for me," she said to him, in a seductively pleading tone. "Fear not that there will be an end, for I will not let you die. But when you have dreamed, you must be more honest with me than you have so far been. Think on my beauty, if you can, and learn to love me just a little, for that will make the path of pain much easier to bear. Only dream for me, and you will find that I can reward as well as punish.

"I need to know the Sphinx's riddle, David—and more than that, I need to know its answer. Find your other mistress for me, and then return to tell me what and where she is. Tell her that I have lived ten thousand years, and that if there is any on this earth who has the wisdom which she needs it is Mandorla the she-wolf. Tell her that, David, and I might ease your hurt for a while. I promise that you will not hurt too badly, for this is only the beginning, and in time, even the harshest of hurts might cost you less, if you will only condescend to learn what I can teach you."

But the reality was harsher than the promise. The pain had not died away before it began to build again, and this time the crescendo was not so soon interrupted.

Lydyard's vision of Satan in Hell was suddenly before him again, in all its dreadful detail, and no matter how he sobbed and cried for the dream to die and fade into the darkness, it would not.

# The Door of the Unreal

GERALD BISS (1876–1922)

BY HALF-PAST EIGHT we were all gathered in the library. Dinner had been a strain on account of the presence of the servants; and we were all glad when it was over. We were all smoking hard at large cigars, which soothed us, as no smoking was the order once we started.

I don't think any one of us was nervous in the accepted sense of the word, but our nerves were as taut as elastic stretched parlous near breaking point: but I think I may say that we were all fit and ready. We were all in rough tweeds and heavy overcoats, as it was quite cold, although the day had been warm enough, and we counted upon the prospect of a considerable wait: and, in addition to our repeaters, we each carried a Browning, a flask, and a powerful electric torch—with the exception of Blenkinsopp and Boodle, who, in their official capacity, would not take rifles.

It had been arranged that either the former at the front or the latter at the back was to give the signal to fire, according to the door from which the exit was made—if any. That was almost the most anxious part of the whole business. I did not for an instant believe that my theory, now accepted without reservation by the others, could be wrong; but, if the line of action should fall out otherwise, it might land us in greater complications and deeper difficulties than ever.

Jevons was left in charge of the house with orders to close up and see everything quiet, to lock the library door after our departure, and to be generally prepared for anything or everything—and, if necessary, to keep up the illusion that we were all in consultation behind the locked library door. At all

Excerpt from Gerald Biss, *The Door of the Unreal* (New York: G. P. Putnam's Sons, Knickerbocker Press, 1920), 285–311.

costs he was to avert suspicion; and Burgess and I knew that we could trust his discretion.

"All ready?" asked Blenkinsopp quietly, as the hall clock chimed a quarter to nine.

We all answered in the affirmative.

"Everyone understand his part?" he went on, "or has anyone any questions to ask? No more talking after this."

We all nodded. There were no questions.

"All right," he said. "Now we will start."

And I will not deny that a keen thrill of anticipation went through me as we silently made our way through the long library window in single file.

Manders, Wellingham, and Verjoyce, under the guidance of Hedges, were to make their way through the woods to the back entrance, and to take cover amongst the trees just inside the garden near the little slip gate. Then Hedges was to work his way round the outside of the garden and join us in the front.

Blenkinsopp, Burgess, and I were to take a wider sweep through the woods and come out in front, where Burgess and Hedges were to take cover under the wall by the gap, facing the front door at an angle, with the moon full on the intervening ground. Blenkinsopp and I were to take up our position under shadow of the last tree of the drive, immediately facing the old iron-studded oak door of Dower House.

I shall never forget that long silent walk through the oppressive blackness of the woods, but it was infinitely less trying than the longer and even more silent, motionless wait after we had once all taken up our allotted positions; and it was a great relief, before ten o'clock, to see Hedges crawl through the gap and disappear under the shadow of the wall, where we knew Burgess to be awaiting him.

I do not think I ever remember a clearer or more lovely night outwardly, than this foul *Walpurgis Nacht*, with all the elemental and superphysical forces of evil out to revel in their great annual orgy of release. The moon was now full, and gave a wonderful white light; and the atmosphere was as clear as crystal.

It was indeed hard to believe that there was evil in the world—and, above all, such evil.

And so the time dragged on, each minute an hour, so it seemed, and the hour aeons. I could hear Blenkinsopp breathing deeply by my side during these interminable minutes that grew into first one hour and then another: and I expect that I was doing the same myself.

It was a relief when I felt his hand on my arm, and he showed me the dial of his luminous watch, indicating half-past eleven; and I nodded. And then my thoughts again turned to the youngsters on the far side of the grim old house, almost forbidding in the cold light, as though it had assumed a sinister aspect with its unconscious infection: and I wondered how they were lasting out through the strain of the silent ordeal. Then my thoughts reverted to the house itself, its history and its architectural beauty: and it seemed a strange, unnatural, almost horrible thought to think that within an hour or two—in all probability—it would be razed to the ground and reduced to a heap of ashes.

And then, as my thoughts wandered momentarily from point to point—it was just a quarter to twelve, Blenkinsopp told me afterwards—I felt his grip tighten upon my arm, and his breathing quicken.

I heard it, too. It was the sound of the clanking chain behind the old oak door with its great studs of iron, which divided the atmosphere of everyday life outside from the elemental drama of evil and unreality within.

"Ah," breathed Blenkinsopp deeply, between his clenched teeth; and I gripped my repeater, my eyes glued fast upon the door.

THEN CAME THE LONGEST WAIT of the lot—seven minutes only, it was by the watch, as long as seven centuries nonetheless—and then came another sound from the direction of the old door: and then, in the clear brightness of the moon, it was pulled slightly ajar, leaving a dark gap to the left, a sinister black fissure in the front of the old house in the full white light.

And then . . . yes, I had been right in my bizarre theory, no fantasy, after all, of an ill-balanced mind . . . out of this black fissure issued a great grey male wolf with the low swinging stride of his species, clearly visible in the brightness of the moonlight.

I dropped on one knee and covered the ill-omened brute with my rifle.

And then . . . I felt a constriction in my throat, and the veins on my temples knotted, as instinctively I wondered how poor old Burgess must be feeling . . . after the great grey male followed a smaller grey female wolf: and I knew that our worst fears were realities, and that the last crowning touch of hell's spite had been put to this piece of devil's work.

Dorothy had metamorphosed.

And in me awoke a burning desire, an intense passion to slay these foul things that had compassed it deliberately and wrought this desecration of her beautiful young body and the damnation of her pure white soul: and it nerved me as nothing else could ever have done.

And then appeared in the wake of the other two a gaunt brown old she-wolf, most sinister of all in the moonlight, and the two older ones formed up, one on either side of the younger one, as though to guide her unaccustomed feet along the dread path of damnation; and with long low sweeping strides they swung across the garden in formation towards the gap in the hedge, the grey male, to my delight, on the offside nearest to me, half a length in front.

Then he half halted as though scenting danger, turning his head first to the right, and then to the left; and as he stood in the incandescent bath of glowing moonlight, momentarily uncertain, and as splendid a target as though it had been daylight, Blenkinsopp's whistle blew—a long shrill blast, sounding clear through the still night.

I drew a bead on the old grey male and fired, and he dropped where he stood; and I thanked God as never before that my right hand had not lost its cunning.

Practically simultaneously two other shots rang out from beneath the shadow of the wall, and the old brown she-wolf dropped in her tracks, while the little one turned round with an almost human cry, yet half a yelp, and began to run back to the house, obviously terror-stricken, and limping in the near hind foot. And, as she reached the doorstep, she gave another even more human cry, stumbled, and dropped.

We all rushed forward from our cover and ran across the garden, Burgess making straight for the old iron-studded door.

Can I describe what met my horror-stricken eyes, one of the most ghastly and gruesome sights God has ever allowed mortal vision to gaze upon, and one that time will never blot out?

There lay the gaunt old she-wolf stark in death, a wolf and nothing but a wolf, with no sign of metamorphosing to her equally repulsive human shape: but the other nearer to me was a terrible and monstrous object, a man's body naked but hairy, with the head of a wolf and the feet of a wolf, not yet dead, but writhing as though in a ghastly convulsion.

As I approached, he snarled viciously at me, baring his fangs and snapping furiously, with blood and froth on his horrid jaws: and he only just missed me. I drew my Browning and fired right at the heart of the foul hybrid creature without a touch of remorse, but rather with a great glow of triumph as I drew the trigger.

And then he gave yet one more convulsive wriggle and struggle: and I found myself standing over and staring down upon the dead body of Professor Lycurgus Wolff, which had housed so long to the detriment of the world and the cost of humanity the dread elemental that had projected itself that night.

"Thank God," I exclaimed fervently; and God knows I never felt more like praying in my life.

And then, as I heard steps racing round the house—it had all been the work of seconds, this climax of hours and weeks—I rushed forward to join Burgess on the steps of the house.

I found him bending over the inanimate form of Dorothy, which he had wrapped round with his big coat and tender, concealing hands: and I felt for him the great horror and great sacredness of the hour of his supreme ordeal.

"Thank God, she was her own true self when I reached her," he said in a strangled voice, "though unconscious. The wound is a mere trifle in the left foot: and I fancy she fainted from the shock. Keep the others back while I attend to it."

And, calling out to the rest to stand back, I gave him a light by my electric torch while he washed the wound with antiseptic he had ready in his pocket, and bound it up with bandages from his first-aid case, which he had not forgotten: and I marveled at the great thoughtfulness and tenderness of this big man in this prodigious test of mortal love. By the light of the torch, as I stood beside him, I noticed the unmistakable footprints of wolves' feet on the old stone step: but I hoped that Burgess in his absorption had overlooked them.

"We must get her away at once up to the house," he said in his firm, concentrated way. "She must remember as little as possible of this awful night, poor child. I won't give her any brandy till I get her right away."

"The C.I.D. men will be here in a moment with the van of petrol and the two-seater," I said. "One of the youngsters will drive you up and back again, if you care to return: and you can put her in Ann's charge—tell her it was the fire, or anything, but not to talk or ask questions. I don't think the wound will need a doctor. At any rate, I sincerely trust not."

The van and the car were on the spot almost immediately; and Wellingham drove off with Burgess beside him with his precious burden in his arms, wrapped round in his coat and mine, with an extra rug which I placed tenderly round her feet.

Then we turned to the grim work which lay in front of us—to make a pyre for the two horrible objects, grim and stark in the garden, and a holocaust of the once dear, but now tainted old house, together with all the elementals and superphysicals, such as would otherwise make it foul and as their abiding place for all time.

IN THE CAR, Burgess told me afterwards in one of his rare moments of expansiveness, the girl had partially come to, but had easily been soothed, snuggling down happily into his arms, as though it had been the most natural thing in the world: and never again was there any doubt or question of how things stood between them.

And it was with a more or less happy heart, after all, that he handed over her sacred body into the tender keep of our splendid little Ann, who understood intuitively, and asked no questions out of love and loyalty to her idolized big brother.

"All explanations afterwards," was all he had said—this Ann told me. "Ask none and give none: but look after my darling for me."

And he was soon on his way back to join us, young Bill Wellingham driving like a man possessed in his desire to miss nothing.

Blenkinsopp had issued his orders; and, as soon as the front door was clear, we all got to work piling up the dry wood in the downstairs rooms and saturating it with petrol. We also soaked the old woodwork of the building, sluicing with petrol the glorious old beams, four centuries old, the priceless paneling, and the carved staircase that was worth its weight in gold, together with the miniature minstrels' gallery, which was such a feature of the house, sung of by architects as often as it had been sung in by musicians. The beds, the curtains, the carpets were saturated with spirit until the smell became almost overwhelming.

The two bodies—one outwardly an old man with a worldwide reputation, the other apparently a she-wolf—were laid upon the special prepared pyres halfway up the staircase, and themselves saturated thoroughly in case anything should go wrong with our plans; so that it might seem that, while Dorothy escaped by her window and injured her foot in so doing, the Professor and Anna had essayed the staircase and been overcome by the consuming flames.

Last, but not least, we raised an immense pyre in the old barn at the side, already half full, as it stood, of inflammable matter: and there we found not only human bones, which we placed on top of the great heap, but a woman's watch, which was afterwards privately identified as the property of Mrs. Bolsover, and a diamond brooch, which was recognized by Wellingham and Verjoyce as a present from Tony to Miss St. Clair, and was actually engraved on the back with the name "Wuffles."

These connecting and convincing proofs have never, I may add, been made public by Scotland Yard, but lie hid in its secret archives—*not* in the superficial Black Museum, a more or less polite pander to the morbid-minded public.

Burgess arrived back just before our preparations were concluded; and it was his own hand that set fire deliberately to the waiting pile, in order that no one else could ever be blamed. It was a wonderful sacrificial act, worthy of an enthusiast, but executed with the coolness and precision of a cricketer, without the least theatrical touch.

In the meantime I had had the whole horrid bed of lycanthropic flowers rooted up and placed upon the pyre in the barn; and I noted to instruct Hedges to see the whole hollow dug over deep, and buried in with quick lime, together with the noxious pools.

We opened the old mullioned windows to create a draft; and each of us did our share of the arson business from one point and another—the hall itself being voluntarily selected by Burgess, while I took the barn as my portion.

And in less time than it takes to write it there was one terrific concentrated blaze, which, within a few minutes, began to light up the skies despite the darkness and dankness of the low-lying hollow, fighting for supremacy with the ill-omened *Walpurgis* moon itself.

And with that caprice of thought that persistently obtrudes at really serious crises, there kept ringing through my head the whole time the historic words of Bishop Latimer to Bishop Ridley—"This day, brother, have we lit such a fire as shall never be put out."

But we dared not tarry long lest we should be caught upon the spot: so, collecting everything that might betray us, we packed the men aboard the van with instructions to return to the garage, while we took cover in the woods until such time as we dared reappear upon the scene and face our story out.

.    .    .

I NEED NOT LABOR DETAIL or dilate upon the rest of that awful night, or rather early morning. Suffice to say, with Blenkinsopp and Boodle on the spot, our story, as we had anticipated, was never questioned. The local police dared not, even if it had occurred to them to do so; and to the reporters, in due course, there was nothing to question with such a splendid three-column story to hand—literally red-hot—and the presses eager to lap it up.

Blenkinsopp drove straight back to town soon after six in the morning, when we had seen the house and barn burnt beyond all telling, the hollow a seething cauldron of furious ashes—angry perhaps, from the elemental fury within. He left Boodle in charge; and I need hardly add that he made things all right up at the Yard.

THE SENSATION and the strain of the next few days were awful, and the reaction upon all of us great: but the worst was over, we all felt, whatever might befall.

Dorothy, with the vigor and recuperative power of youth, made wonderful progress, and her wounded foot was soon on the road to convalescence under the care of "Doctor" Burgess and "Nurse" Ann; and there we were saved taking an extra person, in the shape of a doctor, into our confidence upon this unpleasant and peculiarly secret subject.

Dorothy herself remembered nothing so far as the actual metamorphosis was concerned, and I doubt little that all along she had been under the hypnotic influence of the old Professor: but she had a mighty strange story to tell of the earlier happenings of the evening.

"We had no meals at all that day, and I was horribly hungry; but Anna said it was *his* orders, and would vouchsafe no further explanation. Then, as it grew dark and night approached, my father—and, oh, thank God, he was not my *real* father, only my stepfather, though he had forbidden me to say so to any one, and I dared not do so before. . . ."

A sudden light broke over my mind. It explained so much. Why had it never occurred to me, I wondered, as it made much that had been so puzzling quite clear.

"My real father was Colonel Cargill, of the Rifle Brigade," she went on; "but he died when I was a baby, and my mother before I was ten. Four years before her death she married Professor Wolff—why I could never make out. I have often thought during the last year that he must have hypnotized her. She was dreadfully unhappy; and I am sure that she was glad to die, if it had not been for me. Then for years I went from one school to another on the Continent and in this country, seeing practically nothing of him or that horrible old Anna Brunnolf"—the poor girl shuddered instinctively—"till they came to this country, when the Professor took me to live with them, refusing to allow me to communicate with any of my school friends or mistresses, and ordering me to call myself 'Dorothea Wolff' and him 'father,' and never on any account to disclose to anyone our real relationship. And I felt compelled against my will to obey him, as I was afraid of him," she concluded with pathetic simplicity.

Burgess's face lightened. There was one load off his mind in the fact that none of the old Professor's tainted blood ran in her veins, and the lycanthropic taint was thus beyond all doubt of question acquired and, therefore, exorcisable.

"Thank God," he said, taking her beautiful hand between his: and she smiled up happily into his eyes from her couch.

"He always had an extraordinary influence over me," she continued, "as over my mother—a ghastly, evil, penetrating influence that seemed to fascinate like a serpent's, and turned one's very soul sick. His eyes were so terrible at times; he had only to look at me, and I dared not cross his slightest wish. You remember that I told you how strange he had been for a fortnight—from the new moon onwards? That was forced from me by your sympathy: and I was in mortal fear after I had spoken. Well, to cut things short, on the evening of the fire, when it became dark all save for the moon, he made me dip my hands and face in special water that he brought with his own hands—strange water that seemed to have a life of its own and was instinctively repulsive. Then he placed round my waist a girdle of dark plaited hair with a queer old gold buckle, and put flowers—these horrible yellow ones with the black pustules, of which Mr. Osgood destroyed one in the garden that afternoon, and red and white ones as well: and then in the old oak hall, empty and lit only by the light of the moon through the mullioned windows, with white chalk he drew a circle some six or seven feet in diameter, and placed me in the center, sprinkling my forehead, my hands, and my breast with some of the same water.

"Then"—and her face grew frightened at the horror of the recollection, and I saw Burgess's grip upon her hand tighten reassuringly—"he began in his rough guttural voice to chant a weird incantation, moving slowly round and round me all the while.

"I felt that he was mad—or worse: but I was fascinated and could not move. Then he went across to the wood fire burning on the open hearth, under the Clympynge coat of arms and took off an iron pot, swinging it like a censer, and sprinkling the whole center of the circle, including myself, with it. . ."

"I know," I broke in, interrupting for the first time—"spring water with hemlock, aloes, opium, mandrake, solanum, poppy seed, asafoetida, and parsley—some or all of the ingredients."

Poor Dorothy shuddered again at the recollection, as she concluded bravely:

"And then it seemed that out of the half darkness there rose a tall, pillarlike phantom: and, as it did so, I must have fainted. It is the last thing I remember until I found myself in Burgess's arms in the car, as though in a dream—a passing recollection—and then in bed with dear Ann nursing me. I have no knowledge of anything in between."

"Thank God," I said with great fervor: "and now you must lie back and rest. Try and forget those horrors; and, above all, don't talk to Ann or any one else about them. Thank God we were in time to save you."

"And there is no trace of . . . of. . . ?" she asked in an awestruck whisper.

"Of neither of them," I struck in quietly, to save her as much as I could: and under my breath added once more, "Thank God."

SO BURGE AND I LEFT HER, and went downstairs to his sanctum.

"I shall marry her, of course, Linc," he said, "whatever may happen. She is not only pure in herself, but certainly untainted in blood or by an unconscious orgy; and it must be my joy and privilege in life to protect her from any ill consequences of the evil wrought by others."

I gripped his hand.

"I know, old friend: and I trust by God's grace to be able to exorcise this impregnated evil, if you will put your trust in me, and her—your most precious possession in the world—in my hands."

"Gladly will I leave it to you," said Burgess most heartily; "for, had it not been for your wonderful intuition and prompt action, I shudder to think what far worse things might have befallen my darling by now—and other innocent people."

And never in our long friendship have I felt so near or so close to the man I regard most in the world.

"I shall always feel," I said quickly, speaking with restraint, "to my dying day that it was given to me by a Higher Power to save not only the soul of Dorothy, but to wipe out this great and subtle danger to this country of yours which I have learnt to love so dearly from such long and close association."

It was getting too much like a melodrama in real life for my liking: so I went over to the sideboard.

"I'll shake you a cocktail, Burge," I said. "It won't do either of us any harm before lunch."

AND THEN IT FELL to my lot to work out the method and ritual of exorcism, and to make my preparations against the next full moon, which fell in the early hours of Wednesday, May 30th. So I decided to anticipate its coming to full by a few hours, and to act on the evening of Tuesday, May 29th, between 8:32 and 9:16, when things were specially favorable to the exorcism of evil spirits and elementals, as that period was dominated by Mercury the most bitter opponent of all such evil things—that is to say, Mercury was in 17 II under the cusp of Seventh House, slightly to south of due west.

And so I laid my plans, while all went well at the house, both the invalids making rapid progress till we had grown more like a happy family party, with the other loyal actors in the recent drama coming to and fro, than a house with the shadow of great horror hanging over it, as we had been whilst awaiting the coming to fullness of the last moon.

Burgess was happier than any day could ever be long, and Dorothy was a different creature, though at times she grew restless, and a strange light would come into her eyes, as the moon approached fullness: but I made her sleep on the side of the house away from it, with blinds and curtains drawn close to keep its baleful light from her sensitive condition, both mental and physical, while each night I closed the windows of her room myself, and fastened them securely with my own hands, placing rye, garlic, and hyssop over every crevice.

Our little Ann and her speedily recovering patient became inseparable under old Nature's wonderful system of mutual attraction; and, as we sat on the terrace with the garden ablaze with its bright armies of tulips in regiments and platoons, with their many-colored "busbies" on their annual full-dress parade, I was the philosopher of the party, smoking my pipe contentedly and banking my hopes on the evening of the twenty-ninth.

I WAS ALL READY when it arrived; and Burgess and I, with Dorothy left the house for an alleged drive in the dusk after an early dinner, at which the poor girl made but a poor pretense: and I could see marked signs of restlessness and both mental and physical stirrings within. And I don't mind confessing that I prayed as I have seldom prayed, as I sat at that dinner table with laughter on my lips, a glass of wine in my hand, and a load of anxiety in my heart.

Dorothy was dressed in the simplest white and only slipped on a light wrap, as it was a warm night: and she sat between us in the two-seater, supported morally as well as physically on both sides. I had explained everything to her, and she was glad to face the ordeal, though not unnaturally a little fearful and nervous: but, at her expressed desire, the ceremony was to be as private as possible.

It did not take us long before we reached the hatefulness of the Dower House hollow, a strange place in the dusk, and merely the empty shell of early associations; and I felt her tremble as we drove up the drive.

"Hold her tight, Burge," I said in a concentrated voice: "and pray as never before for your great love's sake."

And while I made my preparations swiftly, everything being arranged ready to hand, they knelt in the dusk under the old trees, which made it almost dark, the moon not yet being very bright or luminous.

First I drew a circle of seven-foot radius just in front of the old stone steps, all charred and scorched, and at the center I made certain magical figures—in yellow chalk—representing Mercury; and round them I drew in white chalk a triangle within a circle of three-foot radius, having the same center as the larger circle.

And then I took Dorothy and bound her securely hand and foot, and made her kneel within the inner circle, whilst round the outer circle I placed at equal distances seven hand lamps burning olive oil. Then I built a rough altar of wood, about a foot to the southeast circumference of the inner circle: and opposite the altar, about a foot and a half to the far side of the circumference of the inner circle, I made a fire of wood, and placed over it a tripod with an iron pot, into which I poured two pints of pure spring water.

Then I added two drachms of sulphur, half an ounce of castoreum, six drachms of opium, three drachms of asafoetida, half an ounce of hypericum, three quarters of an ounce of ammonia, and half an ounce of camphor. And, when I had stirred and mixed it thoroughly, I added a portion of mandrake root, and a fungus.

Then, dipping a cup in the hot liquid, I dashed it over Dorothy, regardless of everything, and I poured the rest round her within the magic circle, calling, in a loud voice, three times upon the Evil Spirit—the unspeakable elemental who had defiled the temple of her body by taking up its dwelling therein.

And at that moment, with a strangled cry, Dorothy fell forward on her face, and a strange grey cloud, formless, yet not without form, seemed to pass upwards like a pyramid of foul smoke, disappearing and disintegrating into the air.

A WEEK LATER Dorothy and Burgess were made man and wife at eight o'clock on a brilliant June morning, with the happy augury of the sun pouring into the old Saxon church on the fringe of Clymping estate; and I had the great honor and happiness of standing beside them as "best man."

And this is the real end and the true story of the appalling mysteries of the Brighton Road, still unrevealed so far as the public are concerned; and by now they have written them off in their short memories amongst the many undiscovered crimes chalked up against Scotland Yard, which is not always so much to blame as they think.

AND NOW MY TASK is finished, thank Heaven. This manuscript, by the unanimous will of all concerned, is to be placed in the custody of the British Museum, and not to be available to the general public for a century—until all the actors in the ghoulish drama are dead and forgotten. Then the whole horrible truth can be revealed to those curious enough to dig up a tragedy a century old.

# PART FOUR

# The Supernatural Werewolf

Supernatural intervention in human life is mysterious. Uncertainty, doubt, and improbability often attend it. When the supernatural is allied with lycanthropy, however, mystery is bathed in fright. The Hebrew Old Testament records a startling instance of transformation as punishment. Nebuchadnezzar, the great king of Babylon, was so bloated with pride about the breadth of his kingdom that he commanded his people to bow down to and worship the enormous statue of himself. Ruler and self-proclaimed god of the world, he walked in his palace one day contemplating his glory, boasting to himself, "Is not this great Babylon, that I have built for the house of the kingdom by the might of my power, and for the honor of my majesty?" But "while the word was in the king's mouth, there fell a voice from heaven, saying . . . thy dwelling shall be with the beasts of the field: they shall make thee to eat grass as oxen, and seven times shall pass over thee, until thou know that the most High ruleth in the kingdom of men" (Daniel 4:30–32). For centuries this story was the centerpiece of discussions about the intervention of God in human life and the possibility of metamorphosis.

In the two stories in this section, supernatural intervention is malevolent, with no hint of beneficence in its interaction with human beings. In Kipling's story, the ancient gods of India disrupt human life by punishing a blasphemer; they transform him into a werewolf. In Leiber's story, urban gods of the modern world "shock to madness" a sensitive human being; their aggressive, physical werewolf omnipresence unnerves him.

Kipling's story reveals the power of Indian gods and of their disciples. It is a story of the religious tensions between the Englishmen living in India who worship the Christian God, and of the native Indians who worship "heathen" gods. Although the Englishmen are inclined to dismiss the pagan gods of the East, even to regard them as nonexistent, the Englishmen are baffled by a sequence of events that can only be attributed to pagan supernatural interference in the life of their friend.

While drunk on New Year's Eve, an Englishman named Fleete defiles the statue of Hanuman, the Monkey-god, by "grinding the ashes of his cigar butt into the forehead of the red stone image of Hanuman." A leper-disciple at the temple observes this desecration, curses Fleete for his blasphemy, and places "the mark of the beast" on Fleete's chest: a leopard rosette that gradually turns black. Fleete's rapid transformation into a werewolf, after being branded, calls forth the ingenuity of his friends to rescue him from a lycanthropic condition unfit for a sophisticated Western human being.

As a werewolf, Fleete develops a voracious appetite for raw meat. Losing human consciousness, he attempts to leap out of a window to join wolves who are howling for him. To prevent him from becoming a member of a wolf pack, his friends truss him up. Then they capture the leper-disciple who put the curse on their friend, and torture him until he removes the "mark of the beast" from their friend. After his return to the human state, Fleete has no recollection of having spent some time as a werewolf. It is only years later that this story can be told by his friends. Although they triumphed in their struggle with a pagan god, they declare that the nature of the torture inflicted on the leper-disciple "is not to be printed."

Kipling's linking of metamorphosis with the power of the heathen Monkey-god Hanuman raises troubling doubts in the Western mind. From an Anglocentric viewpoint, the heathen gods are only gods of "stone and brass," powerless superstitious creations of a mendacious culture. On the other hand, Fleete's two friends cannot deny the blood-curdling power of Hanuman, who seized Fleete's human soul and replaced it with the soul of a beast.

In Leiber's story, the modern world has created its own gods in the form of werewolves who smell like garbage and exude the foul, oily fluids of industrialized society. In a technological world, where human life is jeopardized by the absence of the need for a beneficent creator god, the self-created gods take on the ominous characteristics of werewolves. They are menacing, bred in a spiritually deprived world, with the power to enter the consciousness of susceptible human beings and to drive them to insanity.

David Lashley is hounded by unseen presences. He sees, hears, and smells something resembling a werewolf wherever he goes: in his room at night, on the streetcar, at work in a department store. Nowhere can he escape the stalking of a werewolf. Even his bedroom, where they sniff all night and exude obnoxious odors, cannot protect him from these supernatural beings. On the streetcar they blow a cold, sick breath on his neck and appear with eyes like molten metal in the placards. In his workplace they slip in as huge dogs and leave greasy, black stains on his sandwiches. Fearing for his sanity, he decides to track down these werewolves to determine whether or not he is hallucinating. Driven by an obsessive fear, he takes a streetcar to the end of the line and finds their lair. The stalking werewolf recognizes him, chases him, captures him, and brutally attacks him. David Lashley smells "a sickening stench" and feels its jaws—"a foul oily fluid splattered his face." Barely escaping with his life, he is rescued by a policeman, who hears him muttering " 'God, God, God,' over and over again."

Leiber's story shows that the terror human beings felt in the past, when werewolves roamed in rural settings attacking and transforming humans into werewolves, is not over.

*The terror still occurs in a modern city, for all its scientific sophistication. Like the gods in Shakespeare's* King Lear *who play an active role in destroying human life, the modern gods in the form of werewolves terrorize, and almost destroy, David Lashley. He might well echo Gloucester, "As flies to wanton boys are we to th' gods, / They kill us for their sport" (IV.1.36–37).*

# The Mark of the Beast

RUDYARD KIPLING (1865–1936)

EAST OF SUEZ, some hold, the direct control of Providence ceases; Man being there handed over to the power of the Gods and Devil of Asia, and the Church of England Providence only exercising an occasional and modified supervision in the case of Englishmen.

This theory accounts for some of the more unnecessary horrors of life in India: it may be stretched to explain my story.

My friend Strickland of the Police, who knows as much of natives of India as is good for any man, can bear witness to the facts of the case. Dumoise, our doctor, also saw what Strickland and I saw. The inference which he drew from the evidence was entirely incorrect. He is dead now; he died in a rather curious manner, which has been elsewhere described.

When Fleete came to India, he owned a little money and some land in the Himalayas, near a place called Dharmsala. Both properties had been left him by an uncle, and he came out to finance them. He was a big, heavy, genial, and inoffensive man. His knowledge of natives was, of course, limited, and he complained of the difficulties of the language.

He rode in from his place in the hills to spend New Year in the station, and he stayed with Strickland. On New Year's Eve there was a big dinner at the club, and the night was excusably wet. When men forgather from the uttermost ends of the Empire, they have a right to be riotous. The Frontier had sent down a contingent o' Catch-'em-Alive-O's who had not seen twenty white faces for a year, and were used to ride fifteen miles to dinner at the next Fort at the risk of a Khyberee bullet where their drinks should lie. They profited by

First published in 1890.

139

their new security, for they tried to play pool with a curled-up hedgehog found in the garden, and one of them carried the marker round the room in his teeth. Half a dozen planters had come in from the south and were talking "horse" to the Biggest Liar in Asia, who was trying to cap all their stories at once. Everybody was there, and there was a general closing up of ranks and taking stock of our losses in dead or disabled that had fallen during the past year.

It was a very wet night, and I remember that we sang "Auld Lang Syne" with our feet in the Polo Championship Cup, and our heads among the stars, and swore that we were all dear friends. Then some of us went away and annexed Burma, and some tried to open up the Sudan and were opened up by Fuzzies in that cruel scrub outside Suakin, and some found stars and medals, and some were married, which was bad, and some did other things which were worse, and the others of us stayed in our chains and strove to make money on insufficient experiences.

Fleete began the night with sherry and bitters, drank champagne steadily up to dessert, then raw, rasping Capri with all the strength of whisky, took Benedictine with his coffee, four or five whiskies and sodas to improve his pool strokes, beer and bones at half-past two, winding up with old brandy. Consequently, when he came out, at half-past three in the morning, into fourteen degrees of frost, he was very angry with his horse for coughing, and tried to leapfrog into the saddle. The horse broke away and went to his stables; so Strickland and I formed a Guard of Dishonor to take Fleete home.

OUR ROAD LAY through the bazaar, close to a little temple of Hanuman, the Monkey-god, who is a leading divinity worthy of respect. All gods have good points, just as have all priests. Personally, I attach much importance to Hanuman, and am kind to his people—the great gray apes of the hills. One never knows when one may want a friend.

There was a light in the temple, and as we passed, we could hear voices of men chanting hymns. In a native temple, the priests rise at all hours of the night to do honor to their god. Before we could stop him, Fleete dashed up the steps, patted two priests on the back, and was gravely grinding the ashes of his cigar butt into the forehead of the red stone image of Hanuman. Strickland tried to drag him out, but he sat down and said solemnly:

"Shee that? 'Mark of the B—beasht! *I* made it. Ishn't it fine?"

In half a minute the temple was alive and noisy, and Strickland, who knew what came of polluting gods, said that things might occur. He, by virtue of his official position, long residence in the country, and weakness for going among the natives, was known to the priests and he felt unhappy. Fleete sat on the ground and refused to move. He said that "good old Hanuman" made a very soft pillow.

Then, without any warning, a Silver Man came out of a recess behind the image of the god. He was perfectly naked in that bitter, bitter cold, and his body shone like frosted silver, for he was what the Bible calls "a leper as white as snow." Also he had no face, because he was a leper of some years' standing and his disease was heavy upon him. We two stooped to haul Fleete up, and the temple was filling and filling with folk who seemed to spring from the earth, when the Silver Man ran in under our arms, making a noise exactly like the mewing of an otter, caught Fleete round the body and dropped his head on Fleete's breast before we could wrench him away. Then he retired to a corner and sat mewing while the crowd blocked all the doors.

The priests were very angry until the Silver Man touched Fleete. That nuzzling seemed to sober them.

At the end of a few minutes' silence, one of the priests came to Strickland and said, in perfect English, "Take your friend away. He was done with Hanuman, but Hanuman has not done with him." The crowd gave room and we carried Fleete into the road.

Strickland was very angry. He said that we might all three have been knifed, and that Fleete should thank his stars that he had escaped without injury.

Fleete thanked no one. He said that he wanted to go to bed. He was gorgeously drunk.

We moved on, Strickland silent and wrathful, until Fleete was taken with violent shivering fits and sweating. He said that the smells of the bazaar were overpowering, and he wondered why slaughterhouses were permitted so near English residences. "Can't you smell the blood?" said Fleete.

We put him to bed at last, just as the dawn was breaking, and Strickland invited me to have another whisky and soda. While we were drinking he talked of the trouble in the temple, and admitted that it baffled him completely. Strickland hates being mystified by natives, because his business in life is to overmatch them with their own weapons. He has not yet succeeded in doing this, but in fifteen or twenty years he will have made some small progress.

"They should have mauled us," he said, "instead of mewing at us. I wonder what they meant. I don't like it one little bit."

I said that the Managing Committee of the temple would in all probability bring a criminal action against us for insulting their religion. There was a section of the Indian Penal Code which exactly met Fleete's offense. Strickland said he only hoped and prayed that they would do this. Before I left I looked into Fleete's room and saw him lying on his right side, scratching his left breast. Then I went to bed cold, depressed, and unhappy, at seven o'clock in the morning.

AT ONE O'CLOCK I rode over to Strickland's house to inquire after Fleete's head. I imagined that it would be a sore one. Fleete was breakfasting and seemed unwell. His temper was gone, for he was abusing the cook for not supplying him with an underdone chop. A man who can eat raw meat after a wet night is a curiosity. I told Fleete this and he laughed.

"You breed queer mosquitoes in these parts," he said. "I've been bitten to pieces, but only in one place."

"Let's have a look at the bite," said Strickland. "It may have gone down since this morning."

While the chops were being cooked, Fleete opened his shirt and showed us, just over his left breast, a mark, the perfect double of the black rosettes—the five or six irregular blotches arranged in a circle—on a leopard's hide. Strickland looked and said, "It was only pink this morning. It's grown black now."

Fleete ran to a glass.

"By Jove!" he said, "this is nasty. What is it?"

We could not answer. Here the chops came in, all red and juicy, and Fleete bolted three in a most offensive manner. He ate on his right grinders only, and threw his head over his right shoulder as he snapped the meat. When he had finished, it struck him that he had been behaving strangely, for he said apologetically, "I don't think I ever felt so hungry in my life. I've bolted like an ostrich."

After breakfast Strickland said to me, "Don't go. Stay here, and stay for the night."

Seeing that my house was not three miles from Strickland's, this request was absurd. But Strickland insisted, and was going to say something when Fleete interrupted by declaring in a shamefaced way that he felt hungry again.

Strickland sent a man to my house to fetch over my bedding and a horse, and we three went down to Strickland's stables to pass the hours until it was time to go out for a ride. The man who has a weakness for horses never wearies of inspecting them; and when two men are killing time in this way they gather knowledge and lies the one from the other.

THERE WERE FIVE HORSES in the stables, and I shall never forget the scene as we tried to look them over. They seemed to have gone mad. They reared and screamed and nearly tore up their pickets; they sweated and shivered and lathered and were distraught with fear. Strickland's horses used to know him as well as his dogs; which made the matter more curious. We left the stable for fear of the brutes throwing themselves in their panic. Then Strickland turned back and called me. The horses were still frightened, but they let us "gentle" and make much of them, and put their heads in our bosoms.

"They aren't afraid of *us*," said Strickland. "D'you know, I'd give three months' pay if *Outrage* here could talk."

But *Outrage* was dumb, and could only cuddle up to his master and blow out his nostrils, as is the custom of horses when they wish to explain things but can't. Fleete came up when we were in the stalls, and as soon as the horses saw him, their fright broke out afresh. It was all that we could do to escape from the place unkicked. Strickland said, "They don't seem to love you, Fleete."

"Nonsense," said Fleete; "my mare will follow me like a dog." He went to her; she was in a loose box; but as he slipped the bars she plunged, knocked him down, and broke away into the garden. I laughed, but Strickland was not amused. He took his moustache in both fists and pulled at it till it nearly came out. Fleete, instead of going off to chase his property, yawned, saying that he felt sleepy. He went to the house to lie down, which was a foolish way of spending New Year's Day.

Strickland sat with me in the stables and asked if I had noticed anything peculiar in Fleete's manner. I said that he ate his food like a beast; but that this might have been the result of living alone in the hills out of reach of society as refined and elevating as ours, for instance. Strickland was not amused. I do not think that he listened to me, for his next sentence referred to the mark on Fleete's breast, and I said that it might have been caused by blister flies, or that it was possibly a birthmark newly born and now visible for the first time. We both agreed that it was unpleasant to look at, and Strickland found occasion to say that I was a fool.

"I can't tell you what I think now," said he, "because you would call me a madman; but you must stay with me for the next few days, if you can. I want you to watch Fleete, but don't tell me what you think till I have made up my mind."

"But I am dining out tonight," I said.

"So am I," said Strickland, "and so is Fleete. At least if he doesn't change his mind."

WE WALKED about the garden smoking, but saying nothing—because we were friends, and talking spoils good tobacco—till our pipes were out. Then we went to wake up Fleete. He was wide awake and fidgeting about his room.

"I say, I want some more chops," he said. "Can I get them?"

We laughed and said, "Go and change. The ponies will be round in a minute."

"All right," said Fleete. "I'll go when I get the chops—underdone ones, mind."

He seemed to be quite in earnest. It was four o'clock, and we had had breakfast at one; still, for a long time, he demanded those underdone chops. Then he changed into riding clothes and went out into the verandah. His pony—the mare had not been caught—would not let him come near. All three horses were unmanageable—mad with fear—and finally Fleete said that he would stay at home and get something to eat. Strickland and I rode out wondering. As we passed the temple of Hanuman, the Silver Man came out and mewed at us.

"He is not one of the regular priests of the temple," said Strickland. "I think I should peculiarly like to lay my hands on him."

There was no spring in our gallop on the racecourse that evening. The horses were stale, and moved as though they had been ridden out.

"The fright after breakfast has been too much for them," said Strickland.

That was the only remark he made through the remainder of the ride. Once or twice I think he swore to himself, but that did not count.

We came back in the dark at seven o'clock, and saw that there were no lights in the bungalow. "Careless ruffians my servants are!" said Strickland.

My horse reared at something on the carriage drive, and Fleete stood up under its nose.

"What are you doing, groveling about the garden?" said Strickland.

But both horses bolted and nearly threw us. We dismounted by the stables and returned to Fleete, who was on his hands and knees under the orange bushes.

"What the devil's wrong with you?" said Strickland.

"Nothing, nothing in the world," said Fleete, speaking very quickly and thickly. "I've been gardening—botanizing you know. The smell of the earth is delightful. I think I'm going for a walk—a long walk—all night."

Then I saw that there was something excessively out of order somewhere, and I said to Strickland, "I am not dining out."

"Bless you!" said Strickland. "Here, Fleete, get up. You'll catch fever there. Come in to dinner and let's have the lamps lit. We'll all dine at home."

Fleete stood up unwillingly, and said, "No lamps—no lamps. It's much nicer here. Let's dine outside and have some more chops—lots of 'em and underdone—bloody ones with gristle."

Now a December evening in Northern India is bitterly cold, and Fleete's suggestion was that of a maniac.

"Come in," said Strickland sternly. "Come in at once."

Fleete came, and when the lamps were brought, we saw that he was literally plastered with dirt from head to foot. He must have been rolling in the garden. He shrank from the light and went to his room. His eyes were horrible to look at. There was a green light behind them, not in them, if you understand, and the man's lower lip hung down.

Strickland said, "There is going to be trouble—big trouble—tonight. Don't change your riding things."

WE WAITED and waited for Fleete's reappearance, and ordered dinner in the meantime. We could hear him moving about his own room, but there was no light there. Presently from the room came the long-drawn howl of a wolf.

People write and talk lightly of blood running cold and hair standing up and things of that kind. Both sensations are too horrible to be trifled with. My heart stopped as though a knife had been driven through it, and Strickland turned white as the tablecloth.

The howl was repeated, and was answered by another howl far across the fields.

That set the gilded roof on the horror. Strickland dashed into Fleete's room. I followed, and we saw Fleete getting out of the window. He made beast noises in the back of his throat. He could not answer us when we shouted at him. He spat.

I don't quite remember what followed, but I think that Strickland must have stunned him with the long bootjack or else I should never have been able to sit on his chest. Fleete could not speak, he could only snarl, and his snarls were those of a wolf, not of a man. The human spirit must have been giving way all day and have died out with the twilight. We were dealing with a beast that had once been Fleete.

The affair was beyond any human and rational experience. I tried to say "hydrophobia," but the word wouldn't come, because I knew that I was lying.

We bound this beast with leather thongs of the punkah-rope, and tied its thumbs and big toes together, and gagged it with a shoehorn, which makes a very efficient gag if you know how to arrange it. Then we carried it into the dining room, and sent a man to Dumoise, the doctor, telling him to come over at once. After we had despatched the messenger and were drawing breath, Strickland said, "It's no good. This isn't any doctor's work." I, also, knew that he spoke the truth.

The beast's head was free, and it threw it about from side to side. Anyone entering the room would have believed that we were curing a wolf's pelt. That was the most loathsome accessory of all.

Strickland sat with his chin in the heel of his fist, watching the beast as it wriggled on the ground, but saying nothing. The shirt had been torn open in the scuffle and showed the black rosette mark on the left breast. It stood out like a blister.

In the silence of the watching we heard something without mewing like a she-otter. We both rose to our feet, and, I answer for myself, not Strickland, felt sick—actually and physically sick. We told each other, as did the men in *Pinafore,* that it was the cat.

Dumoise arrived, and I never saw a little man so unprofessionally shocked. He said that it was a heartrending case of hydrophobia, and that nothing could be done. At least any palliative measures would only prolong the agony. The beast was foaming at the mouth. Fleete, as we told Dumoise, had been bitten by dogs once or twice. Any man who keeps half a dozen terriers must expect a nip now and again. Dumoise could offer no help. He could only certify that Fleete was dying of hydrophobia. The beast was then howling, for it had managed to spit out the shoehorn. Dumoise said that he would be ready to certify to the cause of death, and that the end was certain. He was a good little man, and he offered to remain with us; but Strickland refused the kindness. He did not wish to poison Dumoise's New Year. He would only ask him not to give the real cause of Fleete's death to the public.

So Dumoise left, deeply agitated; and as soon as the noise of the cart wheels had died away, Strickland told me, in a whisper, his suspicions. They were so wildly improbable that he dared not say them out aloud; and I, who entertained all Strickland's beliefs, was so ashamed of owning to them that I pretended to disbelieve.

"Even if the Silver Man had bewitched Fleete for polluting the image of Hanuman, the punishment could not have fallen so quickly."

As I was whispering this the cry outside the house rose again, and the beast fell into a fresh paroxysm of struggling till we were afraid that the thongs that held it would give way.

"Watch!" said Strickland. "If this happens six times I shall take the law into my own hands. I order you to help me."

He went into his room and came out in a few minutes with the barrels of an old shotgun, a piece of fishing line, some thick cord, and his heavy wooden bedstead. I reported that the convulsions had followed the cry by two seconds in each case, and the beast seemed perceptibly weaker.

Strickland muttered, "But he can't take away the life! He can't take away the life!"

I said, though I knew that I was arguing against myself, "It may be a cat. It must be a cat. If the Silver Man is responsible, why does he dare to come here?"

Strickland arranged the wood on the hearth, put the gun barrels into the glow of the fire, spread the twine on the table and broke a walking stick in two. There was one yard of fishing line, gut, lapped with wire, such as is used for *mahseer*-fishing, and he tied the two ends together in a loop.

Then he said, "How can we catch him? He must be taken alive and unhurt."

I said that we must trust in Providence, and go out softly with polo sticks into the shrubbery at the front of the house. The man or animal that made the cry was evidently moving round the house as regularly as a night watchman. We could wait in the bushes till he came by and knock him over.

Strickland accepted this suggestion, and we slipped out from a bathroom window into the front verandah and then across the carriage drive into the bushes.

In the moonlight we could see the leper coming round the corner of the house. He was perfectly naked, and from time to time he mewed and stopped to dance with his shadow. It was an unattractive sight, and thinking of poor Fleete, brought to such degradation by so foul a creature, I put away all my doubts and resolved to help Strickland from the heated gun barrels to the loop of twine—from the loins to the head and back again—with all tortures that might be needful.

The leper halted in the front porch for a moment and we jumped out on him with the sticks. He was wonderfully strong, and we were afraid that he might escape or be fatally injured before we caught him. We had an idea that lepers were frail creatures, but this proved to be incorrect. Strickland knocked his legs from under him and I put my foot on his neck. He mewed hideously, and even through my riding boots I could feel that his flesh was not the flesh of a clean man.

He struck at us with his hand and feet-stumps. We looped the lash of a dog whip round him under the armpits and dragged him backwards into the hall and so into the dining room where the beast lay. There we tied him with trunk straps. He made no attempt to escape, but mewed.

When we confronted him with the beast the scene was beyond descrip-tion. The beast doubled backwards into a bow as though he had been poi-soned with strychnine, and moaned in the most pitiable fashion. Several other things happened also, but they cannot be put down here.

"I think I was right," said Strickland. "Now we will ask him to cure the case."

But the leper only mewed. Strickland wrapped a towel round his hand and took the gun barrels out of the fire. I put the half of the broken walking stick through the loop of fishing line and buckled the leper comfortably to Strick-land's bedstead. I understood then how men and women and little children can endure to see a witch burnt alive; for the beast was moaning on the floor, and though the Silver Man had no face, you could see horrible feelings passing through the slab that took its place, exactly as waves of heat play across red-hot iron—gun barrels for instance.

Strickland shaded his eyes with his hands for a moment and we got to work. This part is not to be printed.

THE DAWN was beginning to break when the leper spoke. His mewings had not been satisfactory up to that point. The beast had fainted from exhaustion and the house was very still. We unstrapped the leper and told him to take away the evil spirit. He crawled to the beast and laid his hand upon the left breast. That was all. Then he fell face down and whined, drawing in his breath as he did so.

We watched the face of the beast, and saw the soul of Fleete coming back into the eyes. Then a sweat broke out on the forehead and the eyes—they were human eyes—closed. We waited for an hour but Fleete still slept. We carried him to his room and bade the leper go, giving him the bedstead, and the sheet on the bedstead to cover his nakedness, the gloves and the towels with which we had touched him, and the whip that had been hooked round his body. He put the sheet about him and went out into the early morning without speaking or mewing.

Strickland wiped his face and sat down. A night-gong, far away in the city, made seven o'clock.

"Exactly four-and-twenty hours!" said Strickland. "And I've done enough to ensure my dismissal from the service, besides permanent quarters in a lunatic asylum. Do you believe that we are awake?"

The red-hot gun barrel had fallen on the floor and was singeing the carpet. The smell was entirely real.

That morning at eleven we two together went to wake up Fleete. We looked and saw that the black leopard-rosette on his chest had disappeared. He was very drowsy and tired, but as soon as he saw us, he said, "Oh! Confound you fellows. Happy New Year to you. Never mix your liquors. I'm nearly dead."

"Thanks for your kindness, but you're over time," said Strickland. "Today is the morning of the second. You've slept the clock round with a vengeance."

The door opened, and little Dumoise put his head in. He had come on foot, and fancied that we were laying out Fleete.

"I've brought a nurse," said Dumoise. "I suppose that she can come in for . . . what is necessary."

"By all means," said Fleete cheerily, sitting up in bed. "Bring on your nurses."

Dumoise was dumb. Strickland led him out and explained that there must have been a mistake in the diagnosis. Dumoise remained dumb and left the house hastily. He considered that his professional reputation had been injured, and was inclined to make a personal matter of the recovery. Strickland went out too. When he came back, he said that he had been to call on the Temple of Hanuman to offer redress for the pollution of the god, and had been solemnly assured that no white man had ever touched the idol and that he was an incarnation of all the virtues laboring under a delusion. "What do you think?" said Strickland.

I said, " 'There are more things . . . ' "

But Strickland hates that quotation. He says that I have worn it threadbare.

One other curious thing happened which frightened me as much as anything in all the night's work. When Fleete was dressed he came into the dining room and sniffed. He had a quaint trick of moving his nose when he sniffed. "Horrid doggy smell, here," said he. "You should really keep those terriers of yours in better order. Try sulphur, Strick."

But Strickland did not answer. He caught hold of the back of a chair, and, without warning, went into an amazing fit of hysterics. It is terrible to see a strong man overtaken with hysteria. Then it struck me we had fought for Fleete's soul with the Silver Man in that room, and had disgraced ourselves as Englishmen forever, and I laughed and gasped and gurgled just as shamefully as Strickland, while Fleete thought that we had both gone mad. We never told him what we had done.

Some years later, when Strickland had married and was a churchgoing member of society for his wife's sake, we reviewed the incident dispassionately, and Strickland suggested that I should put it before the public.

I cannot myself see that this step is likely to clear up the mystery; because, in the first place, no one will believe a rather unpleasant story, and, in the second, it is well known to every right-minded man that the gods of the heathen are stone and brass, and any attempt to deal with them otherwise is justly condemned.

# The Hound

**FRITZ LEIBER (1910–1992)**

DAVID LASHLEY HUDDLED the skimpy blankets around him and dully watched the cold light of morning seep through the window and stiffen in his room. He could not recall the exact nature of the terror against which he had fought his way to wakefulness, except that it had been in some way gigantic and had brought back to him the fear-ridden helplessness of childhood. It had lurked near him all night and finally it had crouched over him and thrust down toward his face.

The radiator whined dismally with the first push of steam from the basement, and he shivered in response. He thought that his shivering was an ironically humorous recognition of the fact that his room was never warm except when he was out of it. But there was more to it than that. The penetrating whine had touched something in his mind without being quite able to dislodge it into consciousness. The mounting rumble of city traffic, together with the hoarse panting of a locomotive in the railroad yards, mingled themselves with the nearer sound, intensifying its disturbing tug at hidden fears. For a few moments he lay inert, listening. There was an unpleasant stench too in the room, he noticed, but that was nothing to be surprised at. He had experienced more than once the strange olfactory illusions that are part of the aftermath of flu. Then he heard his mother moving around laboriously in the kitchen, and that stung him into action.

"Have you another cold?" she asked, watching him anxiously as he hurriedly spooned in a boiled egg before its heat should be entirely lost in the chilly plate. "Are you sure?" she persisted. "I heard someone sniffling all night."

In *Weird Tales* (1942).

"Perhaps father—" he began.

She shook her head. "No, he's all right. His side was giving him a lot of pain yesterday evening, but he slept quietly enough. That's why I thought it must be you, David. I got up twice to see, but"—her voice became a little doleful—"I know you don't like me to come poking into your room at all hours."

"That's not true!" he contradicted. She looked so frail and little and worn, standing there in front of the stove with one of father's shapeless bathrobes hugged around her, so like a sick sparrow trying to appear chipper, that a futile irritation, an indignation that he couldn't help her more, welled up within him, choking his voice a little. "It's that I don't want you getting up all the time and missing your sleep. You have enough to do taking care of father all day long. And I've told you a dozen times that you mustn't make breakfast for me. You know the doctor says you need all the rest you can get."

"Oh, *I'm* all right," she answered quickly, "but I was sure you'd caught another cold. All night long I kept hearing it—a sniffling and a snuffling—"

Coffee spilled over into the saucer as David set down the half-raised cup. His mother's words had reawakened the elusive memory, and now that it had come back he did not want to look it in the face.

"It's late, I'll have to rush," he said.

She accompanied him to the door, so accustomed to his hastiness that she saw in it nothing unusual. Her wan voice followed him down the dark apartment stair: "I hope a rat hasn't died in the walls. Did you notice the nasty smell?"

And there he was out of the door and had lost himself and his memories in the early morning rush of the city. Tires singing on asphalt. Cold engines coughing, then starting with a roar. Heels clicking on the sidewalk, hurrying, trotting, converging on streetcar intersections and elevated stations. Low heels, high heels, heels of stenographers bound downtown, and of war workers headed for the outlying factories. Shouts of newsboys and glimpses of headlines: "AIR BLITZ ON . . . BATTLESHIP SUNK . . . BLACKOUT EXPECTED HERE . . . DRIVEN BACK."

But sitting in the stuffy solemnity of the streetcar, it was impossible to keep from thinking of it any longer. Besides, the stale medicinal smell of the yellow woodwork immediately brought back the memory of that other smell. David Lashley clenched his hands in his overcoat pockets and asked himself how it was possible for a grown man to be so suddenly overwhelmed by a fear from childhood. Yet in the same instant he knew with acute certainty that this was no childhood fear, this thing that had pursued him up the years, growing ever more vast and menacing, until, like the demon wolf Ferris at Ragnorak, its gaping jaws scraped heaven and earth, seeking to open wider. This thing that had dogged his footsteps, sometimes so far behind that he forgot its existence, but now so close that he could feel its cold sick breath on his neck. Werewolves? He had read up on such things at the library, fingering dusty books in uneasy fascination, but what he had read made them seem innocuous and without significance—dead superstitions—in comparison with this thing that was part and parcel of the great sprawling cities and chaotic people of the twentieth century, so much a part that he, David Lashley, winced at the endlessly varying howls and growls of traffic and industry—sounds at once animal and mechanical; shrank back with a start from the sight of headlights at night—those dazzling unwinking eyes; trembled uncontrollably if he heard the scuffling of rats in an alley or caught sight in the evenings of the shadowy forms of lean mongrel dogs looking for food in vacant lots. "Sniffling and snuffling," his mother had said. What better words could you want to describe the inquisitive, persistent pryings of the beast that had crouched outside the bedroom door all night in his dreams and then finally pushed through to plant its dirty paws on his chest. For a moment he saw, superimposed on the yellow ceiling and garish advertising placards of the streetcar, its malformed muzzle . . . the red eyes like thickly scummed molten metal . . . the jaws slavered with thick black oil . . .

Wildly he looked around at his fellow passengers, seeking to blot out that vision, but it seemed to have slipped down into all of them, infecting them, giving their features an ugly canine cast—the slack, receding jaw of an otherwise pretty blonde, the narrow head and wide-set eyes of an unshaven mechanic returning from the night shift. He sought refuge in the open newspaper of the man sitting beside him, studying it intently without regard for the impression of rudeness he was creating. But there was a wolf in the cartoon, and he quickly turned away to stare through the dusty pane at the stores sliding by. Gradually the sense of oppressive menace lifted a little. But the cartoon had established another contact in his brain—the memory of a cartoon from the First World War. What the wolf or hound in that earlier cartoon had represented—war, famine, or the ruthlessness of the enemy—he could not say, but it had haunted his dreams for weeks, crouched in corners, and waited for him at the head of the stairs. Later he had tried to explain to friends the horrors that may lie in the concrete symbolisms and personifications of a cartoon if interpreted naively by a child, but had been unable to get his idea across.

The conductor growled out the name of a downtown street, and once again he lost himself in the crowd, finding relief in the never-ceasing movement, the brushing of shoulders against his own. But as the time clock emitted its delayed musical bong! and he turned to stick his card in the rack, the girl at the desk looked up, and remarked, "Aren't you going to punch in for your dog, too?"

"My dog?"

"Well, it was there just a second ago. Came in right behind you, looking as if it owned you—I mean you owned it." She giggled briefly through her nose. "One of Mrs. Montmorency's mastiffs come to inspect conditions among the working class, I presume."

He continued to stare at her blankly. "A joke," she explained patiently, and returned to her work.

"I've got to get a grip on myself," he found himself muttering tritely as the elevator lowered him noiselessly to the basement.

He kept repeating it as he hurried to the locker room, left his coat and lunch, gave his hair a quick careful brushing, hurried again through the still-empty aisles, and slipped in behind the socks-and-handkerchiefs counter. "It's just nerves. I'm not crazy. But I've got to get a grip on myself."

"Of course you're crazy. Don't you know that talking to yourself and not noticing anybody is the first symptom of insanity?"

Gertrude Rees had stopped on her way over to neckties. Light brown hair, painstakingly waved and ordered, framed a serious not-too-pretty face.

"Sorry," he murmured. "I'm jittery." What else could you say? Even to Gertrude.

She grimaced sympathetically. Her hand slipped across the counter to squeeze his for a moment.

But even as he watched her walk away, his hands automatically setting out the display boxes, the new question was furiously hammering in his brain. What else could you say? What words could you use to explain it? Above all, to whom could you tell it? A dozen names printed themselves in his mind and were as quickly discarded.

One remained. Tom Goodsell. He would tell Tom. Tonight, after the first-aid class.

Shoppers were already filtering into the basement. "He wears size eleven, madam? Yes, we have some new patterns. These are silk and lisle." But their ever-increasing numbers gave him no sense of security. Crowding the aisles, they became shapes behind which something might hide. He was continually peering past them. A little child who wandered behind the counter and pushed at his knee, gave him a sudden fright.

Lunch came early for him. He arrived at the locker room in time to catch hold of Gertrude Rees as she retreated uncertainly from the dark doorway.

"Dog," she gasped. "Huge one. Gave me an awful start. Talk about jitters! Wonder where he could have come from? Watch out. He looked nasty."

But David, impelled by sudden recklessness born of fear and shock, was already inside and switching on the light.

"No dog in sight," he told her.

"You're crazy. It must be there." Her face, gingerly poked through the doorway, lengthened in surprise. "But I tell you I—Oh, I guess it must have pushed out through the other door."

He did not tell her that the other door was bolted.

"I suppose a customer brought it in," she rattled on nervously. "Some of them can't seem to shop unless they've got a pair of Russian wolfhounds. Though that kind usually keeps out of the bargain basement. I suppose we ought to find it before we eat lunch. It looked dangerous."

But he hardly heard her. He had just noticed that his locker was open and his overcoat dragged down on the floor. The brown paper bag containing his lunch had been torn open and the contents rummaged through, as if an animal had been nosing at it. As he stopped, he saw that there were greasy, black stains on the sandwiches, and a familiar stale stench rose to his nostrils.

That night he found Tom Goodsell in a nervous, expansive mood. The latter had been called up and would start for camp in a week. As they sipped coffee in the empty little restaurant, Tom poured out a flood of talk about old times. David would have been able to listen better, had not the uncertain, shadowy shapes outside the window been continually distracting his attention. Eventually he found an appropriate opportunity to turn the conversation down the channels which absorbed his mind.

"The supernatural beings of a modern city?" Tom answered, seeming to find nothing out of the way in the question. "Sure, they'd be different from the ghosts of yesterday. Each culture creates its own ghosts. Look, the Middle Ages built cathedrals, and pretty soon there were little gray shapes gliding around at night to talk with the gargoyles. Same thing ought to happen to us, with our skyscrapers and factories." He spoke eagerly, with all his old poetic flair, as if he'd just been meaning to discuss this very matter. He would talk about anything tonight. "I'll tell you how it works, Dave. We begin by denying all the old haunts and superstitions. Why shouldn't we? They belong to the era of cottage and castle. They can't take root in the new environment. Science goes materialistic, proving that there isn't anything in the universe except tiny bundles of energy. As if, for that matter, a tiny bundle of energy mightn't mean anything.

"But wait, that's just the beginning. We go on inventing and discovering and organizing. We cover the earth with huge structures. We pile them together in great heaps that make old Rome and Alexandria and Babylon seem almost toy-towns by comparison. The new environment, you see, is forming."

David stared at him with incredulous fascination, profoundly disturbed. This was not at all what he had expected or hoped for—this almost telepathic prying into his most hidden fears. He had wanted to talk about these things— yes—but in a skeptical reassuring way. Instead, Tom sounded almost serious. David started to speak, but Tom held up his finger for silence, aping the gesture of a schoolteacher.

"Meanwhile, what's happening inside each one of us? I'll tell you. All sorts of inhibited emotions are accumulating. Fear is accumulating. Horror is accumulating. A new kind of awe of the mysteries of the universe is accumulating. A psychological environment is forming, along with the physical one. Wait, let me finish. Our culture becomes ripe for infection. From somewhere. It's just like a bacteriologist's culture—I didn't intend the pun—when it gets to the right temperature and consistency for supporting a colony of germs. Similarly, our culture suddenly spawns a horde of demons. And, like germs, they have a peculiar affinity for our culture. They're unique. They fit in. You wouldn't find the same kind any other time or place.

"How would you know when the infection had taken place? Say, you're taking this pretty seriously, aren't you? Well, so am I, maybe. Why, they'd haunt us, terrorize us, try to rule us. Our fears would be their fodder. A parasite-host relationship. Supernatural symbiosis. Some of us—the sensitive ones—would notice them sooner than others. Some of us might see them without knowing what they were. Others might know about them without seeing them. Like me, eh?"

"What was that? I didn't catch your remark. Oh, about werewolves. Well, that's a pretty special question, but tonight I'd take a crack at anything. Yes, I think there'd be werewolves among our demons, but they wouldn't be much like the old ones. No nice clean fur, white teeth and shining eyes. Oh, no. Instead you'd get some nasty hound that wouldn't surprise you if you saw it nosing at a garbage pail or crawling out from under a truck. Frighten and terrorize you, yes. But surprise, no. It would fit into the environment. Look as if it belonged in a city and smell the same. Because of the twisted emotions that would be its food, your emotions and mine. A matter of diet."

Tom Goodsell chuckled loudly and lit another cigarette. But David only stared at the scarred counter. He realized he couldn't tell Tom what had happened this morning—or this noon. Of course, Tom would immediately scoff and be skeptical. But that wouldn't get around the fact that Tom had already agreed—agreed in partial jest perhaps, but still agreed. And Tom himself confirmed this, when in a more serious friendlier voice, he said:

"Oh, I know I've talked a lot of rot tonight, but still, you know, the way things are, there's something to it. At least, I can't express my feelings any other way."

They shook hands at the corner, and David rode the surging streetcar home through a city whose every bolt and stone seemed subtly infected, whose every noise carried shuddering overtones. His mother was waiting up for him, and after he had wearily argued with her about getting more rest and seen her off to bed, he lay sleepless himself, all through the night, like a child in a strange house, listening to each tiny noise and watching intently each changing shape taken by the shadows.

That night nothing shouldered through the door or pressed its muzzle against the windowpane.

Yet he found that it cost him an effort to go down to the department store next morning, so conscious was he of the thing's presence in the faces and forms, the structures and machines around him. It was as if he were forcing himself into the heart of a monster. Detestation of the city grew within him. As yesterday, the crowded aisles seemed only hiding places, and he avoided the locker room. Gertrude Rees remarked sympathetically on his fatigued look, and he took the opportunity to invite her out that evening. Of course, he told himself while they sat watching the movie, she wasn't very close to him. None of the girls had been close to him—a not-very-competent young man tied down to the task of supporting parents whose little reserve of money had long ago dribbled away. He had dated them for a while, talked to them, told them his beliefs and ambitions, and then one by one they had drifted off to marry other men. But that did not change the fact that he needed the wholesomeness Gertrude could give him.

And as they walked home through the chilly night, he found himself talking inconsequentially and laughing at his own jokes. Then, as they turned to one another in the shadowy vestibule and she lifted her lips, he sensed her features altering queerly, lengthening. "A funny sort of light here," he thought as he took her in his arms. But the thin strip of fur on her collar grew matted and oily under his touch, her fingers grew hard and sharp against his back, he felt her teeth pushing out against her lips, and then a sharp, pricking sensation as of icy needles.

Blindly he pushed away from her, then saw—and the sight stopped him dead—that she had not changed at all or that whatever change had been was now gone.

"What's the matter, dear?" he heard her ask startedly. "What's happened? What's that you're mumbling? Changed, you say? What's changed? Infected with it? What do you mean? For heaven's sake, don't talk that way. You've done it to me, you say? Done what?" He felt her hand on his arm, a soft hand now. "No, you're not crazy. Don't think of such things. But you're neurotic and maybe a little batty. For heaven's sake, pull yourself together."

"I don't know what happened to me," he managed to say, in his right voice again. Then, because he had to say something more: "My nerves all jumped, like someone had snapped them."

He expected her to be angry, but she seemed only puzzledly sympathetic, as if she liked him but had become afraid of him, as if she sensed something wrong in him beyond her powers of understanding or repair.

"Do take care of yourself," she said doubtfully. "We're all a little crazy now and then, I guess. My nerves get like wires too. Good night."

He watched her disappear up the stairs. Then he turned and ran.

At home his mother was waiting up again, close to the hall radiator to catch its dying warmth, the inevitable shapeless bathrobe wrapped about her. Because of a new thought that had come to the forefront of his brain, he avoided her embrace and, after a few brief words, hurried off toward his room. But she followed him down the hall.

"You're not looking at all well, David," she told him anxiously, whispering because father might be asleep. "Are you sure you're not getting flu again? Don't you think you should see the doctor tomorrow?" Then she went on quickly to another subject, using that nervously apologetic tone with which he was so familiar. "I shouldn't bother you with it, David, but you really must be more careful of the bedclothes. You'd laid something greasy on the coverlet and there were big, black stains."

He was pushing open the bedroom door. Her words halted his hand only for an instant. How could you avoid the thing by going one place rather than another?

"And one thing more," she added, as he switched on the lights. "Will you try to get some cardboard tomorrow to black out the windows? They're out of it at the stores around here and the radio says we should be ready."

"Yes, I will. Good night, Mother."

"Oh, and something else," she persisted, lingering uneasily just beyond the door. "That really must be a dead rat in the walls. The smell keeps coming in waves. I spoke to the real estate agent, but he hasn't done anything about it. I wish you'd speak to him."

"Yes. Good night, Mother."

He waited until he heard her door softly close. He lit a cigarette and slumped down on the bed to try and think as clearly as he could about something to which everyday ideas could not be applied.

Question One (and he realized with an ironic twinge that it sounded melodramatic enough for a dime novel): Was Gertrude Rees what might be called, for want of a better term, a werewolf? Answer: Almost certainly not, in any ordinary sense of the word. What had momentarily come to her had been something he had communicated to her. It had happened because of his presence. And either his own shock had interrupted the transformation or else Gertrude Rees had not proved a suitable vehicle of incarnation for the thing.

Question Two: Might he not communicate the thing to some other person? Answer: Yes. For a moment his thinking paused, as there swept before his mind's eye kaleidoscopic visions of the faces which might, without warning, begin to change in his presence: His mother, his father, Tom Goodsell, the prim-mouthed real estate agent, a customer at the store, a panhandler who would approach him on a rainy night.

Question Three: Was there any escape from the thing? Answer: No. And yet—there was one bare possibility. Escape from the city. The city had bred the thing; might it not be chained to the city? It hardly seemed to be a reasonable possibility; how could a supernatural entity be tied down to one locality? And yet—he stepped quickly to the window and, after a moment's hesitation, jerked it up. Sounds which had been temporarily blotted out by his thinking now poured past him in quadrupled volume, mixing together discordantly like instruments tuning up for some titanic symphony—the racking surge of streetcar and elevated, the coughing of a locomotive in the yards, the hum of tires on asphalt and the growl of engines, the mumbling of radio voices, the faint mournful note of distant horns. But now they were no longer separate sounds. They all issued from one cavernous throat—a single moan, infinitely penetrating, infinitely menacing. He slammed down the window and put his hands to his ears. He switched out the lights and threw himself on the bed, burying his head in the pillows. Still the sound came through. And it was then he realized that ultimately, whether he wanted to or not, the thing would drive him from the city. The moment would come when the sound would begin to penetrate too deeply, to reverberate too unendurably in his ears.

The sight of so many faces, trembling on the brink of an almost unimaginable change, would become too much for him. And he would leave whatever he was doing and go away.

That moment came a little after four o'clock next afternoon. He could not say what sensation it was that, adding its straw-weight to the rest, drove him to take the step. Perhaps it was a heaving movement in the rack of dresses two counters away; perhaps it was the snoutlike appearance momentarily taken by a crumpled piece of cloth. Whatever it was, he slipped from behind the counter without a word, leaving a customer to mutter indignantly, and walked up the stairs and out into the street, moving almost like a sleepwalker yet constantly edging from side to side to avoid any direct contact with the crowd engulfing him. Once in the street, he took the first car that came by, never noting its number, and found himself an empty place in the corner of the front platform.

With ominous slowness at first, then with increasing rapidity the heart of the city was left behind. A great gloomy bridge spanning an oily river was passed over, and the frowning cliffs of the buildings grew lower. Warehouses gave way to factories, factories to apartment buildings, apartment buildings to dwellings which were at first small and dirty white, then large and mansionlike but very much decayed, then new and monotonous in their uniformity. People of different economic status and racial affiliation filed in and emptied out as the different strata of the city were passed through. Finally the vacant lots began to come, at first one by one, then in increasing numbers, until the houses were spaced out two or three to a block.

"End of the line," sang out the conductor, and without hesitation David swung down from the platform and walked on in the same direction that the streetcar had been going. He did not hurry. He did not lag. He moved as an automaton that had been wound up and set going, and will not stop until it runs down.

The sun was setting smokingly red in the west. He could not see it because of a tree-fringed rise ahead, but its last rays winked at him from the windowpanes of little houses blocks off to the right and left, as if flaming lights had been lit inside. As he moved they flashed on and off like signals. Two blocks further on the sidewalk ended, and he walked down the center of a muddy lane. After passing a final house, the lane also came to an end, giving way to a narrow dirt path between high weeds. The path led up the rise and through the fringe of trees. Emerging on the other side, he slowed his pace and finally stopped, so bewilderingly fantastic was the scene spread out before him. The sun had set, but high cloud banks reflected its light, giving a spectral glow to the landscape.

Immediately before him stretched the equivalent of two or three empty blocks, but beyond that began a strange realm that seemed to have been plucked from another climate and another geological system and set down here outside the city. There were strange trees and shrubs, but, most striking of all, great uneven blocks of reddish stone which rose from the earth at unequal intervals and culminated in a massive central eminence fifty or sixty feet high.

As he gazed, the light drained from the landscape, as if a cloak had been flipped over the earth, and in the sudden twilight there rose from somewhere in the region ahead a faint howling, mournful and sinister, but in no way allied to the other howling that had haunted him day and night. Once again he moved forward, but now impulsively toward the source of the new sound.

A small gate in a high wire fence pushed open, giving him access to the realm of rocks. He found himself following a gravel path between thick shrubs and trees. At first it seemed quite dark, in contrast to the open land behind him. And with every step he took, the hollow howling grew closer. Finally the path turned abruptly around a shoulder of rock, and he found himself at the sound's source.

A ditch of rough stone about eight feet wide and of similar depth separated him from a space overgrown with short, brownish vegetation and closely surrounded on the other three sides by precipitous, rocky walls in which were the dark mouths of two or three caves. In the center of the open space were gathered a half-dozen white-furred canine figures, their muzzles pointing toward the sky, giving voice to the mournful cry that had drawn him here.

It was only when he felt the low iron fence against his knees and made out the neat little sign reading, ARCTIC WOLVES, that he realized where he must be—in the famous zoological gardens which he had heard about but never visited, where the animals were kept in as nearly natural conditions as was feasible. Looking around, he noted the outlines of two or three low inconspicuous buildings, and some distance away he could see the form of a uniformed guard silhouetted against a patch of dark sky. Evidently he had come in after hours and through an auxiliary gate that should have been locked.

Swinging around again, he stared with casual curiosity at the wolves. The turn of events had the effect of making him feel stupid and bewildered, and for a long time he pondered dully as to why he should find these animals unalarming and even attractive.

Perhaps it was because they were so much a part of the wild, so little of the city. That great brute there, for instance, the biggest of the lot, who had come forward to the edge of the ditch to stare back at him. He seemed an incarnation of primitive strength. His fur so creamy white—well, perhaps not so white; it seemed darker than he had thought at first, streaked with black—or was that due to the fading light? But at least his eyes were clear and clean, shining faintly like jewels in the gathering dark. But no, they weren't clean; their reddish gleam was thickening, scumming over, until they looked more like two tiny peepholes in the walls of a choked furnace. And why hadn't he noticed before that the creature was obviously malformed? And why should the other wolves draw away from it and snarl as if afraid?

Then the brute licked its black tongue across its greasy jowls, and from its throat came a faint familiar growl that had in it nothing of the wild, and David Lashley knew that before him crouched the monster of his dreams, finally made flesh and blood.

With a choked scream he turned and fled blindly down the gravel path that led between thick shrubs to the little gate, fled in panic across empty blocks, stumbling over the uneven ground and twice falling. When he reached the fringe of trees he looked back, to see a low, lurching form emerge from the gate. Even at this distance he could tell that the eyes were those of no animal.

It was dark in the trees, and dark in the lane beyond. Ahead the street lamps glowed, and there were lights in the houses. A pang of helpless terror gripped him when he saw there was no streetcar waiting, until he realized— and the realization was like the onset of insanity—that nothing whatever in the city promised him refuge. This—everything that lay ahead—was the thing's hunting ground. It was driving him in toward its lair for the kill.

Then he ran, ran with the hopeless terror of a victim in the arena, of a rabbit loosed before greyhounds, ran until his sides were walls of pain and his gasping throat seemed aflame, and then still ran. Over mud, dirt, and brick, and then onto the endless sidewalks. Past the neat suburban dwellings which in their uniformity seemed like monoliths lining some avenue of Egypt. The streets were almost empty, and those few people he passed stared at him as at a madman.

Brighter lights came into view, a corner with two or three stores. There he paused to look back. For a moment he saw nothing. Then it emerged from the shadows a block behind him, loping unevenly with long strides that carried forward with a rush, its matted fur shining oilily under a street lamp. With a croaking sob he turned and ran on.

The thing's howling seemed suddenly to increase a thousandfold, becoming a pulsating wail, a screaming ululation that seemed to blanket the whole city with sound. And as that demoniac screeching continued, the lights in the houses began to go out one by one. Then the streetlights vanished in a rush, and an approaching streetcar was blotted out, and he knew that the sound did not come altogether or directly from the thing. This was the long-predicted blackout.

He ran on with arms outstretched, feeling rather than seeing the intersections as he approached them, misjudging his step at curbs, tripping and falling flat, picking himself up to stagger on half stunned. His diaphragm contracted to a knot of pain that tied itself tighter and tighter. Breath rasped like a file in his throat. There seemed no light in the whole world, for the clouds had gathered thicker and thicker ever since sunset. No light, except those twin points of dirty red in the blackness behind.

A solid edge of darkness struck him down, inflicting pain on his shoulder and side. He scrambled up. Then a second solid obstacle in his path smashed him full in the face and chest. This time he did not rise. Dazed, tortured by exhaustion, motionless, he waited its approach.

First a padding of footsteps, with the faint scraping of claws on cement. Then a snuffling. Then a sickening stench. Then a glimpse of red eyes. And then the thing was upon him, its weight pinning him down, its jaws thrusting at his throat. Instinctively his hand went up, and his forearm was clamped by teeth whose icy sharpness stung through the layers of cloth, while a foul oily fluid splattered his face.

At that moment light flooded them, and he was aware of a malformed muzzle retreating into the blackness, and of weight lifted from him. Then silence and cessation of movement. Nothing, nothing at all—except the light flooding down. As consciousness and sanity teetered in his brain, his eyes found the source of light, a glaring white disk only a few feet away. A flashlight, but nothing visible in the blackness behind it. For what seemed an eternity, there was no change in the situation—himself supine and exposed upon the ground in the unwavering circle of light.

Then a voice from the darkness, the voice of a man paralyzed by supernatural fear. "God, God, God," over and over again. Each word dragged out with prodigious effort.

An unfamiliar sensation stirred in David, a feeling almost of security and relief.

"You—saw it then?" he heard issue from his own dry throat. "The hound? the—wolf?"

"Hound? Wolf?" The voice from behind the flashlight was hideously shaken. "It was nothing like that. It was—" Then the voice broke, became earthly once more. "Good grief, man, we must get you inside."

# PART FIVE

# The Victimized Werewolf

The word victim *is today frequently associated with abuse. One of the worst kinds of abuse is by a person infected with AIDS deliberately inflicting a victim with the virus. Since infection comes through blood contact, the unwary victim is doomed. In this section lycanthropy falls into the disease category: two unwilling victims are infected by a deliberate werewolf attack and are metamorphosed into werewolves. The prognosis is death.*

*Lycanthropy, like all diseases, has its strategies. It infects its victims with murderous impulses that cannot be controlled or cured. The victims become killers, even though they abhor killing. They have panic attacks about killing someone they love. Those who love the werewolf victims watch in horror as the disease turns their loved ones into voracious predators.*

*In earlier medical treatises, lycanthropy (however it was contracted) was regarded as a disease with a specific diagnosis and with a number of more or less successful remedies. The seventh-century Alexandrian physician, Paulos Aigina, for example, prescribed baths, purging, opening of a vein, control of diet to alleviate the suffering of the werewolf, and opium rubbed on the patient's nostrils to insure uninterrupted sleep (since werewolves did most of their hunting at night).*

*Of the two werewolves in this section, one is a young male who becomes a werewolf when he is bitten by an old male werewolf, and the other is a young Teuton male in medieval Britain who carries lycanthropy in his genes. Both are victims. One is blessed with a cure; the other is not. For both of them, the disease harms the body and inflicts desolation on the soul.*

*Derleth and Schorer's story takes place in a hunting lodge in Upper Michigan where a brother and a sister are vacationing. A menacing man lives deep in the woods, and a wolf threatens the small community where no wolves have been seen for many years. People in the community are suspicious about the connection between the two. In the full moon the wolf kills cattle, and in one full moon he bites the young male vacationer, inflicting on him severe lacerations and contaminating his blood. But this is no ordinary wolf and no ordinary wolf bite. The wolf is a werewolf, and once the blood of the old wolf has been transfused into the young man's veins, the victim suffers the symptoms and effects of lycanthropy.*

*Each night the young werewolf joins the old werewolf in his killings; each day the victim becomes more emaciated physically and more disturbed mentally. What is unusual about this* victimized werewolf is that he is not only aware of his metamorphosis, but that he remembers what he has done. Deep in his consciousness he is repelled by the loss of his humanity. Although he is powerless to overcome the blood lust that penetrates his soul in the full moon, upon restoration by day he despises himself for killing animals, for slitting their throats and licking up their blood, and for devouring their flesh. Appealing to his sister to help him, he pleads with her to tie him up each evening before he metamorphoses. The degradation accompanying the disease almost destroys both victim and sister. Neither is equipped to find a cure.

Help and hope come from the outside. The narrator, who is visiting this region, is puzzled by the reclusiveness of his neighbors. Attempting to be friendly, he is rebuffed by the sister when he knocks at their door. Peering through a crack in the curtain, he is shocked to see a huge wolf tied up in the corner of the room. He knows instinctively that the wolf is the metamorphosed brother. The sister finally comes in desperation to the narrator for help. The only cure is to kill the old werewolf with a silver bullet. The narrator goes into town, has a silver bullet fashioned, and returns to the cabin. When the old werewolf skulks around the cabin howling for the young werewolf to join him, the narrator shoots and kills the old werewolf. The brother is cured, the disease eradicated by the death of the virulent carrier.

Field's young victim, Harold, has inherited the disease of metamorphosis from his cruel grandfather, Siegfried the Teuton. Since this disease is genetic, the grandson has no weapons against periodically becoming a marauding werewolf, killing cattle and humans, and destroying the tranquillity of the community. A victim werewolf, Harold can find no remedies for his genetically inherited lycanthropy.

Meanwhile, a werewolf is ravaging the community: "Wheresoever he went he attacked and devoured mankind, spreading terror and desolation round about, and the dream readers said that the earth would not be freed from the werewolf until some man offered himself a voluntary sacrifice to the monster's rage." As the feast of Ste. AElfreda approaches, Harold explains to the lovely Yseult that he must travel to Normandy upon a mission so he cannot attend the feast. Not revealing to her that he is the werewolf and that he will be in the grove killing as many as he can, he pleads with her not to go. Before parting and saying his last good-bye, Harold gives Siegfried's magic spear to Yseult, the only weapon that can kill the werewolf and eradicate the disease, and he instructs her to use the spear should the werewolf attack in the sacred grove.

The night of the meeting arrives, and the grove is filled with revelers. Suddenly the werewolf appears, killing as many people as he can. They run for their lives. Yseult, however, has no choice but to stay and throw the spear at the werewolf. A supernatural force carries the spear to the heart of the werewolf and kills him.

As the savior of the community, Yseult insists upon finding Harold and telling him *about how she killed the werewolf with his spear. She finds him sleeping peacefully in his bed, except that his heart has been pierced with a spear and his body is covered with blood. He is at peace because he is dead. Harold's death is a redemptive act—he has supplied the weapon that will release him from his genetic lycanthropy; and because he will have no offspring, the genes will not be transmitted to another unfortunate victim. Though dead, he is no longer victim but victor.*

# The Woman at Loon Point

AUGUST W. DERLETH (1909–1971)
AND MARK SCHORER (1908–1977)

I MET LARAMIE SHAW not long after my arrival at my father's hunting lodge at the base of Loon Point in Upper Michigan last autumn. Three days after, to be exact. Even before that, I had heard that long-deserted Loon Lodge was inhabited, and the natives of Lacroit village, south of my father's cabin, had spoken of the Shaws—"that Laramie, who walks as if she's scared of something," and "that young man, Jim, who's gettin' sicker and sicker instead of better, as he ought." And they spoke of how the Shaws had never been seen either hunting or fishing, but kept to their lodge, where they had been ever since spring. The inhabitants of Loon Lodge were, in fact, a local mystery.

I had been walking along the shore of the Point most of that afternoon, and admit hoping that I might meet at least one of the Shaws. I had kept to the fairly well-defined path leading along the lake shore, and had stepped off it only for a few moments to examine a dead bird on the beach, when I heard quick footsteps behind me. I swung around and saw the girl coming out of the forest. She caught sight of my movement and stopped, instinctively taking a step backward. Her eyes were dark and startled and filled with sudden fear. Her cheeks were flushed with the wind, but the rest of her face, except for her large and brooding mouth, was astonishingly pale. She wore an old hunting jacket, and beneath this a plain black dress, the skirt of which was flapping around her legs in the wind. In an instant her eyes dropped, the fear went out of them, and she passed me without a nod, despite my raising my cap to her. I watched her until she vanished around a bend not far away.

In *Weird Tales* (December 1936).

Why had she been afraid?

That night I went into the village to find out more about the Shaws. But my intentions were sidetracked by a topic which, though it had been current for some time, was still far more important to the natives gathered in the village store than the slight mystery of the Shaws.

For some time the villagers had been aware of a wolf in the vicinity. Though the animal had appeared but seldom, it had made several efforts to attack different natives. It had been shot at, of course, and though one woodsman swore that he had wounded the beast, it had been seen loping about subsequent to the shot. Wolves had long been uncommon in northern Michigan, and for years in the immediate past no wolf had been seen near Lacroit. The occasion for the recurrence of this oft-discussed topic that evening was the report that a hunter had spied the beast the previous night on Loon Point, had, indeed, heard it howl, and had shot at it before it had made off into the underbrush. Only when the villagers had talked themselves out was I able to introduce the topic of the Shaws.

But if they had been disappointed in my inability to contribute anything to their wolf-lore, I was much more so in the scant information they were able to give me. No one knew where the Shaws had come from, though the majority of them thought Chicago. They had arrived in late April, both in good health and excellent spirits, and had taken the lodge for two months, meaning to return to the city at the end of that time. It was the girl who had started the story of the wolf's presence by arriving in the village one morning early for a doctor, saying that her brother, who had left Loon Lodge just before dawn, had been attacked and severely lacerated by a wolf. The doctor later admitted that the young man had certainly been bitten by an animal of some kind.

From that time on the boy was seen no more, though before that he had been out quite often, usually alone, but sometimes with a tramp-like individual who apparently lived some distance along the isolated coast above Loon Point. The girl came into Lacroit only when it was absolutely necessary, and struck everyone as looking afraid—glancing over her shoulder all the time, in a strained way, and nervous. When the two months had passed, Laramie Shaw had appeared in Lacroit and had taken Loon Lodge indefinitely. That was the substance of what I learned.

Yet I was curiously disturbed by the concluding aside of the storekeeper's wife—"Thet Shaw girl used to whistle and sing all the time—now she don't.

She don't even smile like she used to. I c'n tell you it ain't a small thing'll make a woman change like that."

WHEN I LEFT Lacroit that night, my mind was filled with thoughts of the Shaws. The chill autumn wind was whistling through the Point's tall pines, and not far away the loons laughed weirdly from the lake. I was in a hurry to reach my lodge, now that darkness had come down in earnest. The distance I had to travel was two miles, and I had gone over three-fourths of the way, when I heard behind me the distinct sound of footsteps. Could—my heart leaped unaccountably—could Laramie Shaw have been out, in the village, perhaps? I stopped to wait. Immediately the footsteps stopped, but not before I had heard them more distinctly. At the same moment I felt myself warned by blind instinct to press on, and my momentary hearing of the walker behind me acquainted me with the fact that it was no human being that followed; for the footsteps were padding, stealthy, and slunk through the dry leaves like those of some predatory beast.

I turned and ran wildly for the lodge, which was still lost in the blackness ahead. I think that perhaps the thing that saved me was the presence of a screened veranda; for I had no sooner flung myself beyond the screen than I saw two eyes glaring balefully at me from the path I had just quitted, and when I lit one of my lamps and held it aloft, I saw the clearly outlined figure of a gigantic wolf staring at me from immediately beyond the enclosing screen! As I watched, it turned and slunk away into the woods.

Next morning the wolf had taken a secondary place in my mind, and the Shaws had again come forward. If my curiosity must be satisfied, why not go boldly to Loon Lodge and declare myself a recent neighbor come to introduce himself? Certainly that seemed much the best plan.

Consequently, I walked to the end of the Point that morning. But I knocked on the door of Loon Lodge in vain; for no one answered. I was certain that one of the heavy curtains which still strangely covered the windows moved a little, as though someone peering out had disturbed it. Accordingly, I knocked louder; still no one replied. I went home more curious than before.

That night, which was overcast by lowering clouds driven across the sky by a booming wind, I determined to force a meeting with the Shaws. The restlessness to which I had been a prey since my futile visit of the morning had grown so that sleep was out of the question. The book I tried to read failed to hold my interest; I was thinking of Laramie Shaw and her frightened eyes, and I saw her face on every page I read. I gave up at last, and set out for Loon Lodge.

The curtains were drawn over the windows of the lodge at the end of the Point, but I could see that a light burned in the cabin; for the curtains were frequently broken by slits and tiny holes through which light glowed. I moved carefully forward, intending to take the Shaws by surprise with a sudden assault upon their door. But as I passed a window I paused. There might be no harm in looking momentarily into the room, for if I rapped, the light might be put out and I might go again unanswered.

I stooped down and looked into the room through a rent in the curtain—and had to clutch at the window ledge to keep from falling back in amazement at what I saw within.

Laramie Shaw was standing in the center of the room, disheveled and distraught, and before her was an animal chained to one wall. For an instant I took the animal to be a large and shaggy police dog, and then I saw and recognized it for what it actually was—*a huge timber wolf!*

I felt immediately that there was something deeply wrong about what I saw. The brute's slavering fangs, its struggles to escape from the binding cords and chain were harmless; for the chain was of steel and the cord was extremely stout. It was as I looked at the rope that I saw how peculiarly the animal was bound—its forelegs tied securely to its chest, the rope having been twisted round and round the body, though surprisingly loose, despite its secureness; its hind legs stretched out and tied together, free of its body. The position in which this manner of binding left the animal was more than strange, but even more amazing was the patent fact that somehow this ferocious beast had been taken alive—and by a woman aided solely by a sick brother!

Abruptly I thought of Jim Shaw. He was not in the room. And if he were sleeping elsewhere in the cabin, surely it was only a miracle that the disturbance made by the brute had not awakened him.

Laramie Shaw stepped suddenly away from the beast, and leaned weakly against the table. Her face came into sight, and I saw that her eyes were still haunted by that strange look of fear I had first seen in the forest. But I saw also a look of repugnance that was not loathing, and a distinct suggestion of pity for the animal at her feet.

The wolf stirred and began to struggle violently.

At that moment a sound from the blackness of the surrounding forest broke into my puzzled thoughts, cutting through the still weirdly recurring laughter of the loons on the lake. It was the call of a timber wolf, a long drawn-out howl echoing through the woods, and from inside Loon Lodge came a feeble answer.

I bent again and looked through the rent in the curtain. I saw the wolf straining futilely at the binding cords. Laramie Shaw stood for a moment waiting; then she slumped into a chair and put her head in her hands. Her shoulders began to shudder—she was weeping!

The call of the wolf sounded again from the forest. I stood for a moment undecided. If the beast threatened to attack me I had an ideal excuse for getting into Loon Lodge, but I might be forced to break my way in. I had little time to consider, however, for the wolf was rapidly coming nearer, though I could now tell that it was approaching from the opposite side of the lodge. Abruptly I dodged away from the cabin and found the path, along which I ran, hoping that the animal would not follow.

Its cries receded into the distance, and I gathered that the animal was still at Loon Lodge. Could it be its mate that the Shaws had caught?

I HAD ALMOST REACHED my cabin, still running easily along the path, when I tripped and went sprawling. For a moment I lay motionless; then I turned cautiously and lit my cigarette lighter. I had tripped over the recently killed carcass of a rabbit. Its throat had been ripped open and its blood had evidently been drunk by the killer; for there were but few drops on the leaves covering the path. I thought at once of a weasel, but certainly no weasel would have ripped open the rabbit's throat as this had been torn. Was it possible that the wolf had paused on its way to Loon Lodge to kill this rabbit? But wolves, I knew, eat their kill.

I went on to my lodge, now doubly welcome after the strange experience I had undergone.

Despite my original intention of airing the Loon Lodge mystery in Lacroit next day, I said nothing about what I had seen. After a short stay in the village, I made my way back along the trail into the forest. I had gone perhaps half the distance to my lodge when I saw before me on the path an emaciated-looking man. He was obviously waiting for me, since he kept his eyes fixed on me.

As I came closer, I saw that he was shabbily dressed, though it was apparent that his clothes had at one time been good. His face held me—deep, black eyes, somehow seeming afire, pale mouth, bloodless cheeks, long stubble on his chin and neck, a heavy mustache on his upper lip. He took a step toward me as I came on, and I saw that he walked with a slight limp.

"I believe you're the young man who has the lodge at the base of the Point?" he said curtly, as I came up to him.

"I'm Jack Durfrey, yes," I said.

"I want a word with you," he went on. His voice had a suggestion of menace in it.

"Walk along?" I asked.

He shook his head. "It'll take only a moment," he went on. "I've seen you about Loon Lodge, and I happen to know that your attentions are unwelcome to the young lady there. I'll thank you to keep away from the Shaws' cabin hereafter."

For a moment I saw red. I controlled myself with an effort and shot back, "You? Who the devil are you to give orders to me?"

"My name," he said in a flat, disdainful voice, "is Henri Letellier. And that doesn't mean anything to you—and won't, unless I find you near Loon Lodge again."

What prevented me from striking out immediately I don't know. Before I could reply, Letellier had stepped back into the dense undergrowth fringing the trail. I took a tentative step forward, thought better of it, and went on my way, in mounting anger.

Almost at once after my return to my cabin, I made my way to Loon Lodge and hid myself in the dense bushes around the clearing in which the lodge stood. The cabin was still tightly closed, but a thin trail of smoke ascending from the chimney gave evidence of life.

I HAD NOT LONG to wait, for suddenly the door opened and a thin young man emerged into the sunlight. He was wearing trousers and an old dressing gown, which was swinging open. His face was pale and bloodless, and his lips were unhealthily gray. His eyes were dark and shone in such a fashion that I could not doubt that he was seriously ill. He stood for a moment leaning against the house, leaving the door ajar. Then he began to move around the lodge, and in a few moments he was lost to sight behind the building.

Then the door swung wide again, and Laramie Shaw came out. She looked much as she had looked the day before, except that she seemed more wan, and her eyes seemed darker. The morning wind from the lake blew at her black hair, which fell straight to her shoulders. With a slight intake of breath I noticed how beautiful she was. She stood looking uneasily around her, then suddenly called in a low quavering voice, "Jim! Oh, Jim!"

The young man came from behind the cabin, and the expression of relief on Laramie Shaw's face was immediate. She looked uneasily around, past him, her eyes embracing the encroaching woods; then she stood aside until her brother entered the cabin again. She followed him.

I crouched in hiding for a few moments more. Then I ventured into the clearing and approached the cabin. There was no reply to my assault on the door of Loon Lodge, but I saw the curtains quiver and knew that I was being watched.

For some time I stood undecided on the stoop, not only mystified but also slightly angered; then I doubled back and hid once more in the dense foliage, where I sat and watched the lodge.

It was some time before Laramie Shaw appeared. She opened the door cautiously and looked out across the clearing. For a few moments she stood framed in the doorway, her head thrown back, her eyes still suspicious. Then she went quickly around to the side of the lodge and began to gather kindling wood.

I left my hiding place and strode rapidly across to the cabin. Before the woman had time to start, I stood waiting, and there was no escape for her then. Slowly, rather thoughtfully, she advanced toward the door, a query on her face.

"You're Miss Shaw?" I asked.

She nodded and looked at me without emotion, waiting.

"I'm Jack Durfrey, your nearest neighbor."

"Yes," she said.

She was obviously reluctant to talk. I waited insistently, determined that she would speak to me. Presently I said, "I've been up to call before. Perhaps you were out, but I don't think so. If it had not been for someone who's apparently your guardian rather rudely warning me away from this place, I wouldn't have come again."

Suddenly she took interest. She looked sharply at me. "Guardian," she repeated. "Was it—?" Her face paled, suddenly, inexplicably.

"Henri Letellier," I said. "That's what he called himself."

She stepped back, dropping the wood she had gathered. For a moment I thought she was going to faint. A low moan escaped her lips. In a moment she had composed herself and was facing me again, defiantly.

Then I tried direct attack. "I want to help you, Miss Shaw," I said.

"What do you mean?" she asked immediately. "I'm not—we're not in need of help—I don't think you've a right to presume that."

I looked hard into her eyes, and she was almost immediately disconcerted.

"I want you to tell me a few things," I went on, "and perhaps I can help."

At this she was definitely disturbed and made an effort to get past me. I caught her arm.

"I saw you last night," I said abruptly.

A cry broke from her lips. She stood away at arm's length, her free hand covering her mouth. Her eyes were wide with unmistakable terror. With an effort she forced the fear from her eyes, brought her hand from her mouth, and attempted to smile.

"I don't think you could have seen me," she said in a low voice.

"Try to believe me," I said gently. "I saw you in your cabin with a bound wolf."

She could not disguise her fright, and yet attempted to laugh, succeeding only in sounding hysterical.

"Both my brother and I went to bed early last night," she said.

"I saw through a rent in the curtain," I persisted.

An angry flush crossed her face. "Go away, please," she said.

"Very well," I said, "but I'll return tonight—and shoot any wolf I see, whether inside the cabin or not."

A torrent of words fell from her lips. "No, no, please! You must not come back here again. Oh, it may be true—no, no, what am I saying? Of course it isn't true, it can't be! But there's a wolf in the forest. I've heard him. You must not be out when he runs. Promise me you won't come back here."

Her voice had gone low, husky, almost sobbing. Tears stood in her eyes. For a moment her emotion disconcerted me.

"I'm sorry," I said. "If you sincerely believe I can't help you, I won't come back."

I heard her breathe an almost inaudible "Thank you," and saw her disappear inside, closing the door behind her.

.     .     .

DESPITE MY PROMISE, I did return to the cabin that night. It had been dark for more than an hour when I arrived at Loon Lodge, but a light glowed from behind the curtains drawn over the windows. I went at once to the closest window, and discovered that the rent through which I had looked into the lodge on the previous night had been repaired. Indeed all the curtains had been carefully sewed and patched. Laramie Shaw obviously did not intend to allow me a second sight of what happened at night in the cabin.

But I heard the growling and struggling of the bound wolf inside; so I knew that it was there.

On the homeward path I heard again the call of the other wolf coming from the direction of Loon Lodge.

The next night there was a full moon. I took up my watch again, but once more failed utterly to learn anything new and was driven to my lodge by the approach of the other animal and my carelessness in bringing an unloaded weapon with me.

On the next two nights my watch was equally futile. But on the third night after the full moon, there was a slight change. The wolf was in the cabin, but not once did it cry out, not once did it struggle to escape. The wolf that haunted the surrounding forest called from afar, making no attempt to approach Loon Lodge. After that, the imprisoned animal became more and more quiet.

During this time, I saw nothing of the Shaws. I tried once again to call, but my knocks went unanswered. Nevertheless, I continued to watch the cabin, and as a result I discovered that the wolf inside became most violent in the week of the full moon, a violence common to all animals.

Eventually, I gave up, though the mystery that brooded over the Shaws lingered in my mind and irritated me by its presence. November had come, and soon I would be leaving again for home.

And then one day, in answer to a furious pounding on my front door shortly after the noon hour, I opened it on Laramie Shaw and looked into her frightened eyes. At once she brushed past me, and closed the door and latched it. Then she turned and faced me, her back to the door, her eyes wild and afraid.

"I've come," she said jerkily. "You were the only one I could go to. I've stood it so long—I can't anymore."

I saw that she was on the verge of collapse, and pushed forward a chair into which I urged her. Her face was the color of chalk. Her hands were clasped in her lap, her fingers twining together and together.

"I want to do anything I can to help you," I said.

SHE DID NOT ANSWER at once. She closed her eyes and leaned back; for an instant I thought she had fainted. But she had not; for presently, with visible effort, she forced herself to tell me of the horrible thing that was making her life a torture.

"Those things you said you saw in our lodge," she began slowly. "They were true. I don't know how to explain them."

She paused and looked helplessly at me. Then she began, at a different point, her voice hysterically hurried.

"We came here on a vacation. We had planned to stay for two months. Not long after our arrival, Jim made the acquaintance of an elderly man whom he met in the woods. Though not very well dressed, this man—you saw him, you told me he had warned you away from us—Henri Letellier, was intelligent and interesting. He had led a long life of vagabondage, and his narratives held Jim.

"One night we asked him into the lodge for supper with us. He ate nothing but meat, and as the meal progressed he got more and more nervous, and began to look around as if suspicious of something. His conduct alarmed me, and even Jim took notice. Then, suddenly, just as the sun was setting, he jumped up and ran from the house without a word of explanation. We were astounded, and naturally Jim went after him.

"Before Jim returned, night had set in, and a moon was glowing above the trees fringing the clearing. And then—with Jim nowhere in sight—I heard the unmistakable howl of a timber wolf from somewhere in the immediate vicinity! Only a split second later I heard Jim crashing through the underbrush, coming toward the lodge. I don't know what I feared, but I ran back into the cabin for Jim's gun.

"Only Providence could have caused me to do that; for when I got outside again, I saw Jim being flung to the ground under the attack of a gigantic timber wolf. I fired and missed, afraid of hitting Jim. But my shot didn't frighten the brute away. It slashed Jim cruelly, dangerously close to his neck. Then I fired again, and that time I struck it—in the leg, I think; for it jumped away and vanished in the forest in a moment.

"I ran to him. He lay moaning on the ground where he had been thrown. I got him into the lodge and bathed the wound and dressed it. Then I went for a doctor. He came and dressed Jim's wound anew, but seemed so incredulous about the scanty details I gave him that we didn't call him again. Fortunately, Jim seemed to be resting easily; so there was no need for the doctor again. Toward morning he developed a strange fever and became restless. I was anxious and became still more so when after a little while he began to make odd, delirious sounds. I bent to listen, and—oh, how can I tell it?—they were animal sounds, unhuman, guttural sounds, and even as I recognized them, there came from Jim's throat what was unmistakably *the low whine of an animal in pain!*"

She paused and covered her face with her hands. "Oh, I can't go on," she sobbed, "I can't—it's so horrible, so unbelievable—you'll think I'm mad."

"Please go on," I said in the most persuasive voice I could summon. I made no move to comfort her, feeling instinctively that she might resent it.

She looked up. "Perhaps you've guessed the frightful thing that happened. That man—Letellier—is a werewolf—a man doomed to become a beast at sundown, doomed to assume the shape of a savage wolf, a beast whose nourishment is the blood of animals and human beings! And his bite was so venomous, so accursed, that it had contaminated Jim, so that Jim, too, must inevitably change and become as Letellier!"

She looked at me with defiant eyes.

"Go on," I said in a tense voice. I did not want her to see any evidence of the turmoil in my mind. I had fleetingly thought that something had unsettled her mind; but too soon I saw that everything I had seen fitted into this inconceivable tale she was relating. Yet I could not easily believe.

"Jim knew," she went on. "He knew what to expect; for he had been transformed into a werewolf completely—he knew of the terrible blood lust that would come over him, knew that soon a nightly change of form would begin. He knew that somehow blood from Letellier's veins had entered his own, thus binding him to Letellier. And he felt that if he could be kept from tasting blood in any form for a long time, the spell could be weakened and broken.

"It was at Jim's demand that I tied and chained him the next night—and every night after." She shuddered. "I didn't want to do it, but Jim insisted. I can't describe my horror and loathing at the sight of the slow change that came over him that night—how before my eyes my brother became a savage beast!"

.    .    .

FOR A FEW MOMENTS she sat in silence that I did not break.

"He was worst in the week of the full moon," she began again. "Then the blood lust in his veins was strongest, and I had the most difficult time with him. It's the sixth month, now. Up to this time Letellier has appeared only on moonlit nights and howled for Jim just beyond the clearing. Jim says that if he can be shot and killed, the spell will be lifted from him by Letellier's death. I tried once or twice to shoot him, but he avoids me—and I'm not a good shot.

"I came to you, because today Letellier surprised me at the lodge—and threatened me. He knows that Jim is escaping him, and that I'm helping him. If I continue, he means to waylay me either when I go to Lacroit, or when I get water or wood. Before this he never came, though I saw him once by day shortly after he had attacked Jim in his nocturnal form. He was limping. I think my bullet caused that limp. That offers definite proof that bullets can and do affect these creatures. At least, a bullet can kill their bodies—but Jim says that it must be a silver bullet to free the evil spirit that animates Letellier. Will you help me?"

Once more she was on the verge of hysteria.

"You and I will do it together," I said.

"Thank you," she said simply.

"I'm going back to Loon Lodge with you at once," I went on, "and when I know you're safe inside, I'm going to Lacroit and have silver bullets made."

OUR JOURNEY BACK to Loon Lodge was rapid, for Laramie Shaw was worried about Jim, not knowing how much power Letellier might have over him by day. But Jim was safe. I left at once for Lacroit, warning Laramie under no conditions to leave the house, for since Letellier might have seen me and guessed that she had sought help, he might lie in wait for her at once.

The hour I spent in the village was nerve-racking. I could not help thinking of Laramie's danger, fearing that she might be drawn from the lodge despite my warning. And my fear for her safety was tinged by an entirely different emotion which the first sight of Laramie Shaw had implanted in my mind.

An old locksmith had no difficulty in making the bullets which were to fit into my pistol, the weapon I could use with the greatest degree of accuracy.

November dusk was threatening from the other side of the lake when I made my way along the shore, and already the early moon had risen. I ran, to reach Loon Lodge before night, but my haste was needless; for the sun was still lingering on the horizon when I emerged into the clearing. As I approached the lodge, I saw from the corner of one eye that someone was lurking in the bushes beyond, but as I spun around to look, he vanished. At the same moment, Laramie, who had seen me coming, threw open the door and with a glad cry ran out toward me.

I ran to her, took her arm almost roughly, and retreated into the cabin. "Someone in the bushes," I warned.

"I know," she said recklessly; "it's Letellier. He's been here ever since you left for Lacroit."

Jim sat in a low chair near the table. He was even paler than he had been when I had seen him a month before. Indeed, he seemed to be in the last stages of some incurable disease.

"Jim, this is Jack Durfrey. He's got the lodge at the base of the Point. He knows, and he's come to help."

Jim put out a weak, uncertain hand, muttering, "Glad to know you."

As I spoke to him, the sun slipped below the horizon, and abruptly, to my horror, a change came over Jim Shaw. He seemed to shrivel, to shrink back against the chair. His head appeared to lengthen, his hair became coarse, and on his shrinking hands appeared a grayish-black mat of hair. His clothes dropped from him. At the same instant a wolf howled from the dusk beyond the lodge.

Then I jerked open the door and fired at the skulking figure in the encroaching shadows. I missed, for the wolf that was Letellier vanished into the underbrush.

I heard Laramie's frightened cry behind me and whirled to see Jim, her brother, a wild animal, snarling and unbound, free for the first time. In the excitement of my coming, Laramie had forgotten to bind him! But, fortunately for both of us, the animal could not throw off the physical weakness of the man, and the wolf was accordingly handicapped. Again came a threatening howl from outside.

I had left the door standing partly open, an act of carelessness for which both Laramie and I might have paid with our souls. It was Laramie's warning cry that saved us. I turned just in time. For the wolf that was Letellier, seeing that Jim was unbound, that the door was open and our backs turned, had run swiftly across the clearing, and was launching itself at me even as I turned. I fired blindly, closing my eyes.

I think no sound was ever more welcome to my ears than the sound of the wolf's body crashing to the earth. With an effort I swung the door to and backed up against it.

I heard Laramie's low cry of joy, and in another moment witnessed the amazing transformation from wolf to man that brought Jim Shaw once more into human shape, a slow, horrible process, suggestive of long-lost, age-old horror.

Then Laramie Shaw sought my arms.

LARAMIE HAS SINCE BECOME my wife.

I admit that at first I had had doubts about her sanity, despite the way in which facts as I knew them fitted into her explanation. But all doubts I had were lost when Jim and I stepped from the lodge later that night to bury the thing that lay just beyond the door. For, though I had clearly shot a timber wolf, the thing we buried was the body of the man who called himself Henri Letellier!

# The Werewolf

EUGENE FIELD (1850–1895)

IN THE REIGN of Egbert the Saxon there dwelt in Britain a maiden named Yseult, who was beloved of all, both for her goodness and for her beauty. But, though many a youth came wooing her, she loved Harold only, and to him she plighted her troth.

Among the other youth of whom Yseult was beloved was Alfred, and he was sore angered that Yseult showed favor to Harold, so that one day Alfred said to Harold: "Is it right that old Siegfried should come from his grave and have Yseult to wife?" Then added he, "Prithee, good sir, why do you turn so white when I speak your grandsire's name?"

Then Harold asked, "What know you of Siegfried that you taunt me? What memory of him should vex me now?"

"We know and we know," retorted Alfred. "There are some tales told us by our grandmas we have not forgot."

So ever after that Alfred's words and Alfred's bitter smile haunted Harold by day and night.

Harold's grandsire, Siegfried the Teuton, had been a man of cruel violence. The legend said that a curse rested upon him, and that at certain times he was possessed of an evil spirit that wreaked its fury on mankind. But Siegfried had been dead full many years, and there was naught to mind the world of him save the legend and a cunning-wrought spear which he had from Brunehilde, the queen. This spear was such a weapon that it never lost its brightness, nor had its point been blunted. It hung in Harold's chamber, and it was the marvel among weapons of that time.

In *Second Book of Tales* (New York: Charles Scribner's Sons, 1911), 243–56.

Yseult knew that Alfred loved her, but she did not know of the bitter words which Alfred had spoken to Harold. Her love for Harold was perfect in its trust and gentleness. But Alfred had hit the truth: the curse of old Siegfried was upon Harold—slumbering a century; it had awakened in the blood of the grandson, and Harold knew the curse that was upon him, and it was this that seemed to stand between him and Yseult. But love is stronger than all else, and Harold loved.

Harold did not tell Yseult of the curse that was upon him, for he feared that she would not love him if she knew. Whensoever he felt the fire of the curse burning in his veins, he would say to her, "Tomorrow I hunt the wild boar in the uttermost forest," or, "Next week I go stag stalking among the distant northern hills." Even so it was that he ever made good excuse for his absence, and Yseult thought no evil things, for she was trustful; ay, though he went many times away and was long gone, Yseult suspected no wrong. So none beheld Harold when the curse was upon him in its violence.

Alfred alone bethought himself of evil things. " 'Tis passing strange," quoth he, "that ever and anon this gallant lover should quit our company and betake himself whither none knoweth. In sooth, 't will be well to have an eye on old Siegfried's grandson."

Harold knew that Alfred watched him zealously, and he was tormented by a constant fear that Alfred would discover the curse that was on him; but what gave him greater anguish was the fear that mayhap at some moment when he was in Yseult's presence, the curse would seize upon him and cause him to do great evil unto her, whereby she would be destroyed or her love for him would be undone forever. So Harold lived in terror, feeling that his love was hopeless, yet knowing not how to combat it.

Now, it befell in those times that the country round about was ravaged of a werewolf, a creature that was feared by all men howe'er so valorous. This werewolf was by day a man, but by night a wolf given to ravage and to slaughter, and having a charmed life against which no human agency availed aught. Wheresoever he went he attacked and devoured mankind, spreading terror and desolation round about, and the dream readers said that the earth would not be freed from the werewolf until some man offered himself a voluntary sacrifice to the monster's rage.

Now, although Harold was known far and wide as a mighty huntsman, he had never set forth to hunt the werewolf, and, strange enow, the werewolf never ravaged the domain while Harold was therein. Whereat Alfred marveled much, and oftentimes he said: "Our Harold is a wondrous huntsman. Who is like unto him in stalking the timid doe and in crippling the fleeing boar? But how passing well doth he time his absence from the haunts of the werewolf. Such valor beseemeth our young Siegfried."

Which being brought to Harold his heart flamed with anger, but he made no answer, lest he betray the truth he feared.

It happened so about that time that Yseult said to Harold, "Wilt thou go with me tomorrow even to the feast in the sacred grove?"

"That can I not do," answered Harold. "I am privily summoned here to Normandy upon a mission of which I shall some time tell thee. And I pray thee, on thy love for me, go not to the feast in the sacred grove without me."

"What say'st thou?" cried Yseult. "Shall I not go to the feast of Ste. AElfreda? My father would be sore displeased were I not there with the other maidens. 'T were greatest pity that I should despite his love thus."

"But do not, I beseech thee," Harold implored. "Go not to the feast of Ste. AElfreda in the sacred grove! And thou would thus love me, go not—see, thou my life, on my two knees I ask it!"

"How pale thou art," said Yseult, "and trembling."

"Go not to the sacred grove upon the morrow night," he begged.

Yseult marveled at his acts and at his speech. Then, for the first time, she thought him to be jealous—whereat she secretly rejoiced (being a woman).

"Ah," quoth she, "thou dost doubt my love," but when she saw a look of pain come on his face she added—as if she repented of the words she had spoken—"or dost thou fear the werewolf?"

Then Harold answered, fixing his eyes on hers, "Thou hast said it; it is the werewolf that I fear."

"Why dost thou look at me so strangely, Harold?" cried Yseult. "By the cruel light in thine eyes one might almost take thee to be the werewolf!"

"Come hither, sit beside me," said Harold tremblingly, "and I will tell thee why I fear to have thee go to the feast of Ste. AElfreda tomorrow evening. Hear what I dreamed last night. I dreamed I was the werewolf—do not shudder, dear love, for 't was only a dream.

"A grizzled old man stood at my bedside and strove to pluck my soul from my bosom.

" 'What would'st thou?' I cried.

" 'Thy soul is mine,' he said, 'thou shalt live out my curse. Give me thy soul—hold back thy hands—give me thy soul, I say.'

" 'Thy curse shall not be upon me,' I cried. 'What have I done that thy curse should rest upon me? Thou shalt not have my soul.'

" 'For my offence shalt thou suffer, and in my curse thou shalt endure hell—it is so decreed.'

"So spake the old man, and he strove with me, and he prevailed against me, and he plucked my soul from my bosom, and he said, 'Go, search and kill'—and—and lo, I was a wolf upon the moor.

"The dry grass crackled beneath my tread. The darkness of the night was heavy and it oppressed me. Strange horrors tortured my soul, and it groaned and groaned jailed in that wolfish body. The wind whispered to me; with its myriad voices it spake to me and said, 'Go, search and kill.' And above these voices sounded the hideous laughter of an old man. I fled the moor—whither I knew not, nor knew I what motive lashed me on.

"I came to a river and I plunged in. A burning thirst consumed me, and I lapped the waters of the river—they were waves of flame, and they flashed around me and hissed, and what they said was, 'Go, search and kill,' and I heard the old man's laughter again.

"A forest lay before me with its gloomy thickets and its somber shadows—with its ravens, its vampires, its serpents, its reptiles, and all its hideous brood of night. I darted among its thorns and crouched amid the leaves, the nettles, and the brambles. The owls hooted at me and the thorns pierced my flesh. 'Go, search and kill,' said everything. The hares sprang from my pathway; the other beasts ran bellowing away, every form of life shrieked in my ears—the curse was on me—I was the werewolf.

"On, on I went with the fleetness of the wind, and my soul groaned in its wolfish prison, and the winds and the waters and the trees bade me, 'Go, search and kill, thou accursed brute; go, search and kill.'

"Nowhere was there pity for the wolf, what mercy, thus, should I, the werewolf, show? The curse was on me and it filled me with hunger and a thirst for blood. Skulking on my way within myself, I cried, 'Let me have blood, oh, let me have human blood, that this wrath may be appeased, that this curse may be removed.'

"At last I came to the sacred grove. Somber loomed the poplars, the oaks frowned upon me. Before me stood an old man—'twas he, grizzled and taunting, whose curse I bore. He feared me not. All other living things fled before me, but the old man feared me not. A maiden stood beside him. She did not see me, for she was blind.

" 'Kill, kill,' cried the old man, and he pointed at the girl beside him.

"Hell raged within me—the curse impelled me—I sprang at her throat. I heard the old man's laughter once more, and then—then I awoke, trembling, cold, horrified."

Scarce was this dream told when Alfred strode the way.

"Now, by'r Lady," quoth he, "I bethink me never to have seen a sorrier twain."

Then Yseult told him of Harold's going away and how that Harold had besought her not to venture to the feast of Ste. AElfreda in the sacred grove.

"These fears are childish," cried Alfred boastfully. "And thou sufferest me, sweet lady, I will bear thee company to the feast, and a score of my lusty yeomen with their good yew bows and honest spears, they shall attend me. There be no werewolf, I trow, will chance about with us."

Whereat Yseult laughed merrily, and Harold said: " 'Tis well, thou shalt go to the sacred grove, and may my love and Heaven's grace forfend all evil."

Then Harold went to his abode, and he fetched old Siegfried's spear back unto Yseult, and he gave it unto her two hands, saying, "Take this spear with thee to the feast tomorrow night. It is old Siegfried's spear, possessing mighty virtue and marvelous."

And Harold took Yseult to his heart and blessed her, and he kissed her upon her brow and upon her lips, saying, "Farewell, oh, my beloved. How wilt thou love me when thou know'st my sacrifice. Farewell, farewell, forever, oh, alder-liefest mine."

So Harold went his way, and Yseult was lost in wonderment.

On the morrow night came Yseult to the sacred grove wherein the feast was spread, and she bore old Siegfried's spear with her in her girdle. Alfred attended her, and a score of lusty yeomen were with him. In the grove there was great merriment, and with singing and dancing and games withal did the honest folk celebrate the feast of the fair Ste. AElfreda.

But suddenly a mighty tumult arose, and there were cries of "The werewolf! The werewolf!" Terror seized upon all—stout hearts were frozen with fear. Out from the further forest rushed the werewolf, wood wroth, bellowing hoarsely, gnashing his fangs, and tossing hither and thither the yellow foam from his snapping jaws. He sought Yseult straight, as if an evil power drew him to the spot where she stood. But Yseult was not afeared; like a marble statue she stood and saw the werewolf's coming. The yeomen, dropping their torches and casting aside their bows, had fled; Alfred alone abided there to do the monster battle.

At the approaching wolf he hurled his heavy lance, but as it struck the werewolf's bristling back the weapon was all to-shivered.

Then the werewolf, fixing his eyes upon Yseult, skulked for a moment in the shadow of the yews, and thinking then of Harold's words, Yseult plucked old Siegfried's spear from her girdle, raised it on high, and with the strength of despair sent it hurtling through the air.

The werewolf saw the shining weapon, and a cry burst from his gaping throat—a cry of human agony. And Yseult saw in the werewolf's eyes the eyes of someone she had seen and known, but 't was for an instant only, and then the eyes were no longer human, but wolfish in their ferocity.

A supernatural force seemed to speed the spear in its flight. With fearful precision the weapon smote home and buried itself by half its length in the werewolf's shaggy breast just above the heart, and then, with a monstrous sigh—as if he yielded up his life without regret—the werewolf fell dead in the shadow of the yews.

Then, ah, then in very truth there was great joy, and loud were the acclaims, while, beautiful in her trembling pallor, Yseult was led unto her home, where the people set about to give great feast to do her homage, for the werewolf was dead, and she it was that had slain him.

But Yseult cried out, "Go, search for Harold—go, bring him to me. Nor eat, nor sleep till he be found."

"Good my lady," quoth Alfred, "how can that be, since he hath betaken himself to Normandy?"

"I care not where he be," she cried. "My heart stands still until I look into his eyes again."

"Surely he hath not gone to Normandy," outspake Hubert. "This very eventide I saw him enter his abode."

They hastened thither—a vast company. His chamber door was barred.

"Harold, Harold, come forth!" they cried, as they beat upon the door, but no answer came to their calls and knockings. Afeared, they battered down the door, and when it fell they saw that Harold lay upon his bed.

"He sleeps," said one. "See, he holds a portrait in his hand—and it is her portrait. How fair he is and how tranquilly he sleeps."

But no, Harold was not asleep. His face was calm and beautiful, as if he dreamed of his beloved, but his raiment was red with the blood that streamed from a wound in his breast—a gaping, ghastly spear wound just above his heart.

# PART SIX

# The Avenging Werewolf

Avenging werewolves take justice into their own hands—or paws. In the first story, a woman is betrayed by her master. He seduces her and then renounces her and their expected child, banishing her to a distant room in the castle. Before her death in childbirth, she commissions the child to claim his birthright and to avenge the wrongs done to both of them.

In the other two stories in this section there is a faithless wife who is instrumental in transforming her husband into a werewolf. The husbands are justifiably angry, feeling that their metamorphosis was a deliberate, personal assault on their humanity. Robbed of human shape and dignity, aliens in the human world, they retain human memory, feelings, and a sense of justice. What validates their existence, even though their humanity is diminished, is their psychological need to punish the perpetrators. These two stories, however, are more than simple tales of misogyny—they show that even though a human being takes on an animal form, he or she does not necessarily engage in degrading acts of lycanthropy. The human spirit transcends the material form in which it is imprisoned. It displays human emotions; it makes moral decisions.

The three werewolves in this section are all mature males. Peter Fleming's werewolf is on a quest to kill all rivals for the inheritance. Marie de France's werewolf, a nobleman, is finally able to punish the wife and all her offspring with banishment and facial disfiguration. Joseph Jacobs's werewolf, a gentle husband, punishes his wife by having her listen to and affirm the truth of his story as he tells it over and over again in her presence.

Fleming's story takes place in a quiet setting in a remote railroad station in the west of England, but the aura of dread hangs over the scene—"a pale leprous flush on the black and beaded window." Although Fleming gives a description of both travelers, it is the traveler with the dark sallow skin, a pointed nose, a sharp and narrow jaw, and deep-set, honey-colored eyes who attracts suspicion. The other traveler is a conventional upper-class young man.

In order to break the silence between two strangers waiting for a train, the upper-class young man tells the traveler with the "dark sallow skin" about strange happenings in the neighborhood. There are mysterious killings by an animal who tears out the throats of his animal and human victims but leaves human footprints at the scene. There is the history of a bastard child born with the features of a werewolf and a dying mother's curse on her seducer.

Although the ending of "The Kill" may seem melodramatic, it is as much a story of human cruelty as it is about werewolf cruelty: it is the story of the abandonment by a powerful male of the mother of their child. Only someone with power equal to or greater than the power of the perpetrator can right this wrong. Only a child, born with the characteristic power of a werewolf, can achieve justice.

Marie de France, who is considered the greatest woman writer of the Middle Ages, has written a psychologically complex story about a nobleman and his wife, a story that reminds the reader of the Hebrew Old Testament story of Samson and Delilah. When Delilah tries to find out the source of Samson's great strength, Samson outwits her several times and thwarts her attempts to discover his secret. He succumbs finally to her daily pressure—"so that his soul was vexed unto death . . . [and] he told her all his heart" (Judges 16:16–17). Delilah betrays him to the Philistines, who put out his eyes and imprison him in Gaza. His retribution occurs when he pulls down the pillars of the arena and causes the death of three thousand Philistines.

Like Delilah, the wife in Marie's story wants to know her husband's secret: he disappears three days a week. When he finally succumbs to her importunate requests disguised as a loving wife's concern for him, and reveals to her that he is the victim of a metamorphosis those three days when he is condemned to live as a werewolf in the forest, she is so horrified that she steals his clothes when he is a werewolf and condemns him to an irreversible life as a werewolf, with no four-day respite each week. The wife then marries a knight, has children with him, and banishes her lawful husband from her heart and thoughts.

This story, however, is more than a surface tale of a treacherous wife, of a husband condemned to a bestial life, of his rescue by the king, and of the revenge of a husband. The story peels away the veneer of civilization and respectability and reveals that the husband's physical transformation is not as revolting as the wife's psychological and moral transformation. By forcing her husband to be a werewolf, she deserves to wear on her face the symbol of her heartlessness and treachery. Her children will inherit the disgrace.

Jacobs's story, rooted in Celtic folklore, is part of a larger story, Morraha. (The story has a number of parallels with the King Arthur story titled Arthur and Gorlagon.) Here the metamorphoses are accomplished with the use of magic. The wife strikes her somewhat eccentric husband (he understands the language of birds and regularly tunes in to their conversations) with a magic rod and turns him into a raven, an old white horse, a fox, and a werewolf. Although he is a gentle, civilized werewolf, he is forced to leave home and journey to a castle where he is accepted into service by a king. The king and queen, however, are bereft of all their children, who have disappeared mysteriously in the night. The one remaining child, guarded by the werewolf until age three, is snatched away in spite of the werewolf's vigilance. Rejected by the king for failing to protect the child, the werewolf leaves the king, returns to his home, and is transformed into a human being by a blow of the same magic rod that transformed him originally.

The story's folkloric structure demands restoration of all the elements in order to give closure to the multiplicity of events. Restoration, as is expected, is accomplished by the werewolf before he initiates his final avenging stratagem. His wife must corroborate his story, testify against herself, and attest to being the author of the insidious plot that reduced her husband to something less than human.

# The Kill

PETER FLEMING (1907–1971)

IN THE COLD WAITING ROOM of a small railway station in the West of England two men were sitting. They had sat there for an hour, and were likely to sit there longer. There was a thick fog outside. Their train was indefinitely delayed.

The waiting room was a barren and unfriendly place. A naked electric bulb lit it with wan, disdainful efficiency. A notice, "No Smoking," stood on the mantelpiece; when you turned it round, it said "No Smoking" on the other side, too. Printed regulations relating to an outbreak of swine fever in 1924 were pinned neatly to one wall, almost, but maddeningly not quite, in the center of it. The stove gave out a hot, thick smell, powerful already, but increasing. A pale leprous flush on the black and beaded window showed that a light was burning on the platform outside, in the fog. Somewhere, water dripped with infinite reluctance onto corrugated iron.

The two men sat facing each other over the stove on chairs of an unswerving woodenness. Their acquaintance was no older than their vigil. From such talk as they had had, it seemed likely that they were to remain strangers.

The younger of the two resented the lack of contact in their relationship more than the lack of comfort in their surroundings. His attitude toward his fellow beings had but recently undergone a transition from the subjective to the objective. As with many of his class and age, the routine, unrecognized as such, of an expensive education, with the triennial alternative of those delights normal to wealth and gentility, had atrophied many of his curiosities. For the first twenty-odd years of his life he had read humanity in terms of rel-

In Peter Fleming, *A Story to Tell and Other Tales* (New York: Charles Scribner's Sons, 1942).

evance rather than reality, looking on people who held no ordained place in his own existence much as a buck in a park watches visitors walking up the drive: mildly, rather resentfully inquiring—not inquisitive. Now, hot in reaction from this unconscious provincialism, he treated mankind as a museum, gaping conscientiously at each fresh exhibit, hunting for the noncumulative evidence of man's complexity with indiscriminate zeal. To each magic circle of individuality he saw himself as a kind of freelance tangent. He aspired to be a connoisseur of men.

There was undoubtedly something arresting about the specimen before him. Of less than medium height, the stranger had yet that sort of ranging leanness that lends vicarious inches. He wore a long black overcoat, very shabby, and his shoes were covered with mud. His face had no color in it, though the impression it produced was not one of pallor; the skin was of a dark sallow, tinged with gray. The nose was pointed, the jaw sharp and narrow. Deep vertical wrinkles, running down toward it from the high cheekbones, sketched the permanent groundwork of a broader smile than the deep-set, honey-colored eyes seemed likely to authorize. The most striking thing about the face was the incongruity of its frame. On the back of his head the stranger wore a bowler hat with a very narrow brim. No word of such casual implications as a tilt did justice to its angle. It was clamped, by something at least as holy as custom, to the back of his skull, and that thin, questing face confronted the world fiercely from under a black halo of nonchalance.

The man's whole appearance suggested *difference* rather than aloofness. The unnatural way he wore his hat had the significance of indirect comment, like the antics of a performing animal. It was as if he was part of some older thing, of which Homo sapiens in a bowler hat was an expurgated edition. He sat with his shoulders hunched and his hands thrust into his overcoat pockets. The hint of discomfort in his attitude seemed due not so much to the fact that his chair was hard as to the fact that it was a chair.

The young man had found him uncommunicative. The most mobile sympathy, launching consecutive attacks on different fronts, had failed to draw him out. The reserved adequacy of his replies conveyed a rebuff more effectively than sheer surliness. Except to answer him, he did not look at the young man. When he did, his eyes were full of an abstracted amusement. Sometimes he smiled, but for no immediate cause.

Looking back down their hour together, the young man saw a field of endeavor on which frustrated banalities lay thick, like the discards of a routed army. But resolution, curiosity, and the need to kill time all clamored against an admission of defeat.

"If he will not talk," thought the young man, "then I will. The sound of my own voice is infinitely preferable to the sound of none. I will tell him what has just happened to me. It is really a most extraordinary story. I will tell it as well as I can, and I shall be very much surprised if its impact on his mind does not shock this man into some form of self-revelation. He is unaccountable without being *outre*, and I am inordinately curious about him."

Aloud he said, in a brisk and engaging manner: "I think you said you were a hunting man?"

The other raised his quick, honey-colored eyes. They gleamed with inaccessible amusement. Without answering, he lowered them again to contemplate the little beads of light thrown through the ironwork of the stove onto the skirts of his overcoat. Then he spoke. He had a husky voice.

"I came here to hunt," he agreed.

"In that case," said the young man, "you will have heard of Lord Fleer's private pack. Their kennels are not far from here."

"I know them," replied the other.

"I have just been staying there," the young man continued. "Lord Fleer is my uncle."

The other looked up, smiled and nodded, with the blind inconsequence of a foreigner who does not understand what is being said to him. The young man swallowed his impatience.

"Would you," he continued, using a slightly more peremptory tone than heretofore,—"would you care to hear a new and rather remarkable story about my uncle? Its denouement is not two days old. It is quite short."

From the fastness of some hidden joke, those light eyes mocked the necessity of a definite answer. At length: "Yes," said the stranger, "I would." The impersonality in his voice might have passed for a parade of sophistication, a reluctance to betray interest. But the eyes hinted that interest was alive elsewhere.

"Very well," said the young man.

Drawing his chair a little closer to the stove, he began:

AS PERHAPS you know, my uncle, Lord Fleer, leads a retired, though by no means an inactive life. For the last two or three hundred years, the currents of contemporary thought have passed mainly through the hands of men whose gregarious instincts have been constantly awakened and almost invariably indulged. By the standards of the eighteenth century, when Englishmen first became self-conscious about solitude, my uncle would have been considered unsociable. In the early nineteenth century, those not personally acquainted with him would have thought him romantic. Today, his attitude toward the sound and fury of modern life is too negative to excite comment as an oddity; yet even now, were he to be involved in any occurrence which could be called disastrous or interpreted as discreditable, the press would pillory him as a "Titled Recluse."

The truth of the matter is, my uncle has discovered the elixir, or, if you prefer it, the opiate, of self-sufficiency. A man of extremely simple tastes, not cursed with overmuch imagination, he sees no reason to cross frontiers of habit which the years have hallowed into rigidity. He lives in his castle (it may be described as commodious rather than comfortable), runs his estate at a slight profit, shoots a little, rides a great deal, and hunts as often as he can. He never sees his neighbors except by accident, thereby leading them to suppose, with sublime but unconscious arrogance, that he must be slightly mad. If he is, he can at least claim to have padded his own cell.

My uncle has never married. As the only son of his only brother, I was brought up in the expectation of being his heir. During the war, however, an unforeseen development occurred.

In this national crisis my uncle, who was of course too old for active service, showed a lack of public spirit which earned him locally a good deal of unpopularity. Briefly, he declined to recognize the war, or, if he did recognize it, gave no sign of having done so. He continued to lead his own vigorous but (in the circumstances) rather irrelevant life. Though he found himself at last obliged to recruit his hunt servants from men of advanced age and uncertain mettle in any crisis of the chase, he contrived to mount them well, and twice a week during the season himself rode two horses to a standstill after the hill foxes which, as no doubt you know, provide the best sport the Fleer country has to offer.

When the local gentry came and made representations to him, saying that it was time he did something for his country besides destroying its vermin by the most unreliable and expensive method ever devised, my uncle was very sensible. He now saw, he said, that he had been standing too aloof from a struggle of whose progress (since he never read the paper) he had been only indirectly aware. The next day he wrote to London and ordered the *Times* and a Belgian refugee. It was the least he could do, he said. I think he was right.

The Belgian refugee turned out to be a female, and dumb. Whether one or both of these characteristics had been stipulated for by my uncle, nobody knew. At any rate, she took up her quarters at Fleer: a heavy, unattractive girl of twenty-five, with a shiny face and small black hairs on the backs of her hands. Her life appeared to be modeled on that of the larger ruminants, except, of course, that the greater part of it took place indoors. She ate a great deal, slept with a will, and had a bath every Sunday, remitting this salubrious custom only when the housekeeper, who enforced it, was away on her holiday. Much of her time she spent sitting on a sofa, on the landing outside her bedroom, with Prescott's "Conquest of Mexico" open on her lap. She read either exceptionally slowly or not at all, for to my knowledge she carried the first volume about with her for eleven years. Hers, I think, was the contemplative type of mind.

The curious, and from my point of view the unfortunate, aspect of my uncle's patriotic gesture was the gradually increasing affection with which he came to regard this unlovable creature. Although, or more probably because, he saw her only at meals, when her features were rather more animated than at other times, his attitude toward her passed from the detached to the courteous, and from the courteous to the paternal. At the end of the war there was no question of her return to Belgium, and one day in 1919 I heard with pardonable mortification that my uncle had legally adopted her, and was altering his will in her favor.

Time, however, reconciled me to be disinherited by a being who, between meals, could scarcely be described as sentient. I continued to pay an annual visit to Fleer, and to ride with my uncle after his big-boned Welsh hounds over the sullen, dark-gray hill country in which—since its possession was no longer assured to me—I now began to see a powerful, though elusive, beauty.

I came down here three days ago, intending to stay for a week. I found my uncle, who is a tall, fine-looking man with a beard, in his usual unassailable good health. The Belgian, as always, gave me the impression of being impervious to disease, to emotion, or indeed to anything short of an act of God. She had been putting on weight since she came to live with my uncle, and was now a very considerable figure of a woman, though not, as yet, unwieldy.

It was at dinner, on the evening of my arrival, that I first noticed a certain *malaise* behind my uncle's brusque, laconic manner. There was evidently something on his mind. After dinner he asked me to come into his study. I detected, in the delivery of the invitation, the first hint of embarrassment I had known him to betray.

The walls of the study were hung with maps and the extremities of foxes. The room was littered with bills, catalogues, old gloves, fossils, rattraps, cartridges, and feathers which had been used to clean his pipe—a stale diversity of jetsam which somehow managed to produce an impression of relevance and continuity, like the debris in an animal's lair. I had never been in the study before.

"Paul," said my uncle as soon as I had shut the door, "I am very much disturbed."

I assumed an air of sympathetic inquiry.

"Yesterday," my uncle went on, "one of my tenants came to see me. He is a decent man, who farms a strip of land outside the park wall, to the northward. He said that he had lost two sheep in a manner for which he was wholly unable to account. He said he thought they had been killed by some wild animal."

My uncle paused. The gravity of his manner was really portentous.

"Dogs?" I suggested, with the slightly patronizing diffidence of one who has probability on his side.

My uncle shook his head judiciously. "This man had often seen sheep which had been killed by dogs. He said that they were always badly torn—nipped about the legs, driven into a corner, worried to death: it was never a clean piece of work. These two sheep had not been killed like that. I went down to see them for myself. Their throats had been torn out. They were not bitten, or nuzzled. They had both died in the open, not in a corner. Whatever did it was an animal more powerful and more cunning than a dog."

I said: "It couldn't have been something that had escaped from a traveling menagerie, I suppose?"

"They don't come into this part of the country," replied my uncle; "there are no fairs."

We were both silent for a moment. It was hard not to show more curiosity than sympathy as I waited on some further revelation to stake out my uncle's claim on the latter emotion. I could put no interpretation on those two dead sheep wild enough to account for his evident distress.

He spoke again, but with obvious reluctance.

"Another was killed early this morning," he said in a low voice, "on the Home Farm. In the same way."

For lack of any better comment, I suggested beating the nearby coverts. There might be some—

"We've scoured the woods," interrupted my uncle brusquely.

"And found nothing?"

"Nothing. . . . Except some tracks."

"What sort of tracks?"

My uncle's eyes were suddenly evasive. He turned his head away.

"They were a man's tracks," he said slowly. A log fell over in the fireplace.

Again a silence. The interview appeared to be causing him pain rather than relief. I decided that the situation could lose nothing through the frank expression of my curiosity. Plucking up courage, I asked him roundly what cause he had to be upset? Three sheep, the property of his tenants, had died deaths which, though certainly unusual, were unlikely to remain for long mysterious. Their destroyer, whatever it was, would inevitably be caught, killed, or driven away in the course of the next few days. The loss of another sheep or two was the worst he had to fear.

When I had finished, my uncle gave me an anxious, almost a guilty look. I was suddenly aware that he had a confession to make.

"Sit down," he said. "I wish to tell you something."

This is what he told me:

A quarter of a century ago, my uncle had had occasion to engage a new housekeeper. With the blend of fatalism and sloth which is the foundation of the bachelor's attitude to the servant problem, he took on the first applicant. She was a tall, black, slant-eyed woman from the Welsh border, aged about thirty. My uncle said nothing about her character, but described her as having "powers." When she had been at Fleer some months, my uncle began to notice her, instead of taking her for granted. She was not averse to being noticed.

One day she came and told my uncle that she was with child by him. He took it calmly enough till he found that she expected him to marry her; or pretended to expect it. Then he flew into a rage, called her a whore, and told her she must leave the house as soon as the child was born. Instead of breaking down, or continuing the scene, she began to croon to herself in Welsh, looking at him sideways with a certain amusement. This frightened him. He forbade her to come near him again, had her things moved into an unused wing of the castle, and engaged another housekeeper.

A child was born, and they came and told my uncle that the woman was going to die; she asked for him continually, they said. As much frightened as distressed, he went through passages long unfamiliar to her room. When the woman saw him, she began to gabble in a preoccupied kind of way, looking at him all the time, as if she were repeating a lesson. Then she stopped, and asked that he should be shown the child.

It was a boy. The midwife, my uncle noticed, handled it with a reluctance almost amounting to disgust.

"That is your heir," said the dying woman, in a harsh, unstable voice. "I have told him what he is to do. He will be a good son to me, and jealous of his birthright." And she went off, my uncle said, into a wild yet cogent rigmarole about a curse, embodied in the child, which would fall on any whom he made his heir over the bastard's head. At last her voice trailed away and she fell back, exhausted and staring.

As my uncle turned to go, the midwife whispered to him to look at the child's hands. Gently unclasping the podgy, futile little fists, she showed him that on each hand the third finger was longer than the second. . . .

Here I interrupted. The story had a certain queer force behind it, perhaps from its obvious effect on the teller. My uncle feared and hated the things he was saying.

"What did that mean?" I asked; "—the third finger longer than the second?"

"It took me a long time to discover," replied my uncle. "My own servants, when they saw I did not know, would not tell me. But at last I found out through the doctor, who had it from an old woman in the village. People born with their third finger longer than their second become werewolves. At least" (he made a perfunctory effort at amused indulgence) "that is what the common people here think."

"And what does that—what is that supposed to mean?" I, too, found myself throwing rather hasty sops to skepticism. I was growing strangely credulous.

"A werewolf," said my uncle, dabbling in improbability without self-consciousness, "is a human being who becomes, at intervals, to all intents and purposes a wolf. The transformation—or the supposed transformation—takes place at night. The werewolf kills men and animals and is supposed to drink their blood. Its preference is for men. All through the Middle Ages, down to the seventeenth century, there were innumerable cases (especially in France) of men and women being legally tried for offenses which they had committed as animals. Like the witches, they were rarely acquitted, but, unlike the witches, they seem seldom to have been unjustly condemned." My uncle paused. "I have been reading books," he explained. "I wrote to a man in London who is interested in these things when I heard what was believed about the child."

"What became of the child?" I asked.

"The wife of one of my keepers took it in," said my uncle. "She was a stolid woman from the North, who, I think, welcomed the opportunity to show what little store she set by the local superstitions. The boy lived with them till he was ten. Then he ran away. I had not heard of him since then till"—my uncle glanced at me almost apologetically—"till yesterday."

We sat for a moment in silence, looking at the fire. My imagination had betrayed my reason in its full surrender to the story. I had not got it in me to dispel his fears with a parade of sanity. I was a little frightened myself.

"You think it is your son, the werewolf, who is killing the sheep?" I said at length.

"Yes. For a boast; or for a warning; or perhaps out of spite, at a night hunting wasted."

"Wasted?"

My uncle looked at me with troubled eyes.

"His business is not with sheep," he said uneasily.

"For the first time I realized the implications of the Welshwoman's curse. The hunt was up. The quarry was the heir to Fleer. I was glad to have been disinherited.

"I have told Germaine not to go out after dusk," said my uncle, coming in pat on my train of thought.

The Belgian was called Germaine; her other name was Vom.

I CONFESS I spent no very tranquil night. My uncle's story had not wholly worked in me that "suspension of disbelief" which someone speaks of as being the prime requisite of good drama. But I have a powerful imagination. Neither

fatigue nor common sense could quite banish the vision of that metamorphosed malignancy ranging, with design, the black and silver silences outside
my window. I found myself listening for the sound of loping footfalls on a
frost-baked crust of beech leaves. . . .

Whether it was in my dream that I heard, once, the sound of howling I do
not know. But the next morning I saw, as I dressed, a man walking quickly up
the drive. He looked like a shepherd. There was a dog at his heels, trotting
with a noticeable lack of assurance. At breakfast my uncle told me that another sheep had been killed, almost under the noses of the watchers. His voice
shook a little. Solicitude sat oddly on his features as he looked at Germaine.
She was eating porridge, as if for a wager.

After breakfast we decided on a campaign. I will not weary you with the
details of its launching and its failure. All day we quartered the woods with
thirty men, mounted and on foot. Near the scene of the kill our dogs picked up
a scent which they followed for two miles and more, only to lose it on the
railway line. But the ground was too hard for tracks, and the men said it could
only have been a fox or a polecat, so surely and readily did the dogs follow it.

The exercise and the occupation were good for our nerves. But late in the
afternoon my uncle grew anxious; twilight was closing in swiftly under a sky
heavy with clouds, and we were some distance from Fleer. He gave final instructions for the penning of the sheep by night, and we turned our horses'
heads for home.

We approached the castle by the back drive, which was little used: a dank,
unholy alley, running the gauntlet of a belt of firs and laurels. Beneath our
horses' hoofs, flints clinked remotely under a thick carpet of moss. Each consecutive cloud from their nostrils hung with an air of permanency, as if be-
queathed to the unmoving air.

We were perhaps three hundred yards from the tall gates leading to the
stable yard when both horses stopped dead, simultaneously. Their heads were
turned toward the trees on our right, beyond which, I knew the sweep of the
main drive converged on ours.

My uncle gave a short, inarticulate cry in which premonition stood aghast
at the foreseen. At the same moment, something howled on the other side of
the trees. There was relish, and a kind of sobbing laughter, in that hateful
sound. It rose and fell luxuriously, and rose and fell again, fouling the night.
Then it died away, fawning on satiety in a throaty whimper.

The forces of silence fell unavailingly on its rear; its filthy echoes still went reeling through our heads. We were aware that feet went loping lightly down the iron-hard drive . . . two feet.

My uncle flung himself off his horse and scrambled down a bank and out into the open. The only figure in sight was motionless.

Germaine Vom lay doubled up in the drive, a solid, black mark against the shifting values of the dusk. We ran forward. . . .

To me she had always been an improbable cipher rather than a real person. I could not help reflecting that she died, as she had lived, in the livestock tradition. Her throat had been torn out.

THE YOUNG MAN leant back in his chair, a little dizzy from talking and from the heat of the stove. The inconvenient realities of the waiting room, forgotten in his narrative, closed in on him again. He sighed, and smiled rather apologetically at the stranger.

"It is a wild and improbable story," he said. "I do not expect you to believe the whole of it. For me, perhaps, the reality of its implications has obscured its almost ludicrous lack of verisimilitude. You see, by the death of the Belgian I am heir to Fleer."

The stranger smiled: a slow, but no longer an abstracted smile. His honey-colored eyes were bright. Under his long black overcoat his body seemed to be stretching itself in sensual anticipation. He rose silently to his feet.

The other found a sharp, cold fear drilling into his vitals. Something behind those shining eyes threatened him with appalling immediacy, like a sword at his heart. He was sweating. He dared not move.

The stranger's smile was now a grin, a ravening convulsion of the face. His eyes blazed with a hard and purposeful delight. A thread of saliva dangled from the corner of his mouth.

Very slowly he lifted one hand and removed his bowler hat. Of the fingers crooked about its brim, the young man saw that the third was longer than the second.

# The Lay of the Were-Wolf

## MARIE DE FRANCE (FL. 1160–1215)

AMONGST THE TALES I tell you once again, I would not forget the lay of the Were-Wolf. Such beasts as he are known in every land. Bisclavaret he is named in Brittany, whilst the Norman calls him Garwal.

It is a certain thing, and within the knowledge of all, that many a christened man has suffered this change, and ran wild in woods, as a Were-Wolf. The Were-Wolf is a fearsome beast. He lurks within the thick forest, mad and horrible to see. All the evil that he may, he does. He goeth to and fro, about the solitary place, seeking man, in order to devour him. Hearken, now, to the adventure of the Were-Wolf that I have to tell.

In Brittany there dwelt a baron who was marvelously esteemed of all his fellows. He was a stout knight, and a comely, and a man of office and repute. Right private was he to the mind of his lord, and dear to the counsel of his neighbors. This baron was wedded to a very worthy dame, right fair to see, and sweet of semblance. All his love was set on her, and all her love was given again to him. One only grief had this lady. For three whole days in every week her lord was absent from her side. She knew not where he went, nor on what errand. Neither did any of his house know the business which called him forth.

On a day when this lord was come again to his house, altogether joyous and content, the lady took him to task, right sweetly, in this fashion,

"Husband," said she, "and fair, sweet friend, I have a certain thing to pray of you. Right willingly would I receive this gift, but I fear to anger you in the asking. It is better for me to have an empty hand, than to gain hard words."

*French Medieval Romances from the Lays of Marie De France*, translated by Eugene Mason (New York: E. P. Dutton 1911), reprinted 1924, 83–90.

When the lord heard this matter, he took the lady in his arms, very tenderly, and kissed her.

"Wife," he answered, "ask what you will. What would you have, for it is yours already?"

"By my faith," said the lady, "soon shall I be whole. Husband, right long and wearisome are the days that you spend away from your home. I rise from my bed in the morning, sick at heart, I know not why. So fearful am I, lest you do aught to your loss, that I may not find any comfort. Very quickly shall I die for reason of my dread. Tell me now, where you go, and on what business! How may the knowledge of one who loves so closely bring you to harm?"

"Wife," made answer the lord, "nothing but evil can come if I tell you this secret. For the mercy of God do not require it of me. If you but knew, you would withdraw yourself from my love, and I should be lost indeed."

When the lady heard this, she was persuaded that her baron sought to put her by with jesting words. Therefore she prayed and required him the more urgently, with tender looks and speech, till he was overborne, and told her all the story, hiding naught.

"Wife, I become Bisclavaret. I enter in the forest, and live on prey and roots, within the thickest of the wood."

After she had learned his secret, she prayed and entreated the more as to whether he ran in his raiment, or went spoiled of vesture.

"Wife," said he, "I go naked as a beast."

"Tell me, for hope of grace, what you do with your clothing?"

"Fair wife, that will I never. If I should lose my raiment, or even be marked as I quit my vesture, then a Were-Wolf I must go for all the days of my life. Never again should I become man, save in that hour my clothing were given back to me. For this reason never will I show my lair."

"Husband," replied the lady to him, "I love you better than all the world. The less cause have you for doubting my faith, or hiding any tittle from me. What savor is here of friendship? How have I made forfeit of your love; for what sin do you mistrust my honor? Open now your heart, and tell what is good to be known."

So at the end, outwearied and overborne by her importunity, he could no longer refrain, but told her all.

"Wife," said he, "within this wood, a little from the path, there is a hidden way, and at the end thereof an ancient chapel, where oftentimes I have bewailed my lot. Near by is a great hollow stone, concealed by a bush, and there is the secret place where I hide my raiment, till I would return to my own home."

On hearing this marvel the lady became sanguine of visage, because of her exceeding fear. She dared no longer to lie at his side, and turned over in her mind, this way and that, how best she could get her from him. Now there was a certain knight of those parts, who, for a great while, had sought and required this lady for her love. This knight had spent long years in her service, but little enough had he got thereby, not even fair words, or a promise. To him the dame wrote a letter, and meeting, made her purpose plain.

"Fair friend," said she, "be happy. That which you have coveted so long a time, I will grant without delay. Never again will I deny your suit. My heart, and all I have to give, are yours, so take me now as love and dame."

Right sweetly the knight thanked her for her grace, and pledged her faith and fealty. When she had confirmed him by an oath, then she told him of his business of her lord—why he went, and what he became, and of his ravening within the wood. So she showed him of the chapel, and of the hollow stone, and of how to spoil the Were-Wolf of his vesture. Thus, by the kiss of his wife, was Bisclavaret betrayed. Often enough had he ravished his prey in desolate places, but from this journey he never returned. His kinsfolk and acquaintance came together to ask of his tidings, when this absence was noised abroad. Many a man, on many a day, searched the woodland, but none might find him, nor learn where Bisclavaret was gone.

The lady was wedded to the knight who had cherished her for so long a space. More than a year had passed since Bisclavaret disappeared. Then it chanced that the King would hunt in the selfsame wood where the Were-Wolf lurked. When the hounds were unleashed they ran this way and that, and swiftly came upon his scent. At the view the huntsman winded on his horn, and the whole pack were at his heels. They followed him from morn to eve, till he was torn and bleeding, and was all adread lest they should pull him down. Now the King was very close to the quarry, and when Bisclavaret looked upon his master, he ran to him for pity and for grace. He took the stirrup within his paws, and fawned upon the prince's foot. The King was very fearful at this sight, but presently he called his courtiers to his aid.

"Lords," cried he, "hasten hither, and see this marvelous thing. Here is a beast who has the sense of man. He abases himself before his foe, and cries for mercy, although he cannot speak. Beat off the hounds, and let no man do him harm. We will hunt no more today, but return to our own place, with the wonderful quarry we have taken."

The King turned him about, and rode to his hall, Bisclavaret following at his side. Very near to his master the Were-Wolf went, like any dog, and had no care to seek again the wood. When the King had brought him safely to his own castle, he rejoiced greatly, for the beast was fair and strong; no mightier had any man seen. Much pride had the King in his marvelous beast. He held him so dear, that he bade all those who wished for his love, to cross the Wolf in naught, neither to strike him with a rod, but ever to see that he was richly fed and kenneled warm. This commandment the Court observed willingly. So all the day the Wolf sported with the lords, and at night he lay within the chamber of the King. There was not a man who did not make much of the beast, so frank was he and debonair. None had reason to do him wrong, for ever was he about his master, and for his part did evil to none. Every day were these two companions together, and all perceived that the King loved him as his friend.

Hearken now to that which chanced.

The King held a high Court, and bade his great vassals and barons, and all the lords of his venery to the feast. Never was there a goodlier feast, nor one set forth with sweeter show and pomp. Amongst those who were bidden came that same knight who had the wife of Bisclavaret for dame. He came to the castle, richly gowned, with a fair company, but little he deemed whom he would find so near. Bisclavaret marked his foe the moment he stood within the hall. He ran towards him, and seized him with his fangs, in the King's very presence, and to the view of all. Doubtless he would have done him much mischief, had not the King called and chidden him, and threatened him with a rod. Once, and twice, again, the Wolf set upon the knight in the very light of day. All men marveled at his malice, for sweet and serviceable was the beast, and to that hour had shown hatred of none. With one consent the household deemed that this deed was done with full reason, and that the Wolf had suffered at the knight's hand some bitter wrong. Right wary of his foe was the knight until the feast had ended, and all the barons had taken farewell of their lord, and departed, each to his own house. With these, amongst the very first, went that lord whom Bisclavaret so fiercely had assailed. Small was the wonder he was glad to go.

Not long while after this adventure, it came to pass that the courteous King would hunt in that forest where Bisclavaret was found. With the prince came his wolf, and a fair company. Now at nightfall the King abode within a certain lodge of that country, and this was known of that dame who before was the wife of Bisclavaret. In the morning the lady clothed her in her most dainty apparel, and hastened to the lodge, since she desired to speak with the King, and to offer him a rich present. When the lady entered in the chamber, neither man or leash might restrain the fury of the Wolf. He became as a mad dog in his hatred and malice. Breaking from his bonds he sprang at the lady's face, and bit the nose from her visage. From every side men ran to the succor of the dame. They beat off the wolf from his prey, and for a little would have cut him in pieces with their swords. But a certain wise counselor said to the King,

"Sire, hearken now to me. This beast is always with you, and there is not one of us all who has not known him for long. He goes in and out amongst us, nor has molested any man, neither done wrong or felony to any, save only to this dame, one only time as we have seen. He has done evil to this lady, and to that knight, who is now the husband of the dame. Sire, she was once the wife of that lord who was so close and private to your heart, but who went, and none might find where he had gone. Now, therefore, put the dame in a sure place, and question her straitly, so that she may tell—if perchance she knows thereof—for what reason this Beast holds her in such mortal hate. For many a strange deed has chanced, as well we know, in this marvelous land of Brittany."

The King listened to these words, and deemed the counsel good. He laid hands upon the knight, and put the dame in surety in another place. He caused them to be questioned right straitly, so that their torment was very grievous. At the end, partly because of her distress, and partly by reason of her exceeding fear, the lady's lips were loosed, and she told her tale. She showed them of the betrayal of her lord, and how his raiment was stolen from the hollow stone. Since then she knew not where he went, nor what had befallen him, for he had never come again to his own land. Only, in her heart, well she deemed and was persuaded, that Bisclavaret was he.

Straightway the King demanded the vesture of his baron, whether this were to the wish of the lady, or whether it were against her wish. When the raiment was brought him, he caused it to be spread before Bisclavaret, but the Wolf made as though he had not seen. Then that cunning and crafty counselor took the King apart, that he might give him a fresh rede.

"Sire," said he, "you do not wisely, nor well, to set this raiment before Bisclavaret, in the sight of all. In shame and much tribulation must he lay aside the beast, and again become man. Carry your wolf within your most secret chamber, and put his vestment therein. Then close the door upon him, and leave him alone for a space. So we shall see presently whether the ravening beast may indeed return to human shape."

The King carried the Wolf to his chamber, and shut the doors upon him fast. He delayed for a brief while, and taking two lords of his fellowship with him, came again to the room. Entering therein, all three, softly together, they found the knight sleeping in the King's bed, like a little child. The King ran swiftly to the bed and taking his friend in his arms, embraced and kissed him fondly, above a hundred times. When man's speech returned once more, he told him of his adventure. Then the King restored to his friend the fief that was stolen from him, and gave such rich gifts, moreover, as I cannot tell. As for the wife who had betrayed Bisclavaret, he bade her avoid his country, and chased her from the realm. So she went forth, she and her second lord together, to seek a more abiding city, and were no more seen.

The adventure that you have heard is no vain fable. Verily and indeed it chanced as I have said. The lay of the Were-Wolf, truly, was written that it should ever be borne in mind.

# The Story of Rough Niall of the Speckled Rock

JOSEPH JACOBS (1854–1916)

WHEN I WAS GROWING UP, my mother taught me the language of the birds; and when I got married I used to be listening to their conversation; and I would be laughing; and my wife would be asking me what was the reason of my laughing, but I did not like to tell her, as women are always asking questions. We went out walking one fine morning, and the birds were arguing with one another. One of them said to another:

"Why should you be comparing yourself with me, when there is not a king nor knight that does not come to look at my tree?"

"What advantage has your tree over mine, on which there are three rods of magic mastery growing?"

When I heard them arguing, and knew that the rods were there, I began to laugh.

"Oh," asked my wife, "why are you always laughing? I believe it is at myself you are jesting, and I'll walk with you no more."

"Oh, it is not about you I am laughing. It is because I understand the language of the birds."

Then I had to tell her what the birds were saying to one another; and she was greatly delighted, and she asked me to go home, and she gave orders to the cook to have breakfast ready at six o'clock in the morning. I did not know why she was going out early, and breakfast was ready in the morning at the hour she appointed. She asked me to go out walking. I went with her. She went to the tree, and asked me to cut a rod for her.

"Oh, I will not cut it. Are we not better without it?"

In *More Celtic Fairy Tales*, ed. Joseph Jacobs (New York: G. P. Putnam's Sons, n.d.).

"I will not leave this until I get the rod, to see if there is any good in it."

I cut the rod and gave it to her. She turned from me and struck a blow on a stone, and changed it; and she struck a second blow on me, and made of me a black raven, and she went home and left me after her. I thought she would come back; she did not come, and I had to go into a tree till morning. In the morning, at six o'clock, there was a bellman out, proclaiming that everyone who killed a raven would get a four-penny bit. At last you could not find man or boy without a gun, nor, if you were to walk three miles, a raven that was not killed. I had to make a nest in the top of the parlor chimney, and hide myself all day till night came, and go out to pick up a bit to support me, till I spent a month. Here she is herself to say if it is a lie I am telling.

"It is not," said she.

Then I saw her out walking. I went up to her, and I thought she would turn me back to my own shape, and she struck me with the rod and made of me an old white horse, and she ordered me to be put to a cart with a man, to draw stones from morning till night. I was worse off then. She spread abroad a report that I had died suddenly in my bed, and prepared a coffin, and waked and buried me. Then she had no trouble. But when I got tired I began to kill everyone who came near me, and I used to go in the haggard every night and destroy the stacks of corn; and when a man came near me in the morning I would follow him till I broke his bones. Everyone got afraid of me. When she saw I was doing mischief, she came to meet me, and I thought she would change me. And she did change me, and made a fox of me. When I saw she was doing me every sort of damage, I went away from her. I knew there was a badger's hole in the garden, and I went there till night came, and I made great slaughter among the geese and ducks. There she is herself to say if I am telling a lie.

"Oh! you are telling nothing but the truth, only less than the truth."

When she had enough of my killing the fowl, she came out into the garden, for she knew I was in the badger's hole. She came to me and made me a wolf. I had to be off, and go to an island, where no one at all would see me, and now and then I used to be killing sheep, for there were not many of them, and I was afraid of being seen and hunted; and so I passed a year, till a shepherd saw me among the sheep and a pursuit was made after me. And when the dogs came near me there was no place for me to escape to from them; but I recognized the sign of the king among the men, and I made for him, and the king cried out to stop the hounds. I took a leap upon the front of the king's saddle, and the woman behind cried out, "My king and my lord, kill him or he will kill you!"

"Oh! he will not kill me. He knew me; he must be pardoned."

The king took me home with him, and gave orders I should be well cared for. I was so wise when I got food, I would not eat one morsel until I got a knife and fork. The man told the king, and the king came to see if it was true, and I got a knife and fork, and I took the knife in one paw and the fork in the other, and I bowed to the king. The king gave orders to bring him drink, and it came; and the king filled a glass of wine and gave it to me.

I took hold of it in my paw and drank it and thanked the king.

"On my honor," said he, "it is some king or other has lost him, when he came on the island; and I will keep him, as he is trained; and perhaps he will serve us yet."

And this is the sort of king he was—a king who had not a child living. Eight sons were born to him and three daughters, and they were stolen the same night they were born. No matter what guard was placed over them, the child would be gone in the morning. A twelfth child now came to the queen, and the king took me with him to watch the baby. The women were not satisfied with me.

"Oh," said the king, "what was all your watching ever good for? One that was born to me I have not; I will leave this one in the dog's care, and he will not let it go."

A coupling was put between me and the cradle, and when everyone went to sleep I was watching till the person woke who attended in the daytime; but I was there only two nights; when it was near the day, I saw a hand coming down through the chimney, and the hand was so big that it took round the child altogether, and thought to take him away. I caught hold of the hand above the wrist, and as I was fastened to the cradle, I did not let go my hold till I cut the hand from the wrist, and there was a howl from the person without. I laid the hand in the cradle with the child, and as I was tired I fell asleep; and when I awoke, I had neither child nor hand; and I began to howl, and the king heard me, and he cried out that something was wrong with me, and he sent servants to see what was the matter with me, and when the messenger came he saw me covered with blood, and he could not see the child; and he went to the king and told him the child was not to be got. The king came and saw the cradle colored with the blood, and he cried out "where was the child gone?" and everyone said it was the dog had eaten it.

The king said: "It is not: loose him, and he will get the pursuit himself."

When I was loosed, I found the scent of blood till I came to a door of the room in which the child was. I went back to the king and took hold of him, and went back again and began to tear at the door. The king followed me and asked for the key. The servant said it was in the room of the stranger woman. The king caused search to be made for her, and she was not to be found. "I will break the door," said the king, "as I can't get the key." The king broke the door, and I went in, and went to the trunk, and the king asked for a key to unlock it. He got no key, and he broke the lock. When he opened the trunk, the child and the hand were stretched side by side, and the child was asleep. The king took the hand and ordered a woman to come for the child, and he showed the hand to everyone in the house. But the stranger woman was gone, and she did not see the king—and here she is herself to say if I am telling lies of her.

"Oh, it's nothing but the truth you have!"

The king did not allow me to be tied anymore. He said there was nothing so much to wonder at as that I cut the hand off, as I was tied.

The child was growing till he was a year old. He was beginning to walk, and no one cared for him more than I did. He was growing till he was three, and he was running out every minute; so the king ordered a silver chain to be put between me and child, that he might not go away from me. I was out with him in the garden every day, and the king was as proud as the world of the child. He would be watching him everywhere we went, till the child grew so wise that he would loose the chain and get off. But one day that he loosed it I failed to find him; and I ran into the house and searched the house, but there was no getting him for me. The king cried to go out and find the child, that had got loose from the dog. They went searching for him, but could not find him. When they failed altogether to find him, there remained no more favor with the king towards me, and everyone disliked me, and I grew weak, for I did not get a morsel to eat half the time. When summer came, I said I would try and go home to my own country. I went away one fine morning, and I went swimming, and God helped me till I came home. I went into the garden, for I knew there was a place in the garden where I could hide myself, for fear my wife should see me. In the morning I saw her out walking, and the child with her, held by the hand. I pushed out to see the child, and as he was looking about him everywhere, he saw me and called out, "I see my shaggy papa. Oh!" said he; "oh, my heart's love, my shaggy papa, come here till I see you!"

I was afraid the woman would see me, as she was asking the child where he saw me, and he said I was up in a tree; and the more the child called me, the more I hid myself. The woman took the child home with her but I knew he would be up early in the morning.

I went to the parlor window, and the child was within, and he playing. When he saw me he cried out, "Oh! my heart's love, come here till I see you, shaggy papa." I broke the window and went in, and he began to kiss me. I saw the rod in front of the chimney, and I jumped up at the rod and knocked it down. "Oh! my heart's love, no one would give me the pretty rod," said he. I hoped he would strike me with the rod, but he did not. When I saw the time was short, I raised my paw, and I gave him a scratch below the knee. "Oh! you naughty, dirty, shaggy papa, you have hurt me so much, I'll give you a blow of the rod." He struck me a light blow, and so I came back to my own shape again. When he saw a man standing before him he gave a cry, and I took him up in my arms. The servants heard the child. A maid came in to see what was the matter with him. When she saw me she gave a cry out of her, and she said, "Oh, if the master isn't come to life again!"

Another came in, and said it was he really. When the mistress heard of it, she came to see with her own eyes, for she would not believe I was there; and when she saw me she said she'd drown herself. But I said to her, "If you yourself will keep the secret, no living man will ever get the story from me until I lose my head." Here she is herself to say if I am telling the truth. "Oh, it's nothing but truth you are telling."

When I saw I was in a man's shape, I said I would take the child back to his father and mother, as I knew the grief they were in after him. I got a ship and took the child with me; and as I journeyed I came to land on an island, and I saw not a living soul on it, only a castle dark and gloomy. I went in to see was there anyone in it. There was no one but an old hag, tall and frightful, and she asked me, "What sort of person are you?" I heard someone groaning in another room, and I said I was a doctor, and I asked her what ailed the person who was groaning.

"Oh," said she, "it is my son whose hand has been bitten from his wrist by a dog."

I knew then that it was he who had taken the child from me, and I said I would cure him if I got a good reward.

"I have nothing; but there are eight young lads and three young women, as handsome as anyone ever laid eyes on, and if you cure him I will give you them."

"Tell me first in what place his hand was cut from him?"

"Oh, it was out in another country, twelve years ago."

"Show me the way, that I may see him."

She brought me into a room, so that I saw him, and his arm was swelled up to the shoulder. He asked me if I would cure him; and I said I would cure him if he would give me the reward his mother promised.

"Oh, I will give it; but cure me."

"Well, bring them out to me."

The hag brought them out of the room. I said I should burn the flesh that was on his arm. When I looked on him, he was howling with pain. I said that I would not leave him in pain long. The wretch had only one eye in his forehead. I took a bar of iron, and put it in the fire till it was red, and I said to the hag, "He will be howling at first, but will fall asleep presently, and do not wake him till he has slept as much as he wants. I will close the door when I am going out." I took the bar with me, and I stood over him, and I turned it across through his eye as far as I could. He began to bellow, and tried to catch me, but I was out and away, having closed the door. The hag asked me, "Why is he bellowing?"

"Oh, he will be quiet presently, and will sleep for a good while, and I'll come again to have a look at him; but bring me out the young men and the young women."

I took them with me, and I said to her, "Tell me where you got them."

"My son brought them with him, and they are all the children of one king."

I was well satisfied, and I had no wish for delay to get myself free from the hag, so I took them on board the ship, and the child I had myself. I thought the king might leave me and the child I nursed myself; but when I came to land, and all those young people with me, the king and queen were out walking. The king was very aged, and the queen aged likewise. When I came to converse with them, and the twelve with me, the king and queen began to cry. I asked, "Why are you crying?"

"It is for good cause I am crying. As many children as these I should have, and now I am withered, grey, at the end of my life, and I have not one at all."

I told him all I went through, and I gave him the child in his hand, and "these are your other children who were stolen from you, whom I am giving to you safe. They are gently reared."

When the king heard who they were, he smothered them with kisses and drowned them with tears, and dried them with fine cloths silken and the hair of his own head, and so also did their mother, and great was his welcome for me, as it was I who found them all. The king said to me, "I will give you the last child, as it is you who have earned him best; but you must come to my court every year, and the child with you, and I will share with you my possessions.

"I have enough of my own, and after my death I will leave it to the child."

I spent a time, till my visit was over, and I told the king all the troubles I went through, only I said nothing about my wife. And now you have the story.

# PART SEVEN

# The Guilty Werewolf

The guilty werewolf has two faces—the face of an ordinary, decent human being and the face of a werewolf. The male werewolves in this section have the ordinary, decent face of a king and of a handsome young man; both have the hidden face of a werewolf. Looking in a mirror, however, the guilty werewolf may see only the face of a human being. Unlike the psychotic werewolf who sees "through a glass darkly" and stares at the face of a werewolf in the mirror, the guilty werewolf hides his true nature (perhaps even from himself) behind his human face. Both werewolves are guilty of brutal, stonyhearted acts that deprive them of their right to be called human beings.

Ovid, one of the greatest classical poets of all times, shows the horror of the cannibalism of King Lycaon, king of Arcadia, who has violated the most basic principles of human existence. There can be no expiation for the crime of eating human flesh. The metamorphosis of Lycaon is narrated by Jupiter, king of the gods, in his council chamber. Jupiter has heard rumors of the degradations practiced by the human race, and especially of the unspeakable crimes committed by Lycaon, whose "offense is rank, it smells to heaven." Lycaon murders the men he takes as his prisoners, has them butchered, and serves them up, roasted and boiled, to his guests, the fragrance of the roasted flesh filling the banquet hall. Lycaon's cannibalism is so appalling to Jupiter, who as a guest is served a dish of human flesh, that he immediately transforms Lycaon into a wolf. Condemned by Jupiter to wearing a werewolf's face, and to being driven by a wolf's voracious appetites, Lycaon carries the weight of unconfessed, unrepented guilt the rest of his life. His conduct banishes him from the human community, and he becomes an alien in a wolf community. Like Cain, he must wander as an outcast from the face of the earth. And like Cain, he will think, "My punishment is greater than I can bear." The appropriate punishment for Lycaon leaves him with unbearable guilt but without access to remorse.

The Transylvanian community that Spariosu and Benedek portray in their story is a moral community. A traditional society, it clearly delineates right from wrong, moral from immoral conduct. The guilty cannot escape the inevitable punishment for their wicked deeds. Having been fathered by a dissolute man, a handsome young son exceeds his father in infamous acts: he seduces vulnerable young women, propagates the country with bastards, takes no responsibility for his offspring, and destroys the peaceful fabric of the community. Werewolves hang around his door and stalk him; they recognize him as one of their own. Looking into the eyes of a young werewolf who attacks him, the guilty one sees his face reflected in the young werewolf's eyes.

One winter Benedek's grandfather told him an old tale when they went into the forest to gather firewood and saw fresh wolf tracks in the snow. In some parts of Transylvania, village people believe that the third, seventh, or twelfth son or daughter, if a bitang (a child born out of wedlock or as the result of incest), can become a werewolf. An acute feeling of guilt or some other form of mental anguish can trigger this frightful transformation. Once they become adults, the unfortunates are periodically seized by madness, when they run into the wilderness and change into wolves. They can be ferocious, attacking anybody or anything in their way. They suffer from this sad condition only while alive and will not return after death.

Although the young man in the story revels in his charm and shows an attractive face to his female conquests, the community cannot wait for the werewolves to claim him, to relocate him in the bestial community to which his guilty acts doom him. Fearful for their lives, the community breathes a sigh of relief when the young man is transformed into a werewolf and joins the werewolf pack that has just killed his dear friend. Already dehumanized by his lack of guilty feelings, he is justly transformed into a ravenous wolf. He can only live with fellow beasts, hunting and being hunted.

# Lycaon's Punishment

OVID (43 B.C.–A.D. 18)

JUPITER, KING OF THE GODS, called the gods to a meeting in his council chamber. "You've been hearing rumors," he said, "about what I did to Lycaon."

All the assembled gods were reluctant to talk about the unbelievable rumors they had heard—rumors of a human being turned into a ferocious wolf. Finally one of the gods got up enough courage to ask, "What did he do?"

"He laid plots against me," said Jupiter. "But that isn't the worst part of my story. You all know, I can handle plots against me."

The gods trembled. They knew how Jupiter handled plots against him. He destroyed the perpetrators with a thunderbolt, or something equally devastating.

Jupiter continued. "Lycaon received the punishment that fits the crime."

The gods relaxed. They were prepared to hear Jupiter's account of the monstrous crime that had caused the drastic punishment.

"Rumors had reached me about what Lycaon was doing to other human beings. I wanted to check out those rumors, hoping that they were false. I went down from Mount Olympus and disguised myself by dressing in human clothes. One afternoon I came to the palace of Lycaon and asked to see him. At first the servant was reluctant to inform Lycaon that someone wanted to see him. For all the servant knew, I might have a dagger under my cloak. Lycaon had enemies everywhere.

"Finally, after I insisted that I had an important message for Lycaon, he agreed to inform him. Lycaon was curious enough to allow me to enter the palace, under guard, and to deliver the important message.

From *Metamorphoses* (adapted and retold by Charlotte F. Otten).

"When I came into his presence, I told him that the message was so important I had to deliver it to him alone. Apparently, I looked harmless to him, so he agreed and dismissed the servant. After the servant left, I said to Lycaon, 'I am Jupiter, King of the Gods. And your King.'

"Lycaon laughed. 'We have men coming here all the time claiming to be gods,' he said, 'but no one has claimed to be Jupiter, King of the Gods. That's the best story I've heard in a long time. I'll have to have proof. Stay overnight and I'll give you a test in the morning.'

"I agreed, knowing that in the dead of night Lycaon would try to kill me.

" 'But first,' Lycaon said, 'you must eat at my banquet table. I'm preparing a great feast for my court. I invite you to be my guest.'

"I accepted his invitation, but while I was pretending to prepare for the banquet, I followed Lycaon. I was careful so that he couldn't detect me following him. But, then, you all know how effective my disguises are."

Jupiter paused. What he discovered was so abhorrent that he found it difficult to talk about it.

"Lycaon went into the part of the palace where prisoners were kept and selected one handsome prisoner. Before the prisoner could react, Lycaon had slit the throat of the hostage. Then Lycaon dragged the body to the kitchen where the cooks butchered the man, still warm, and selected the tougher parts for boiling and the choice parts for roasting over an open fire. Soon the palace was filled with the delicious smells of roasting flesh, the flesh of a human being that would be served at the banquet."

The gods gasped. This was cannibalism, the worst kind of violence. It was the kind of savagery that was an abomination in the eyes of the gods and of human beings. Such savagery in the human race could not be tolerated. The gods wondered what punishment could suit a crime so repugnant as this.

Jupiter gave them time to reflect on this monstrosity. Then he went on. "Lycaon set the banquet meat on the table, bragging that this was the best meat, the most succulent meat, we would ever taste. No sooner had he done this than I, with my avenging flames, brought the house crashing down in instantaneous fire. Everything that I had heard about Lycaon was true. This was not the first time he had eaten human flesh.

"Lycaon escaped the fire—I wanted him to escape since death by fire was too good for him—and he ran to what he thought was the safety of the countryside. He thought he was free of me. It took a while before he realized what had happened to him.

"First, he discovered that he could not speak. He could make only howling noises. Then he saw that I had changed his clothes into bristling hairs, his arms to legs, and his jaws into the jaws of a wolf. He had acted like a beast. He deserved to be one."

The gods agreed. The punishment did indeed fit the crime. "Has he metamorphosed completely into a wolf?" they wondered. "Do wolves accept him?"

"No," replied Jupiter. "That would be too light a punishment. I made sure that wolves won't have him. He still has the consciousness of a human being. I won't ever let him forget that he is human, but he can act only like the beast he is in his heart—ferocious, violent, uncivilized. He will always be painfully aware that he has lost his humanity but that he isn't fit to be a wolf."

"So, then," the gods asked, "what is he? both man and wolf?"

"Yes, he is a man-wolf, a werewolf, forever," said Jupiter. "And let him be a warning to all human beings. Those who act like cannibals will suffer the same fate."

# The Bitang

MIHAI I. SPARIOSU AND DEZSÖ BENEDEK

IN A REMOTE HAMLET in the Transylvanian Alps there once dwelt a lonely old woman with her only son, born out of wedlock. The youth was so good-looking that everyone called him Nicholas the Handsome. He could sing and dance well, and he was a fine storyteller. Whenever he attended a wedding or christening, he was sure to turn it into a memorable event. So folks from all over the valley started hiring him to entertain their guests at festive occasions. And since he was so handsome, rarely did he leave a party without someone to share his bed. Gradually the young man's ways became more and more dissolute.

The old woman felt very ashamed of her son's loose conduct. Whenever Nicholas was away, she sat home alone crying quietly. "He's turned out just like his dead father," she would sigh, wiping her tears. And in vain did she beg him to change his ways. The older her son grew, the looser he became, and the rumor even reached her that he had fathered several children. Finally Nicholas's mother could no longer bear her shame and died of a broken heart.

Some years later Nicholas grew tired of feasting and merrymaking and decided to slow down a little. He bought himself a flock of sheep and a small farm at the edge of the forest. He tended his flock all day and made a good living by selling sheep's cheese in the neighboring villages. But he still preferred skirt chasing to marrying and raising a family.

One crisp winter afternoon Nicholas was coming back from a nearby village. Climbing up a steep ravine, his skis strapped to his back, he thought he

In *Ghosts, Vampires, and Werewolves* (New York: Orchard Books, 1994), 14–19.

saw a dark shadow darting behind the bushes on the hilltop. When he arrived at the spot, he looked around but saw nothing alarming. He put on his skis and continued through the forest. Yet he had an uncanny feeling that someone was following him.

As Nicholas came within sight of his farm, he was relieved and stopped to rest for a minute. Suddenly he felt a sharp blow on the back of his head and fell down in the snow. A fierce growl told him he was being attacked by a wolf.

Luckily the high collar of the coat Nicholas was wearing prevented the beast from breaking his neck, but its sharp fangs tore deep into his skin. Nicholas rolled a few yards down the snowy slope and, shaking his attacker loose, drew his dagger. Blinded by the snow in his eyes, he stabbed wildly at the air around him until he realized the wolf was gone. Then he rose, trembling, to his feet and ran all the way home.

Around midnight Nicholas was still washing his neck wounds with strong chamomile tea when he heard a wolf's howl under his bedroom window. The sheep started to bleat in their pen, and the dog barked furiously. Soon the barking turned into a pitiful yelp, and all became quiet. Nicholas stayed up most of the rest of the night, sick with worry. Finally, just before daybreak, he fell asleep, exhausted.

Stepping out on the porch the next day, Nicholas saw that the snow in his front yard was full of wolf tracks. "There must have been dozens of them," he whispered anxiously, and went to check on his horse and sheep. The farm animals were all right, but near the stable lay his dog's spiked collar in a huge puddle of frozen blood. Horrified, Nicholas picked up the collar and ran back into the house, where he remained for the rest of the day.

The following morning Nicholas had to go to the village again. He tried to bandage his wounded neck by wrapping a piece of cloth around it, but the cloth was too short to be tied together. Looking for something to hold it in place, he came upon the steel-spiked dog collar. This should do nicely, he thought, fitting the collar over his bandage.

The collar's sharp steel spikes made him look so fierce that Nicholas was startled when he glanced at himself in the mirror. Disguising the collar with a thick woolen scarf, he went to the stable to get his horse. Soon he was on his way to the village.

Just before a clearing where there stood the cabin of an old woodcutter and his son, Nicholas's horse spooked, throwing him into a snowbank. A huge gray wolf leaped out of the thick underbrush and, growling savagely, tore into the horse's neck.

Nicholas ran for his life. He pounded desperately on the cabin door and rushed inside as soon as the woodcutter's son opened it for him. Gasping for breath, Nicholas told the son, who was one of his old carousing companions, about the savage beast that had been stalking him relentlessly for two days.

"This is very odd," said Nicholas's friend while putting on his winter coat. "Lone wolves rarely attack humans in broad daylight, and even more rarely so close to their homes." Then he grabbed his gun and filled his pockets with ammunition. "Let's see if we can teach him a lesson."

"Why go out there, son?" said the old woodcutter, who until then had been sitting quietly by the warm brick stove. "This doesn't concern you. Besides, what Nicholas needs is not a shotgun but a priest and holy water. Wasn't he sired by Michael the Handsome? Like father, like son."

Nicholas was about to ask the old woodcutter what he meant by these strange words, but his friend intervened.

"Oh, never mind my old man," said the son. "His head is full of superstitions and silly tales. Let's go and get that wolf of yours."

"In God's name, son, don't leave the house, I beg you."

"Go back to sleep, Father, We'll hear your stories after dinner."

Ignoring the old woodcutter's warning, the two men opened the heavy oak door and stepped onto the porch. The brisk mountain air was filled with the sickly odor of fresh blood, and from the woods nearby there came menacing howls. Shaking like a leaf, Nicholas walked behind the woodcutter's son.

As in a dream, Nicholas saw his former attacker leap out of nowhere and land on top of his friend, bringing him down in the snow. The man's agonizing shriek was cut short as the wolf's fangs tore open his throat. When it was all over, the wolf put its front paws on the corpse and, lifting its bloodstained muzzle toward the sky, howled fiercely. Several other wolves then rushed out of the woods and started devouring the human flesh.

Nicholas felt he was about to collapse, but he tried to compose himself. Grabbing his friend's gun, he started racing back toward the cabin. Behind him he heard again the leader's horrifying howl, echoed instantly by the whole pack. Nicholas did not have to turn around to know they were now pursuing him. In his haste he neglected to take care with his footing; he flipped and fell on his back, only a few steps away from the cabin.

The lead wolf went for his throat, pressing its jaws past the barrel of the gun. As the beast bit down on his neck, Nicholas could hear its teeth crack on the steel spikes of the dog collar. Its mouth torn to shreds, the wolf recoiled.

Still on his back, Nicholas fired both barrels of the shotgun at his attacker. The blast caught the wolf in the chest and threw it back into the other charging beasts. Nicholas rose to his feet and ran to the cabin door.

"Let me in," he screamed, banging his fists on the door.

"Go away, you murderer," said the old man inside.

"Help me!" Nicholas shrieked. "Help me—let me in!"

"Why don't you ask them for help? Just look behind you."

Nicholas cast a quick glance behind him and froze. The wolves had moved back a few yards, and, huddled in the snow, there lay a human form. Nicholas felt as though he were losing his mind.

"What's all this about, old man?" he shouted through the door. "What's going on?"

"Only wretched sinners like you forget that a seventh son born out of wedlock joins the unclean and turns into a wolf," said the old man inside.

"What?" whispered Nicholas.

"Go look at him. He's much like yourself, for he's a *bitang*, one of your bastard sons."

Nicholas felt rage and fear billowing inside him. He started kicking the cabin door as hard as he could.

"Old man, you're mad. Let me in before they tear me to pieces."

"I wish they would. But they rarely harm one of their own. Now go away before I shoot you."

Overwhelmed, Nicholas turned around and staggered over to the corpse in the snow. It had been a slender, handsome youth, but now his lips were torn and bloody, his chest carved open by the gun blast. Nicholas gazed into the lad's cloudy eyes and there, giving him unbearable pain, he discovered his own young image. Sobbing, he fell to his knees and bent over the lifeless boy.

"Go away, *bitang!* You are cursed." Nicholas heard the old man's angry voice. The door opened slightly, and a bullet whizzed past him.

Filled with shame and remorse, Nicholas tried to stand up, but he could not. He tried again, but dropped back in the snow on all fours. With horror he saw that his arms were now covered with dark gray fur. Before his very eyes, his hands shriveled up and changed into paws.

The dog collar grew tight and stifling around his stiffening, thick neck. As he tried to shake it loose, its clasp snapped, and the collar fell into the snow. Letting out a long howl, he disappeared into the forest, followed by his pack of wolves.

# PART EIGHT

# The Unabsolved Werewolf

Werewolves have human souls. Whatever the cause of their metamorphosis, they continue to have spiritual needs. These needs include the human need for expiation of crimes done as werewolves. Only a proper burial can assure the werewolves of redemption. Unburied werewolves remain outcasts in a perpetual state of disquiet. Although as werewolves they abrogated the rights to a human burial, in death they do not want to have their bodies dumped into an unmarked pit, or, worse, to lie uncovered, to be exposed to predators, with dogs licking up their blood, their flesh molding in the rain, their bones bleaching in the sun. The need for a proper burial lingers in the soul and propels werewolves to make post-death appearances to those who may be willing to grant them absolution through burial. They cannot rest in peace until the solemnities and ceremonies of burial validate the remnant of their humanness.

There are four unabsolved werewolves in this section: a family (father, mother, and daughter) and a young American Indian male. The family of werewolves died in a fire thirty years earlier, and their bones were dumped unceremoniously into mounds in their barnyard. The family of werewolves is condemned to wandering destructively until a guileless person loves the daughter and frees them by conducting an Anglican Prayer Book burial. The young American Indian werewolf committed a crime against the tribe. He killed a wolf, the totem of his tribe, and, as punishment, was denied entrance into the happy hunting grounds. His bones were thrown into a pit in the ground; his head and tomahawk were buried separately. After death he reappears as a werewolf to a camper at a remote lake, begging (with werewolf gestures, bereft of human language) for the restoration and peace of a proper burial.

The family of werewolves portrayed in "The Phantom Farmhouse" is confronted by Mr. Weatherby, a clergyman recovering from a serious illness who is the narrator of the story. As he is recovering, he takes walks in the Maine countryside and discovers a farmhouse with a hospitable family. Even though the family has strange characteristics—each member has an unusually long forefinger, sharply pointed blood-red nails, and a strange throaty voice—he is drawn to the beautiful daughter and falls in love with her. Meanwhile, killer dogs without tails are roaming the countryside tearing out the throats of sheep, dogs, and other animals; human beings narrowly escape these marauding werewolves. The daughter, overcome by Mr. Weatherby's love, pleads with him to come at dawn and to read the Prayer Book Order for the Burial of the Dead over three mounds in the thicket behind the corncrib. When Mr. Weatherby informs his friends at the sanatorium about his decision to acquiesce to the request of a person who is rumored to have died thirty years earlier, he is urged not to risk his life for a werewolf. Disregarding their warnings, he reads the Order for Burial of the Dead over the frenzied howlings of the hounds of hell. As soon as he has completed the service, the hounds cease their howling. Grace, love, and peace are restored in the benediction. The house and its inhabitants dissolve into mist. Christian burial, administered by one who is capable of loving even a werewolf, absolves these three perturbed werewolves. Requiescat in pace.

The story "Running Wolf" combines Algernon Blackwood's love of nature, of solitude in woods and forest, with his observations on the psychic powers of human beings. Blackwood had no doubt that a human spirit could live on a hundred years after death and make its presence felt in the shape of a werewolf. The sympathetic trout fisherman in the story is, according to Blackwood, an "average man, who either through a flash of terror or beauty becomes stimulated into extrasensory experience."

One evening the fisherman senses the presence of a wolf lurking in the shadows of his campfire. He concludes that this is no ordinary wolf, "for it was, after all, no dog its appearance aped, but something nearer to himself, and more familiar still. It sat there with the pose, the attitude, the gesture in repose of something almost human. And then, with a second shock of biting wonder, it came to him like a revelation. The wolf sat beside that campfire as a man might sit."

With this revelation, all his fear disappears, and the fisherman develops a symbiotic relationship with his werewolf visitor. Gaining confidence, the werewolf leads the fisherman to scattered bones, a severed head, and a tomahawk, indicating that he wishes to have the skeleton and head reunited in a proper burial. The plea for absolution from a hundred-year-old guilt is heard and understood by the fisherman. He reunites bones and head in this simple burial ceremony and enables the werewolf to find eternal peace in the happy hunting grounds. In the end, the fisherman knows that he has "pleased and satisfied" the werewolf and that "he had now fulfilled its purpose in a great measure."

# The Phantom Farmhouse

## SEABURY QUINN (1889–1969)

I HAD BEEN at the new Briarcliff Sanitarium nearly three weeks before I actually saw the house.

Every morning, as I lay abed after the nurse had taken my temperature, I wondered what was beyond the copse of fir and spruce at the turn of the road. The picture seemed incomplete without chimneys rising among the evergreens. I thought about it so much I finally convinced myself there really was a house in the wood. A house where people lived and worked and were happy.

All during the long, trying days when I was learning to navigate a wheelchair, I used to picture the house and the people who lived in it. There would be a father, I was sure; a stout, good-natured father, somewhat bald, who sat on the porch and smoked a cob pipe in the evening. And there was a mother, too; a waistless plaid-skirted mother with hair smoothly parted over her forehead, who sat beside the father as he rocked and smoked, and who had a brown workbasket in her lap. She spread the stocking feet over her outstretched fingers and her vigilant needle spied out and closed every hole with a cunning no mechanical loom could rival.

Then there was a daughter. I was a little hazy in my conception of her; but I knew she was tall and slender as a hazel wand, and that her eyes were blue and wide and sympathetic.

Picturing the house and its people became a favorite pastime with me during the time I was acquiring the art of walking all over again. By the time I was able to trust my legs on the road, I felt I knew my way to my vision-friends'

In *Weird Tales* (October 1923).

home as well as I knew the byways of my own parish; though I had as yet not set foot outside the sanitarium.

Oddly enough, I chose the evening for my first long stroll. It was unusually warm for September in Maine, and some of the sturdier of the convalescents had been playing tennis during the afternoon. After dinner they sat on the veranda, comparing notes on their respective cases of influenza, or matching experiences in appendicitis operations.

After building the house bit by bit from my imagination, as a child pieces together a picture puzzle, I should have been bitterly disappointed if the woods had proved empty; yet when I reached the turn of the road and found my dream house a reality, I was almost afraid. Bit for bit and part for part, it was as I had visualized it.

A long, rambling, comfortable-looking farmhouse it was, with a wide porch screened by vines, and a whitewashed picket fence about the little clearing before it. There was a tumbledown gate in the fence, one of the kind that is held shut with a weighted chain. Looking closely, I saw the weight was a disused ploughshare. Leading from gate to porch was a path of flat stones, laid unevenly in the short grass, and bordered with a double row of clam shells. A lamp burned in the front room, sending out cheerful golden rays to meet the silver moonlight.

A strange, eerie sensation came over me as I stood there. Somehow, I felt I had seen that house before; many, many times before; yet I had never been in that part of Maine till I came to Briarcliff, nor had anyone ever described the place to me. Indeed, except for my idle dreams, I had had no intimation that there was a house in those pines at all.

"Who lives in the house at the turn of the road?" I asked the fat man who roomed next to me.

He looked at me as blankly as if I had addressed him in Choctaw, then countered, "What road?"

"Why, the south road," I explained. "I mean the house in the pines—just beyond the curve, you know."

If such a thing had not been obviously absurd, I should have thought he looked frightened at my answer. Certainly his already prominent eyes started a bit further from his face.

"Nobody lives there," he assured me. "Nobody's lived there for years. There isn't any house there."

I became angry. What right had this fellow to make my civil question the occasion for an ill-timed jest? "As you please," I replied. "Perhaps there isn't any house there for *you*; but I saw one there last night."

"My God!" he ejaculated, and hurried away as if I'd just told him I was infected with smallpox.

Later in the day I overheard a snatch of conversation between him and one of his acquaintances in the lounge.

"I tell you it's so," he was saying with great earnestness. "I thought it was a lot of poppycock, myself; but that clergyman saw it last night. I'm going to pack my traps and get back to the city, and not waste any time about it, either."

"Rats!" his companion scoffed. "He must have been stringing you."

Turning to light a cigar, he caught sight of me. "Say, Mr. Weatherby," he called, "you didn't mean to tell my friend here that you really saw a house down by those pines last night, did you?"

"I certainly did," I answered, "and I tell you, too. There's nothing unusual about it, is there?"

"Is there?" he repeated. "*Is* there? Say, what'd it look like?"

I described it to him as well as I could, and his eyes grew as wide as those of a child hearing the story of Bluebeard.

"Well, I'll be a Chinaman's uncle!" he declared as I finished. "I sure will!"

"See here," I demanded. "What's all the mystery about that farmhouse? Why shouldn't I see it? It's there to be seen, isn't it?"

He gulped once or twice, as if there were something hot in his mouth, before he answered:

"Look here, Mr. Weatherby, I'm telling you this for your own good. You'd better stay in nights; and you'd better stay away from those pines in particular."

Nonplussed at this unsolicited advice, I was about to ask an explanation, when I detected the after-tang of whisky on his breath. I understood, then, I was being made the butt of a drunken joke by a pair of racecourse followers.

"I'm very much obliged, I'm sure," I replied with dignity, "but if you don't mind, I'll choose my own comings and goings."

"Oh, go as far as you like"—he waved his arms wide in token of my complete free-agency—"go as far as you like. I'm going to New York."

And he did. The pair of them left the sanitarium that afternoon.

.    .    .

A SLIGHT RECURRENCE of my illness held me housebound for several days after my conversation with the two sportively inclined gentlemen, and the next time I ventured out at night the moon had waxed to the full, pouring a flood of light upon the earth that rivaled midday. The minutest objects were as readily distinguished as they would have been before sunset; in fact, I remember comparing the evening to a silver-plated noon.

As I trudged along the road to the pine copse, I was busy formulating plans for intruding into the family circle at the farmhouse, devising all manner of pious frauds by which to scrape acquaintance.

"Shall I feign having lost my way, and inquire direction to the sanitarium; or shall I ask if some mythical acquaintance, a John Squires, for instance, lives there?" I asked myself as I neared the turn of the road.

Fortunately for my conscience, all these subterfuges were unnecessary, for as I neared the whitewashed fence, a girl left the porch and walked quickly to the gate, where she stood gazing pensively along the moonlit road. It was almost as if she were coming to meet me, I thought, as I slackened my pace and assumed an air of deliberate casualness.

Almost abreast of her, I lessened my pace still more, and looked directly at her. Then I knew why my conception of the girl who lived in that house had been misty and indistinct. For the same reason the venerable John had faltered in his description of the New Jerusalem until his vision in the Isle of Patmos.

From the smoothly parted hair above her wide, forget-me-not eyes, to the hem of her white cotton frock, she was as slender and lovely as a Rossetti saint; as wonderful to the eye as a medieval poet's vision of his lost love in paradise. Her forehead, evenly framed in the beaten bronze of her hair, was wide and high, and startlingly white, and her brows were delicately penciled as if laid on by an artist with a camel's hair brush. The eyes themselves were sweet and clear as forest pools mirroring the September sky, and lifted a little at the corners, like an Oriental's, giving her face a quaint, exotic look in the midst of these Maine woods.

So slender was her figure that the swell of her bosom was barely perceptible under the light stuff of her dress, and, as she stood immobile in the nimbus of moon rays, the undulation of the line from her shoulders to ankles was what painters call a "curve of motion."

One hand rested lightly on the gate, a hand as finely cut as a bit of Italian sculpture, and scarcely less white than the limed wood supporting it. I noticed idly that the forefinger was somewhat longer than its fellows, and that the nails were almond shaped and very pink—almost red—as if they had been rouged and brightly polished.

No man can take stock of a woman thus, even in a cursory, fleeting glimpse, without her being aware of the inspection, and in the minute my eyes drank up her beauty, our glances crossed and held.

The look she gave back was as calm and unperturbed as though I had been nonexistent; one might have thought I was an invisible wraith of the night; yet the faint suspicion of a flush quickening in her throat and cheeks told me she was neither unaware nor unappreciative of my scrutiny.

Mechanically, I raised my cap, and, wholly without conscious volition, I heard my own voice asking: "May I trouble you for a drink from your well? I'm from the sanitarium—only a few days out of bed, in fact—and I fear I've overdone myself in my walk."

A smile flitted across her rather wide lips, quick and sympathetic as a mother's response to her child's request, as she swung the gate open for me.

"Surely—" she answered, and her voice had all the sweetness of the south wind soughing through her native pines—"surely you may drink at our well, and rest yourself, too—if you wish."

She preceded me up the path, quickening her pace as she neared the house, and running nimbly up the steps to the porch. From where I stood beside the old-fashioned well, fitted with windlass and bucket, I could hear the sound of whispering voices in earnest conversation. Hers I recognized, lowered though it was, by the flutelike purling of its tones; the other two were deeper, and, it seemed to me, hoarse and throaty. Somehow, odd as it seemed, there was a canine note in them, dimly reminding me of the muttering of not too friendly dogs—such fractious growls I had heard while doing missionary duty in Alaska, when the savage, half-wolf malamutes were not fed promptly at the relay stations.

Her voice rose a trifle higher, as if in argument, and I fancied I heard her whisper, "This one is mine, I tell you; mine. Go to your own hunting."

An instant later there was a reluctant assenting growl from the shadow of the vines curtaining the porch, and a light laugh from the girl as she descended the steps, swinging a bright tin cup in her hand. For a second she looked at me, as she sent the bucket plunging into the stone-curbed well; then she announced, in explanation: "We're great hunters here, you know. The season is just in, and Dad and I have the worst quarrels about whose game is whose."

She laughed in recollection of their argument, and I laughed with her. I had been quite a Nimrod as a boy, myself, and well I remembered the heated controversies as to whose charge of shot was responsible for some luckless bunny's demise.

The well was very deep, and my breath was coming fast by the time I had helped her wind the bucket-rope upon the windlass; but the water was cold as only spring-fed well water can be. As she poured it from the bucket it shone almost like foam in the moonlight, and seemed to whisper with a half-human voice, instead of gurgling as other water does when poured.

I had drunk water in nearly every quarter of the globe; but never such water as that. Cold as the breath from a glacier: limpid as visualized air, it was yet so light and tasteless in substance that only the chill in my throat and the sight of the liquid in the cup told me that I was doing more than going through the motions of drinking.

"And now, will you rest?" she invited, as I finished my third draft. "We've an extra chair on the porch for you."

Behind the screen of vines I found her father and mother seated in the rays of the big kitchen lamp. They were just as I had expected to find them; plain, homely, sincere country folk, courteous in their reception and anxious to make a sick stranger welcome. Both were stout, with the comfortable stoutness of middle age and good health; but both had surprisingly slender hands. I noticed, too, that the same characteristic of an overlong forefinger was apparent in their hands as in their daughter's and that both their nails were trimmed to points and stained almost a brilliant red.

"My father, Mr. Squires," the girl introduced, "and my mother, Mrs. Squires."

I could not repress a start. There people bore the very name I had casually thought to use when inquiring for some imaginary person. My lucky stars had surely guided me away from that attempt to scrape an acquaintance. What a figure I should have cut if I had actually asked for Mr. Squires!

Though I was not aware of it, my curious glance must have stayed longer on their reddened nails than I had intended, for Mrs. Squires looked deprecatingly at her hands. "We've all been turning, putting up fox grapes"—she included her husband and daughter with a comprehensive gesture. "And the stain just won't wash out; has to wear off, you know."

I spent, perhaps, two hours with my newfound friends, talking of everything from the best methods of potato culture to the surest way to landing a nine-pound bass. All three joined in the conversation and took a lively interest in the topics under discussion. After the vapid talk of the guests at the sanitarium, I found the simple, interested discourse of these country people as stimulating as wine, and when I left them it was with a hearty promise to renew my call at an early date.

"Better wait until after dark," Mr. Squires warned. "We'd be glad to see you any time; but we're so busy these fall days, we haven't much time for company."

I took the broad hint in the same friendly spirit it was given.

It must have grown chillier than I realized while I sat there, for my new friends' hands were clay-cold when I took them in mine at parting.

Homeward bound, a whimsical thought struck me so suddenly I laughed aloud. There was something suggestive of the dog tribe about the Squires family, though I could not for the life of me say what it was. Even Mildred, the daughter, beautiful as she was, with her light eyes, her rather prominent nose and her somewhat wide mouth, reminded me in some vague way of a lovely silver collie I had owned as a boy.

I struck a tassel of dried leaves from a cluster of weeds with my walking stick as I smiled at the fanciful conceit. The legend of the werewolf—those horrible monsters, formed as men, but capable of assuming bestial shape at will, and killing and eating their fellows, was as old as mankind's fear of the dark, but no mythology I had ever read contained a reference to dog people.

Strange fancies strike us in the moonlight, sometimes.

September ripened to October, and the moon, which had been as round and bright as an exchange-worn coin when I first visited the Squires house, waned as thin as a shaving from a silversmith's lathe.

I became a regular caller at the house in the pines. Indeed, I grew to look forward to my nightly visits with those homely folk as a welcome relief from the tediously gay companionship of the oversophisticated people at the sanitarium.

My habit of slipping away shortly after dinner was the cause of considerable comment and no little speculation on the part of my fellow convalescents. It was Miss Leahy who pushed the impudent curiosity further than any of the rest, however. One evening, as I was setting out, she met me at the gate and announced her intention of going with me. "You must have found something *dreadfully* attractive to take you off every evening this way, Mr. Weatherby," she hazarded as she pursed her rather pretty, rouged lips at me and caught step with my walk. "We girls really *can't* let some little country lass take you away from us, you know. We simply can't."

I made no reply. It was scarcely possible to tell a pretty girl, even such a vain little flirt as Sara Leahy, to go home and mind her business. Yet that was just what I wanted to do. But I would not take her with me; to that I made up my mind. I would stop at the turn of the road, just out of sight of the farmhouse, and cut across the fields. If she wanted to accompany me on a cross-country hike in high-heeled slippers, she was welcome to do so.

Besides, she would tell the others that my wanderings were nothing more mysterious than nocturnal exploration of the nearby woods; which bit of misinformation would satisfy the busybodies at Briarcliff and relieve me of the espionage to which I was subjected, as well.

I smiled grimly to myself as I pictured her climbing over fences and ditches in her flimsy party frock and beaded pumps, and lengthened my stride toward the woods at the road's turn.

We marched to the limits of the field bordering the Squires' grove in silence, I thinking of the mild revenge I should soon wreak upon the pretty little busybody at my side, Miss Leahy, and she too intent on holding the pace I set to waste breath in conversation.

As we neared the woods she halted, an expression of worry, almost fear, coming over her face.

"I don't believe I'll go any farther," she announced.

"No?" I replied, a trifle sarcastically. "And is your curiosity so easily satisfied?"

"It's not that." She turned half round, as if to retrace her steps. "I'm afraid of those woods."

"Indeed?" I queried. "And what is there to be afraid of? Bears, Indians, or wildcats. I've been through them several times without seeing anything terrifying." Now she had come this far, I was anxious to take her through the fields and underbrush.

"No-o," Miss Leahy answered, a nervous quaver in her voice. "I'm not afraid of anything like that; but—oh, I don't know what you call it. Pierre told me all about it the other day. Some kind of dreadful thing—loop—loop—something or other. It's a French word, and I can't remember it."

I was puzzled. Pierre Geronte was the ancient French-Canadian gardener at the sanitarium, and, like all doddering old men, would talk for hours to anyone who would listen. Also, like all *habitants*, he was full of wild folklore his ancestors brought overseas with them generations ago.

"What did Pierre tell you?" I asked.

"Why, he said that years ago some terrible people lived in these woods. They had the only house for miles 'round; and travelers stopped there for the night, sometimes. But no stranger was ever seen to leave that place, once he went in. One night the farmers gathered about the house and burned it, with the family that lived there. When the embers had cooled down they made a search, and found nearly a dozen bodies buried in the cellar. That was why no one ever came away from that dreadful place.

"They took the murdered men to the cemetery and buried them; but they dumped the charred bodies of the murderers into graves in the barnyard, without even saying a prayer over them. And Pierre says—Oh, look! *Look!*"

She broke off her recital of the old fellow's story, and pointed a trembling hand across the field to the edge of the woods. A second more and she shrank against me, clutching at my coat with fear-stiffened fingers and crying with excitement and terror.

I looked in the direction she indicated, myself a little startled by the abject fear that had taken such sudden hold on her.

Something white and ungainly was running diagonally across the field from us, skirting the margin of the woods and making for the meadow that adjoined the sanitarium pasture. A second glance told me it was a sheep; probably one of the flock kept to supply our table with fresh meat.

I was laughing at the strength of the superstition that could make the girl see a figure of horror in an innocent mutton that had strayed away from its fellows and was scared out of its silly wits, when something else attracted my attention.

Loping along in the trail of the fleeing sheep, somewhat to the rear and a little to each side, were two other animals. At first glance they appeared to be a pair of large collies; but as I looked more intently, I saw that these animals were like nothing I had ever seen before. They were much larger than any collie—nearly as high as St. Bernards—yet shaped in a general way like Alaskan sledge dogs—huskies.

The farther one was considerably the larger of the two, and ran with a slight limp, as if one of its hind paws had been injured. As nearly as I could tell in the indifferent light, they were a rusty brown color, very thick-haired and unkempt in appearance. But the strangest thing about them was the fact that both were tailless, which gave them a terrifyingly grotesque look.

As they ran, a third form, similar to the other two in shape, but smaller, slender as a greyhound, with much lighter-hued fur, broke from the thicket of short brush edging the wood and took up the chase, emitting a series of short, sharp yelps.

"Sheep killers," I murmured, half to myself. "Odd. I've never seen dogs like that before."

"They're not dogs," wailed Miss Leahy against my coat. "They're not dogs. Oh, Mr. Weatherby, let's go away. Please, please take me home."

She was rapidly becoming hysterical, and I had a difficult time with her on the trip back. She clung whimpering to me, and I had almost to carry her most of the way. By the time we reached the sanitarium, she was crying bitterly, shivering, as if with a chill, and went in without stopping to thank me for my assistance.

I turned and made for the Squires farm with all possible speed, hoping to get there before the family had gone to bed. But when I arrived the house was in darkness, and my knock at the door received no answer.

As I retraced my steps to the sanitarium, I heard faintly, from the fields beyond the woods, the shrill, eerie cry of the sheep-killing dogs.

A TORRENT OF RAIN held us marooned the next day. Miss Leahy was confined to her room, with a nurse in constant attendance and the house doctor making hourly calls. She was on the verge of a nervous collapse, he told me, crying with a persistence that bordered on hysteria, and responding to treatment very slowly.

An impromptu dance was organized in the great hall and half a dozen bridge tables set up in the library; but as I was skilled in neither of these rainy day diversions I put on a waterproof and patrolled the veranda for exercise.

On my third or fourth trip around the house, I ran into old Geronte shuffling across the porch, wagging his head and muttering portentously to himself.

"See here, Pierre," I accosted him, "what sort of nonsense have you been telling Miss Leahy about those pine woods down the south road?"

The old fellow regarded me unwinkingly with his beady eyes, wrinkling his age-yellowed forehead for all the world like an elderly baboon inspecting a new sort of edible. "*M'sieur* goes out alone much at nights, *n'est-ce pas?*" he asked, at length.

"Yes, Monsieur goes out alone much at night," I echoed, "but what Monsieur particularly desires to know is what sort of tales have you been telling Mademoiselle Leahy. *Comprenez vous?*"

The network of wrinkles about his lips multiplied as he smiled enigmatically, regarding me askance from the corners of his eyes.

"*M'sieur* is *Anglais*," he replied. "He would not understand—or believe."

"Never mind what I'd believe," I retorted. "What is this story about murder and robbery being committed in those woods? Who were the murderers, and where did they live? Hein?"

For a few seconds he looked fixedly at me, chewing the end of senility between his toothless gums, then, glancing carefully about, as if he feared being overheard, he tiptoed up to me and whispered:

"*M'sieur* mus' stay indoors these nights. W'en the moon, she shine, yes; w'en she not show her face, no. There are evil things abroad at the dark of the moon, *M'sieur*. Even las' night they keel t'ree of my bes' sheep. Remembair, *M'sieur*, the *loup-garou*, he is out when the moon hide her light."

And with that he turned and left me; nor could I get another word from him save his cryptic warning, "Remembair, *M'sieur*, the *loup-garou*. Remembair."

In spite of my annoyance, I could not get rid of the unpleasant sensation the old man's words left with me. The *loup-garou*—werewolf—he had said, and to prove his goblin-wolf's presence, he had cited the death of his three sheep.

As I paced the rain-washed porch, I thought of the scene I had witnessed the night before, when the sheep killers were at their work.

"Well," I reflected, "I've seen the *loup-garou* on his native heath at last. From causes as slight as this, no doubt, the horrible legend of the werewolf had sprung. Time was when all France quaked at the sound of the *loup-garou's* hunting call and the bravest knights in Christendom trembled in their castles and crossed themselves fearfully because some renegade shepherd dog quested his prey in the night. On such a foundation are the legends of a people built."

Whistling a snatch from *Pinafore* and looking skyward in search of a patch of blue in the clouds, I felt a tug at my raincoat sleeve, such as a neglected terrier might give. It was Geronte again.

. . .    .

"*M'SIEUR*," he began in the same mysterious whisper, "the *loup-garou* is a ver-
ity, certainly. I, myself, have nevair seen him"—he paused to bless himself—
"but my cousin, Baptiste, was once pursued by him. Yes.

"It was near the shrine of the good Sainte Anne that Baptiste lived. One
night he was sent to fetch the cure for a dying woman. They rode fast through
the trees, the cure and my cousin Baptiste, for it was at the dark of moon, and
the evil forest folk were abroad. And as they galloped, there came a *loup-garou*
from the woods, with eyes as bright as hellfire. It followed hard, this tailless
hound from the devil's kennel; but they reached the house before it, and the
cure put his book, with the Holy Cross on its cover, at the doorstep. The *loup-
garou* wailed under the windows like a child in pain until the sun rose; then it
slunk back to the forest.

"When my cousin Baptiste and the cure came out, they found its hand
marks in the soft earth around the door. Very like your hand, or mine, they
were, *M'sieur*; save that the first finger was longer than the others."

"And did they find the *loup-garou?*" I asked, something of the old man's
earnestness communicated to me.

"Yes, *M'sieur*; but of course," he replied gravely. "T'ree weeks before a
stranger, drowned in the river, had been buried without the office of the
Church. W'en they opened his grave they found his fingernails as red as blood,
and sharp. Then they knew. The good cure read the burial office over him, and
the poor soul that had been snatched away in sin slept peacefully at last."

He looked quizzically at me, as if speculating whether to tell me more;
then, apparently fearing I would laugh at his outburst of confidence, started
away toward the kitchen.

"Well, what else, Pierre?" I asked, feeling he had more to say.

"*Non, non, non*," he replied. There is nothing more, *M'sieur.* I did but want
*M'sieur* should know my own cousin, Baptiste Geronte, had seen the *loup-garou*
with his very eyes."

"Hearsay evidence," I commented as I went in to dinner.

DURING THE RAINY WEEK that followed, I chafed at my confinement like
a privileged convict suddenly deprived of his liberties, and looked wistfully
down the south road as any prisoned gipsy ever gazed upon the open trail.

The quiet home circle at the farmhouse, the unforced conversation of the old folks, Mildred's sweet companionship, all beckoned me with an almost irresistible force. For in this period of enforced separation I discovered what I had dimly suspected for some time. I loved Mildred Squires. And, loving her, I longed to tell her of it.

No lad intent on visiting his first sweetheart ever urged his feet more eagerly than I when the curtains of the rain had at last drawn up, I hastened toward the house at the turn of the road.

As I hoped, yet hardly dared expect, Mildred was standing at the gate to meet me as I rounded the curve, and I yearned toward her like a hummingbird seeking its nest.

She must have read my heart in my eyes, for her greeting smile was as tender as a mother's as she bends above her babe.

"At last you have come, my friend," she said, putting out both hands in welcome. "I am very glad."

We walked silently up the path, her fingers still resting in mine, her face averted. At the steps she paused, a little embarrassment in her voice as she explained, "Father and mother are out; they have gone to a—meeting. But you will stay?"

"Surely," I acquiesced. And to myself I admitted my gratitude for this chance of Mildred's unalloyed company alone.

We talked but little that night. Mildred was strangely distrait, and, much as I longed to, I could not force a confession of my love from my lips. Once, in the midst of a long pause between our words, the cry of the sheep killers came faintly to us, echoed across the fields and woods, and as the weird, shrill sound fell on our ears, she threw back her head, with something of the gesture of a hunting dog scenting its quarry.

Toward midnight she turned to me, a panic of fear having apparently laid hold of her.

"You must go!" she exclaimed, rising and laying her hand on my shoulder.

"But your father and mother have not returned," I objected. "Won't you let me stay until they get back?"

"Oh, no, no," she answered, her agitation increasing. "You must go at once—please." She increased her pressure on my shoulder, almost as if to shove me from the porch.

Taken aback by her sudden desire to be rid of me, I was picking up my hat, when she uttered a stifled little scream and ran quickly to the edge of the porch, interposing herself between me and the yard. At the same moment I heard a muffled sound from the direction of the front gate, a sound like a growling and snarling of savage dogs.

I leaped forward, my first thought being that the sheep killers I had seen the other night had strayed to the Squires place. Crazed with blood, I knew, they would be almost as dangerous to human beings as to sheep, and every nerve in my sickness-weakened body cried out to protect Mildred.

To my blank amazement, as I looked from the porch I beheld Mr. and Mrs. Squires walking sedately up the path, talking composedly together. There was no sign of the dogs or any other animals about.

As the elderly couple neared the porch, I noticed that Mr. Squires walked with a pronounced limp, and that both their eyes shone very brightly in the moonlight, as though they were suffused with tears.

They greeted me pleasantly enough; but Mildred's anxiety seemed increased, rather than diminished, by their presence, and I took my leave after a brief exchange of civilities.

On my way back I looked intently in the woods bordering the road for some sign of the house of which Pierre had told Miss Leahy; but everywhere the pines grew as thickly as though neither axe nor fire had ever disturbed them.

"Geronte is in his second childhood," I reflected, "and like an elder child, he loves to terrify his juniors with fearsome witch-tales."

Yet an uncomfortable feeling was with me till I saw the gleam of the sanitarium's lights across the fields; and as I walked toward them it seemed to me that more than once I heard the baying of the sheep killers in the woods behind me.

A buzz of conversation, like the sibilant arguments of a cloud of swarming bees, greeted me as I descended the stairs to breakfast next morning.

It appeared that Ned, one of the pair of great mastiffs attached to the sanitarium, had been found dead before his kennel, his throat and brisket torn open and several gaping wounds in his flanks. Boris, his fellow, had been discovered whimpering and trembling in the extreme corner of the doghouse, the embodiment of canine terror.

Speculation as to the animal responsible for the outrage was rife, and, as usual, it ran the gamut of possible and impossible surmises. Every sort of beast from a grizzly bear to a lion escaped from the circus was in turn indicted for the crime, only to have a complete alibi straightway established.

The only one having no suggestion to offer was old Geronte, who stood sphinxlike in the outskirts of the crowd, smiling sardonically to himself and wagging his head sagely. As he caught sight of me he nodded sapiently, as if to include me in the joint tenancy to some weighty secret.

Presently he worked his way through the chattering group and whispered, "M'sieur, he was here last night— and with him was the other tailless one. Come and see."

Plucking me by the sleeve, he led me to the rear of the kennels, and, stooping, pointed to something in the moist earth. "You see?" he asked, as if a printed volume lay for my reading in the mud.

"I see that someone has been on his hands and knees here," I answered, inspecting the hand prints he indicated.

"*Something,*" he corrected, as if reasoning with an obstinate child. "Does not M'sieur behol' that the first finger is the longest?"

"Which proves nothing," I defended. "There are many hands like that."

"Oh—yes?" he replied with that upward accent of his. "And where has M'sieur seen hands like that before?"

"Oh, many times," I assured him somewhat vaguely, for there was a catch at the back of my throat as I spoke. Try as I would, I could recall only three pairs of hands with that peculiarity.

His little black eyes rested steadily on me in an unwinking stare, and the corners of his mouth curved upward in a malicious grin. It seemed, almost, as if he found a grim pleasure in thus driving me into a corner.

"See here, Pierre," I began testily, equally annoyed at myself and him, "you know as well as I that the *loup-garou* is an old woman's tale. Someone was looking here for tracks, and left his own while doing it. If we look among the patients here, we shall undoubtedly find a pair of hands to match these prints."

"God forbid!" he exclaimed, crossing himself. "That would be an evil day for us, M'sieur. Here, Bor-ees," he snapped his fingers to the surviving mastiff, "come and eat."

The huge beast came wallowing over to him with the ungainly gait of all heavily muscled animals, stopping on his way to make a nasal investigation of my knees. Scarcely had his nose come into contact with my trousers when he leaped back, every hair in his mane and along his spine stiffly erect, every tooth in his great mouth bared in a savage snarl. But instead of the mastiff's fighting growl, he emitted only a low, frightened whine, as though he were facing some animal of greater power than himself, and knew his own weakness.

"Good heavens!" I cried, thoroughly terrified at the friendly brute's sudden hostility.

"Yes, *M'sieur*," Geronte cut in quickly, putting his hand on the dog's collar and leading him a few paces away. "It is well you should call upon the heavenly ones; for surely you have the odor of hell upon your clothes."

"What do you mean?" I demanded angrily. "How dare you—?"

He raised a thin hand deprecatingly. "*M'sieur* knows that he knows," he replied evenly; "and what I also know."

And leading Boris by the collar, he shuffled to the house.

MILDRED WAS WAITING for me at the gate that evening, and again her father and mother were absent at one of their meetings.

We walked silently up the path and seated ourselves on the porch where the waning moon cast oblique rays through the pine branches.

I think Mildred felt the tension I was drawn to, for she talked trivialities with an almost feverish earnestness, stringing her sentences together and changing her subjects as a Navajo rug weaver twists and breaks her threads.

At last I found an opening in the abattis of her small talk.

"Mildred," I said, very simply for great emotions tear the ornaments from our speech, "I love you, and I want you for my wife. Will you marry me, Mildred?" I laid my hand on hers. It was cold as lifeless flesh, and seemed to shrink beneath my touch.

"Surely, dear, you must have read the love in my eyes," I urged, as she averted her face in silence. "Almost from the night I first saw you, I've loved you! I—"

"O-o-h, don't!" Her interruption was a strangled moan, as if wrung from her by my words.

I leaned nearer her. "Don't you love me, Mildred?" I asked. As yet she had not denied it.

For a moment she trembled, as if a sudden chill had come on her, then, leaning to me, she clasped my shoulders in her arms, hiding her face against my jacket.

"John, John, you don't know what you say," she whispered, as though a sob had torn the words before they left her lips. Her breath was on my cheek, moist and cold as air from a vault.

I could feel the litheness of her through the thin stuff of her gown, and her body was as devoid of warmth as a dead thing.

"You're cold," I told her, putting my arms about her shieldingly. "The night has chilled you."

A convulsive sob was her only answer.

"Mildred," I began again, putting my hand beneath her chin and lifting her face to mine, "tell me, dear, what is the matter?" I lowered my lips to hers.

With a cry that was half scream, half weeping, she thrust me suddenly from her, pressing her hands against my breast and lowering her head until her face was hidden between her outstretched arms. I, too, started back, for in the instant our lips were about to meet, hers had writhed back from her teeth, like a dog's when he is about to spring, and a low, harsh noise, almost a growl, had risen in her throat.

"For God's sake," she whispered hoarsely, agony in every note of her shaking voice, "never do that again!" she whispered hoarsely. "Oh, my dear, dear love, you don't know how near to a horror worse than death you were."

"A—horror—worse—than death?" I echoed dully, pressing her cold little hands in mine. "What do you mean, Mildred?"

"Loose my hands," she commanded with a quaint reversion to the speech of our ancestors, "and hear me. I do love you. I love you better than life. Better than death. I love you so I have overcome something stronger than the walls of the grave for your sake, but John, my very love, this is our last night together. We can never meet again. You must go, now, and not come back until tomorrow morning."

"Tomorrow morning?" I repeated blankly. What wild talk was this?

Heedless of my interruption, she hurried on. "Tomorrow morning, just before the sun rises over those trees, you must be here, and have your prayer book with you."

I listened speechless, wondering which of us was mad.

"By that corncrib there"—she waved a directing hand—"you will find three mounds. Stand beside them and read the office for the burial of the dead. Come quickly, and pause for nothing on the way. Look back for nothing; heed no sound from behind you. And for your own safety, come no sooner than to allow yourself the barest time to read your office."

Bewildered, I attempted to reason with the mad woman; begged her to explain this folly; but she refused all answer to my fervid queries, nor would she suffer me to touch her.

Finally, I rose to go. "You will do what I ask?" she implored.

"Certainly not," I answered firmly.

"John, John, have pity!" she cried, flinging herself to the earth before me and clasping my knees. "You say you love me. I only ask this one favor of you; only this. Please, for my sake, for the peace of the dead and the safety of the living, promise you will do this thing for me."

Shaken by her abject supplication, I promised, though I felt myself a figure in some grotesque nightmare as I did it.

"Oh, my love, my precious love," she wept, rising and taking both my hands. "At last I shall have peace, and you shall bring it to me. No," she forbade as I made to take her in my arms at parting. "The most I can give you, dear, is this." She held her icy hands against my lips. "It seems so little, dear; but oh! it is so much."

Like a drunkard in his cups, I staggered along the south road, my thoughts gone wild with the strangeness of the play I had just acted.

Across the clearing came the howls of the sheep killers, a sound I had grown used to of late. But tonight there was a deeper, fiercer *timbre* in their bay; a note that boded ill for man as well as beast. Louder and louder it swelled; it was rising from the field itself, now, drawing nearer and nearer the road.

I turned and looked. The great beasts I had seen pursuing the luckless sheep the other night were galloping toward me. A cold finger seemed traced down my spine; the scalp crept and tingled beneath my cap. There was no other object of their quest in sight. I was their elected prey.

My first thought was to turn and run; but a second's reasoning told me this was worse than useless. Weakened with long illness, with an uphill road to the nearest shelter, I should soon be run down.

No friendly tree offered asylum; my only hope was to stand and fight. Grasping my stick, I spread my feet, bracing myself against their charge.

And as I waited their onslaught, there came from the shadow of the pines the shriller, sharper cry of the third beast. Like the crest of a flying, wind-lashed wave, the slighter, silver-furred brute came speeding across the meadow, its ears laid back, its slender paws spurning the sod daintily. Almost, it seemed as if the pale shadow of a cloud were racing toward me.

The thing dashed slantwise across the field, its flight converging on the line of the other two's attack. Midway between me and them it paused; hairs bristling, limbs bent for a spring.

My eyes went wide with incredulity. It was standing in my defense.

All the savageness of the larger beasts' hunting cry was echoed in the smaller creature's bay, and with it a defiance that needed no interpretation.

The attackers paused in their rush; halted, and looked speculatively at my ally. They took a few tentative steps in my direction; and a fierce, almost an articulate curse, went up from the silver-haired beast. Slowly the tawny pair circled and trotted back to the woods.

I hurried toward the sanitarium, grasping my stick firmly in readiness for another attack.

But no further cries came from the woods, and once, as I glanced back, I saw the light-haired beast trotting slowly in my wake, looking from right to left, as if to ward off danger.

Half an hour later I looked from my window toward the house in the pines. Far down the south road, its muzzle pointed to the moon, the bright-furred animal crouched and poured out a lament to the night. And its cry was like the wail of a child in pain.

Far into the night I paced my room, like a condemned convict when the vigil of the death watch is on him. Reason and memory struggled for the mastery; one urging to give over my wild act, the other bidding me obey my promise to Mildred.

Toward morning I dropped into a chair, exhausted with my objectless marching. I must have fallen asleep, for when I started up the stars were dimming in the zenith, and bands of slate, shading to amethyst slanted across the horizon.

A moment I paused, laughing cynically at my fool's errand, then, seizing cap and book, I bolted down the stairs, and ran through the paling dawn to the house in the pines.

There was something ominous and terrifying in the two-toned pastel of the house that morning. Its windows stared at me with blank malevolence, like the half-closed eyes of one stricken dead in mortal sin. The little patches of hoarfrost on the lawn were like leprous spots on some unclean thing. From the trees behind the clearing an owl hooted mournfully, as if to say, "Beware, beware," and the wind soughing through the black pine boughs echoed the refrain ceaselessly.

Three mounds, sunken and weed-grown, lay in the unkempt thicket behind the corncrib. I paused beside them, throwing off my cap and adjusting my stole hastily. Thumbing the pages to the committal service, I held the book close, that I might see the print through the morning shadows, and commenced: "I know that my redeemer liveth. . ."

Almost beside me, under the branches of the pines, there rose such a chorus of howls and yelps, I nearly dropped my book. Like all the hounds in the kennels of hell, the sheep killers clamored at me, rage and fear and mortal hatred in their cries. Through the bestial cadences, too, there seemed to run a human note; the sound of voices heard before beneath these very trees. Deep and throaty, and raging mad, two of the voices came to me, and, like the tremolo of a violin lightly played in an orchestra of brass, the shriller cry of a third beast sounded.

As the hubbub rose at my back, I half turned to fly. Next instant I grasped my book more firmly and resumed my office, for like a beacon in the dark, Mildred's words flashed on my memory: *"Look back for nothing; heed no sound behind you."*

"Man that is born of a woman hath but a short time to live and is full of misery . . . deliver us from all our offenses . . . O, Lord, deliver us not into the bitter pains of eternal death . . ." and to such an accompaniment, surely, as no priest ever before chanted the office, I pressed through the brief service to the final *Amen.*

Tiny grouts of moisture stood out on my forehead, my breath struggled in my throat as I gasped out the last word. My nerves were frayed to shreds and my strength nearly gone as I let fall my book, and turned upon the beasts among the trees.

They were gone. Abruptly as it had begun, their clamor stopped, and only the rotting pine needles, lightly gilded by the morning sun, met my gaze. A light touch fell in the palm of my open hand, as if a pair of cool, sweet lips had laid a kiss there.

A vaporlike swamp-fog enveloped me. The outbuildings, the old, stone-curbed well where I had drunk the night I first saw Mildred, the house itself— all seemed fading into mist and swirling away in the morning breeze.

"Eh, eh, eh; but *M'sieur* will do himself an injury, sleeping on the wet earth!" Old Geronte bent over me, his arm beneath my shoulders. Behind him, great

Boris, the mastiff, stood wagging his tail, regarding me with doggish good humor.

"Pierre," I muttered thickly, "how came you here?"

"This morning, going to my tasks, I saw *M'sieur* run down the road like a thing pursued. I followed quickly, for the woods hold terrors in the dark, *M'sieur.*"

I looked toward the farmhouse. Only a pair of chimneys, rising stark and bare from a crumbling foundation, were there. Fence, well, barn—all were gone, and in their place a thicket of sumac and briars, tangled and overgrown as though undisturbed for thirty years.

"The house, Pierre! Where is the house?" I croaked, sinking my fingers into his withered arm.

" 'Ouse?" he echoed. "Oh, but of course. There is no 'ouse here, *M'sieur;* nor has there been for years. This is an evil place, *M'sieur;* 't is best we quit it, and that quickly. There be evil things that run by night—"

"No more," I answered, staggering toward the road, leaning heavily on him. "I brought them peace, Pierre."

He looked dubiously at the English prayer book I held. A Protestant clergyman is a thing of doubtful usefulness to the orthodox French-Canadian. Something of the heartsick misery in my face must have touched his kind old heart, for at last he relented, shaking his head pityingly and patting my shoulder gently as one would soothe a sorrowing child.

"Per'aps, *M'sieur*," he conceded. "Per'aps; who shall say no? Love and sorrow are the purchase price of peace. Yes. Did not *le bon Dieu* so buy the peace of the world?"

# Running Wolf

## ALGERNON BLACKWOOD (1869–1951)

THE MAN WHO ENJOYS an adventure outside the general experience of the race, and imparts it to others, must not be surprised if he is taken for either a liar or a fool, as Malcolm Hyde, hotel clerk on a holiday, discovered in due course. Nor is "enjoy" the right word to use in describing his emotions; the word he chose was probably "survive."

When he first set eyes on Medicine Lake, he was struck by its still, sparkling beauty, lying there in the vast Canadian backwoods; next, by its extreme loneliness; and lastly—a good deal later, this—by its combination of beauty, loneliness, and singular atmosphere, due to the fact that it was the scene of his adventure.

"It's fairly stiff with big fish," said Morton of the Montreal Sporting Club. "Spend your holidays there—up Mattawa way, some fifteen miles west of Stony Creek. You'll have it all to yourself except for an old Indian who's got a shack there. Camp on the east side—if you'll take a tip from me." He then talked for half an hour about the wonderful sport; yet he was not otherwise very communicative, and did not suffer questions gladly, Hyde noticed. Nor had he stayed there very long himself. If it was such a paradise as Morton, its discoverer and the most experienced rod in the province, claimed, why had he himself spent only three days there?

"Ran short of grub," was the explanation offered; but to another friend he had mentioned briefly, "flies," and to a third, so Hyde learned later, he gave the excuse that his half-breed "took sick," necessitating a quick return to civilization.

In *Tales of the Uncanny and the Supernatural* (London: Peter Nevill, 1949). No copyright given.

Hyde, however, cared little for the explanations; his interest in these came later. "Stiff with fish" was the phrase he liked. He took the Canadian Pacific train to Mattawa, laid in his outfit at Stony Creek, and set off thence for the fifteen-mile canoe trip without a care in the world.

Traveling light, the portages did not trouble him; the water was swift and easy, the rapids negotiable; everything came his way, as the saying is. Occasionally he saw big fish making for the deeper pools, and was sorely tempted to stop; but he resisted. He pushed on between the immense world of forests that stretched for hundreds of miles, known to deer, bear, moose, and wolf, but strange to any echo of human tread, a deserted and primeval wilderness. The autumn day was calm, the water sang and sparkled, the blue sky hung cloudless overall, ablaze with light. Toward evening he passed an old beaver dam, rounded a little point, and had his first sight of Medicine Lake. He lifted his dripping paddle; the canoe shot with silent glide into calm water. He gave an exclamation of delight, for the loveliness caught his breath away.

Though primarily a sportsman, he was not insensible to beauty. The lake formed a crescent, perhaps four miles long, its width between a mile and half a mile. The slanting gold of sunset flooded it. No wind stirred its crystal surface. Here it had lain since the redskins' god first made it; here it would lie until he dried it up again. Towering spruce and hemlock trooped to its very edge, majestic cedars leaned down as if to drink, crimson sumacs shone in fiery patches, and maples gleamed orange and red beyond belief. The air was like wine, with the silence of a dream.

It was here the red men formerly "made medicine," with all the wild ritual and tribal ceremony of an ancient day. But it was of Morton, rather than of Indians, that Hyde thought. If this lonely, hidden paradise was really stiff with big fish, he owed a lot to Morton for the information. Peace invaded him, but the excitement of the hunter lay below.

He looked about him with quick, practiced eye for a camping place before the sun sank below the forests and the half-lights came. The Indian's shack, lying in full sunshine on the eastern shore, he found at once; but the trees lay too thick about it for comfort, nor did he wish to be so close to its inhabitant. Upon the opposite side, however, an ideal clearing offered. This lay already in shadow, the huge forest darkening it toward evening; but the open space attracted. He paddled over quickly and examined it. The ground was hard and dry, he found, and a little brook ran tinkling down one side of it into the lake.

This outfall, too, would be a good fishing spot. Also it was sheltered. A few low willows marked the mouth.

An experienced camper soon makes up his mind. It was a perfect site, and some charred logs, with traces of former fires, proved that he was not the first to think so. Hyde was delighted. Then, suddenly, disappointment came to tinge his pleasure. His kit was landed, and preparations for putting up the tent were begun, when he recalled a detail that excitement had so far kept in the background of his mind—Morton's advice. But not Morton's only, for the storekeeper at Stony Creek had reinforced it. The big fellow with straggling moustache and stooping shoulders, dressed in shirt and trousers, had handed him out a final sentence with the bacon, flour, condensed milk, and sugar. He had repeated Morton's half-forgotten words: "Put yer tent on the east shore, I should," he had said at parting.

He remembered Morton, too, apparently. "A shortish fellow, brown as an Indian and fairly smelling of the woods. Traveling with Jake, the half-breed." That assuredly was Morton. "Didn't stay long, now, did he," he added to himself in a reflective tone.

"Going Windy Lake way, are yer? Or Ten Mile Water, maybe?" he had inquired of Hyde.

"Medicine Lake."

"Is that so?" the man said, as though he doubted it for some obscure reason. He pulled at his ragged moustache a moment. "Is that so, now?" he repeated. And the final words followed him downstream after a considerable pause—the advice about the best shore on which to put his tent. All this now suddenly flashed back upon Hyde's mind with a tinge of disappointment and annoyance, for when two experienced men agreed, their opinion was not to be lightly disregarded. He wished he had asked the storekeeper for more details. He looked about him, he reflected, he hesitated. His ideal camping-ground lay certainly on the forbidden shore. What in the world, he wondered, could be the objection to it?

But the light was fading; he must decide quickly one way or the other. After staring at his unpacked dunnage, and the tent, already half erected, he made up his mind with a muttered expression that consigned both Morton and the storekeeper to less pleasant places. "They must have *some* reason," he growled to himself; "fellows like that usually know what they're talking about. I guess I'd better shift over to the other side—for tonight, at any rate."

He glanced across the water before actually reloading. No smoke rose from the Indian's shack. He had seen no sign of a canoe. The man, he decided, was away. Reluctantly, then, he left the good camping ground and paddled across the lake, and half an hour later his tent was up, firewood collected, and two small trout were already caught for supper. But the bigger fish, he knew, lay waiting for him on the other side by the little outfall, and he fell asleep at length on his bed of balsam boughs, annoyed and disappointed, yet wondering how a mere sentence could have persuaded him so easily against his own better judgment. He slept like the dead; the sun was well up before he stirred.

But his morning mood was a very different one. The brilliant light, the peace, the intoxicating air, all this was too exhilarating for the mind to harbor foolish fancies, and he marveled that he could have been so weak the night before. No hesitation lay in him anywhere. He struck camp immediately after breakfast, paddled back across the strip of shining water, and quickly settled in upon the forbidden shore, as he now called it, with a contemptuous grin. And the more he saw of the spot, the better he liked it. There was plenty of wood, running water to drink, an open space about the tent, and there were no flies. The fishing, moreover, was magnificent. Morton's description was fully justified, and "stiff with big fish" for once was not an exaggeration.

The useless hours of the early afternoon he passed dozing in the sun, or wandering through the underbrush beyond the camp. He found no sign of anything unusual. He bathed in a cool, deep pool; he reveled in the lonely little paradise. Lonely it certainly was, but the loneliness was part of its charm; the stillness, the peace, the isolation of this beautiful backwoods lake delighted him. The silence was divine. He was entirely satisfied.

After a brew of tea, he strolled toward evening along the shore, looking for the first sign of a rising fish. A faint ripple on the water, with the lengthening shadows, made good conditions. *Plop* followed plop, as the big fellows rose, snatched at their food, and vanished into the depths. He hurried back. Ten minutes later he had taken his rods and was gliding cautiously in the canoe through the quiet water.

So good was the sport, indeed, and so quickly did the big trout pile up in the bottom of the canoe, that despite the growing lateness, he found it hard to tear himself away. "One more," he said, "and then I really will go." He landed that "one more," and was in the act of taking off the hook, when the deep silence of the evening was curiously disturbed. He became abruptly aware that someone watched him. A pair of eyes, it seemed, were fixed upon him from some point in the surrounding shadows.

Thus, at least, he interpreted the odd disturbance in his happy mood; for thus he felt it. The feeling stole over him without the slightest warning. He was not alone. The slippery big trout dropped from his fingers. He sat motionless, and stared about him.

Nothing stirred; the ripple on the lake had died away; there was no wind; the forest lay a single purple mass of shadow; the yellow sky, fast fading, threw reflections that troubled the eye and made distances uncertain. But there was no sound, no movement; he saw no figure anywhere. Yet he knew that someone watched him, and a wave of quite unreasoning terror gripped him. The nose of the canoe was against the bank. In a moment, and instinctively, he shoved it off and paddled into deeper water. The watcher, it came to him also instinctively, was quite close to him upon that bank. But where? And who? Was it the Indian?

Here, in deeper water, and some twenty yards from the shore, he paused and strained both sight and hearing to find some possible clue. He felt half ashamed, now that the first strange feeling passed a little. But the certainty remained. Absurd as it was, he felt positive that someone watched him with concentrated and intent regard. Every fiber in his being told him so; and though he could discover no figure, no new outline on the shore, he could even have sworn in which clump of willow bushes the hidden person crouched and stared. His attention seemed drawn to that particular clump.

The water dripped slowly from his paddle, now lying across the thwarts. There was no other sound. The canvas of his tent gleamed dimly. A star or two were out. He waited. Nothing happened.

Then, as suddenly as it had come, the feeling passed, and he knew that the person who had been watching him intently had gone. It was as if a current had been turned off; the normal world flowed back; the landscape emptied as if someone had left a room. The disagreeable feeling left him at the same time, so that he instantly turned the canoe in to the shore again, landed, and, paddle in hand, went over to examine the clump of willows he had singled out as the place of concealment. There was no one there, of course, nor any trace of recent human occupancy. No leaves, no branches stirred, nor was a single twig displaced; his keen and practiced sight detected no sign of tracks upon the ground. Yet, for all that, he felt positive that a little time ago someone had crouched among these very leaves and watched him. He remained absolutely convinced of it. The watcher, whether Indian hunter, stray lumberman, or wandering half-breed, had now withdrawn, a search was useless, and dusk was falling. He returned to his little camp, more disturbed perhaps then he cared to acknowledge. He cooked his supper, hung up his catch on a string, so that no prowling animal could get at it during the night, and prepared to make himself comfortable until bedtime. Unconsciously, he built a bigger fire than usual, and found himself peering over his pipe into the deep shadows beyond the firelight, straining his ears to catch the slightest sound. He remained generally on the alert in a way that was new to him.

A man under such conditions and in such a place need not know discomfort until the sense of loneliness strikes him as too vivid a reality. Loneliness in a backwoods camp brings charm, pleasure, and a happy sense of calm until, and unless, it comes too near. It should remain an ingredient only among other conditions; it should not be directly, vividly noticed. Once it has crept within short range, however, it may easily cross the narrow line between comfort and discomfort, and darkness is an undesirable time for the transition. A curious dread may easily follow—the dread lest the loneliness suddenly be disturbed, and the solitary human feel himself open to attack.

For Hyde, now, this transition had been already accomplished; the too intimate sense of his loneliness had shifted abruptly into the worst condition of no longer being quite alone. It was an awkward moment, and the hotel clerk realized his position exactly. He did not quite like it. He sat there, with his back to the blazing logs, a very visible object in the light, while all about him the darkness of the forest lay like an impenetrable wall. He could not see a yard beyond the small circle of his campfire; the silence about him was like the silence of the dead. No leaf rustled, no wave lapped; he himself sat motionless as a log.

Then again he became suddenly aware that the person who watched him had returned, and that same intent and concentrated gaze as before was fixed upon him where he lay. There was no warning; he heard no stealthy tread or snapping of dry twigs, yet the owner of those steady eyes was very close to him, probably not a dozen feet away. This sense of proximity was overwhelming.

It is unquestionable that a shiver ran down his spine. This time, moreover, he felt positive that the man crouched just beyond the firelight, the distance he himself could see being nicely calculated, and straight in front of him. For some minutes he sat without stirring a single muscle, yet with each muscle ready and alert, straining his eyes in vain to pierce the darkness, but only succeeding in dazzling his sight with the reflected light. Then, as he shifted his position slowly, cautiously, to obtain another angle of vision, his heart gave two big thumps against his ribs and the hair seemed to rise on his scalp with the sense of cold that gave him gooseflesh. In the darkness facing him, he saw two small and greenish circles that were certainly a pair of eyes, yet not the eyes of Indian hunter, or of any human being. It was a pair of animal eyes that stared so fixedly at him out of the night. And this certainty had an immediate and natural effect upon him.

For, at the menace of those eyes, the fears of millions of long dead hunters since the dawn of time woke in him. Hotel clerk though he was, heredity surged through him in an automatic wave of instinct. His hand groped for a weapon. His fingers fell on the iron head of his small camp axe, and at once he was himself again. Confidence returned; the vague, superstitious dread was gone. This was a bear or wolf that smelt his catch and came to steal it. With beings of that sort he knew instinctively how to deal, yet admitting by this very instinct, that his original dread had been of quite another kind.

"I'll damned quick find out what it is," he exclaimed aloud, and snatching a burning brand from the fire, he hurled it with good aim straight at the eyes of the beast before him.

The bit of pitch-pine fell in a shower of sparks that lit the dry grass this side of the animal, flared up a moment, then died quickly down again. But in that instant of bright illumination he saw clearly what his unwelcome visitor was. A big timber wolf sat on its hindquarters, staring steadily at him through the firelight. He saw its legs and shoulders, he saw its hair, he saw also the big hemlock trunks lit up behind it, and the willow scrub on each side. It formed a vivid, clear-cut picture shown in clear detail by the momentary blaze. To his amazement, however, the wolf did not turn and bolt away from the burning log, but withdrew a few yards only, and sat there again on its haunches, staring, staring as before. Heavens, how it stared! He "shoo-ed" it, but without effect; it did not budge. He did not waste another good log on it, for his fear was dissipated now; a timber wolf was a timber wolf, and it might sit there as long as it pleased, provided it did not try to steal his catch. No alarm was in him anymore. He knew that wolves were harmless in the summer and autumn, and even when "packed" in the winter, they would attack a man only when suffering desperate hunger. So he lay and watched the beast, threw bits of stick in its direction, even talked to it, wondering only that it never moved. "You can stay there forever, if you like," he remarked to it aloud, "for you cannot get at my fish, and the rest of the grub I shall take into the tent with me!"

The creature blinked its bright green eyes, but made no move.

Why, then, if his fear was gone, did he think of certain things as he rolled himself in the Hudson Bay blankets before going to sleep? The immobility of the animal was strange, its refusal to turn and bolt was still stranger. Never before had he known a wild creature that was not afraid of fire. Why did it sit and watch him, as with purpose in its gleaming eyes? How had he felt its presence earlier and instantly? A timber wolf, especially a solitary wolf, was a timid thing, yet this one feared neither man nor fire. Now, as he lay there wrapped in his blankets inside the cozy tent, it sat outside beneath the stars, beside the fading embers, the wind chilly in its fur, the ground cooling beneath its planted paws, watching him, steadily watching him, perhaps until the dawn.

It was unusual, it was strange. Having neither imagination nor tradition, he called upon no store of racial visions. Matter of fact, a hotel clerk on a fishing holiday, he lay there in his blankets, merely wondering and puzzled. A timber wolf was a timber wolf and nothing more. Yet this timber wolf—the idea haunted him—was different. In a word, the deeper part of his original uneasiness remained. He tossed about, he shivered sometimes in his broken sleep; he did not go out to see, but he woke early and unrefreshed.

Again with the sunshine and the morning wind, however, the incident of the night before was forgotten, almost unreal. His hunting zeal was uppermost. The tea and fish were delicious, his pipe had never tasted so good, the glory of this lonely lake amid primeval forests went to his head a little; he was a hunter before the Lord, and nothing else. He tried the edge of the lake, and in the excitement of playing a big fish knew suddenly that it, the wolf, was there. He paused with the rod exactly as if struck. He looked about him, he looked in a definite direction. The brilliant sunshine made every smallest detail clear and sharp—boulders of granite, burned stems, crimson sumac, pebbles along the shore in neat, separate detail—without revealing where the watcher hid. Then, his sight wandering farther inshore among the tangled undergrowth, he suddenly picked up the familiar, half-expected outline. The wolf was lying behind a granite boulder, so that only the head, the muzzle, and the eyes were visible. It merged in its background. Had he not known it was a wolf, he could never have separated it from the landscape. The eyes shone in the sunlight.

There it lay. He looked straight at it. Their eyes, in fact, actually met full and square. "Great Scott!" he exclaimed aloud, "why, it's like looking at a human being!"

From that moment unwittingly, he established a singular personal relation with the beast. And what followed confirmed this undesirable impression, for the animal rose instantly and came down in leisurely fashion to the shore, where it stood looking back at him. It stood and stared into his eyes like some great wild dog, so that he was aware of a new and almost incredible sensation—that it courted recognition.

"Well! well!" he exclaimed again, relieving his feelings by addressing it aloud, "if this doesn't beat everything I ever saw! What d'you want, anyway?"

He examined it now more carefully. He had never seen a wolf so big before; it was a tremendous beast, a nasty customer to tackle, he reflected, if it ever came to that. It stood there absolutely fearless and full of confidence. In the clear sunlight he took in every detail of it—a huge, shaggy, lean-flanked timber wolf, its wicked eyes staring straight into his own, almost with a kind of purpose in them. He saw its great jaws, its teeth, and its tongue hung out, dropping saliva a little. And yet the idea of its savagery, its fierceness, was very little in him.

He was amazed and puzzled beyond belief. He wished the Indian would come back. He did not understand this strange behavior in an animal. Its eyes, the odd expression in them, gave him a queer, unusual, difficult feeling. Had his nerves gone wrong, he almost wondered.

The beast stood on the shore and looked at him. He wished for the first time that he had brought a rifle. With a resounding smack he brought his paddle down flat upon the water, using all his strength, till the echoes rang as from a pistol shot that was audible from one end of the lake to the other. The wolf never stirred. He shouted, but the beast remained unmoved. He blinked his eyes, speaking as to a dog, a domestic animal, a creature accustomed to human ways. It blinked its eyes in return.

At length, increasing his distance from the shore, he continued fishing, and the excitement of the marvelous sport held his attention—his surface attention, at any rate. At times he almost forgot the attendant beast; yet whenever he looked up, he saw it there. And worse; when he slowly paddled home again, he observed it trotting along the shore as though to keep him company. Crossing a little bay, he spurted, hoping to reach the other point before his undesired and undesirable attendant. Instantly the brute broke into that rapid, tireless lope that, except on ice, can run down anything on four legs in the woods. When he reached the distant point, the wolf was waiting for him. He raised his paddle from the water, pausing a moment for reflection; for his very close attention—there were dusk and night yet to come—he certainly did not relish. His camp was near; he had to land; he felt uncomfortable even in the sunshine of broad day, when, to his keen relief, about half a mile from the tent, he saw the creature suddenly stop and sit down in the open. He waited a moment, then paddled on. It did not follow. There was no attempt to move; it merely sat and watched him. After a few hundred yards, he looked back. It was still sitting where he left it. And the absurd, yet significant, feeling came to him that the beast divined his thought, his anxiety, his dread, and was now showing him, as well as it could, that it entertained no hostile feeling and did not meditate attack.

He turned the canoe toward the shore; he landed; he cooked his supper in the dusk; the animal made no sign. Not far away it certainly lay and watched, but it did not advance. And to Hyde, observant now in a new way, came one sharp, vivid reminder of the strange atmosphere into which his commonplace personality had strayed: he suddenly recalled that his relations with the beast, already established, had progressed distinctly a stage further. This startled him, yet without the accompanying alarm he must certainly have felt twenty-four hours before. He had an understanding with the wolf. He was aware of friendly thoughts toward it. He even went so far as to set out a few big fish on the spot where he had first seen it sitting the previous night. "If he comes," he thought, "he is welcome to them. I've got plenty, anyway." He thought of it now as "he."

Yet the wolf made no appearance until he was in the act of entering his tent a good deal later. It was close on ten o'clock, whereas nine was his hour, and late at that, for turning in. He had, therefore, unconsciously been waiting for him. Then, as he was closing the flap, he saw the eyes close to where he had placed the fish. He waited, hiding himself, and expecting to hear sounds of munching jaws; but all was silence. Only the eyes glowed steadily out of the background of pitch darkness. He closed the flap. He had no slightest fear. In ten minutes he was sound asleep.

He could not have slept very long, for when he woke up he could see the shine of a faint red light through the canvas, and the fire had not died down completely. He rose and cautiously peeped out. The air was very cold; he saw his breath. But he also saw the wolf, for it had come in, and was sitting by the dying embers, not two yards away from where he crouched behind the flap. And this time, at these very close quarters, there was something in the attitude of the big wild thing that caught his attention with a vivid thrill of startled surprise and a sudden shock of cold that held him spellbound. He stared, unable to believe his eyes; for the wolf's attitude conveyed to him something familiar that at first he was unable to explain. Its pose reached him in the terms of another thing with which he was entirely at home. What was it? Did his sense betray him? Was he still asleep and dreaming?

Then, suddenly, with a start of uncanny recognition, he knew. Its attitude was that of a dog. Having found the clue, his mind then made an awful leap. For it was, after all, no dog its appearance aped, but something nearer to himself, and more familiar still. Good heavens! It sat there with the pose, the attitude, the gesture in repose of something almost human. And then, with a second shock of biting wonder, it came to him like a revelation. The wolf sat beside that campfire as a man might sit.

Before he could weigh his extraordinary discovery, before he could examine it in detail or with care, the animal, sitting in this ghastly fashion, seemed to feel his eyes fixed on it. It slowly turned and looked him in the face, and for the first time Hyde felt a full-blooded superstitious fear flood through his entire being. He seemed transfixed with that nameless terror that is said to attack human beings who suddenly face the dead, finding themselves bereft of speech and movement. This moment of paralysis certainly occurred. Its passing, however, was as singular as its advent. For almost at once he was aware of something beyond and above this mockery of human attitude and pose, something that ran along unaccustomed nerves and reached his feeling, even perhaps his heart. The revulsion was extraordinary, its result still more extraordinary and unexpected. Yet the fact remains. He was aware of another thing that had the effect of stilling his terror as soon as it was born. He was aware of appeal, silent, half expressed, yet vastly pathetic. He saw in the savage eyes a beseeching, even a yearning, expression that changed his mood as by magic from dread to natural sympathy. The great grey brute, symbol of cruel ferocity, sat there beside his dying fire and appealed for help.

The gulf betwixt animal and human seemed in that instant bridged. It was, of course, incredible. Hyde, sleep still possibly clinging to his inner being with the shades and half shapes of dream yet about his soul, acknowledged, how he knew not, the amazing fact. He found himself nodding to the brute in half consent, and instantly, without more ado, the lean grey shape rose like a wraith and trotted off swiftly, but with stealthy tread, into the background of the night.

When Hyde woke in the morning, his first impression was that he must have dreamed the entire incident. His practical nature asserted itself. There was a bite in the fresh autumn air; the bright sun allowed no half-lights anywhere; he felt brisk in mind and body. Reviewing what had happened, he came to the conclusion that it was utterly vain to speculate; no possible explanation of the animal's behavior occurred to him; he was dealing with something entirely outside his experience. His fear, however, had completely left him. The odd sense of friendliness remained. The beast had a definite purpose, and he himself was included in that purpose. His sympathy held good.

But with the sympathy there was also an intense curiosity. "If it shows itself again," he told himself, "I'll go up close and find out what it wants." The fish laid out the night before had not been touched.

It must have been a full hour after breakfast when he next saw the brute; it was standing on the edge of the clearing, looking at him in the way now become familiar. Hyde immediately picked up his axe and advanced toward it boldly, keeping his eyes fixed straight upon its own. There was nervousness in him, but kept well under; nothing betrayed it; step by step he drew nearer until some ten yards separated them. The wolf had not stirred a muscle as yet. Its jaws hung open, its eyes observed him intently; it allowed him to approach without a sign of what its mood might be. Then, with these ten yards between them, it turned abruptly and moved slowly off, looking back first over one shoulder and then over the other, exactly as a dog might do, to see if he was following.

A singular journey it was they then made together, animal and man. The trees surrounded them at once, for they left the lake behind them, entering the tangled bush beyond. The beast, Hyde noticed, obviously picked the easiest track for him to follow; for obstacles that meant nothing to the four-legged expert, yet were difficult for a man, were carefully avoided with an almost uncanny skill, while yet the general direction was accurately kept. Occasionally there were windfalls to be surmounted; but though the wolf bounded over these with ease, it was always waiting for the man on the other side after he had laboriously climbed over. Deeper and deeper into the heart of the lonely forest they penetrated in this singular fashion, cutting across the arc of the lake's crescent, it seemed to Hyde; for after two miles or so, he recognized the big rocky bluff that overhung the water at its northern end. This outstanding bluff he had seen from his camp, one side of it falling sheer into the water; it was probably the spot, he imagined, where the Indians held their medicine-making ceremonies, for it stood out in isolated fashion, and its top formed a private plateau not easy of access. And it was here, close to a big spruce at the foot of the bluff upon the forest side, that the wolf stopped suddenly and for the first time since its appearance gave audible expression to its feelings. It sat down on its haunches, lifted its muzzle with open jaws, and gave vent to a subdued and long-drawn howl that was more like the wail of a dog than the fierce barking cry associated with a wolf.

By this time Hyde had lost not only fear, but caution too; nor, oddly enough, did this warning howl revive a sign of unwelcome emotion in him. In that curious sound he detected the same message that the eyes conveyed—appeal for help. He paused, nevertheless, a little startled, and while the wolf sat waiting for him, he looked about him quickly. There was young timber here; it had once been a small clearing, evidently. Axe and fire had done their work, but there was evidence to an experienced eye that it was Indians and not white men who had once been busy here. Some part of the medicine ritual, doubtless, took place in the little clearing, thought the man, as he advanced again towards his patient leader. The end of their journey, he felt, was close at hand.

He had not taken two steps before the animal got up and moved very slowly in the direction of some low bushes that formed a clump just beyond. It entered these, first looking back to make sure that its companion watched. The bushes hid it; a moment later it emerged again. Twice it performed this pantomime, each time, as it reappeared, standing still and staring at the man with as distinct an expression of appeal in the eyes as an animal may compass, probably. Its excitement, meanwhile, certainly increased, and this excitement was, with equal certainty, communicated to the man. Hyde made up his mind quickly. Gripping his axe tightly, and ready to use it at the first hint of malice, he moved slowly nearer to the bushes, wondering with something of a tremor what would happen.

If he expected to be startled, his expectation was at once fulfilled; but it was the behavior of the beast that made him jump. It positively frisked about him like a happy dog. It frisked for joy. Its excitement was intense, yet from its open mouth no sound was audible. With a sudden leap, then, it bounded past him into the clump of bushes, against whose very edge he stood, and began scraping vigorously at the ground. Hyde stood and stared, amazement and interest now banishing all his nervousness, even when the beast, in its violent scraping, actually touched his body with its own. He had, perhaps, the feeling that he was in a dream, one of those fantastic dreams in which things may happen without involving an adequate surprise; for otherwise the manner of scraping and scratching at the ground must have seemed an impossible phenomenon. No wolf, no dog certainly, used its paws in the way those paws were working. Hyde had the odd, distressing sensation that it was hands, not paws, he watched. And yet, somehow, the natural adequate surprise he should have felt was absent. The strange action seemed not entirely unnatural. In his heart some deep hidden spring of sympathy and pity stirred instead. He was aware of pathos.

The wolf stopped in its task and looked up into his face. Hyde acted without hesitation then. Afterwards he was wholly at a loss to explain his own conduct. It seemed he knew what to do, divined what was asked, expected of him. Between his mind and the dumb desire yearning through the savage animal there was intelligent and intelligible communication. He cut a stake and sharpened it, for the stones would blunt his axe-edge. He entered the clump of bushes to complete the digging his four-legged companion had begun. And while he worked, though he did not forget the close proximity of the wolf, he paid no attention to it; often his back was turned as he stooped over the laborious clearing away of the hard earth; no uneasiness or sense of danger was in him anymore. The wolf sat outside the clump and watched the operations. Its concentrated attention, its patience, its intense eagerness, the gentleness and docility of the grey, fierce, and probably hungry brute, its obvious pleasure and satisfaction, too, at having won the human to its mysterious purpose— these were colors in the strange picture that Hyde thought of later when dealing with the human herd in his hotel again. At the moment he was aware chiefly of pathos and affection. The whole business was, of course, not to be believed, but that discovery came later, too, when telling it to others.

The digging continued for fully half an hour before his labor was rewarded by the discovery of a small whitish object. He picked it up and examined it—the finger-bone of a man. Other discoveries then followed quickly and in quantity. The *cache* was laid bare. He collected nearly the complete skeleton. The skull, however, he found last, and might not have found at all but for the guidance of his strangely alert companion. It lay some few yards away from the central hole now dug, and the wolf stood nuzzling the ground with its nose before Hyde understood that he was meant to dig exactly in that spot for it. Between the beast's very paws his stake struck hard upon it. He scraped the earth from the bone and examined it carefully. It was perfect, save for the fact that some wild animal had gnawed it, the teeth-marks being still plainly visible. Close beside it lay the rusty iron head of a tomahawk. This and the smallness of the bones confirmed him in his judgment that it was the skeleton not of a white man, but of an Indian.

During the excitement of the discovery of the bones one by one, and finally of the skull, but, more especially, during the period of intense interest while Hyde was examining them, he had paid little if any attention to the wolf. He was aware that it sat and watched him, never moving its keen eyes for a single moment from the actual operations, but sign or movement it made none at all. He knew that it was pleased and satisfied, he knew also that he had now fulfilled its purpose in a great measure. The further intuition that now came to him, derived, he felt positive, from his companion's dumb desire, was perhaps the cream of the entire experience to him. Gathering the bones together in his coat, he carried them, together with the tomahawk, to the foot of the big spruce where the animal had first stopped. His leg actually touched the creature's muzzle as he passed. It turned its head to watch, but did not follow, nor did it move a muscle while he prepared the platform of boughs upon which he then laid the poor worn bones of an Indian who had been killed, doubtless, in sudden attack or ambush, and to whose remains had been denied the last grace of proper tribal burial. He wrapped the bones in bark; he laid the tomahawk beside the skull; he lit the circular fire round the pyre, and the blue smoke rose upward into the clear bright sunshine of the Canadian autumn morning till it was lost among the mighty trees far overhead.

In the moment before actually lighting the little fire he had turned to note what his companion did. It sat five yards away, he saw, gazing intently, and one of its front paws was raised a little from the ground. It made no sign of any kind. He finished the work, becoming so absorbed in it that he had eyes for nothing but the tending and guarding of his careful ceremonial fire. It was only when the platform of boughs collapsed, laying their charred burden gently on the fragrant earth among the soft wood ashes, that he turned again, as though to show the wolf what he had done, and seek, perhaps, some look of satisfaction in its curiously expressive eyes. But the place he searched was empty. The wolf had gone.

He did not see it again; it gave no sign of its presence anywhere; he was not watched. He fished as before, wandered through the bush about his camp, sat smoking round his fire after dark, and slept peacefully in his cozy little tent. He was not disturbed. No howl was ever audible in the distant forest, no twig snapped beneath a stealthy tread, he saw no eyes. The wolf that behaved like a man had gone forever.

It was the day before he left that Hyde, noticing smoke rising from the shack across the lake, paddled over to exchange a word or two with the Indian, who had evidently now returned. The redskin came down to meet him as he landed, but it was soon plain that he spoke very little English. He emitted the familiar grunts at first; then bit by bit Hyde stirred his limited vocabulary into action. The next result, however, was slight enough, though it was certainly direct:

"You camp there?" the man asked, pointing to the other side.

"Yes."

"Wolf come?"

"Yes."

"You see wolf?"

"Yes."

The Indian stared at him fixedly a moment, a keen, wondering look upon his coppery, creased face.

"You 'fraid wolf?" he asked after a moment's pause.

"No," replied Hyde, truthfully. He knew it was useless to ask questions of his own, though he was eager for information. The other would have told him nothing. It was sheer luck that the man had touched on the subject at all, and Hyde realized that his own best role was merely to answer, but to ask no questions. Then, suddenly, the Indian became voluble. There was awe in his voice and manner.

"Him no wolf. Him big medicine wolf. Him spirit wolf."

Whereupon he drank the tea the other had brewed for him, closed his lips tightly, and said no more. His outline was discernible on the shore, rigid and motionless, an hour later, when Hyde's canoe turned the corner of the lake three miles away, and landed to make the portages up the first rapid of his homeward stream.

It was Morton, who, after some persuasion, supplied further details of what he called the legend. Some hundred years before, the tribe that lived in the territory beyond the lake began their annual medicine-making ceremonies on the big rocky bluff at the northern end; but no medicine could be made. The spirits, declared the chief medicine man, would not answer. They were offended. An investigation followed. It was discovered that a young brave had recently killed a wolf, a thing strictly forbidden, since the wolf was the totem animal of the tribe. To make matters worse, the name of the guilty man was Running Wolf. The offence being unpardonable, the man was cursed and driven from the tribe:

"Go out. Wander alone among the woods, and if we see you we slay you. Your bones shall be scattered in the forest, and your spirit shall not enter the Happy Hunting Grounds till one of another race shall find and bury them."

"Which meant," explained Morton laconically, his only comment on the story, "probably forever."

# PART NINE

# The Voluntary Werewolf

There are human beings who find peace in being a werewolf—not the kind of werewolf who revels in violence and power but the kind of werewolf who feels human flesh as a prison. Preferring the animal state to the human, the voluntary werewolf finds that in the life of wolf there is the absence of human discord, strife, and meaninglessness. In this section there are two werewolves in various states of transformation. Each rejects being human and consciously works at becoming a wolf. Each longs for the time when she and he can shuffle off these human coils and participate fully in the life of a wolf. The exception in this section is the one werewolf who has never metamorphosed into a she-werewolf but pretends that she has. She collaborates in finding a real wolf substitute for herself. The truth of the matter is, however, that through this deception she exposes the fraudulent claims of a guest to possessing the supernatural power to transform one species into another.

Saki's "The She-Wolf" is a story not of transformation but of revelation. His characters are shallow, skeptical humans who think that metamorphosing into a wolf would be a delightful diversion, a pleasant relief from the boredom of human life. At a house party where he is a guest, Leonard Bilsiter, who claims to have gained supernatural powers while traveling in Russia, is suspected of being a charlatan, although his aunt testifies that she has seen him turn a vegetable marrow into a wood pigeon. Desiring to enliven her party, his hostess challenges Bilsiter to use his supernatural powers: " 'I wish you would turn me into a wolf, Mr. Bilsiter,' said his hostess at luncheon the day after his arrival."

Without his intervention, his hostess disappears and then reappears as a she-wolf before the eyes of all the guests. When the frightened guests plead with him to metamorphose her back into her human shape, he is unable to do so. Stripped of his pretense to transformative power, Bilsiter has no choice but to accept the claim of another guest to having metamorphosed the hostess into a werewolf, and then having restored her to human shape. The pretentious antics of one guest have been replaced by the ungenerous connivings of three others.

Although the story appears to be about the tension between credulity and belief, about the soullessness of modern society that looks for evidence of the supernatural at conventional dinner parties, Saki's story reveals the rootlessness of moderns who seek mystic sensations and supernatural powers in the absence of the underpinnings of a deeper, more spiritual earlier society.

When Jane Yolen's scientists in her futuristic story "Green Messiah" think about werewolves, they think about the possibility of metamorphosing humans into wolves in order to replenish the world's declining wolf populations. The failure of conservation movements such as Greenpeace in the seventies and eighties provides the challenge to a genetic research team to develop a radical scientific approach to the repopulation of the wild. Since previous attempts on the part of biologists and environmentalists have been unsuccessful, these scientists are attempting an experiment in metamorphosis: a genetically engineered conversion of a human being into a wolf. Believing that not all human beings are descended from apes but that some are descended from wolves, the scientists choose a woman whose genetic makeup matches the descriptions of werewolves in legend and medicine. The subject of their experiment, Lupe de Diega, a resident of Brooklyn whose ancestors came from Spain, has some of the physiognomic features of wolves, and hence is considered an ideal subject for this experiment.

Given injections of hallucinogens, she gradually develops into a werewolf. Although the researchers do not detect it, the transformation is for her a satisfying, nonregressive one. She remembers the Goya print of Spanish werewolves on her grandmother's kitchen wall and recognizes her kinship to those in the picture. Having always felt like an outsider in human society, she begins to feel the joy that transformation brings. With the final metamorphosis, she slips out of the shackles of research and, unmonitored, enters into a life free of human egotistical interference.

Bruce Elliott's story is a reversal. A caged wolf who lives happily in a zoo and who fathers a number of cubs has metamorphosed into a human being. Having become a maladjusted wolfwere, he is placed in a mental institution for rehabilitation. Although he conforms only reluctantly to human attempts to make him an acceptable member of human society, he is considered rehabilitated. Human life, however, with all its contradictions and veiled instincts, puzzles him. What he misses most is the simple, deep love between him and his wolf mate and their unswerving devotion to their cubs.

Using the human skills that he has developed in the institution, he discovers that the key to being metamorphosed back into a wolf is in a library. Buried in books on lycanthropy there are formulas for turning a human being into a werewolf. Through strong volition and the successful use of one of these formulas, he is successful in reacquiring his wolf shape.

Elliott's innovative approach to metamorphosis destabilizes the prevailing view on lycanthropy—that being a werewolf is degradation and that being a human being is preferable to being a wolf. Elliott portrays the emotional intensity of the wolf as a contradiction to the human assumption that animal emotions are less intense than and inferior to those of human beings. To choose to be a wolf rather than a human being is for humans an unthinkable choice, but for the wolfwere it is the only choice. Bred in his bones is the knowledge that being a wolf is not a debased state but a state where love of one's mate and one's offspring is the core of one's being.

# The She-Wolf

SAKI (H. H. MUNRO, 1870–1916)

LEONARD BILSITER was one of those people who have failed to find this world attractive or interesting, and who have sought compensation in an "unseen world" of their own experience or imagination—or invention. Children do that sort of thing successfully, but children are content to convince themselves, and do not vulgarize their beliefs by trying to convince other people. Leonard Bilsiter's beliefs were for "the few," that is to say, anyone who would listen to him.

His dabblings in the unseen might not have carried him beyond the customary platitudes of the drawing-room visionary if accident had not reinforced his stock-in-trade of mystical lore. In company with a friend, who was interested in a Ural mining concern, he had made a trip across eastern Europe at a moment when the great Russian railway strike was developing from a threat to a reality; its outbreak caught him on the return journey, somewhere on the further side of Perm, and it was while waiting for a couple of days at a wayside station in a state of suspended locomotion that he made the acquaintance of a dealer in harness and metalware, who profitably whiled away the tedium of the long halt by initiating his English traveling companion in a fragmentary system of folklore that he had picked up from Trans-Baikal traders and natives. Leonard returned to his home circle garrulous about his Russian strike experiences, but oppressively reticent about certain dark mysteries, which he alluded to under the resounding title of Siberian Magic. The reticence wore off in a week or two under the influence of an entire lack of general curiosity, and Leonard began to make more detailed allusions to the

In *Beasts and Super-Beasts* (New York: Viking 1914).

enormous powers which this new esoteric force, to use his own description of it, conferred on the initiated few who knew how to wield it. His aunt, Cecilia Hoops, who loved sensation perhaps rather better than she loved the truth, gave him as clamorous an advertisement as anyone could wish for by retailing an account of how he had turned a vegetable marrow into a wood pigeon before her very eyes. As a manifestation of the possession of supernatural powers, the story was discounted in some quarters by the respect accorded to Mrs. Hoops' powers of imagination.

However divided opinion might be on the question of Leonard's status as a wonder worker or a charlatan, he certainly arrived at Mary Hampton's house party with a reputation of pre-eminence in one or other of those professions, and he was not disposed to shun such publicity as might fall to his share. Esoteric forces and unusual powers figured largely in whatever conversation he or his aunt had a share in, and his own performances, past and potential, were the subject of mysterious hints and dark avowals.

"I wish you would turn me into a wolf, Mr. Bilsiter," said his hostess at luncheon the day after his arrival.

"My dear Mary," said Colonel Hampton, "I never knew you had a craving in that direction."

"A she-wolf, of course," continued Mrs. Hampton; "it would be too confusing to change one's sex as well as one's species at a moment's notice."

"I don't think one should jest on these subjects," said Leonard.

"I'm not jesting, I'm quite serious, I assure you. Only don't do it today; we have only eight available bridge players, and it would break up one of our tables. Tomorrow we shall be a larger party. Tomorrow night, after dinner—"

"In our present imperfect understanding of these hidden forces I think one should approach them with humbleness rather than mockery," observed Leonard, with such severity that the subject was forthwith dropped.

Clovis Sangrail had sat unusually silent during the discussion on the possibilities of Siberian Magic; after lunch he sidetracked Lord Pabham into the comparative seclusion of the billiard room and delivered himself of a searching question.

"Have you such a thing as a she-wolf in your collection of wild animals? A she-wolf of moderately good temper?"

Lord Pabham considered. "There is Louisa," he said, "a rather fine specimen of the timber wolf. I got her two years ago in exchange for some Arctic foxes. Most of my animals get to be fairly tame before they've been with me very long; I think I can say Louisa has an angelic temper, as she-wolves go. Why do you ask?"

"I was wondering whether you would lend her to me for tomorrow night," said Clovis, with the careless attitude of one who borrows a collar stud or a tennis racquet.

"Tomorrow night?"

"Yes, wolves are nocturnal animals, so the late hours won't hurt her," said Clovis, with the air of one who had taken everything into consideration; "one of your men can bring her over from Pabham Park after dusk, and with a little help he ought to be able to smuggle her into the conservatory at the same moment that Mary Hampton makes an unobtrusive exit."

Lord Pabham stared at Clovis for a moment in pardonable bewilderment; then his face broke into a wrinkled network of laughter.

"Oh, that's your game, is it? You are going to do a little Siberian Magic on your own account. And is Mrs. Hampton willing to be a fellow conspirator?"

"Mary is pledged to see me through with it, if you will guarantee Louisa's temper."

"I'll answer for Louisa," said Lord Pabham.

By the following day the house party had swollen to larger proportions, and Bilsiter's instinct for self-advertisement expanded duly under the stimulant of an increased audience. At dinner that evening he held forth at length on the subject of unseen forces and untested powers, and his flow of impressive eloquence continued unabated while coffee was being served in the drawing room preparatory to a general migration to the card room. His aunt ensured a respectful hearing for his utterances, but her sensation-loving soul hankered after something more dramatic than mere vocal demonstration.

"Won't you do something to *convince* them of your powers, Leonard?" she pleaded; "change something into another shape. He can, you know, if he only chooses to," she informed the company.

"Oh, do," said Mavis Pellington earnestly, and her request was echoed by nearly everyone present. Even those who were not open to conviction were perfectly willing to be entertained by an exhibition of amateur conjuring.

Leonard felt that something tangible was expected of him.

"Has anyone present," he asked, "got a three-penny bit or some small object of no particular value—?"

"You're surely not going to make coins disappear, or something primitive of that sort?" said Clovis contemptuously.

"I think it very unkind of you not to carry out my suggestion of turning me into a wolf," said Mary Hampton, as she crossed over to the conservatory to give her macaws their usual tribute from the dessert dishes.

"I have already warned you of the danger of treating these powers in a mocking spirit," said Leonard solemnly.

"I don't believe you can do it," laughed Mary provocatively from the conservatory; "I dare you to do it if you can. I defy you to turn me into a wolf."

As she said this she was lost to view behind a clump of azaleas.

"Mrs. Hampton—"began Leonard with increased solemnity, but he got no further. A breath of chill air seemed to rush across the room, and at the same time the macaws broke forth into earsplitting screams.

"What on earth is the matter with those confounded birds, Mary!" exclaimed Colonel Hampton; at the same moment an even more piercing scream from Mavis Pellington stampeded the entire company from their seats. In various attitudes of helpless horror or instinctive defense they confronted the evil-looking grey beast that was peering at them from amid a setting of fern and azalea.

Mrs. Hoops was the first to recover from the general chaos of fright and bewilderment.

"Leonard," she screamed shrilly to her nephew, "turn it back into Mrs. Hampton at once! It may fly at us at any moment. Turn it back!"

"I—I don't know how to," faltered Leonard, who looked more scared and horrified than anyone.

"What!" should Colonel Hampton, "you've taken the abominable liberty of turning my wife into a wolf, and now you stand there calmly and say you can't turn her back again!"

To do strict justice to Leonard, calmness was not a distinguishing feature of his attitude at the moment.

"I assure you I didn't turn Mrs. Hampton into a wolf; nothing was farther from my intentions," he protested.

"Then where is she, and how came that animal into the conservatory?" demanded the Colonel.

"Of course we must accept your assurance that you didn't turn Mrs. Hampton into a wolf," said Clovis politely, "but you will agree that appearances are against you."

"Are we to have all these recriminations with that beast standing there ready to tear us to pieces?" wailed Mavis indignantly.

"Lord Pabham, you know a good deal about wild beasts—" suggested Colonel Hampton.

"The wild beasts that I have been accustomed to," said Lord Pabham, "have come with proper credentials from well-known dealers, or have been bred in my own menagerie. I've never before been confronted with an animal that walks unconcernedly out of an azalea bush, leaving a charming and popular hostess unaccounted for. As far as one can judge from *outward* characteristics," he continued, "it has the appearance of a well-grown female of the North American timber wolf, a variety of the common species *Canis lupus.*"

"Oh, never mind its Latin name," screamed Mavis, as the beast came a step or two further into the room; "can't you entice it away with food, and shut it up where it can't do any harm?"

"If it is really Mrs. Hampton, who has just had a very good dinner, I don't suppose food will appeal to it very strongly," said Clovis.

"Leonard," beseeched Mrs. Hoops tearfully, "even if this *is* none of your doing can't you use your great powers to turn this dreadful beast into something harmless before it bites us all—a rabbit or something?"

"I don't suppose Colonel Hampton would care to have his wife turned into a succession of fancy animals as though we were playing a round game with her," interposed Clovis.

"I absolutely forbid it," thundered the Colonel.

"Most wolves that I've had anything to do with have been inordinately fond of sugar," said Lord Pabham; "if you like I'll try the effect on this one."

He took a piece of sugar from the saucer of his coffee cup and flung it to the expectant Louisa, who snapped it in midair. There was a sigh of relief from the company; a wolf that ate sugar when it might at the least have been employed in tearing macaws to pieces had already shed some of its terrors. The sigh deepened to a gasp of thanksgiving when Lord Pabham decoyed the animal out of the room by a pretended largesse of further sugar. There was an instant rush to the vacated conservatory. There was no trace of Mrs. Hampton except the plate containing the macaws' supper.

"The door is locked on the inside!" exclaimed Clovis, who had deftly turned the key as he affected to test it.

Everyone turned towards Bilsiter.

"If you haven't turned my wife into a wolf," said Colonel Hampton, "will you kindly explain where she has disappeared to, since she obviously could not have gone through a locked door? I will not press you for an explanation of how a North American timber wolf suddenly appeared in the conservatory, but I think I have some right to inquire what has become of Mrs. Hampton."

Bilsiter's reiterated disclaimer was met with a general murmur of impatient disbelief.

"I refuse to stay another hour under this roof," declared Mavis Pellington.

"If our hostess has really vanished out of human form," said Mrs. Hoops, "none of the ladies of the party can very well remain. I absolutely decline to be chaperoned by a wolf!"

"It's a she-wolf," said Clovis soothingly.

The correct etiquette to be observed under the unusual circumstances received no further elucidation. The sudden entry of Mary Hampton deprived the discussion of its immediate interest.

"Someone has mesmerized me," she exclaimed crossly; "I found myself in the game larder, of all places, being fed with sugar by Lord Pabham. I hate being mesmerized, and the doctor has forbidden me to touch sugar."

The situation was explained to her, as far as it permitted of anything that could be called explanation.

"Then you *really* did turn me into a wolf, Mr. Bilsiter?" she exclaimed excitedly.

But Leonard had burned the boat in which he might now have embarked on a sea of glory. He could only shake his head feebly.

"It was I who took that liberty," said Clovis; "you see, I happen to have lived for a couple of years in northeastern Russia, and I have more than a tourist's acquaintance with the magic craft of that region. One does not care to speak about these strange powers, but once in a way, when one hears a lot of nonsense being talked about them, one is tempted to show what Siberian magic can accomplish in the hands of someone who really understands it. I yielded to that temptation. May I have some brandy? The effort has left me rather faint."

If Leonard Bilsiter could at that moment have transformed Clovis into a cockroach and then have stepped on him he would gladly have performed both operations.

# Green Messiah

JANE YOLEN (1939– )

"IT'S QUITE SIMPLE, REALLY," Professor Magister was saying. "With the world's population of wild carnivores falling rapidly, the predator-to-prey ratio is way out of balance. A world so out of balance is a world that may die. It's our only hope, really."

Lupe stopped listening. The press conference went on and on and on, but she simply turned her attention inward. She already knew the entire speech Magister would give the reporters. He'd been practicing it on all his coworkers and volunteers. He'd remind them how the conservation movement of the seventies and eighties, Greenpeace and all the rest, had failed. How out of that dismal failure had grown a new movement, connecting all the old fragmented groups: Green Messiah. How Green Messiah had dedicated itself to repopulating the wild kingdoms by means of genetic experimentation developed at the Asimov Institute. How she, Lupe de Diega, had been one of the Chosen Ones, the volunteers, the Green Messengers, because genetically she'd matched the old legends. Dark-haired, long-fingered, yellow-eyed, with a slash of the single eyebrow across her forehead, that was Lupe. All those things that had caused her to be teased and hated for years were now her passport to fame. She would be in all the history books, not for what she was—but for what she would become. Lupe de Diega, the first girl to be genetically changed into wolf.

"Legends," the professor was stating in his deep, resonant voice, "are merely signposts to long-forgotten facts. Our ancestors were leaving us mes-

Jane Yolen, "Green Messiah," in *Werewolves*, ed. Jane Yolen and Martin H. Greenberg (New York: Harper and Row, 1988), 189–200.

sages, but we did not—*could not*—read them. The Ages of Reason and Cynicism did not allow us to believe that the past could so inform the future."

The reporters in the audience stirred uneasily. Though word of the experiments had already leaked out, they were there for facts, not speeches. Sensing that, Dr. Magister seemed to shake himself all over and begin again.

"Green Messiah looked behind the legends to the facts," he said.

Lupe saw that the reporters were concentrating again.

"Just as we now understand that herbalists knew things long before modern medicine re-proved them acceptable, like belladonna and penicillin, so too the old folktales carried biologic history within the body of the story. Green Messiah followed those tracks. Werewolves, the old stories warned, were people who had fingers of a single length, who had eyebrows that met in the middle, who had hair growing in their palms. We saw the possibility that this was a real genetic link with humanity's past."

Lupe's eyes narrowed. She could feel her breathing deepen. She opened her mouth and panted shallowly. Then, realizing that some of the reporters were staring at her, she forced herself to close her mouth and listen to Magister again.

"Those stories of the *loup-garou*, the werewolf, were left over from thousands of years of human memory. Our forebears remembered something we did not—that not all humans are descended from apes. Some, it seems, are descended from *Canis lupus*, the wolf. Not even Darwin suspected that! We at Green Messiah are breeding the race backward, but in days, not in decades."

He smiled over at Lupe. She did not smile back. A wolf smile means something entirely different, and she had had enough treatments already to be uncomfortable with the lifting of lips that in humans was used to signify happiness. She shrugged her shoulders in response, restraining the impulse to wag her as yet nonexistent tail.

Magister looked back at the audience. He was a good speaker. He knew how to play the crowd. "And so, my friends of the press, may I present to you the young woman with whom our first hopes lie, Ms. Lupe de Diega, a resident of Brooklyn whose ancestors came from Spain but one generation past. In a matter of a few months, she will become a full-grown werewolf, capable of changing from human to wolf and back again, capable of bringing to the dying breed new life."

Hands went up all over the auditorium and Lupe sat back against her chair. A raised hand seemed threatening these days. Then she stopped herself and stared around. Her nostrils flared slightly. She caught a faint scent in the air, but it was neither anger nor fear. It was, perhaps, curiosity. Then she chided herself mentally. Surely *curiosity* had no smell.

The professor allowed questions, singling out a man halfway toward the back. The man stood so his question might be better heard.

"Will she change on—um—the full moon?"

"Don't be absurd," said Magister, but with a laugh so as not to affront the man. "The notion of a werewolf changing on the full moon is simply"—he smiled, letting them all in on the joke—"moonshine and malarkey. That's a good example of the folk mind at work, disguising, making metaphoric. Do what we of Green Messiah trained ourselves to do, Mr. uh—"

"Hyatt, sir, of UPI."

"Mr. Hyatt. Read *behind* the legends. Ask yourself: What does the full moon represent?"

Lupe thought of the moon, round and beckoning. It represented freedom. *She* knew that, even if Magister did not. For a professor he was very stupid. Very stupid indeed.

"How about magic and mystery?" called out a man from the back.

"The pull of the tides?" shouted another.

"Get your minds away from mysticism," said Magister. "Think of facts."

A reporter from *MS.* magazine raised her hand and stood. "Do you mean that the female's monthly or moon cycle is linked to this change?"

"*Bingo!*" Magister said. "That was our best guess."

"What about males?" called out a man behind a television camera.

"We aren't quite sure yet," Magister admitted. "That is why we're starting with Ms. de Diega. We expect she'll bring us back information that will help us figure out what links the male werewolf to his change. If, indeed, there *are* male werewolves. There is one theory that werewolves are only female."

There was an enormous explosion of sounds from the reporters and this time Lupe did smile.

"How does *she* feel about it?" the UPI reporter, Hyatt, called out.

"Why don't you ask *her* directly?" Magister responded. He came over to Lupe murmuring. "Steady, Lupe, steady, girl. Just come to the microphone. I'll be right by your side. It's going very well. Nothing to be afraid of."

She stood in a single graceful motion and followed at his heels.

"Speak, Lupe," he instructed.

The microphone had a cold, metal scent. She spoke into it, her voice deep and steady. "I wait. I hope. I am ready." The echo coming back to her from the corners of the auditorium made her tremble.

Magister's hand on the small of her back, through the thin cotton dress, calmed her. She had nothing more to say.

"Good girl," he whispered, giving her a little push. She returned to her chair.

THE REST OF THE CONFERENCE went as planned. Magister brought out maps and charts, and the graduate students handed out photocopied material to the audience so that they could follow along and print accurately what Green Messiah was doing. But Lupe's attention was drawn to a small bird that had, somehow, gotten trapped in the room and was frantically beating against a window. She felt her body straining toward it. It took all her concentration not to whine.

The bird finally swooped toward the back and out through an open door, losing itself somewhere in the maze of halls outside. Lupe lost interest once it had disappeared and turned her head toward Magister. He was just finishing.

"And so, this summer, we will take Ms. de Diega up to an undisclosed taiga or coniferous forest region in northern Canada where moose, elk, and a number of species of deer are abundant, as well as squirrels, marmots, chipmunks, rats, mice, moles, shrews, and hares. But where, alas, the wolf population is now minimal.

"There we shall give her a collar that will allow us to track her movements. We'll help her remove her clothes, and give her the last of the series of injections of the Green Messiah serum to facilitate her change.

"We expect the change to be complete within hours and then Ms. de Diega—Lupe—will be off to find her dwindling pack. With her human mind, she will easily become dominant wolf and guide her fellow canines to a richer and more fruitful heritage than they could otherwise have known."

A single hand was raised in the auditorium.

"Can you be sure?" the reporter asked.

Magister smiled. "Nothing in life is *sure*. However, we have looked at this from all the angles, and Ms. de Diega will report back once a month to us with her findings. And we shall, of course, keep you all apprised of her progress." With a nod to Will Sheddery, his top graduate student, Magister closed the conference and escorted Lupe off the stage.

LUPE WAS SURPRISED at how quickly the spring months went by. Her sense of time had become peculiar, tied less to the clock and more to the rising and setting of the sun. She found it harder and harder to get up in the morning and do her regular calisthenics with Emma, her trainer. She seemed to need more sleep, but in shorter snatches.

Magister visited her daily to chart her bodily functions and to ask her questions. Her temperature had risen, her senses of smell and hearing had heightened, her ability to pay attention to his nonsense had grown less and less. Often he had to call her name two or three times to get her attention, and when she turned her head toward him slowly, she would narrow her eyes to signal she was listening. More and more often, she hated to talk.

"Lupe," his deep voice called her.

She couldn't be bothered responding.

"Lupe!"

This time the sharp tone caused her to look up.

"You *must* pay attention. We are less than a week away from your last shot and the Change. We *must* retain a part of your humanity. Otherwise you can do us no good."

She let her head flop back down on her hands. She couldn't understand why Magister wanted to bother her now. Now was naptime. Later would be better.

Someone yanked her head up. It was Will. She lifted her lip at him, trying to snarl. The sound was too human and not nearly threatening enough. It was all she could manage.

"Look at her, sir!" Will was saying. "She's as bad as the Duane girl was. You thought that was because Duane was subnormal to begin with. But Lupe tested normal, even in the 120 range, very bright indeed."

Magister made a snorting sound. "Hmmmph. I don't think it's lack of intelligence, Will. Just a different intelligence. It's time we started thinking of her as a canine, and not as a human." He turned his head. "Emma—bring me that can. The red one. That's right." He held out his hand and the dark-haired trainer placed the can in it.

Opening the top, Magister took out a twisted piece of dried meat. "Lupe!" he said, dangling the strip by her nose.

Lupe sat up. It had taken him long enough! she thought. This time she listened, nodding her head at the appropriate pauses, and chewing with what she hoped was a thoughtful expression on her face.

IT WAS ONE of those brilliant summer days that only the Canadian taiga south of the tundra seemed to produce, the sky beyond the forest a solid blue edging off to a bleached muslin color at the horizon. Snowcapped mountains thrust angrily upward and nearby an aggressive stream tumbled noisily over its rocks.

Lupe's hand went to the collar around her neck. She had told them over and over it was too tight, but no one had listened. Will had smugly informed her that it would fit the wolf just fine. She had bitten back the reply that *she* was the wolf.

Standing barefooted, the light cotton robe wrapped firmly around her, Lupe lifted her face to the slight breeze. She could smell an old scent of weasel and, overlaying it, wolverine. She wrinkled her nose, touched the collar once more, nervously waiting.

Magister came over to her. He smiled, not expecting any return on it. "Well, Lupe, this is the day. Our day."

"*My* day," she growled.

"Your success belongs to all of us. Green Messiah lives as you live," he said, his voice smooth and without affect. She knew he would not use the scolding voice now. Too much was on the line.

She nodded. It took great effort. Too much was on the line for her, too.

"We will withdraw now, to beyond that stand of pines. When you are ready, my dear, cast aside the robe and let the Change take you. You will know when it begins." He reached out and patted her hand awkwardly. She was in between now and she knew he was uncomfortable with her. Inside she was more wolf than woman, outside more woman than wolf. What she needed was integration. He was right. She would know when it began.

Magister signaled to the twelve graduate students and the two Green Messiah doctors with an almost imperceptible hand movement. They finished packing the equipment and loaded it onto the trucks.

Each of them, in turn, came to shake hands with Lupe. Only Emma gave her a hug. Will Sheddery barely touched her.

Magister was last. He held both her hands in his. "Go well, Lupe. Hunt the wind," he whispered. "And don't worry. We will track you with the collar. If there's any trouble, we'll be there for you at once."

Then he got into the last of the trucks and they rumbled across the stone-strewn field.

Lupe could hardly wait for them to leave. She had been ready for over an hour, her thighs wet with blood. Even before the last of the trucks was out of sight, she had ripped off the robe. Standing in the warmth of the sun, she raised her arms up, threw her head back, and began to sing.

Magister had not known, but *she* had known. There was more to the old tales than he suspected. She had memorized the spell from a book she'd found in his library, one of the fairy tales he'd dismissed. The words had settled comfortably in her mouth the very first time she'd spoken them. For she was not any old werewolf, she was *lobombre*, a Spanish werewolf. Like the one in the Goya print that her grandmother had on her kitchen well.

> *Lobombre.*
> *Sing wolf. Howl.*
> *The mouth knows the morning,*
> *The teeth the afternoon,*
> *But the heart knows midnight,*
> *And all the predations of the moon.*
> *Sing wolf. Howl.*

She sang it first in Spanish, then in English, and then, when the full Change came over her, in Wolf. Her eyes narrowed and she could see the wind. Her ears, now long, could hear the grass grow. She felt her hands tighten, the nails lengthen. Before they were completely paws, she reached up and ripped the collar from her throat, throwing it away from her.

When she could wave her plumed tail from side to side, she put her head back and howled. Then she raced off to the copse of trees, far away from the place where Magister and his students waited, to follow the bright steady scent of the pack.

# Wolves Don't Cry

BRUCE ELLIOTT (1915–1973)

THE NAKED MAN behind the bars was sound asleep. In the cage next to him a bear rolled over on its back, and peered sleepily at the rising sun. Not far away a jackal paced springily back and forth as though essaying the impossible, trying to leave its own stench far behind. Flies were gathered around the big bone that rested near the man's sleeping head. Little bits of decaying flesh attracted the insects and their hungry buzzing made the man stir uneasily. Accustomed to instant awakening, his eyes flickered and simultaneously his right hand darted out and smashed down at the irritating flies.

They left in a swarm, but the naked man stayed frozen in the position he had assumed. His eyes were on his hand. He was still that way when the zoo attendant came close to the cage. The attendant, a pail of food in one hand, a pail of water in the other, said, "Hi Lobo, up and at 'em, the customers'll be here soon." Then he too froze. Inside the naked man's head strange ideas were stirring. His paw, what had happened to it? Where was the stiff gray hair? The jet-black steel-strong nails? And what was the odd fifth thing that jutted out from his paw at right angles? He moved it experimentally. It rotated. He'd never been able to move his dew claw, and the fact that he could move this fifth extension was somehow more baffling than the other oddities that were puzzling him.

"You goddamn drunks!" the attendant raved. "Wasn't bad enough the night a flock of you came in here, and a girl bothered the bear and lost an arm

First published in *The Magazine of Fantasy and Science Fiction* (1954). Permission from Scott Meredith Literary Agency, Inc., 845 Third Avenue, New York, NY 10022, agents for the estate of Bruce Elliott.

for her trouble, no, that wasn't bad enough. Now you have to sleep in my cages! And where's Lobo? What have you done with him?"

The naked figure wished the two-legged would stop barking. It was enough trouble trying to figure out what had happened without the angry short barks of the two-legged who fed him, interfering with his thoughts.

Then there were many more of the two-leggeds and a lot of barking, and the naked one wished they'd all go away and let him think. Finally the cage opened and the two-leggeds tried to make him come out of his cage. He retreated hurriedly on all fours to the back of his cage toward his den.

"Let him alone," the two-legged who fed him barked. "Let him go into Lobo's den. He'll be sorry!"

Inside the den, inside the hollowed-out rock that so cleverly approximated his home before he had been captured, he paced back and forth, finding it bafflingly uncomfortable to walk on his naked feet. His paws did not grip the ground the way they should and the rock hurt his new soft pads.

The two-legged ones were getting angry, he could smell the emotion as it poured from them, but even that was puzzling, for he had to flare his nostrils wide to get the scent, and it was blurred, not crisp and clear the way he ordinarily smelled things. Throwing back his head, he howled in frustration and anger. But the sound was wrong. It did not ululate as was its wont. Instead he found to his horror that he sounded like a cub, or a female.

What had happened to him?

Cutting one of his soft pads on a stone, he lifted his foot and licked at the blood.

His pounding heart almost stopped.

This was no wolf blood.

Then the two-legged ones came in after him and the fight was one that ordinarily he would have enjoyed, but now his heart was not in it. Dismay filled him, for the taste of his own blood had put fear in him. Fear unlike any he had ever known, even when he was trapped that time, and put in a box, and thrown onto a wheeled thing that had rocked back and forth, and smelled so badly of two-legged things.

This was a new fear, and a horrible one.

Their barking got louder when they found that he was alone in his den. Over and over they barked, not that he could understand them. "What have you done with Lobo? Where is he? Have you turned him loose?"

It was only after a long time, when the sun was riding high in the summer sky, that he was wrapped in a foul-smelling thing and put in a four-wheeled object and taken away from his den.

He would never have thought, when he was captured, that he would ever miss the new home that the two-leggeds had given him, but he found that he did, and most of all, as the four-wheeled thing rolled through the city streets, he found himself worrying about his mate in the next cage. What would she think when she found him gone, and she just about to have a litter? He knew that most males did not worry about their young, but wolves were different. No mother wolf ever had to worry, the way female bears did, about a male wolf eating his young. No indeed; wolves were different.

And being different, he found that worse than being tied up in a cloth and thrown in the back of a long, wheeled thing was the worry he felt about his mate, and her young-to-be.

But worse was to come: When he was carried out of the moving thing, the two-legged ones carried him into a big building and the smells that surged in on his outraged nostrils literally made him cringe. There was sickness, and stenches worse than he had ever smelled, and above and beyond all other smells the odor of death was heavy in the long white corridors through which he was carried.

Seeing around him as he did ordinarily in grays and blacks and whites, he found that the new sensations that crashed against his smarting eye balls were not to be explained by anything he knew. Not having the words for red, and green, and yellow, for pink and orange and all the other colors in a polychromatic world, not having any idea of what they were, just served to confuse him even more miserably.

He moaned.

The smells, the discomfort, the horror of being handled, were as nothing against the hurt his eyes were enduring.

Lying on a flat hard thing he found that it helped just to stare directly upwards. At least the flat covering ten feet above him was white, and he could cope with that.

The two-legged thing sitting next to him had a gentle bark, but that didn't help much.

The two-legged said patiently over and over again, "Who are you? Have you any idea? Do you know where you are? What day is this?"

After a while the barks became soothing, and nude no longer, wrapped now in a long wet sheet that held him cocoonlike in its embrace, he found that his eyes were closing. It was all too much for him.

He slept.

The next awakening was if anything worse than the first.

First he thought that he was back in his cage in the zoo, for directly ahead of him he could see bars. Heaving a sigh of vast relief, he wondered what had made an adult wolf have such an absurd dream. He could still remember his puppyhood when sleep had been made peculiar by a life unlike the one he enjoyed when awake. The twitchings, the growls, the sleepy murmurs—he had seen his own sons and daughters go through them and they had reminded him of his youth.

But now the bars were in front of him and all was well.

Except that he must have slept in a peculiar position. He was stiff, and when he went to roll over he fell off the hard thing he had been on and crashed to the floor.

Bars or no bars, that was not his cage.

That was what made the second wakening so difficult. For, once he had fallen off the hospital bed, he found that his limbs were encumbered by a long garment that flapped around him as he rolled to all fours and began to pace fearfully back and forth inside the narrow confines of the cell that he now inhabited.

Worse yet, when the sound of his fall reached the ears of a two-legged one, he found that some more two-legs hurried to his side and he was forced, literally forced into an odd garment that covered his lower limbs.

Then they made him sit on the end of his spine and it hurt cruelly, and they put a metal thing in his right paw, and wrapped the soft flesh of his paw around the metal object and holding both, they made him lift some kind of slop from a round thing on the flat surface in front of him.

That was bad, but the taste of the mush they forced into his mouth was grotesque.

Where was his meat? Where was his bone? How could he sharpen his fangs on such food as this? What were they trying to do? Make him lose his teeth?

He gagged and regurgitated the slops. That didn't do the slightest bit of good. The two-leggeds kept right on forcing the mush into his aching jaws. Finally, in despair, he kept some of it down.

Then they made him balance on his hind legs.

He'd often seen the bear in the next cage doing this trick and sneered at the big fat oaf for pandering to the two-leggeds by aping them. Now he found that it was harder than he would have thought. But finally, after the two-leggeds had worked with him for a long time, he found that he could, by much teetering, stand erect.

But he didn't like it.

His nose was too far from the floor, and with whatever it was wrong with his smelling, he found that he had trouble sniffing the ground under him. From this distance he could not track anything. Not even a rabbit. If one had run right by him, he thought, feeling terribly sorry for himself, he'd never be able to smell it, or if he did, be able to track it down, no matter how fat and juicy, for how could a wolf run on two legs?

They did many things to him in the new big zoo, and in time he found that, dislike it as much as he did, they could force him by painful expedients to do many of the tasks they set him.

That, of course, did not help him to understand why they wanted him to do such absurd things as encumber his legs with cloth that flapped and got in the way, or balance precariously on his hind legs, or any of the other absurdities they made him perform. But somehow he surmounted everything and in time even learned to bark a little the way they did. He found that he could bark *hello* and *I'm hungry* and, after months of effort, ask *why can't I go back to the zoo?*

But that didn't do much good, because all they ever barked back was *because you're a man.*

Now of many things he was unsure since that terrible morning, but of one thing he was sure: he *was* a wolf.

Other people knew it too.

He found this out on the day some outsiders were let into the place where he was being kept. He had been sitting, painful as it was, on the tip of his spine, in what he had found the two-leggeds called a chair, when some shes passed by.

His nostrils closed at the sweet smell that they had poured on themselves, but through it he could detect the real smell, the female smell, and his nostrils had flared, and he had run to the door of his cell, and his eyes had become red as he looked at them. Not so attractive as his mate, but at least they were covered with fur, not like the peeled ones that he sometimes saw dressed in stiff white crackling things.

The fur-covered ones had giggled just like ripening she-cubs, and his paws had ached to grasp them, and his jaws ached to bite into their fur-covered necks.

One of the fur-covered two-leggeds had giggled, "Look at that wolf!"

So some of the two-leggeds had perception and could tell that the ones who held him in this big strange zoo were wrong, that he was not a man, but a wolf.

Inflating his now puny lungs to the utmost, he had thrown back his head and roared out a challenge that in the old days, in the forest, would have sent a thrill of pleasure through every female for miles around. But instead of that bloodcurdling, stomach-wrenching roar, a little barking, choking sound came from his throat. If he had still had a tail it would have curled down under his belly as he slunk away.

The first time they let him see himself in what they called a mirror he had moaned like a cub. Where was his long snout, the bristling whiskers, the flat head, the pointed ears? What was this thing that stared with dilated eyes out of the flat shiny surface? White-faced, almost hairless save for a jet-black bar of eyebrows that made a straight line across his high round forehead, small-jawed, small-toothed—he knew with a sinking sensation in the pit of his stomach that even a year-old would not hesitate to challenge him in the mating fights.

Not only challenge him but beat him, for how could he fight with those little canines, those feeble white hairless paws?

Another thing that irritated him, as it would any wolf, was that they kept moving him around. He would no sooner get used to one den and make it his own but what they'd moved him to another one.

The last one that contained him had no bars.

If he had been able to read his chart he would have known that he was considered on the way to recovery, that the authorities thought him almost "cured" of his aberration. The den with no bars was one that was used for limited liberty patients. They were on a kind of parole basis. But he had no idea of what the word meant and the first time he was released on his own cognizance, allowed to make a trip out into the "real" world, he put out of his mind the curious forms of "occupational therapy" with which the authorities were deviling him.

His daytime liberty was unreal and dragged by in a way that made him almost anxious to get back home to the new den.

He had all but made up his mind to do so, when the setting sun conjured up visions which he could not resist. In the dark he could get down on all fours!

Leaving the crowded city streets behind him he hurried out into the suburbs where the spring smells were making the night air exciting.

He had looked forward so to dropping on all fours and racing through the velvet spring light that when he did so, only to find that all the months of standing upright had made him too stiff to run, he could have howled. Then too the clumsy leather things on his back paws got in the way, and he would have ripped them off, but he remembered how soft his new pads were, and he was afraid of what would happen to them.

Forcing himself upright, keeping the curve in his back that he had found helped him to stand on his hind legs, he made his way cautiously along a flat thing that stretched off into the distance.

The four-wheeler that stopped near him would ordinarily have frightened him. But even his new weak nose could sniff through the rank acrid smells of the four-wheeler and find, under the too sweet something on the two-legged female, the real smell, so that when she said, "Hop in, I'll give you a lift," he did not run away. Instead he joined the she.

Her bark was nice, at first.

Later, while he was doing to her what her scent had told him she wanted done, her bark became shrill, and it hurt even his new dull ears. That, of course, did not stop him from doing what had to be done in the spring.

The sounds that still came from her got fainter as he tried to run off on his hind legs. It was not much faster than a walk, but he had to get some of the good feeling of the air against his face, of his lungs panting; he had to run.

Regret was in him that he would not be able to get food for the she, and be near her when she whelped, for that was the way of a wolf; but he knew too that he would always know her by her scent, and if possible when her time came he would be at her side.

Not even the spring running was as it should be, for without the excitement of being on all fours, without the nimbleness that had been his, he found that he stumbled too much, there was no thrill.

Besides, around him, the manifold smells told him that many of the two-leggeds were all jammed together. The odor was like a miasma and not even the all-pervading stench that came from the four-wheelers could drown it out.

Coming to a halt, he sat on his haunches, and for the first time he wondered if he were really, as he knew he was, a wolf, for a salty wetness was making itself felt at the corners of his eyes.

Wolves don't cry.

But if he were not a wolf, what then was he? What *were* all the memories that crowded his sick brain?

Tears or no, he knew that he was a wolf. And being a wolf, he must rid himself of this soft pelt, this hairlessness that made him sick at his stomach just to touch it with his too soft pads.

This was his dream, to become again as he had been. To be what was his only reality, a wolf, with a wolf's life and a wolf's loves.

That was his first venture into the reality of the world at large. His second day and night of "limited liberty" sent him hurrying back to his den. Nothing in his wolf life had prepared him for what he found in the midnight streets of the big city. For he found that bears were not the only males from whom the shes had to protect their young. . . .

And no animal of which he had ever heard could have moaned, as he heard a man moan, "If only pain didn't hurt so much . . ." and the strangled cries, the thrashing of limbs, the violence, and the sound of a whip. He had never known that humans used whips on themselves too. . . .

The third time out, he tried to drug himself the way the two-leggeds did by going to a big place where, on a screen, black and white shadows went through imitations of reality. He didn't go to a show that advertised it was in full glorious color, for he found the other shadows in neutral grays and blacks and whites gave a picture of life the way his wolf eyes were used to looking at it.

It was in this big place where the shadows acted that he found that perhaps he was not unique. His eyes glued to the screen, he watched as a man slowly fell to all fours, threw his head back, bayed at the moon, and then, right before everyone, turned into a wolf!

A *werewolf*, the man was called in the shadow play. And if there were werewolves, he thought, as he sat frozen in the middle of all the seated two-leggeds, then of course there must be weremen (would that be the word?) . . . and he was one of them. . . .

On the screen the melodrama came to its quick, bloody, foreordained end and the werewolf died when shot by a silver bullet. . . . He saw the fur disappear from the skin, and the paws change into hands and feet.

All he had to do, he thought, as he left the theater, his mind full of his dream, was to find out how to become a wolf again, without dying. Meanwhile, on every trip out without fail he went to the zoo. The keepers had become used to seeing him. They no longer objected when he threw little bits of meat into the cage to his pups. At first his she had snarled when he came near the bars, but after a while, although still puzzled, and even though she flattened her ears and sniffed constantly at him, she seemed to become resigned to having him stand as near the cage as he possibly could.

His pups were coming along nicely, almost full-grown. He was sorry, in a way, that they had to come to wolfhood behind bars, for now they'd never know the thrill of the spring running, but it was good to know they were safe, and had full bellies, and a den to call their own.

It was when his cubs were almost ready to leave their mother that he found the two-leggeds had a place of books. It was called a *library*, and he had been sent there by the woman in the hospital who was teaching him and some of the other aphasics how to read and write and speak.

Remembering the shadow play about the werewolf, he forced his puzzled eyes to read all that he could find on the baffling subject of lycanthropy.

In every time, in every clime, he found that there were references to two-leggeds who had become four-leggeds, wolves, tigers, panthers . . . but never a reference to an animal that had become a two-legged.

In the course of his reading, he found directions whereby a two-legged could change himself. They were complicated and meaningless to him. They involved curious things like a belt made of human skin, with a certain odd number of nail heads arranged in a quaint pattern on the body of the belt. The buckle had to be made under peculiar circumstances, and there were many chants that had to be sung.

It was essential, he read in the crabbed old books, that the two-legged desirous of making the change go to a place where two roads intersected at a specific angle. Then, standing at the intersection, chanting the peculiar words, feeling the human skin belt, the two-legged was told to divest himself of all clothing, and then to relieve his bladder.

Only then, the old books said, could the change take place.

He found that this heart was beating madly when he finished the last of the old books.

For if a two-legged could become a four-legged, surely . . .

After due thought, which was painful, he decided that a human skin belt would be wrong for him. The man in the fur store looked at him oddly when he asked for a length of wolf fur long and narrow, capable of being made into a belt. . . .

But he got the fur, and he made the pattern of nail heads, and he did the things the books had described.

It was lucky, he thought as he stood in the deserted zoo, that not far from the cages he had found two roads that cut into each other in just the manner that the books said they should.

Standing where they crossed, his clothes piled on the grass nearby, the belt around his narrow waist, his fingers caressing its fur, his human throat chanting the meaningless words, he found that standing naked was a cold business, and that it was easy to void his bladder as the books had said he must.

Then it was all over.

He had done everything just as he should.

At first nothing happened, and the cold white moon looked down at him, and fear rode up and down his spine that he would be seen by one of the two-leggeds who always wore blue clothes, and he would be taken and put back into that other zoo that was not a zoo, even though it had bars on the windows.

But then an aching began in his erect back, and he fell to all fours, and the agony began, and the pain blinded him to everything, to all the strange functional changes that were going on, and it was a long, long time before he dared open his eyes.

Even before he opened them, he could sense that it had happened, for crisp and clear through the night wind he could smell as he knew he should be able to smell. The odors came and they told him old stories.

Getting up on all fours, paying no attention to the clothes that now smelled foully of the two-leggeds, he began to run. His strong claws scrabbled at the cement, and he hurried to the grass and it was wonderful and exciting to feel the good feel of the growing things under his pads. Throwing his long head back he closed his eyes and from deep, deep inside he sang a song to the wolves' god, the moon.

His baying excited the animals in the cages so near him, and they began to roar, and scream, and those sounds were good too.

Running through the night, aimlessly, but running, feeling the ground beneath his paws was good . . . so good. . . .

And then through the sounds, through all the baying and roaring and screaming from the animals, he heard his she's voice, and he forgot about freedom and the night wind and cool white moon, and he ran back to the cage where she was.

The zoo attendants were just as baffled when they found the wolf curled up outside the cage near the feeding trough as they had been when they had found the man in the wolf's cage.

The two-legged who was his keeper recognized him, and he was allowed to go back into his cage and then the ecstasy, the spring-and-fall time ecstasy of being with his she . . .

Slowly, as he became used to his wolfhood again, he forgot about the life outside the cage, and soon it was all a matter that only arose in troubled dreams. And even then his she was there to nuzzle him and wake him if the nightmares got too bad.

Only once after the first few days did any waking memory of his two-legged life return, and that was when a two-legged she passed by his cage pushing a small four-wheeler in front of her.

Her scent was familiar.

So too was the scent of the two-legged cub.

Darting to the front of his cage, he sniffed long and hard.

And for just a moment the woman who was pushing the perambulator that contained her bastard looked deep into his yellow eyes and she knew, as he did, who and what he was.

And the very, very last thought he had about the matter was one of infinite pity for his poor cub, who some white moonlit night was going to drop down on all fours and become furred . . . and go prowling through the dark—in search of what, he would never know. . . .